# SHOT
## TO HELL

# SHOT TO HELL

### A PERLEY GATES WESTERN

# WILLIAM W. JOHNSTONE

## *and* J. A. Johnstone

# PINNACLE BOOKS
## Kensington Publishing Corp.

www.kensingtonbooks.com

PINNACLE BOOKS are published by

Kensington Publishing Corp.
119 West 40th Street
New York, NY 10018

PUBLISHER'S NOTE
Following the death of William W. Johnstone, the Johnstone family is working with a carefully selected writer to organize and complete Mr. Johnstone's outlines and many unfinished manuscripts to create additional novels in all of his series like The Last Gunfighter, Mountain Man, and Eagles, among others. This novel was inspired by Mr. Johnstone's superb storytelling.

All Kensington titles, imprints, and distributed lines are available at special quantity discounts for bulk purchases for sales promotions, premiums, fund-raising, educational, or institutional use. Special book excerpts or customized printings can also be created to fit specific needs. For details, write or phone the office of the Kensington sales manager: Kensington Publishing Corp., 119 West 40th Street, New York, NY 10018, attn: Sales Department; phone 1-800-221-2647.

PINNACLE BOOKS, the Pinnacle logo, and the WWJ steer head logo are Reg. U.S. Pat. & TM Off.

ISBN-13: 978-0-7860-4368-2
ISBN-10: 0-7860-4368-7

First printing: February 2020

10  9  8  7  6  5  4  3  2  1

Printed in the United States of America

Electronic edition:
ISBN-13: 978-0-7860-4369-9 (e-book)
ISBN-10: 0-7860-4369-5 (e-book)

# CHAPTER 1

"I'll sit down and have a cup of coffee with you," Rachael Parker said to her husband, "now that we're not so busy." She filled his cup and poured one for herself, then sat down at the table with him after she returned the pot to the stove. "What's the occasion for this unexpected visit? I'm surprised Rooster let you come into town by yourself."

Tom laughed. "He didn't. He's down at Wheeler's gettin' a few things we needed to finish fixin' the roof on that shack of his. I told him he could come and get somethin' to eat here, but he said he'd druther not. Said he'd get somethin' to eat at the Buffalo Hump. Said the hotel dinin' room was a little too fancy for him." Tom laughed again just thinking about the odd little man who worked with him at the farm. "Said he's gonna get him some of that meatloaf Ida makes."

Rachael shook her head and commented, "It's a wonder he ain't dead as much as he eats in that saloon. There's no telling what that woman mixes up in that meatloaf."

"Rooster says it's that heapin' portion of gunpowder she mixes in with it, that and the hot pepper, that gives it a kick," Tom said with another chuckle. "Probably not the same recipe Bess uses here in the fancy hotel dinin' room."

"I don't know if Bess even has a recipe for meat loaf," Rachael said. "If she does, she hasn't sprung it on us yet." She smiled at her husband, grateful that he had not fought her on her ambitious partnership with her sister. The hotel that Emma had built, with money that she and Possum Smith had acquired, already showed signs of success. And Rachael was especially proud of the dining room's apparent acceptance, since that was her part of the partnership. Although at first, Tom was not in favor of the two women trying to run a hotel and dining room, Rachael believed he was actually very proud of her. He seemed content with the situation as it now stood. He worked every day with Rooster Crabb on the farm but came to the hotel at the end of the day, having supper and then breakfast the next morning before going back to work. It seemed to be working out for them.

"Here you go, Tom," Kitty Lowery sang out when she placed his plate on the table before him. "When I told Bess it was for you, she put an extra piece of cornbread on it. She knows how you love cornbread." The cheerful young woman suddenly sprouted a deep frown when she glanced toward the door. "Uh-oh," she muttered. "Here comes some more of Ned Stark's men. Looks like you're gonna have to remind them about the rule, Rachael."

Rachael released a tired sigh and got to her feet. "I'll be back in a minute," she said, then hurried to intercept the two men. "You fellows looking for some dinner?" Rachael made a point to speak politely.

Curly Williams paused while he looked her up and

down before responding. "Yes, ma'am, and anything else you're sellin'."

Ignoring the obvious insult, Rachael maintained her polite reception. "You gentlemen probably missed the sign that requests you leave your firearms on the table by the door. So, if you'll leave those pistols on the table, I'd be happy to have you eat with us."

"I'd like to see somebody try to take my gun from me," Quirt Taylor replied.

"I'm afraid that's one of the rules we have in the hotel dining room," Rachael said. "It's for the comfort of the other customers, so if you don't want to leave your weapons on the table, we refuse to serve you."

"I say to hell with your damn rules," Curly spat. "They don't apply to us." He took a step to the side, preparing to walk past her, but she stepped to block him. "You'd best get the hell outta my way, woman." Rachael shook her head and pointed to the weapons table by the door.

Watching the confrontation from his table, Tom decided he had heard enough of the crude affront to his wife. He got to his feet and walked up beside Rachael. "You boys got a lotta rough bark on you, ain'tcha? I expect it's been a while since you've talked to a respectable woman, so you most likely don't know any better. Look around in here. You don't see anybody else wearin' a gun, do you? So who do you think is gonna shoot you?" He pointed to the weapons table. "Just leave your weapons on that table and they'll be right there when you finish eatin'."

Curly didn't say anything for a long moment while he eyed Tom up and down. When he finally spoke, he offered a suggestion. "Why don't you stick that table where the sun don't shine?"

"I think you'd better leave," Rachael said.

"To hell with 'em," Quirt Taylor said, noticing that everyone in the dining room was staring at them. "We don't wanna eat this crap they serve in here, anyway." He took hold of Curly's elbow and pulled him toward the door. Aside to him, he muttered low, "Ned don't want us to stir up no trouble with the town folks. They'll be hollerin' for the sheriff."

"Let 'em holler," Curly blurted defiantly, but he allowed himself to be pulled out the door, knowing Quirt was right. Ned had a working arrangement with Sheriff John Mason, an arrangement that was beneficial to both Ned and Mason.

Rachael took Tom by the arm and walked him back to his table. "Now, don't get all upset about that. They just make a lot of noise, and I don't want you getting yourself to worrying about me." She sat back down at the table while he finished eating.

"I just don't like people talkin' to you like that," Tom said.

"I know," she said and gave him a little peck on his cheek. "But don't worry yourself about that bunch that works for Ned Stark. They don't usually show up here at the hotel. They eat at the Buffalo Hump. I don't know how those two wandered in here today, but they're gone, so that's the end of that."

"I reckon I'd best go get Rooster," he said. "He oughta be about through eatin' his meatloaf by now. I'd like to finish up that roof before supper tonight. If I'm a little late, you'll know Rooster had too much liquid refreshments with his dinner."

"If you're late, I'll keep a plate in the oven for you," she said as she walked him to the door.

\* \* \*

There was a pretty good crowd in the Buffalo Hump for this time of day. That was usually the indication that a cattle herd was passing nearby on its way to market, but it was not the time of the year for cattle drives. Most likely a lot more drifters were attracted to the little town of Bison Gap, Tom thought. He paused just inside the door and looked at Jimmy McGee behind the bar. Jimmy nodded to him and pointed toward a small table in the back corner of the saloon. Tom returned the nod to Jimmy and walked back to the table where Rooster was hunched over a plate of food. "Gunpowder meatloaf?" Tom asked.

"Nah, beef stew," Rooster answered. "She didn't make no meatloaf today."

"You 'bout ready to get on back and finish that roof? You don't wanna have another rain catch you before it's done."

"I'm finished," Rooster declared and pushed the plate away from him. "The tar and stuff's in the wagon. I parked it around back. Lemme pay Jimmy on the way out." He pushed his chair back and stood up, released a loud belch, and followed Tom to the bar.

"Well, lookee here," Curly Williams said and immediately got up on his feet, "if it ain't that jasper from the hotel."

Quirt Taylor turned to see where Curly was looking. "Damned if it ain't," he said. Then, when Curly headed for the bar where Tom was waiting for Rooster to settle up with Jimmy, Quirt called after him. "What are you fixin' to do?"

"Just wanna say 'howdy' to our friend from the hotel," Curly answered. When Rooster was finished, Tom turned to leave, only to come face-to-face with the man he had confronted in the dining room. "Howdy, Tater Head," Curly said. "What you doin' runnin' around without that little woman to protect you? Don't you know we got rules in this saloon, just like you've got rules in that dinin' room?" Tom wasn't prepared to confront the two drifters. He hadn't noticed them sitting at a small table beyond the end of the long bar. Curly didn't wait to hear his response and continued to press him. "I notice you're wearin' a gun now, so I'll tell you about the rules we got in here. If a man's wearin' a gun, he better be ready to use it. Else, he ain't no man a-tall. So I'm fixin' to let you show us you're man enough to wear that gun in here with all us men. Whaddaya say, Tater Head?"

"I say you're just tryin' to make trouble for no good reason a-tall," Tom answered, having no intention to respond to the bully's challenge. "You ready, Rooster?" He stepped aside and started to walk around Curly, but the determined bully quickly stepped in front of him.

"You ain't walkin' outta here till I say you can," Curly said, much to his partner's amusement.

"Make him crawl outta here on his hands and knees," Quirt encouraged.

"All right," Tom said. "You've had your fun with me, but I ain't havin' a duel with you just so you can entertain your friend. So I'll be leavin' now." He looked back at Rooster, who was looking undecided as to what he should do. "Come on, Rooster." When he turned back again, it was to find Curly, right up in his face, the mocking grin gone from his face, replaced by a grim, threatening glare.

"You'll go when I say you can go," Curly warned him, his voice almost a growl. "Now, you ask me real polite-like, 'Please, Mr. Williams, can I crawl outta here, like the yellow-bellied dog I am?'" All talking in the saloon stopped when everybody became aware of the confrontation between the two.

"You can go to hell," Tom responded.

Rooster, still uncertain what he should do, dropped his hand down to rest on the handle of his pistol. That was as far as he got before Quirt caught his eye and shook his head to warn him, his smirk conveying a message that he hoped Rooster would test him. With no choice but to watch, he lifted his hand and looked back in time to see Tom take a step backward. What followed next left Rooster gasping in disbelief. Curly drew his six-gun and fired. Tom doubled over, shot in the stomach. He dropped to his knees while fumbling to find his pistol before Curly put the fatal shot in his forehead.

The silence in the saloon was deafening, broken only by the sound of Tom's body as it keeled over to land on the floor. Rooster pushed past Quirt to rush to Tom's side, but one look told him Tom was gone. He glared up accusingly at Curly, who responded with a smug grin. "He shouldn'ta tried for it," Curly said, loud enough for the benefit of everyone in the saloon. "He made that move for his gun, but I was too fast for him."

"That's a fact," Quirt confirmed, equally as loud. "I seen him go for that gun. Everybody did." He looked around at the still speechless spectators to see if anyone had the guts to disagree. No one did until

Jimmy McGee finally said someone should go fetch the sheriff.

"I'll go," Rooster volunteered and hurried out the door, intent upon getting the sheriff there before Curly and Quirt decided to ride out of town. Hurrying across the open area between the jail and the saloon, he met the sheriff coming out the door of his office.

"I heard the shots," Sheriff Mason said. "What happened?" He was already aware that Curly Williams and Quirt Taylor were in town, and he was hoping it had nothing to do with either of them.

"Curly Williams shot Tom Parker down!" Rooster answered. "Shot him down in cold blood, murdered him!"

"I'll take care of it," the sheriff assured him and hurried along to the saloon. He went in the door, with Rooster right on his heels, to find everyone in the saloon still standing and staring at Tom's body, most of them in disbelief. He looked at once to Curly and Quirt, standing at the bar, the only customers casually having a drink of whiskey. "Curly?" Mason asked.

"Yep, I done it, Sheriff," Curly freely confessed. "He didn't give me no choice. When I saw him reach for that forty-four he's carryin', I had to go for mine. I reckon this was my lucky day, 'cause it turned out I was faster'n him."

"That's a fact, Sheriff," Quirt immediately attested. "I saw the whole thing. I was standin' right there beside 'em. That feller made out like he was fixin' to leave and then he reached for that gun. Look there, he got it halfway outta his holster. He came in here lookin' for me and Curly. We was in the dinin' room at the hotel a little while ago and there was words between him and Curly. That feller didn't like the way Curly talked to the lady that runs the place, and I reckon he decided to come after Curly when we walked outta there peaceful."

"That's a damn lie!" Rooster blurted. "Tom Parker ain't never drew down on anybody. Everybody in this town can tell you that." He looked at the sheriff in desperation. "Hell, you know that, Sheriff." He pointed a finger at Curly. "He tried to get Tom to draw, but Tom wouldn't do it—told him he wouldn't do it—so that feller shot him down!" Rooster ignored the menacing warnings on the faces of Curly and Quirt, to plead with Mason. Then a thought struck him that something else didn't look right and it occurred to him what it was. "When I left here to go get you, Tom's gun wasn't halfway outta his holster like that. They musta done that!" He glared up at them.

"Just calm down, Rooster," the sheriff told him. "Anybody else actually see what happened?"

No one volunteered except the bartender. "I think it happened the way Rooster said it did," Jimmy said.

"I was standin' between him and the bartender," Quirt declared. "There ain't no way he coulda seen him reach for that gun, but I saw him when he done it."

There was no doubt in anyone's mind, including the sheriff's, that Rooster's version was what had actually happened there. And he was not happy with the situation that two of Ned Stark's men had created. "Tom Parker was a good man," Mason began, "but sometimes any man can get to thinkin' dangerous things, things that they wouldn't normally do. I don't see how this could be looked at in any way other than an unfortunate thing, but it is a case of self-defense, pure and simple. We're all sad to see Tom Parker go this way." He turned to address Curly. "I expect it would be best if you boys get on your horses and ride on outta town."

Curly started to object to the suggestion, but Quirt stepped in before he could say anything. "Yes, sir, Sheriff, we don't want no trouble, we're goin'." He grabbed Curly by his elbow and pulled him toward the door.

When they were gone, Mason said to Jimmy McGee, "I'll go tell Floyd Jenkins to come get the body."

"No," Rooster spoke up, although still in a state of shock over Mason's failure to lock Curly up for the shooting. Totally disgusted by the lack of backbone in all the men who had witnessed the cold-blooded murder, he paused to glare at them. They all saw the same thing he had just witnessed, but this was the state of things in Bison Gap since Ned Stark and his gang had moved in. "I'll take care of Tom. I'll bury him, myself," he declared.

"Somebody needs to go tell Rachael up at the dinin' room," Jimmy said.

"I'll do that, too," Rooster said.

"I don't know, Rooster," Jimmy said, looking at the body. "It might be too much for Rachael to see him like that, with that hole in his forehead. Might be Floyd could fix him up a little bit, so it wouldn't look as bad as it does now."

Rooster reconsidered after Jimmy said that. It wouldn't be a very pleasant remembrance for her to carry with her for the rest of her life. And it would be worse for Tom's two daughters to see him this way. "I expect you're right," he decided. "I think it best if I take Tom back to the farm and bury him after Floyd nails him up in a coffin. I'll take him to Floyd's shop, if somebody will help me put him in the wagon." He had half-a-dozen volunteers to carry Tom out to the wagon. "Much obliged," he told them after Tom's body was laid in the back of his wagon. He climbed up into the wagon seat and drove the team of horses up the street to Floyd Jenkins's barbershop. Behind the barbershop, the building was located where Floyd practiced his undertaker chores as well as a little doctoring. Rooster got down from the wagon and walked around to the back of it. "I reckon I need to apologize, partner. I wasn't able to help you, but I was as surprised as you was when that dry-gulcher shot you. I reckon I'll be fixin' that roof by myself."

After agreeing with Floyd on a price to close Tom up in a pine box, Rooster left to take care of the part he dreaded the most, telling Rachael about her husband's death. When he walked into the hotel dining room, there were only a couple of people still eating. Kitty Lowery was near the back of the room, but he didn't see Rachael. When Kitty turned around and saw him, she didn't say anything, but pointed toward the kitchen door as if she knew why he was there. He nodded in return and walked inside the kitchen, where he saw Rachael sitting at the end of the kitchen table. She was weeping and Bess was standing by her, her hand on Rachael's shoulder. Hearing him come in, they both turned to see him. Seeing the dwarflike little man there with his hat in his hand respectfully, his solid white bearded face bowed in sorrow, Rachael broke into a series of sobs. "Somebody's done told you," Rooster guessed.

"Richard Hoover," Bess said. She said the postmaster sent his young son up to tell Rachael right after the shooting.

Rooster walked into the kitchen and stood before the table. "I'm sorry, Rachael. I woulda been here to tell you, but I took Tom to Floyd's first." She looked up to ask why, reacting just as he had at first. "I had to, Rachael, I didn't want you and the girls to see Tom like that. I left him with Floyd, and he's gonna put him in a coffin and close it up. He's already got a couple built, so he said I could pick Tom up in about an hour." When she started to protest, he said, "It's better for you to remember Tom like he was the last time you saw him. I don't think it's a good idea to leave the lid off that coffin. I figured I'd take him back to the farm to bury him, but I'll take him to the cemetery here in town, if you druther."

Rachael didn't have to think about it. "No, I know Tom would rather be laid to rest out there where he loved to work with you. Thank you, Rooster, for taking care of him."

To hear her thanks was painful to Rooster. "Not a-tall, ma'am," he insisted. "I'm just sorry as I can be that I weren't no help to him. It happened before either one of us could do anythin' about it."

"Don't you worry yourself about it," she said. "There wasn't anything you could have done to prevent it. Those two outlaws were determined to get even with Tom for standing up to them in here. If they hadn't gotten him in the saloon, it would have been somewhere else." She shook her head as she recalled the confrontation there in the dining room. "Where are those two now? Are they in jail?"

"No, ma'am, and that's the sorry part of it. John Mason said it was self-defense, and he ran 'em outta town."

Rachael was fairly startled, unable to believe what

he told her. "Self-defense? Surely, there must be some mistake. Mason didn't arrest them at all?"

"No, ma'am," Rooster answered. He hesitated before saying more, but decided she probably suspected the same as other folks had. "There's been some talk around town that the sheriff always goes easy on Ned Stark's men."

"I've heard that, too," Rachael said, getting too angry to cry, "but this is murder! How can he go easy on murder?"

"Yes, ma'am, it is," Rooster agreed, "it's murder, but I don't know what to do about it."

The days that followed that fateful afternoon were hard indeed for Rachael and her daughters, as well as for Rooster. Emma agreed with her sister to close the dining room down for half a day in order for Rachael to hold a funeral service for Tom at the recently built Baptist church. It was the first funeral service held in the new church, led by the Reverend Harvey Poole. Tom was buried near Rooster's cabin in a meadow where he, Rachael, and Emma had lived in a couple of tents when they first came to Bison Gap.

It was no less sorrowful for the bowlegged little elf, Rooster Crabb. He could not count any friends beyond those he had acquired during the last eight months of his life. And now, one of them was dead, and at such a young age. He had two more whom he considered to be his closest friends, Perley Gates and Possum Smith. It was mainly these two who had transformed his existence as an often-bullied little man to one of some respect—although he acknowledged that it was a minor portion of respect—but far more than it was before Perley Gates came into his life. He wished Perley and Possum were there now, but they were a long way away in northeast Texas. He thought they would want to know what happened to Tom, so he decided to send them a letter.

# CHAPTER 2

*Dear Perley,*

*I thought you'd want to know that Tom Parker was shot down yesterday in the Buffalo Hump Saloon. A man named Curly Williams killed him. The sheriff said it was self-defense, but it wasn't. I was there and I saw it. It was murder. Emma and Rachael are working hard at the hotel, but they are afraid there are too many bad people in town since you were sheriff. Everybody wishes you were here now. Say howdy to Possum. Emma wrote this letter for me. I can't write.*

> *Your friend,*
> *Rooster Crabb*

Perley looked at the date and said to Possum, "He wrote this letter almost two weeks ago. Look at that date." He held it out for Possum to see.

Possum just shook his head. "I can't read neither. I know my numbers, though, and I see the number twelve."

"That's right," Perley said, "and today's the twenty-fifth. So Tom got killed two weeks ago." He shook his head. "I declare, that's a downright shame. I know

Rachael must be really sufferin' over it. And the girls,"
he said, "Alice and Melva, that's a terrible thing for
them to deal with." He paused when he thought of
six-year-old Alice, who was determined to marry him
when she grew up to be sixteen.

"Can I see the letter?" Possum asked and Perley
handed it to him. Possum unfolded the single page
and studied it intently.

"I thought you said you can't read and write,"
Perley couldn't resist reminding him.

"I can't," Possum replied while he continued to
study the letter. "Somethin' I always said I was gonna
get around to, but I never did." He folded it back
again and handed it to Perley. "Emma writes with a
fine hand." He considered that for a few moments
before continuing. "That letter makes me think ol'
Rooster's feelin' down and out. I reckon he's on his
own again, like he was when we found him."

"You mean when he found us, don't you?" Perley
japed, since Possum was about to miss Bison Gap
before Rooster came along and put them on the right
path to the little town.

"You ain't never gonna forget that, are you?"
Possum responded. "I told you I'd never been there
before." Perley laughed and Possum paused to think
about it for a few moments. "You know, maybe I
shoulda stayed down there with Rooster, at least till
Emma and Rachael got that hotel up and runnin'."
He gave Perley a businesslike glance. "After all, I own
half interest in that hotel. All the money I've ever had
went into it. And it ain't the easiest thing to do to
make a hotel pay off in that territory, even for a man.
Two women tryin' it, I musta been crazy to leave it
with 'em."

"They're two pretty smart women," Perley said. "If any two women could do it, I'd put my money on them." He was thinking that Possum might be right in thinking he should have stayed to help run the hotel. But he didn't want to remind Possum that he wanted to tag along with him back to the Triple-G. He had to admit that he was more than a little concerned for Emma and Rachael, too. They had become close friends to him in the time he had spent with them, and he hated to think any of his friends were in trouble. He had a feeling that he should do something to help his friends in Bison Gap, but he didn't know what in the world that might be. He had held the temporary job of sheriff there for a short time until they found a man for the job. Ralph Wheeler, the mayor, had lined up a man who was a foreman for some big cattle ranch and also had some law-enforcement experience. His rambling thoughts were interrupted when Possum asked a question.

"We gonna eat, or just stand out here lookin' at the wagon?"

"We're gonna eat," Perley said at once. "That's the only reason I came into town with you in the first place. I wanted to eat at the Paris Diner." He jumped down from the wagon and waited for Possum to tie the horses.

"Why do they call this place the Paris Diner?" Possum wondered. "Is that supposed to be short for dinner? They serve breakfast and supper, too, don't they?"

"I don't know," Perley replied. "Maybe Beulah ain't too good at spellin'." Then he had to explain that dinner had two n's while diner had only one. "The important thing is she knows how to cook."

* * *

"Howdy, Perley," Becky Morris sang out cheerfully when they walked in. "I shoulda known you'd be in town, because we're serving pork chops today. And I know how you love pork chops."

"Well, we did pick a good day to come in, didn't we?" Perley responded. He enjoyed a good pork chop occasionally, since they didn't raise hogs on the Triple-G. His late father had made that an iron rule, no hogs on his ranch.

"I'll get you some coffee," Becky said and went to the kitchen to get the pot.

"Did I hear you say Perley was out there?" Lucy Tate asked when Becky walked in. "Do you want me to wait on him? You waited on him last time he was here." Grinning mischievously, she winked at Beulah.

"Kiss my foot, Lucy," Becky responded. "So what if I like Perley? He and I are good friends." She picked up the coffeepot and looked at Beulah.

"I'm already filling two plates, honey," Beulah said. "Don't pay Lucy no mind. Perley's a good friend to have."

Lucy waited until Becky left the kitchen to comment. "But he ain't got the sense to know Becky's ready to be more than his pal."

"Give him time," Beulah said as she set the two plates on the sideboard. "They're both still young. And when the time's right, he'll pick the right girl, and my money's on Becky."

"You're awful quiet, Possum," Perley commented. "That sure ain't like you. What's got your mind turnin', Bison Gap?"

"Yeah, as a matter of fact," Possum answered, then

paused while Becky placed the hot coffee on the table.

She smiled sweetly and said, "I'll be right back with your pork chops."

Possum continued. "I'm thinkin' I need to go back down to Bison Gap, Perley. It ain't just because I put all my money into that hotel with Emma. I reckon I just thought everything would be all right with Tom there to take care of things. And now, I don't know. I just can't help thinkin' they need somebody right now. I know I ain't much, but at least I wouldn't let anybody take advantage of 'em, if I knew they was tryin' to."

Perley could see that Possum really was serious about it. "That's about three hundred miles from here. It'd take you a week to ride down there."

"Hell, I know how far it is," Possum said and paused again when Becky brought their food and asked if they needed anything else. Perley told her they didn't, and Possum went on. "I figure I won't be missed here on the Triple-G. Hell, it's summer and the crew ain't doin' nothin' but ridin' herd, anyway. I just don't want you to feel like I'm lettin' you down, since you let me tag along with you and got me hired on with the crew. I know you didn't need another man."

"You got no reason to feel bad about quittin'," Perley said. "You've done a fine job while you were here, and I'm sure you'll get your job back if you want it. I'll tell Rubin you've gotta go back to help some folks. Won't be any problem at all. Now, let's enjoy these pork chops before they get cold."

They ate their dinner almost in silence, since it was obvious Possum was doing a lot of deep thinking. Had it not been for the frequent visits to their table by

Becky, there would have been no dinner conversation at all. Most of that was between Becky and Perley. When they got up to leave, Perley left the money on the table and Becky hurried over to say good-bye. "Don't be a stranger, Perley," she said. "We're always glad to see you." Then remembering her manners, she said, "And you, too, Possum."

"Thank you, ma'am," Possum replied. His mind distracted from Bison Gap for that moment, he shook his head while looking at the two young people. *She's a fine-looking little filly,* he thought, *and Perley hasn't the slightest notion that she's taken a shine to him. That boy needs my help when it comes to women. I gotta talk to him about it.* By the time they were outside, and on the wagon, however, his mind had moved back to Bison Gap and the troubles down there. He was especially concerned for Emma. He had taken it upon himself to escort her down from Kansas after her husband, Dan, had been killed. And now, she was the sole manager of the hotel in Bison Gap, and she with a baby to care for. He had to make sure she could stand up to the task, now that Tom Parker was dead.

When they got back to the Triple-G, Possum drove the wagon up to the back of the house to unload some supplies they had picked up for the kitchen. When they had brought in the last of the kitchen supplies, Perley said, "Come on, we'll see if Rubin's still here." He walked into the dining room and found both his brothers, Rubin and John, still sitting at the dinner table, drinking coffee. Their wives were just beginning the chore of clearing the dishes from the table. "Well, don't tell me you've decided to eat with the family today," John greeted him. It was still a tradition for both Rubin's and John's families to eat together in the main house. Perley, more times than not, ate with the ranch hands in the bunkhouse.

"Nope," Perley answered. "Possum and I ate in town. I just wanted to tell you that Possum has to go back to Bison Gap to take care of some problems that came up down there."

"Is that so?" Rubin asked. "I hope it ain't something serious, Possum. If you're worried about leavin' us, don't. We ain't pushed this time of year, anyway. And if you're concerned about a job when you come back, you've got one." Possum said he appreciated it, and Rubin asked, "You leavin' right away?"

"We might as well leave in the mornin'," Perley answered for him.

Both Rubin and John reacted in surprise. So did Possum. "You're goin' with him?" John asked.

"Yeah, I figured I might as well, since Bison Gap's about three hundred miles from here, and Possum's liable to wind up in Oklahoma or somewhere, if I ain't there to keep him on track."

Long accustomed to Perley's unpredictable ways, both his brothers couldn't be totally surprised to hear he was going to head out on another adventure. "Knowin' you," Rubin said, "I'm pretty sure you're not goin' just to make sure Possum doesn't take the wrong trail. Somethin' down there that concerns you, too?"

"I reckon you could say that," Perley replied. "There are some folks down there that Possum and I got pretty close to, and we wanna help them, if that's what they need." He went on to explain in a little more detail what had recently happened, including the death of Tom Parker.

"So what are you figurin' to do, go back to being

the sheriff again?" John asked, not at all sure Perley
was doing a smart thing.

"No, nothin' like that at all," Perley stated, emphat-
ically. "We're just gonna see what help Emma and
Rachael might need to stay in business." Trying to
lighten the conversation a little then, he said, "Mostly
I wanted to help 'em because Rachael has the same
name as my mother." Hearing that, his mother, the
widow, Rachael Gates, threw her head back and
laughed. Proud as she was of his serious-minded elder
brothers, she held a special place in her heart for her
youngest son and the way he seemed to float through
life as if following every breeze that stirred him.

"Well, we'll try to run the ranch without you again,"
Rubin stated facetiously. "Damn it, Perley, you be careful. Possum, watch his back."

"You can count on that," Possum responded, still
surprised that Perley was going with him.

Perley walked around to the end of the table, opposite Rubin's place at the head, and gave his mother a
peck on the cheek. "I will," he said when she whispered for him to be careful. Then he and Possum
went outside to deliver the rest of the supplies to the
barn and the bunkhouse.

Back in the dining room, John shook his head
slowly and commented. "I'm thinkin' there's another
cow pie waitin' for him, and if . . ."

That was as far as he got before his wife, Martha,
interrupted to finish it for him, ". . . there wasn't but
one cow pie it the whole state of Texas, Perley would
step in it."

"That's right," John said, and he and Rubin chuckled.

* * *

Since he and Possum were leaving early the following morning, Perley ate supper with the family that night. When morning came, they set out before Ollie Dinkler had breakfast ready for the crew in the bunkhouse, Perley on his bay gelding named Buck and Possum on a gray he called Dancer, for the gelding's tendency to strut when trotting. They took one packhorse. Since they had bought no provisions for their trip when they were in Paris the day before, they planned to stop at Tyson's Store, which was about twenty-four miles away on the Sulphur River. They would pick up supplies for the trip and have breakfast there while the horses rested.

After they had bought the supplies they needed at Tyson's and the horses were rested, they started out for Bison Gap. Not sure if there was a better way, they opted to follow the same trail they had taken when they left Bison Gap to ride back to the Triple-G. They skirted the towns of Dallas and Fort Worth, having no reason to want to visit either town. With the main objective to reach Bison Gap as quickly as they could, they pushed their horses to make the distance in six and a half days.

Riding two weary horses and leading another, Perley and Possum crossed the bridge over the creek north of the town late in the afternoon of the seventh day of travel. The first thing that met their eye was the new church, standing some thirty yards or so from Wheeler's Merchandise Store, which used to be the first building on the north side of town. "Can't be all bad news," Possum commented, "if they've built a church. That's a humdinger, too, with a bell tower and a steeple." He started to say more but interrupted himself when he spotted another new structure farther down the street. "There she is!" he exclaimed. "There's Emma's hotel!" He nudged the gray with his heels, but the weary horse gave him no more than two or three steps before settling back into a slow walk.

"That's Emma's and your hotel," Perley reminded him.

"Right, that's right," Possum uttered softly to himself, finding it difficult to imagine himself half-owner. Now that he was looking at a real building, instead of a vague possibility in his mind, it seemed even more unlikely. A square, two-story building with a porch across the front, on the first and second floor, with a single-story wing on one side that Perley figured to be the kitchen and dining room. Possum was struck speechless while he gaped at it.

"Well, I've gotta say, it's an elegant hotel," Perley said.

"What's it say?" Possum asked and pointed at a long freshly painted sign hung across the porch at the entrance.

Perley read it for him. "It says, Bison House Hotel."

"I swear," Possum chuckled and repeated it. "Bison House Hotel. That's a good name, ain't it?" Perley allowed that he thought so. Making no effort to hide his excitement, Possum said, "Bison Hotel kinda sounds like they're sayin' it's a hotel for buffalo."

"Bison *House*," Perley emphasized, enjoying Possum's childlike reaction to his investment. It wasn't hard to guess that his friend had never owned anything of any real value before. "Why don't we go in and see if there's anybody in there we know?"

Leaving their horses at the hitching rail, they walked up three steps to the wide porch and Possum paused to look at the six rocking chairs lined up there. Perley started to go to the door but stopped when Possum sat down in one of the chairs to try it out. He looked up at Perley and grinned like a child at Christmas. After a few experimental rocks, Possum jumped up and led the way into the lobby of the hotel.

Behind the check-in desk, Wilbur Ross gazed with a critical eye at the two strangers looking tired and unshaven, no doubt after days on the back of a horse. Remembering his boss's instructions, however, he maintained a courteous attitude. "May I help you gentlemen?"

Thoroughly enjoying himself, Possum stepped up to the desk. "Yeah, me and my partner might wanna try your hotel out." Wilbur's initial thought was that he wished he had the courage to tell them they were in the wrong place—that they should go down to the saloon with the rest of Ned Stark's gang. But he asked instead, "What kind of accommodations are you looking for?"

"Accommodations?" Possum echoed as if offended. "We don't want no accommodations. We want a room. Where's the owner of this hotel? I wanna talk to the owner."

"I'm sorry, sir." Wilbur remained calm, although Perley was about to reach the point where he thought Possum had had enough fun at the desk clerk's expense. "The owner isn't available right now," Wilbur informed him, clearly confused by the stranger's attitude.

"Whaddaya mean she ain't available?" Possum went on. "Emma Slocum, that's her name, ain't it? I wanna see Emma Slocum," he demanded.

Wilbur was beside himself trying to decide what to do when the door to an office behind him suddenly opened and an irritated owner charged toward the desk. "I'm Emma Slocum! What is the problem out here?" Then she looked beyond the clerk and squealed, "Perley Gates! And Possum Smith!" She rushed around the desk to embrace them both, with an arm around each one. "What are you two doing here?" She took a step back to look at them, still finding it hard to believe it was really them. Behind her, a young girl came out of the office leading a toddler by the hand. "This is Barbara Cooper," Emma quickly informed them. "She's Rex Cooper's daughter and she helps me tend Danny." Seeing the question in their expressions, she said, "Rex opened a harness shop here not long after you left."

"Well, I'll be . . ." Perley started when he looked at the toddler, "already walkin'." When he and Possum had left Bison Gap, Emma's baby was just crawling. "I'm pleased to meet you, Barbara. I reckon as busy as Emma is, she needs help with a young'un." Barbara smiled politely.

"We got that letter you wrote for Rooster," Possum said, "and figured we'd take a little ride down here to see how you're doin'. That was sorry news about Tom."

While Possum and Emma were talking, Perley walked over to the desk, where Wilbur was still shaking his head in disbelief. "My name's Perley," he said to the clerk. "I reckon I oughta apologize for my partner japin' you like that. He doesn't mean any harm. He was just hopin' we could surprise Emma."

"Well, it sure looks like you've surprised her, all right, and I'll admit he had me going," Wilbur said.

"I thought you both must be drunk." He paused, then asked, "Did she say his name was Possum Smith?" Perley nodded. "He's half-owner of the hotel!" Wilbur exclaimed. "And I came close to shooting him."

"You did?" Perley asked, seeing no evidence of a weapon on him or on the desk. "Why do you say that?"

"Perley," Wilbur said before answering the question. "You're Perley Gates. I've heard a lot of talk about you. You were the sheriff here for a little while."

"That's a fact, but how were you gonna shoot Possum? You ain't wearin' a gun."

"See that little wire grille in the front of the desk?" Wilbur asked. Perley nodded. "Come around here on this side," Wilbur said and stepped aside to give him room.

Perley stepped around to the other side and discovered a sawed-off shotgun lying on a shelf under the desk, the muzzle looking at the wire grille. "Well, I'll be . . ." Perley started. "That woulda made a pretty big mess of ol' Possum."

Wilbur nodded thoughtfully. "I hope I never have to use it. It was Emma's idea. Rooster Crabb sawed the barrel off, so it would fit on the shelf. We thought we needed to have some kind of protection. There's been a few robberies in town in the last few months, and you never know when you might get hit." That was as much time as they had to talk before Emma came over to collar Perley.

"Rachael's gonna be tickled to see you two saddle tramps. Come on. I'll go to the dining room with you." She grabbed his arm and gave it a squeeze, making no attempt to hide her pleasure to see them. With a few quick instructions to Barbara, she left her to take care of her son and started to the dining room.

"If the dining room is as fancy as the hotel, she might not let us in till we get cleaned up," Perley said.

"Well, we do have a washroom for our guests," Wilbur offered, "if you're going to be staying in the hotel. And you have time before supper." After Possum's charade, he wasn't sure if they were going to take a room or not.

"Of course, they're staying in the hotel," Emma insisted. Then she looked at Perley. "Aren't you?"

"I don't know." Perley hesitated. "Maybe we oughta ride on out and stay with Rooster. Besides, it wouldn't do to take up one of your rooms that a payin' customer might want." He grinned at her. "And I know you ain't gonna charge us."

"Where'd you get that idea?" Emma responded and raised an eyebrow.

"I know sure as hell that I ain't gonna pay," Possum announced. "You can just put me in my half of the hotel."

"Your half of the hotel's in the back," Emma japed him. "Come on. Let's go see Rachael." They followed her down a hallway to the dining room door.

Rachael's reaction upon seeing them was another version of the one they had gotten from Emma, even though secondary in excitement to that from her two daughters. Alice and Melva both squealed their delight in seeing Perley and ran to greet him. Rachael was totally surprised to see them and couldn't wait to show them around the dining room and kitchen, until they expressed their offers of sympathy for the loss of her husband. In the span of a few seconds' time, she went from excitement to sorrow to anger when she told them how Tom was murdered. "Rooster was with him," she concluded. "He saw the whole thing and he said all Tom did was start to walk out."

"Accordin' to what you're sayin', there were a lot of people in the saloon, watchin' this business between Tom and the fellow that shot him," Perley said. "What did they say happened?"

"Nobody had a say about it," Rachael claimed. "Sheriff Mason didn't ask anybody what happened. The only witness he talked to was Quirt Taylor, Curly's friend. Both of them are Ned Stark's men, I might add." She paused then to keep her emotions from getting away from her again, aware that her daughters were listening. "What's done is done, I keep telling myself, so let me show you around my part of the hotel."

Hearing Rachael's retelling of the incident that took Tom's life was troubling to Perley. He followed them around while they toured the dining room and the kitchen, with Alice and Melva hanging on his shirt-sleeves. They met Rachael's cook, Bess Curry, and Kitty Lowery, a waitress. But his mind was still on Tom's death. When he and Possum had left Bison Gap about eight months before, Ralph Wheeler, the mayor, was very confident in the ability of his new sheriff to keep the peace. If Rooster's account of the incident in the saloon was accurate—and he had no reason to doubt it—then it seemed awfully strange that the sheriff didn't talk to other witnesses. He decided he'd like to meet the new sheriff to hear his version of the shooting. He knew he'd see Ralph Wheeler about the job his sheriff was doing. Emma broke into his thoughts then with a suggestion.

"We've got plenty of time before supper," Emma said. "Why don't you two stay here tonight? You can ride down the creek to Rooster's and bring him back here for supper. I know he'd get his feelings hurt if we didn't let him know you were here right away."

"He used to come in here to eat with Tom half the time," Rachael said, "but it took him a while to get used to it. He used to think it was too fancy for him." She chuckled when she recalled, "He would eat at the Buffalo Hump when he came into town. I'm sure we'll see him in here more often while you two are here."

"That sounds like a good idea to me," Possum responded at once. "We'll have us a big ol' supper together and see if Bess, here, is a decent cook." He gave her a playful wink. "It'd have to be pretty bad not to beat mine and Perley's cookin' I've been eatin' for the last week. But we'll take the cheapest rooms you've got, so we don't tie up your best rooms. That all right with you, Perley?"

"That's fine by me," Perley answered. "We've got time to get Rooster and leave the horses at the stable, and still have time to clean up a little before supper."

"All right, then," Possum declared, "we'd best quit dillydallyin' and get on out to Rooster's."

# CHAPTER 3

Using a bucket to water a small patch of tomato plants in the little garden he tended close to his barn, Rooster paused when he caught sight of two riders on the trail beside the creek. When they turned off the trail, onto the path to his place, he put his bucket down and walked over to the corral and the rifle propped against the corner post. He had not always been so cautious when the infrequent visitor happened upon his cabin. But ever since Tom Parker's blatant murder and the ensuing fuss that Rooster had raised about it, he had been given advice that it would be best if he let the dead lie. Some of that advice had not been so subtle, to the point where he had developed a habit of keeping his rifle close at hand, no matter what he was doing.

With his rifle now in hand, he remained standing next to the corner pole in case he suddenly needed some cover while he focused on the path leading down to his cabin. "Great God A-mighty!" He suddenly blurted when he identified his unexpected visitors, scarcely able to believe it. "Hooooeee!" he yelled to attract their attention, sounding more like he was calling his hogs, and he ran to meet them at the cabin. Perley and Possum both chuckled to see the little man charging out to meet them, his bowlegs striding more like the crab that served as his last name. "I swear," Rooster crowed, "I didn't believe my eyes for a minute there!"

Perley and Possum dismounted to receive the handshaking and backslapping greeting from their friend. An uninformed observer of the reunion might have thought it had been many years since they had last seen each other. Perley couldn't help feeling that Rooster had serious concerns about his safety, based upon his reaction to their return. He couldn't express his appreciation enough for their presence when, according to him, the town was going to hell as fast as it could. He told them right away that he worried for Emma and Rachael and the fact that Ned Stark and his men had taken to hanging around Bison Gap. "Who the hell is Ned Stark?" Possum asked.

"He's got a cattle ranch on three hundred acres about three miles south of here. There's thousands of acres to the west of that tract that ain't nothin' but open range, and I think the feller that built the ranch house planned to graze his cattle there. The problem is Stark's got a crew that's way too many for a ranch that size. It seems like his cowhands have too much time on their hands 'cause they hit Bison Gap and the saloon right regular. He ain't too particular about the brand on his cows, either. I took a little ride down that way one day, just to see what kinda operation he was runnin'. I didn't see no herd of cattle grazin' anywhere, not near the creek anywhere, and that's the only real water close to that ranch house. Before I turned around and came back, I saw half a dozen cows gathered in the trees near the creek, and that's all the cows I saw." He paused to nod his confirmation to that. "Now, hold on," he said when Possum started to comment. "Two days later, I heard none of his men were in town 'cause they was fixin' to drive a herd of about four hundred cows to market. Now where'd them cows come from? Maybe he's got a secret way to raise 'em in two days' time."

"Might be you were lucky you didn't get shot," Possum said.

"Well, let me tell you, I ain't been nowhere near the place ever since this business with Tom," Rooster replied.

They talked about that for a while and could only come to the same conclusion Rooster had arrived at before—Sheriff John Mason had some kind of arrangement with Ned Stark. Perley finally reminded them that Emma and Rachael were expecting them back at the hotel for supper. "We need time to take our horses to the stable," he said. "And I'd like to clean up a little before we eat."

Horace Brooks walked out of the stable to meet them when they pulled up in front. "Well, howdy, Perley," he said. "Didn't expect to see you and Possum back in Bison Gap. Thought you were gone from here for good." He paused to nod at Rooster. "Rooster," he acknowledged.

"Howdy, Horace," Perley replied. "You know Possum's half owner of the hotel, so he needed to come back and make sure it got built." Perley thought that was as good a reason as any.

"That's right," Horace said. "I'd plumb forgot about

that. Looks like the women are doin' a pretty good job of runnin' it. You wantin' to stable your horses?"

"Yep," Perley answered, "for tonight, anyway, then we'll see after that. We might go out and stay with Rooster after tonight. They've been rode pretty hard today, better give 'em a portion of oats."

"How long are you gonna be in town?" Horace asked.

"Don't know yet," Perley answered as he and Possum took their saddlebags and rifles off the horses. "We'll be at the hotel tonight, if you need to find us." They took the saddles off and turned the horses out into the corral. Then when Horace showed them which stalls they would use, Perley unloaded the pack-horse and left the saddles and the packs in the stall. The horses taken care of, they walked back up the street to the hotel with Rooster leading his horse.

"Well, I'll be . . ." Perley started as they walked past a lot that had been vacant when he and Perley were there before. "First Bank of Texas," he read.

"That's right," Rooster said, "we didn't have no bank when you left here." He stroked his beard as he thought about it. "I can't figure out where they get money to put in a bank. Ain't nobody got any money around here." Neither of his companions had an answer for him.

"And there's the harness and saddle shop next door," Perley noticed, then reminded Possum that was Rex Cooper, whose daughter was nanny to Emma's son. It was surprising to see the signs of growth in the remote prairieland where Bison Gap was born.

When they reached the hotel, Wilbur Ross put them in separate rooms downstairs, in the back. This only when they insisted they didn't want the more expensive rooms upstairs in the front. "Closer to the kitchen," Possum said. Once they checked in, Possum and Rooster went out to the porch to sit in the rocking chairs while Perley made use of the hotel's washroom. Before he was finished, Rachael came out to the porch and told Possum and Rooster that supper was ready and the dining room was open. "Too bad about Perley," Possum said. "Might not be nothin' left, if you give me and Rooster a head start."

Rachael had a special table set in the back of the dining room with a reserved sign in the middle of it, in honor of her special guests. She led them in and seated them. Thinking Perley would be along any minute, Bess and Kitty put the food on the table and served the coffee. "He's gettin' all prettied up to eat with you ladies," Possum japed.

"He always was kinda tidy," Emma remarked, then frowned when she looked toward the door. "Oh, no, not tonight," she murmured.

Hearing her, Rachael asked what was wrong and Emma nodded toward the door. Rachael gasped when she realized who had just walked in. "Quirt Taylor! The nerve of that sidewinder to show up here. I thought Sheriff Mason told him to get out of town."

"What's he coming back here for, anyway," Emma whispered, "instead of the saloon?"

With their backs to the front door, Rooster and Possum were unaware of the unwelcome guest, their attention captured by the generous supper before them. They were not to be oblivious of him for very long, however, for he had spotted the private party in the back of the room. Brushing Kitty aside when she tried to intercept him, Quirt swaggered back to their table.

"Looks like you've got a party goin' on back here," Quirt smirked. "You gotta empty chair there, maybe I'll join you."

"You're not invited," Emma said.

"Why not?" he asked. "I left my shootin' iron on the table back there at the door. Ain't that the rule?"

"Sheriff ran you and that sorry trash you run with outta town," Rooster said, already heating up. "You ain't got no business in here, or anywhere else in Bison Gap."

Quirt favored him with a sarcastic grin. "You might wanna watch your mouth, you little dung weevil. You've already shot your mouth off about that business in the Buffalo Hump. That was Curly that done for her husband, not me." Turning to grin at Rachael then, he said, "Curly told me to give you a kiss for him."

"Get out of my dining room," Rachael demanded.

Her obvious anger seemed to please him. Apparently, it was his sole reason for coming to the dining room, and he stood there, enjoying her frustration. Unnoticed, because of the disturbance at the table, Perley walked up behind him. "Pardon me, but you're standin' in front of my chair, and my supper's gettin' cold." He had no idea who the man was, or what the excited conversation was about. As soon as Quirt turned around to face him, however, he realized it was not a friendly discussion.

"Who the hell are you?" Quirt blurted.

"I'm Perley," he answered.

"You're what?" Quirt responded, not sure he had heard him correctly.

"That's my name, Perley," he repeated.

"Your name's Pearly?"

"That's right, Perley Gates. What's your name?"

"Pearly Gates?" Quirt laughed. "That's even better. Well, Pearly Gates, if you don't wanna see them Pearly Gates right quick, you'd best set down in that chair and keep your mouth shut."

"That's Quirt Taylor, Perley," Rooster exclaimed. "He's the varmint who hangs around with Curly Williams. He's the one who lied to the sheriff about Tom goin' for his gun."

"There you go, runnin' your mouth again." Quirt pointed a finger at Rooster. "You're a dead man. You just ain't smart enough to know it."

"I reckon you've overstayed your welcome, Mister," Perley said calmly when he threatened Rooster. "It's time for you to walk on outta here, before we have to call the sheriff."

"Is that so?" Quirt replied. "I think maybe you're right. Maybe you oughta go get the sheriff. I'll tell you what, I'll wait outside for you and we'll go get the sheriff together. Whaddaya say to that?"

"Might be the best thing at that," Perley answered. "Might be a good idea to let the sheriff decide what to do."

"All right," Quirt said, struggling to keep from laughing, "Mr. Pearly Gates, I'll wait for you outside. Don't make me wait, or I'll come in and drag your ass out of here." He turned around and headed for the door. "Pearly Gates," they heard him mumble to himself and chuckle as he picked up his pistol and replaced it in his holster.

*Cow pie*, Perley couldn't help thinking as he followed Quirt to the door. He had a pretty good idea what was going to be waiting for him outside the hotel, but he couldn't take a chance on a crazy gunman shooting up the dining room. He went to the table and strapped on his gun belt. "Perley, don't!" Rachael cried out, suddenly realizing he was actually going to answer Quirt's challenge. As if her cry was a signal, everyone jumped up from the table to rush to the door. Possum and Rooster both grabbed their weapons from the table, ready to come to Perley's defense.

"Whoa!" Perley blurted and held up his hand. "I ain't sure what this fellow is up to, but I don't think he wants to walk down to the sheriff's office with me. Possum, if you and Rooster want to help me, go out the front door of the hotel and see if there's anyone else out there. I don't wanna walk into a firin' squad. If he's by himself, like he says, I'd rather just handle it, myself, so there won't be lead flyin' all over the place. All right?"

"Whatever you say, Perley," Possum answered and looked at Rooster to make sure he was in agreement. Rooster nodded. They strapped their guns on and went through the door to the hallway connecting the hotel and the dining room.

"You ladies stay inside," Perley said, then walked out the door.

Outside, Perley stopped in the shadow of the doorway to take a look at what he might be walking into, not at all sure he was doing a smart thing. Waiting for him, just as he said he would, Quirt was standing about fifteen yards from the door. Smiling in the fading light of sunset, his weapon holstered, he motioned for Perley to come forward. "Don't be shy, Pearly, come on out and we'll go to see the sheriff, unless you wanna just settle it between us. Just you and me, man-to-man. Whaddaya say?"

"I think it would be a whole lot better if we just go talk to the sheriff, like we said," Perley answered. "I'd rather do that. That's better than somebody gettin' killed, ain't it?"

"No, Pearly, I don't think that'll do any good. I think we'd best settle it right now. So you just walk out away from that door and stand right there." He pointed to a spot about fifteen yards in front of him.

"We don't have to do this," Perley said.

"Yes, we do," Quirt snapped, getting impatient with Perley's reluctance to face him. "You drag your yellow behind out here, or I'm gonna shoot you down in that doorway."

Perley walked out to the spot designated and stopped. "You're sure?"

"Damn you!" Quirt swore. "Turn and face me!"

Perley started to turn around, but before he had turned halfway, Quirt reached for his pistol. Hearing the sound of Quirt's hand on the handle of the Colt .44, Perley placed a bullet in the center of Quirt's chest while in the process of turning around. Quirt's pistol dropped from his hand and he stared in disbelief at the ugly hole in his shirt before he sank to his knees, then fell forward.

Standing by the front corner of the hotel, Possum said to Rooster, "I told you so."

"I didn't see him draw," Rooster declared. "One second he was standin' sideways, the next second I heard the shot." He shook his head and swore. "Damn!"

They walked out from behind the corner. "You all right, Perley?" Possum called out. "There weren't nobody else back here, just that crazy fool."

"I tried to talk him out of it, but he was determined

to have it out," Perley said as Possum and Rooster walked up to stand over the body.

Possum couldn't help wondering if Perley's seeming reluctance to shoot was in fact a planned ploy to frustrate his adversary to the point where he was prone to shoot in anger—which might cause careless concentration. *Nah,* he told himself. *Perley don't think that deep.*

"I was plannin' to just hit him in the shoulder, but he jumped the gun on me and I didn't have much time to aim," Perley explained.

"Looks to me like your aim was pretty damn good," Rooster declared as he stared down at the hole in the middle of Quirt's chest. "Wonder what in the world he came up here to the hotel for. Just to make mischief, I reckon."

"I reckon," Perley said. "Now, I expect we'd best really go get the sheriff."

Possum thought he knew why Quirt called Perley out, but he didn't share it with them. Quirt called Perley out because he looks so young and innocent that he appears to be an easy target for a gunman like Quirt. *Well, Quirt,* Possum thought, *more than likely it wasn't the first mistake you ever made.* He turned to see Emma and Rachael coming out the door, now that there appeared to be no more shots following the one. Soon a small crowd of spectators gathered to see the origin of the shot fired, unusual in that it came from the hotel and not the saloon. It was a while later that Sheriff John Mason arrived on the scene, after one of the spectators evidently told him someone had been killed.

Mason walked up to stand over the body. "Quirt Taylor," he mumbled low. He looked up then at Perley,

Possum, and Rooster, in that order. Then he brought his gaze back to focus on Perley. "Who are you?"

"My name's Perley Gates," he replied.

Mason's gaze remained on Perley for a long moment. He was familiar with the name. He had heard it enough since he was hired as sheriff. But the pleasant-looking young man standing before him looked nothing at all like he had imagined Perley Gates to look. Mason looked around again before asking, "Can somebody tell me what happened here?"

"Just like it looks, Sheriff," Rooster spoke up. "That piece of trash layin' there came into the dinin' room where we was fixin' to eat supper, lookin' to cause trouble. He called Perley outside to face him in a gun-fight." He paused then to point down at the body. "He lost. And that was after he tried to shoot before Perley had even turned around."

"Anybody else see it?" Mason asked.

"I did," Possum immediately replied. "It happened just like Rooster said.

"I saw it," Emma spoke up, "just like he said."

"I saw it," Rachael followed, "just like Rooster said."

To everyone's surprise, one other witness stepped forward. "What they said is the way it happened," Harvey Poole, the Baptist minister, said. "I was on my way back to the church when I saw the dead man and that man," he pointed to Perley, "about to have a duel. But the dead man didn't wait for him to turn around before he tried to shoot him. It's a sin to take another man's life, but I have to believe the one still standing was given no choice."

"Thank you, Reverend," Mason said, while thinking to himself he was going to have to tell Ned Stark he couldn't very well discredit the witnesses. "Well, I reckon there's no doubt it was self-defense. I'll get Floyd Jenkins to come get the body." He turned back to Perley then. "What brings you back to town, Mr. Gates?"

"As you probably know, Possum and I spent some time here and we thought we'd come back to see how our friends are doin'. Maybe you know Possum is half-owner in the new hotel, and he naturally wanted to see how Emma and Rachael were gettin' along. I mean, it being kind of unusual for two ladies to build a hotel. Looks to me like they're doin' everything right, though. What do you think, Sheriff?"

"I reckon I'd have to agree with you," Mason said. "They're doin' a lot better than a lot of people expected."

"I think they're concerned about seein' more roughnecks and troublemakers in town durin' the last few months," Perley went on, interested to hear the sheriff's comments on the subject. "Sounds to me like most of the trouble comes from fellows like this one and his friends who ride for Ned Stark. Must make your job harder."

Mason hesitated, not sure what this seemingly guileless young man's reasons for being in town really were. He decided to play along until he knew more about him. "Your friends are right," he said. "There have been some incidents in town lately, but no more than most other cow towns, I suspect. I know that face-off between Tom Parker and Curly Williams was hard for Rachael Parker to take, but it was just one of those things that happen when men are drinkin'. I am truly sorry for Rachael."

"That fellow, Curly Williams, he rides for Ned

Stark, right?" Perley asked. "Same as this one who came after me."

Mason was rapidly becoming uncomfortable with Perley's questions, but he attempted to hide his impatience. "Yes, I believe they did work for Stark, but I expect it's just a coincidence. As far as Tom Parker's death, I couldn't arrest Curly Williams for that any more than I can arrest you for Quirt Taylor's. I'm afraid Bison Gap is like every other cow town in Texas—can't help attractin' cowhands with time and money on their hands. Now, if you don't have any more questions, I'll get back to my job to try to keep the peace."

"Thank you, Sheriff," Perley said. "I 'preciate you takin' the time to talk to me. I hope you don't have to get called out for any more trouble tonight." He started back to the dining room where his friends had already gone. On the way, he considered the conversation he had just had with the sheriff. He didn't talk like a rotten sheriff who was in cahoots with an obvious outlaw cattleman. He wondered if he was as rotten as Rooster maintained.

It was a sober supper party that returned to the table. Bess stood near the end of the table, hands on hips, as she looked over the plates of food now getting cold. Seeing her concern, Rachael said, "It'll be fine, Bess. Those potatoes needed a little cooling-off, anyway."

"Hell," Rooster said, "pour some of that molasses on 'em and you won't know the difference." He picked up the bottle to demonstrate. When Perley sat down, Rooster said, "I reckon you just got a real welcome back from Ned Stark, and you had a little talk with our sheriff, too."

"I doubt Ned Stark had anything to do with it," Perley said and waved off the molasses when Rooster offered it to him. "Ned Stark doesn't even know who I am."

"He does now," Possum remarked. "At least, he will when ol' Quirt don't show up for breakfast in the mornin'." He paused to cut off another big bite of steak. "I wish he'd had the courtesy to wait till after supper before he showed up, though."

Rachael offered to dump the cold food and fill their plates with hot food, but everyone protested, especially after Bess commented. "If I do, there ain't gonna be food enough to feed the few payin' customers still comin' in." She and Kitty kept the coffee cups filled, however, and Bess put a new tray of biscuits in the oven. The discussion on the possible ties between Sheriff John Mason and outlaw Ned Stark continued until Rachael called it time to clean up after supper and prepare the kitchen for breakfast in the morning. Since the hotel desk was already closed for the night, Emma stayed to talk a while longer with Possum and Perley before they decided to go to bed. Since it was late, Emma offered Rooster a cot in Possum's room, but he had the problem of what to do about his horse. Perley offered to take it down to the stable for the night, knowing Horace Brooks used to stay there until late. So Perley took Rooster's black gelding down to the stable, arriving just as Horace was closing up. When he returned to the hotel, Rooster was already asleep in Possum's room.

# CHAPTER 4

Sheriff John Mason looked up from his desk when he heard the front door open. "I figured I might be seein' you sometime today," he said to Ned Stark. He was a little surprised to see Ned this early in the morning, however, and he commented on it.

"I needed a couple of things from the store," Stark replied. "And I figured as long as I was here, I'd let Floyd give me a shave and trim up my hair and mustache." That didn't surprise Mason. Stark was vain about his appearance. "While I was there, I paid Floyd to bury Quirt Taylor."

"I don't have a bottle here in the office," Mason said, not sure, if the visit was friendly or not. "But I could offer you a cup of coffee."

"No, thanks," Stark said, then got right to the reason he was there. "I lost a man here last night. Quirt Taylor was a good man. I hate to lose him. How did it happen? The story I got this mornin' was he got gunned down in a face-off with some stranger. The first question that came to my mind was, was it a fair fight? Quirt was pretty damn fast with a handgun, maybe as fast as Curly Williams. I wouldn't know

which one to bet on, if they were facin' each other."
He continued without waiting for Mason's answers.
"Next question I would ask is, who the hell is this
fellow, and what's he doin' in Bison Gap? I don't see
anybody in any of those cells in there. Did you have to
shoot him?" He finally sat down in a chair in front of
Mason's desk and waited for the sheriff's answers to
his questions.

"Things ain't always easy to fix," Mason attempted
to explain. "In the first place, your man went into the
hotel dinin' room where this fellow was eatin' supper
and told him to face him outside or he was gonna
shoot him in there. And all that in front of a room
half full of folks eatin' supper. Accordin' to the witnesses outside, Quirt tried to draw on him while he
was still turnin' around to face him. The fellow cut
him down before Quirt could get off a shot. End of
story. Quirt was just unlucky to challenge a man that's
evidently fast as greased lightnin'. I figure he got what
he asked for."

"Oh, you do, do ya?" Stark responded. "Why didn't
you arrest him?"

"'Cause one of the witnesses was the damn preacher,"
Mason shot back. "If I'da thrown that fellow in jail,
I'da been next Sunday's sermon. I had to let him go,
just like I let Curly go."

"Damn it, Mason, I'm payin' you good money to
keep my men out of jail," Stark fumed.

"And I've been doin' that for all the hell-raisers and
bar fights. Your end of our deal was you'd make sure
there was no shootin' up the town and no killin' of
any of the town folk. First, Curly comes in here and
shoots Tom Parker down. Now Quirt challenges a
stranger in the dinin' room of the hotel."

"What's he doin in Bison Gap, anyway?" Stark asked. "Is he just passin' through?"

"Hell, I don't know," Mason replied in frustration, "I asked him that, but he ain't really a stranger. He was the temporary sheriff for a couple of weeks before I got here. Ralph Wheeler tried to give him this job, but he didn't want it. He says him and Possum Smith just came to town to see how the hotel is doin'. Smith is half-owner of the hotel."

"Maybe this gunslinger is Smith's bodyguard," Stark suggested.

"I don't think so," the sheriff said.

"What's his name? Maybe I've heard of him."

"Perley Gates," Mason answered.

"What?" Stark responded, thinking he hadn't heard correctly. "Sounded like you said Pearly Gates."

"I did," Mason said. "Perley Gates."

"Pearly Gates," Stark repeated. "He's japin' you. That ain't his real name. He made that up. I'll bet if you look through your Wanted papers, you might find a description of somebody just like him."

"I already thought of that," Mason said. "I looked through 'em this mornin' and there wasn't anything close to this fellow. Besides, I told you, he was the sheriff here for a couple of weeks. He spells it P-e-r-l-e-y."

Stark was not convinced. "Is he stayin' at the hotel?" Mason said that he was, as far as he knew. "I think I'd like to take a look at this gunslinger," Stark went on. "Maybe I'll have some dinner in the hotel dinin' room to see if Mr. Perley Gates shows up. I've never been in that hotel, or the dinin' room, either." He got up from his chair. "It'll be a little bit before dinnertime, though, so I think I'll go over to the Buffalo Hump for a drink of whiskey. You want a little drink?"

"Thanks just the same, Ned," Mason responded, "but I don't think it's such a good idea for folks to see us drinkin' together in the saloon. I'm doin' my best to show these folks I'm tryin' to look out for 'em. And everybody in town knows nine outta ten times it's your boys that are raising the most hell in Bison Gap."

Stark shook his head slowly, looking at Mason with a scornful expression. "One of these days you're gonna wind up with the people of this town tellin' you what time you can use the outhouse. Never mind who you drink whiskey with." He paused at Mason's shaving mirror over the washstand to see that his hat was sitting squarely on his head, then went out the door.

At about the same time Stark left the sheriff's office, Possum Smith walked into Emma's office at the hotel to see what she was up to. "You look like you've got nothing to do," Emma said.

"Well, that just goes to show you that you don't know what a visitin' hotel partner does. I've been busy all mornin'. I inspected the dinin' room this mornin' and tested the cookin'. After that, I was busy right up to now, testin' the comfort of the rockin' chairs on the front porch. Now I'm checkin' to make sure the president's office is functionin' like it's supposed to."

She laughed, then asked, "Would you like to look at the ledger, so you can see how much money we've taken in and how much we've spent? That'll tell you if we're likely to show a profit for the year, or if we're gonna go in the hole."

"No, Ma'am," he said. "I trust you. If I didn't, I'da never invested my money with you." That seemed to please her, so he didn't have to tell her he couldn't read or write.

"All right," she replied, "but you know you can look at the books any time you choose." He grinned and nodded.

"Where did Perley and Rooster get to?" she asked then.

"Rooster had to go home to take care of his hogs and chickens. Perley went along with him. They said they'd be back here to eat dinner with us."

"Rooster will probably appreciate the help," Emma said. "He's working pretty hard to keep up with everything Tom had started. He's always raised hogs, but Tom had planted a big garden to supply vegetables for the hotel dining room. And he added the chickens for eggs and some as fryers. So Rooster's got his hands full. I hope it's not too much for him, because it gives our dining room something to serve besides beef and pork."

"That oughta been my part in this partnership, I reckon, helpin' Rooster, maybe takin' Tom's place, since he ain't here no more. But I swear, Emma, if I was to work at farmin' all day long, I likely couldn't raise nothin' more than a blister. I just ain't good at it. I reckon I could get by, if we switched over and started to raise cattle."

"You're an investing partner," she told him. "And don't think that money you invested with Rachael and me didn't help put the hotel in the shape it's in." She could see that he was genuinely concerned that he wasn't carrying half the load, and she was about to reassure him further when Perley and Rooster walked in. She glanced up at the clock and greeted them. "Right on time," she announced. "The dining room should be opening in five minutes. Come on, we might as well go on in."

They found that Rachael had kept the three small tables together to make one larger reserved table for them. Alice and Melva hurried to claim the chairs on either side of the one Perley chose, earning a warning from Rachael to behave. "If you don't, you'll be eating in the kitchen." When everyone was seated, she said that she wouldn't join them right away because she would be busy helping Bess and Kitty. When everything was running smoothly, she would join the party later. "I have to be on my toes when the owners of the hotel are here," she joked. Then she looked at the clock on the wall and announced, "Time to open up," and left to unlock the outside door.

There were six or seven customers waiting to come in. Rachael greeted each one, telling them to sit at any of the small tables around the room. One of the last she greeted was a single man, his jacket open, revealing a gun belt. "I'm sorry, sir," she said, "I have to ask you to leave your weapon on this table by the door."

"Oh, yes, ma'am," he responded politely. "I didn't notice the sign on it. I've never been in here before, so I didn't think about the gun." He immediately unbuckled the gun belt, wrapped his pistol and holster up in it, and placed it on the table. "How's that?" He asked, cheerfully.

"Thank you, sir. You can sit anywhere you like and Kitty will take care of you."

She started to leave him to choose a table, but he stopped her with a question. "What's the big table at the back where they're sittin'?" She told him it was a party of family and friends who were visiting. "Oh, so they're some of your folks, right?"

"That's right," Rachael said, then excused herself to greet some more customers coming in. Stark gave her a smile, then walked back to seat himself at the closest table to the one reserved.

Bess and Kitty kept the food coming, determined that no one should leave the table wanting more. The conversation revolved around Perley's report on the impressive work Tom and Rooster had done on the plot of ground beyond Rooster's cabin. The noise of their talking never reached a boisterous level, so as not to disturb the peaceful atmosphere of the dining room. It made it difficult for the man eating alone at a table near them to hear what was being said, however, even when he leaned toward them. He studied the men at the table, trying to decide which one might be Perley Gates. One at a time he watched them. The short gnarly elf-like man had to be ruled out, and he guessed him to be the one called Rooster. The young, boyish-looking man who was constantly engaging the two little girls in small conversation was possibly the little girls' father. Consequently, he was not a candidate. That left the other older man with the beard streaked with gray and a long gray braid of hair down his back. He looked capable of handling a firearm, but he couldn't picture him as the gunslinger who took Quirt Taylor down. Stark decided that Perley Gates had evidently not attended the dinner. It was a disappointment, for he had really hoped to get a look at the man. He decided, *what the hell, it's damn fine eating.*

When he finished his dinner, Kitty came to take the dishes away and asked if he would like more coffee. He said that he might as well. He was in no hurry.

When she brought the pot back to the table, he asked, "Who do the two little girls belong to?"

"That's Alice and Melva," Kitty answered. "They're Rachael Parker's daughters. Rachael's the manager of the dining room."

"Is that her husband sitting between the little girls?" Stark asked.

"Oh, no, sir," Kitty replied. "Rachael's husband is dead. He was shot down by a murdering outlaw, leaving those little girls without a father."

Stark fought off an urge to chuckle when he realized he had forgotten her husband was the man Curly shot in the saloon. "That fellow sittin' between 'em looks like he could take on the job as their daddy."

Kitty smiled at the thought. "I don't hardly think so," she said, "not Perley Gates."

That caught Stark's attention right away. "That's who?" He asked to make sure he had heard correctly. "Perley Gates?"

She smiled warmly. "That's right, that's his name. Everybody asks him to repeat it." She left him then to fill other coffee cups.

*Perley Gates,* he said to himself, thinking how looks could be deceptive. In spite of the thought, he found it hard to believe the man he was looking at now could have taken Quirt Taylor. There had to be some unusual factor in play. Quirt must have been drunk. He hadn't thought to ask Sheriff Mason if Quirt was drunk or not. The more he thought about it, the more the man interested him. He decided he'd like a closer look, so he gulped the last swallow of his coffee and got up from the table. He picked up his hat from the back of the chair next to his and placed it carefully on his head, making sure it was sitting squarely. Then he casually walked over to the table in the back.

There was a pause in the conversation when the stranger approached and stood by the table. With their backs toward the front of the room, Possum and Rooster were puzzled when Emma paused in mid-sentence, until the stranger spoke. "Just thought I'd tell you I've never been in here before, and I think the food was mighty fine." His remarks were aimed at Rachael, but his focus was on Perley Gates.

"Why, thank you, sir," Rachael responded. "We're always glad to know we've pleased our customers." Possum and Rooster turned to see who she was thanking. Rooster, the only one at the table who had ever seen Ned Stark, froze immediately, speechless for a long moment.

"Not at all," Stark returned, then added, "And I'm sorry to hear about your husband."

Rooster shot up from his chair. "Ned Stark!" He blurted. "You got your nerve comin' in here!" His outburst brought an air of alarm over the whole table. "Get your sorry ass outta here!"

Rachael stood up as well, her face twisted in anger. "Ned Stark," she repeated the name as if it was bitter on her tongue. "Get out of my dining room. We don't serve people like you in here." Her voice, though calm, was heavy with the tension of her fury.

Stark responded with a smile. "Not a very nice way to treat a payin' customer. I have to say the food was good, though." He made a sweeping look across the table. "I ain't the one who shot your husband. That was Curly Williams," he couldn't resist saying, then turned and walked toward the door, satisfied that he had amused himself as well as getting a good look at

Perley Gates. And in his assessment of the man, he was more convinced than ever that Quirt Taylor's death by that man's hand was an accident. Quirt must have been drunk. Without stopping, he picked up his gun belt and walked out the door in better spirits than when he had walked in. He was no longer worried about a possible threat to him or his men. *Not from two old codgers and an innocent-looking young man,* he thought. *And Perley Gates never once opened his mouth, the whole time I was jawing with that lady that runs the place. Maybe I'll turn Curly loose again.*

When he left the hotel, Stark went by Wheeler's Merchandise to buy a few articles he needed, like a new shaving mug and soap, and a new razor strop. The mayor waited on him, providing more amusement for Stark with the cool reception he displayed. Wheeler was one of the few merchants in town who had done business with Stark, even though they all knew who he was. And most of them had had encounters with his men. When he paid for his purchases, he was prompted to remark, "You ain't ever very talkative when I come in your store, but you always take my money."

"Our town would be a much better place to live and work in if that wild bunch of hands working for you didn't raise so much hell," Wheeler felt the need to reply.

Stark shrugged. "Well, you know how it is when hardworkin' ranch hands get a chance to come to town. They can't help lettin' off a little steam and havin' a drink or two. You and your fellow merchants ought not complain. My boys spend a lotta money in your town."

"Most of the time, it's not enough to pay for the damage they do," Wheeler replied.

Standing at the end of the counter, silently listening to their conversation, Cora Wheeler stared at the man who employed the wild, lawless gang of troublemakers that had recently picked Bison Gap as their playground. When he turned to her and said, "Good day, ma'am," she simply turned and walked out of the room. He chuckled, pleased by her reaction. "Be seein' you, Mayor," he said to Wheeler and walked out of the store.

He made one more stop before leaving town and that was at the Buffalo Hump, where he had left his horse. One little shooter for the road, he decided, and tied his purchases on his saddle horn, then went inside. When he walked up to the bar, Jimmy McGee greeted him soberly, "Mr. Stark."

"Gimme a double shot of corn whiskey," Stark ordered. Jimmy poured it and set it on the bar, then watched as Stark sipped a little of it before tossing the rest down. "Wanted to make sure it's the good stuff." He tossed two bits on the bar and started to walk out, satisfied with the fear he thought he saw in every face in Bison Gap. He stopped at the door when he heard his name called. When he looked back, he saw Henry Lawrence, the owner of the Buffalo Hump, coming from the back office.

"Wonder if I could have a word with you, Mr. Stark?" Lawrence asked.

"Sure, what's on your mind?" Stark replied.

"I'd like to talk to you about some of the damage we've suffered here just since you moved your cattle operation close to Bison Gap," Henry said. "I've got some figures here of the damages we've suffered durin' that time that were all caused by your men, and I'd like to talk to you about paying for some of them."

"Why do ya wanna talk to me about 'em?" Stark asked.

"'Cause they're your employees," Lawrence answered.

"Hell, they work for me," Stark declared. "They ain't my children. I ain't got nothin' to do with what they do on their own time. Maybe you oughta talk to the sheriff about your problem."

"I was just hoping you might want to do the right thing," Lawrence said.

"I always do the right thing," Stark said with a smirk, "the right thing for me." He walked on out the door. They could hear him chuckling to himself as he stepped up on his horse and pulled away from the hitching rail.

In the hotel dining room, Emma and Possum were still trying to calm Rachael down. Her anger had sustained her until he walked out the door, then she began to fall apart. Still grieving the loss of her husband, she had not been prepared to be confronted with the man she held responsible for Tom's death. If Ned Stark had never moved to this part of the country, Tom would still be alive. It had been bad enough when she only had a name to hate, when he was almost like a spirit who was not a real person. But now that spirit had taken physical form and she had a real person to hate. She could not rid her mind's eye of his leering face. Seeing the distress in the faces of the two little girls as they witnessed their mother's trauma, Emma left her long enough to take the girls to her room in the hotel to stay with Barbara and the baby.

Of no use in situations such as this, there was nothing Perley could think to do, other than to grab Rachael's elbow when she threatened to collapse. He eased her back down in her chair, but she wanted to leave the dining room and the gaping eyes of the startled customers. He persuaded her to wait until Emma came back to help her and stood by her until she did. Then with Emma leading the way, he walked her back into the hotel to her room.

When he returned to the dining room, he was met by Kitty, who was waiting for him. "Rooster and Possum got their guns and went after Stark!" She exclaimed as soon as he walked in.

"Uh-oh," Perley responded. He picked up his gun belt and ran out the door to the street. Rooster's horse was missing, so he jumped on Buck and galloped down to the stable. He found them there, Rooster waiting while Possum saddled his horse.

When he saw Perley, Rooster shouted, "Come on, Perley! We're goin' after that stinkin' devil!"

"And do what, if you catch him, shoot him?"

"Well, you heard what he said to Rachael," Rooster replied.

"Yeah, he oughta have his ass kicked for that," Perley said. "But if you kill him, you're sure as hell gonna be arrested and probably hanged for it. Then who's gonna raise the hogs and the chickens for the dinin' room? From what you've told me, it doesn't seem to make much sense to go ridin' into a whole nest of gunslingers and ask 'em politely to please don't interfere while you shoot their boss. Do you know where Stark's ranch house is?"

"Well, no, not exactly," Rooster admitted, "but it's somewhere on that three hundred acres runnin' up against the creek." Possum, having saddled his horse and led him out of the stable, stopped to listen to the discussion.

"Stark said some disrespectful things in there, and I admire you wantin' to make him pay for it. But I just hate to see you and Possum ride into his stronghold to get killed and give him something else to crow about." Rooster made a face like he was thinking about it, so Perley went on. "We just got here. This business with Stark's men is just startin'. It started with me havin' to shoot Quirt Taylor. You think it's gonna end there? I hate to tell you, but it ain't, and we've got a lot better chance of fightin' Stark's men on our ground. The next move is theirs, and I expect they'll come lookin' for me, 'cause I'm the one who shot Quirt."

"I don't know, Rooster," Possum spoke up. "Maybe Perley's right it don't make much sense to go ridin' into that big outlaw camp after Stark."

"I think Stark would be tickled pink if you two went ridin' into his camp," Perley said.

"Hell," Rooster swore, "I reckon you're right. I ain't got no sense. Let's go back to the hotel."

"I wish we'da talked this thing over before I went to the trouble to come down here and saddle my horse," Possum complained and turned the gray around to go back in the stable. After Perley said he was going to leave Buck there, too, Possum said, "You might as well leave yours here, Rooster. You can sleep on that cot another night."

Horace Brooks stood just inside the stable door, watching the discussion, but not sure what they were debating. "You gonna leave 'em or not?" he asked.

# CHAPTER 5

"Well, boys," Ned Stark announced when he rode back into the small ranch he and his men had settled in after killing the original occupants. "I had the pleasure of meetin' Mr. Perley Gates, himself, the badass gunslinger who shot Quirt Taylor. And I wanna tell you, he had me shiverin' in my boots."

Suspecting the boss was japing them, Curly Williams responded. "He did, huh? Where'd you see him?"

"I went into the Bison House Hotel and had me some dinner at the dinin' room," Stark answered.

"The hell you did," Curly shot back, certain he was japing them then. "Did you say howdy to the widow Parker?"

"I surely did, and as a matter of fact, I told her you said to tell her howdy, too."

"I know you're lyin' now," Curly said. "And where was Mr. Perley Gates while you was tellin' her all that?"

"He was settin' at the table with her, her and the woman that runs the hotel, and that little cuss called Rooster, and another old gray-haired jasper." He went on to paint the whole picture for the eight men gathered around the table near the fireplace. "I tell you what," he concluded, "that was a bunch of real unhappy people when I left there."

"Yeah," Eli Priest asked, "what about Perley Gates? What did he do while you was dealin' all that horse manure?"

"He was settin' on the other side of the table from me, playin' pattycakes with two little girls about five or six years old. I looked right at him and he never said a word."

"You sure that was him?" Curly asked. "Perley Gates, the gunslinger that beat Quirt Taylor, man-to-man?" Stark nodded and smiled. "How do you know that was him? Did you ask him?"

"Didn't have to," Stark answered. "Girl that works in the dining room told me who he was, so I knew who he was before I walked back to their table."

"Yeah, well I wanna see him," Curly said. "Me and Quirt has been ridin' together for a helluva long time, so I've got somethin' I need to settle with Perley Gates. I know how fast Quirt was, so there's somethin' that ain't right about that gunfight."

"Well, why don't you ride on into town and settle it?" Stark asked.

"I was fixin' to soon as I heard about it, but you said it was best to stay outta town 'cause you didn't want the sheriff to get his drawers in a tangle. You said stay outta town," Curly insisted.

"I ain't tellin' you to stay outta town now." He paused while he thought about it for a moment. "I'll tell you what. I ain't about to let him get away with shootin' one of my men. Curly, I'm givin' you a huntin' license, by yourself, for one day only. That's tomorrow. And that's because you and Quirt was such good friends. So Perley Gates is all yours tomorrow, but you better get him. 'Cause if you don't, it's gonna be open season on him, and anybody that gets him will collect a hundred bucks from me." His announcement was met with loud whoops and grunts of enthusiasm. One hundred dollars was a lot of money just to kill one man.

Curly grinned and declared, "Boys, I'll be ridin' into town early in the mornin'. I've got a man I've gotta see."

"You better make sure you get him, Curly, 'cause I need me a hundred dollars," Slim Garrett declared. He was immediately challenged by the rest of the gang.

"Maybe you'd best get him, Curly," Jim Duncan said. "If you don't, we're gonna have everyone of us bumpin' into each other, runnin' around that town, lookin' for that jasper."

Stark spoke up then. "Jim's right, I can't have all of you hittin' that town at the same time lookin' for that prairie rat. You're gonna have to use some sense and catch him off to the side somewhere. Don't go ridin' down the street, shootin' at the stores and shops. You'd have a company of Rangers down here, and I ain't ready to leave this setup we've got here." He looked back at Curly then. "Curly, you get him to stand up to you in a gunfight, if you can. I wanna make that sheriff think I'm still coverin' his ass."

Back in town, at the Bison House dining room, there was a somewhat less lighthearted atmosphere at the supper table, with Emma wondering what would happen next to spoil what was supposed to be a special gathering of her closest friends and family. What would come from the Ned Stark gang to spoil this night's meal? There was very little chatter beyond comments on Bess's fine supper, and none at all from Rachael. To break the blanket of awkward silence, Perley commented to Possum that he thought he would take Buck to see John Payne in the morning for some new shoes. Possum said he had decided to go out to Rooster's cabin with him in the morning to help him with his pump. "He's thinkin' his well might be runnin' dry," he said, "but I doubt it." No one dawdled over coffee before retiring for the night.


Perley got up well before breakfast the next morning. The dining room wasn't open yet, so he went out to sit on the porch till it was time. He found Possum already there in one of the rocking chairs he had admired when they first arrived. "Rooster still in bed?" Perley asked.

"Yep," Possum answered. "He was still sawin' logs when I left the room. When he comes outta there, he'll swear he was awake when I left, though. You watch and see if he don't. He always likes to say he gets up before anybody else does." They sat in silence for a few moments, watching the new day arrive. Then Possum broached an issue that he was concerned about. "You know, partner, I'm feelin' a little bit worried about ol' Rooster. I mean, with the habit he's got of poppin' off about Ned Stark and his men. With him livin' out there by himself, it'd be too damn easy to shoot him down without anybody noticin' he was dead for a day or two. That's the main reason I'm goin' out to his place with him this mornin'."

"I know what you mean," Perley said. "I've had

some thoughts about that, too, but I don't think we could talk him into movin' into town."

"I know that's so," Possum said at once. "I told him last night he oughta stay in town every night, at least for a while. But he swore nobody was gonna chase him offa his own land. Besides, he's got work out there. He can't just walk off and leave it."

"He's right about that," Perley said. "It's a lot for one man to handle, especially if he's ridin' back and forth to town every day."

"Even if he did that, it'd still be easy to pick him off comin' or goin'," Possum insisted.

"Pick who off?" Rooster interrupted. They hadn't heard him open the screen door. "Pick who off, comin' or goin'?" He asked again with a pretty good idea they were talkin' about him.

"You, you old coot," Possum answered. "It wouldn't take much to plug you, ridin' that little trail by the creek."

"Might not be as easy as you think," Rooster stated defiantly. "I guarantee ya, it'll cost 'em if they come snoopin' around my place."

It was this attitude that worried Perley. He was afraid Rooster would invite trouble with his open defiance of Ned Stark. "It's always smart to keep a sharp eye out, and don't make a lot of noise," he said.

"Like I did this mornin'," Possum said, "when I walked outta the room and left you sleepin'." He looked at Perley and winked.

"Hell, I was awake when you got up," Rooster claimed at once, "been awake for half an hour."

"Is that a fact?" Possum asked. "How come you never said somethin'?"

"I was thinkin' and I didn't feel like jawin' with you

first thing," he maintained. Possum looked at Perley and shook his head as if to say, *what are we gonna do with him?*

"You gonna get your horse shod this mornin'?" Rooster asked Perley.

"Yep," Perley answered. "I think I'd better while I've got a chance. Buck oughta remember John Payne. He fit him with new shoes when we were down here before."

The conversation was cut short then when Alice opened the screen door and announced, "Mama said to tell you that breakfast is ready."

"I need to get back to my place for good," Rooster grumbled. "Half the day's gone waitin' around here to eat."

They were glad to see that Rachael seemed to be back to her cheerful self this morning, as she scurried around preparing for the usual early breakfast customers soon to start showing up. One of them was John Payne, the blacksmith. A single man, Payne had an arrangement with Rachael to eat breakfast every morning for a set monthly rate. As a rule, he made his own dinner, since it wasn't always convenient to leave his shop in the middle of the day. And supper was split between the hotel and the Buffalo Hump. On this morning, Perley joined him at his table to let him know he needed to have Buck shoed. Payne offered to go to the stable and get the bay gelding, to save Perley the trouble. But Perley told him he was going to the stable, anyway, so he'd bring Buck to him. He was reluctant to tell Payne that Buck sometimes acted up a little when someone other than Perley tried to lead him anywhere. On the other hand, as long as Perley led the horse somewhere, Buck never gave anybody any trouble—unless they tried to ride him. Then they usually figured out why Perley named him Buck.

"I'll bring Buck in about half an hour," Perley said when Payne finished his breakfast and got up to leave. "Is that all right?"

"That'll do just fine," Payne answered. "It'll take me a little while to get ready to work, anyway, but I'll get to him right away." Perley picked up his cup and returned to the reserved table to finish his coffee between Alice and Melva.

"Mornin', Horace," Perley greeted the owner of the stable.

"Mornin'," Horace returned. "You fixin' to head out somewhere?"

"Nope. No need to bother with my saddle. I'm just gonna take Buck over to John Payne's shop. It's time to get him some new shoes." Perley slipped his bridle on the big bay's head, led him out of the stall, then out of the stable and up the street toward the blacksmith shop.

As he walked the short distance to John Payne's forge, a lone rider passed him on the street, heading in the direction of the Buffalo Hump Saloon, which was on the opposite side of the creek. He paid no attention to the young man leading the horse, just as Perley gave him no more than a brief glance. When he reached the blacksmith, however, he found Payne pausing to watch the rider as he crossed the bridge to the saloon and went inside. "Little early in the day to start drinkin' whiskey," Perley commented.

"Most likely goin' to get some breakfast at Ida

Wicks's table," Payne said. "That's Curly Williams. He's the man who shot Tom Parker in that saloon a few weeks ago. I wonder what John Mason is gonna do when he finds out Curly's back in town. He ordered him out, for good, I hoped. You don't usually see any of Ned Stark's men in town this early in the day. He can't be up to anything good. I wonder if I oughta go tell the sheriff Curly's in town?"

Perley's mind was also working on what Curly's appearance in town might mean, as far as him and his friends were concerned. He could offer to go alert the sheriff, or he could just let things happen as they naturally played out. The only thing he knew for sure was that he was determined to be ready to act should he see Curly heading to the hotel. "I don't know, John," he finally answered Payne's question. "He might wanna know that Curly's back in town. I can go tell him, if you want to get started on my horse."

"Might be best, at that," Payne said. "You go tell Sheriff Mason and I'll start on Buck." He turned his attention immediately to the horse. He lifted each hoof to check its condition. "They look in pretty good shape, shouldn't take more'n an hour to get you fixed up."

"Good," Perley said. "I'll be back after I tell the sheriff he's got company." He left then and walked up the street to the sheriff's office. He walked across the same bridge Curly had just ridden across because the jail was also on that side of Oak Creek.

Sheriff John Mason walked to the front door of his office with a cup of coffee in hand and looked across the creek at the main street of Bison Gap. It was still early morning when everything was peaceful. He hoped it stayed that way and had turned away to go back to fill his cup when a man walking across the bridge caught his eye. He paused when he identified the man as Perley Gates and wondered if he was heading to the Buffalo Hump. A glance at the front of the saloon found one horse tied at the rail. He shifted his gaze back to Perley and saw him pass by the saloon, evidently coming to see him. The sheriff had already heard about Ned Stark's visit to the hotel dining room, so he assumed Perley Gates was on his way to complain to him about it. It was hard enough to keep the peace, he thought, without Stark stirring up more trouble. He went back inside, placed his coffee cup on the dry sink, and sat down at his desk to await Perley's visit.

"Mornin', Sheriff," Perley greeted him when he walked into the office.

"Mr. Gates," Mason acknowledged. "What can I do for you?"

"Nothin' for me, Sheriff," Perley answered. "I left my horse with the blacksmith. He's gettin' new shoes, and the blacksmith thought you might like to know that Curly Williams just rode back in town. He's at the saloon right now, if you're interested." Perley paused, waiting for Mason's response. When there was no immediate reaction, Perley sought to remind him. "You know, since you ran him out of town for murderin' Tom Parker."

Mason reacted then. "It was not ruled a murder," he said. "I ran Curly outta town because there mighta been trouble from some people who didn't see it that way." He could see his day already ruined by the appearance of Curly Williams. Ned Stark had assured him that he would keep Curly out of town. Now, what the hell was he doing back here? "What?" He said when he realized he had been distracted by his thoughts when Perley was talking.

"I said, that's right, it wasn't ruled a murder," Perley answered. "Knowin' Tom as I did, it would take a lot for me to picture him respondin' to any challenge to participate in a gunfight. You musta thought so, too."

"I had to go with what the witnesses saw," Mason declared.

"Right you are, Sheriff, that's the only thing you can do." He turned to leave. "Like I said, I just walked over because John Payne said I oughta tell you that all your witnesses to that shoot-out just rode in on one horse."

"Tell Payne I said much obliged," Mason said as Perley walked out the door. He remained sitting at his desk after Perley had gone, trying to make up his mind what he should do. It appeared that Curly was calling his bluff. He had depended upon Ned to control his hotheaded gunman. Now, with Ned's aggressive visit to the hotel last night, coupled with Curly showing up the very next morning, it would seem that Ned was backing out of his agreement with him. Still uncertain, he drew his .44 and broke it open to make sure it was fully loaded, the act no more than a nervous reflex. He got up from the desk then and walked to the door to look toward the saloon again, hoping the horse would be gone, but it was still there. Looking toward the bridge, he saw Perley just as he reached the other side, heading to the blacksmith. He told himself that he had to believe Stark had not backed out of their deal, and that Curly was acting in disobedience of Ned's orders. It all came down to the fact that he was going to have to take some action to show Curly and his friends they could not run over the town as long as he was sheriff.

Moving slow and deliberately, still hoping Curly might get on his horse and ride out of town, Mason walked out of his office and locked the door. Down the steps, he paused, then started walking toward the Buffalo Hump. Curly's flea-bitten gray gelding was still tied at the rail when he walked into the saloon. Sitting at a table on the side of the room, Curly sat, eating a steak breakfast. He looked up when Mason walked in. "Well, here comes the sheriff," Curly remarked in his usual sarcastic way. "Howdy, Sheriff. Sit down and have a cup of coffee, or a drink of likker, if that's what you need."

Not sure of himself, or how he should handle the situation, Mason sat down opposite him. Jimmy McGee walked over to the table. "You want anything, Sheriff?"

Mason said no, so Jimmy turned around and went back to the bar, leaving the sheriff looking at the sleazy, taunting smile on Curly's face for several long moments before he made himself speak. "What are you doin' back here in town, Curly? Does Ned know you're here? We had a deal, and you're supposed to stay outta town."

"Hold on there, Sheriff, don't get all lathered up. Sure, Ned knows I'm in town. I've got a job to do. Perley Gates, I'm lookin' for him. He gunned down one of our men, and Ned ain't gonna stand for that. And he picked me to take care of him, 'cause Quirt Taylor was a friend of mine. You want me outta town? The quickest way to do that is to tell me where I can find Perley Gates."

"I don't need another killin' in this town right

now," Mason protested. "Damn it, Ned knows that. We had a deal."

"Well, the deal changed when that dirty dog shot Quirt. When I get Perley Gates, the deal can go back on." He paused, waiting for Mason's reply to that, but Mason still hesitated. "Let me put it to ya straight, Sheriff, I'm gonna settle with Perley Gates, no matter who I have to go through to do it." He dropped his hand into his lap. "And that's the reason I've got this .44 under the table, lookin' straight at you."

"Hold on!" Mason blurted. "He's at the blacksmith right now. You mighta passed him when you rode in, 'cause he was in my office just a few minutes ago." The words came out of his mouth like vomit from a drunk.

Curly flashed that cynical smile. "Good boy, Sheriff, now that wasn't so hard, was it? Now, I reckon I've gotta go see the blacksmith." He got up from the chair. There was no pistol in his lap and Mason immediately despised himself for his moment of cowardice. He stood up as well, watching Curly as he swaggered by the bar, tossing some money on the bar as he passed. Suddenly, Mason felt the weight of his firearm in his holster, and as Curly approached the door, the sheriff's hand quivered as he stared at the outlaw's broad back. At that moment, it seemed that Curly knew what he was thinking, for he suddenly spun around to face Mason, his pistol drawn and leveled at the startled sheriff. Curly grinned, eased the hammer back down, and holstered the weapon. "See you later, Sheriff," he said and was out the door.

Mason felt the need to hold on to the back of the chair, his knees having been drained of all their strength. "That son of a bitch is crazy," Jimmy said.

"Whaddaya gonna do about what he said about Perley? He's talkin' like he's just gonna shoot him down."

Mason was trying to think fast to keep from looking like he didn't know what to do. "I'm gonna go after him," he said, "to make sure nothin' like that happens. He's lookin' to call Perley Gates out. If Perley accepts his challenge, then it's just between the two of 'em. But if Perley won't fight him, then I'll have to arrest Curly if he tries to kill him."

"Arrest him, hell," Jimmy blurted. "Shoot the varmint!"

"Maybe I'll do that," Mason said as he ran out the door. When he got outside, however, he stopped to think again when he could still see Curly riding down toward the blacksmith. "I might need my rifle," he muttered. "I'd best get it." He turned and ran to his office. Inside, he took the Henry rifle out of the rack on the wall and checked to see if the magazine was loaded. He cranked a cartridge into the chamber, then stopped to think again. *It's gonna be too late by the time I get down there,* he thought. *I'm not gonna be in time to stop it. The best thing to do is wait here till I find out what happened, and then I can do whatever has to be done.* He sat down at his desk and fumbled with a cabbage-size rock that he used for a paperweight, waiting for someone to come to alert him.

# Chapter 6

Perley sat on a nail keg, watching Payne work on Buck's hooves, and the blacksmith was commenting on the condition of them and the fact that there was not any abnormal growth around the old shoes. "Looks like you take pretty good care of him," Payne said.

"He takes pretty good care of me," Perley replied.

"He's a fine-lookin' gelding," Payne commented. "Why'd you name him Buck?"

"'Cause he does," Perley said. When Payne laughed, Perley shrugged and explained. "Buck's got it in his head that nobody ain't supposed to ride him but me. I don't know why. I never told him that."

Payne smiled. "So, if I hopped on his back when I'm done, and just rode him around the shop a couple of times to see how his new shoes feel, he'd buck me off?"

"Well, you're welcome to try it and see. I would expect he might test your flyin' ability, to tell you the truth."

Payne cocked his head and grinned. "I've broke more'n a few horses in my time."

"That so?" Perley responded. "That's right, I remember Rooster tellin' me you used to work on a cattle ranch." He started to say more but hesitated when it appeared something had attracted Payne's attention. Judging by the frown on his face, Perley guessed it was something serious. So he turned around to see what had caught the blacksmith's eye. There was a rider approaching them, and Perley realized it was the same man who rode past him when he was leading Buck to the shop. "Curly?" he asked.

"Yeah," Payne answered, "and it looks like he's comin' here. What did Sheriff Mason say when you told him Curly was in town?"

"He just said to tell you he was much obliged for the information," Perley answered. "That was it—didn't say anything about what he was gonna do—just much obliged." While they waited, Perley studied the approaching killer as best he could, for he had never seen Curly before, except for the brief few seconds when he rode past him. Payne was obviously concerned to see him coming to his shop. He wanted nothing to do with him or any of the others who rode for Stark. Perley felt obliged to free Payne of any worry about trouble from the gunman. "I'm pretty sure he's come lookin' for me," Perley said. "I was the unlucky son of a gun who had to shoot Quirt Taylor, so I reckon he's come to complain about it."

"Complain about it?" Payne exclaimed. "He ain't the kind to come talk to you about somethin'. Unless you want the same thing Tom Parker got, you'd do well to run out the back before he gets any closer."

"That is one option," Perley said, then turned to look behind Payne's forge at over two hundred yards of open prairie with not a tree in sight. "That doesn't seem like a good option, though, with me on foot and him on a horse. So I might as well sit right here and wait for him. He might not want to start too much trouble, since the sheriff's office is right across the creek."

"It's too late now, anyway," Payne said. "Where the hell's the sheriff?"

Curly rode the flea-bitten gray right up in the middle of Payne's shop area before pulling it to a stop. "Mornin', boys," he greeted them, seeming to be greatly pleased to be there. "You'd be the blacksmith," he said, looking at Payne and having seen him in town before. "But you, settin' on that nail keg, I ain't never seen you before."

"You saw me just a little while ago," Perley said, "when I was leadin' my horse up here from the stable. I reckon you forgot."

Perley's answer seemed to amuse Curly. He threw his right leg over the gray's neck and slid from the saddle to land facing Perley. "So, what might your name be?"

"My name's Perley Gates."

Curly's grin grew wider, as if he had just hit the jackpot. "Perley Gates," he echoed, "just like them Pearly Gates in Heaven, right?"

"That's right," Perley said. "Only it ain't spelled the same."

"Well, Perley, you need to get your ass off of that nail keg. Me and you have got some business to take care of."

"Is that a fact? What kinda business?"

"Oh, it won't take long," Curly went on, savoring every second of it and wishing it would take longer. "You see, Perley, Quirt Taylor was a close friend of mine, and folks tell me that you were the one who shot him."

"That is a fact," Perley allowed. "That was too bad about Quirt. He just wouldn't listen to reason. But I am sorry that you lost a friend, so I apologize for that and I hope that will satisfy you."

"Are you just plumb loco?" Curly wondered. "You're gonna have to pay for shootin' Quirt. And this time, there ain't gonna be no tricks or anything—just you and me face-to-face. Then we'll see if you was fast enough to beat Quirt in a fair fight."

"That's all you're really interested in, ain't it? Whether you're better with a gun than I am? Ain't that about it?" His questions brought the sarcastic grin back to Curly's face. "That's what I thought," Perley continued. "There's a better way to find out which one of us is the best shot." He turned to Payne and asked, "John, have you got any matchsticks you could let us borrow?"

Trapped in a stupor of fascination of this insane preamble to a gunfight, Payne was jerked out of it for a moment. "Matchsticks? Yeah, I've got matches."

"Good. All right, Curly, here's what we'll do, we'll stick some matches up on that board layin' over against the fence and see which one of us can light the most matches with six shots out of our pistols. Whoever hits the most of 'em wins, and he'll be the best shot."

Finally feeling that he was being played for a fool, Curly suddenly had enough of what he saw as complete nonsense and obvious cowardice on Perley's part. "I'm tired of your games, you yellow belly. Stand up and get ready to use that weapon you're wearin', or I'll shoot you down settin' on that damn keg."

Getting serious, Perley warned, "You're gettin' ready to make the same mistake your friend did. Even though you are guilty for the outright murder of Tom Parker, I'm willin' to let you go, if you turn around and get on that horse, leave this town, and don't ever come back."

"Why, you mouthy piece of dirt," Curly raged and drew his pistol. Perley dropped off the nail keg, onto one knee, pulling his .44 as he did, putting one round into Curly's chest, and a second round in his head. Curly had gotten his pistol cocked, but that was as far as he got before being struck dead.

Payne was stricken speechless by what he had just witnessed, hardly believing it possible that Perley was still alive. He stared at the body of the feared gunman, then back at Perley, then back at the body again. "I saw it, but I don't believe it," he muttered to himself. "How in the world did you . . . ?" He started but trailed off, still caught in disbelief.

Perley didn't try to explain, for he didn't understand, himself. He had always been fast with a six-gun ever since he was a kid, for no reason he could explain. He never practiced. When the moment demanded it, he never consciously thought about what he was doing, it just happened. His brother John compared Perley's lightning-fast reactions to a magician's sleight of hand and advised him not to try to figure it out. "You got a gift," John told him, "just be glad you've got it." It was hard for Perley to be thankful for a gift that usually ended up with him shooting somebody.

The two shots were enough to bring the sheriff out

of his office to stand on his front steps and listen for more shots. Since the shots were so close together, he pictured both men managing to get off a shot. The question was, who was the unlucky one who got off the last shot? After a few minutes and no more shots, he figured that whatever happened was now over and he could safely investigate it. Still holding his rifle, he strode forcefully toward the bridge and the blacksmith shop beyond. The first thing he noticed as he approached was Curly's flea-bitten gray, walking unattended away from the forge. He stopped the horse and dropped the reins to the ground as Payne walked out to meet him. "I heard shots," Mason declared.

Payne shook his head and repeated what he had said to himself before. "I saw it, but I don't believe it."

The sheriff looked beyond Payne to see Perley standing over the body. "Curly?" He asked in total disbelief.

"Yep," Payne answered. "Perley shot him twice."

"Face on?" Mason asked.

"Face on," Payne confirmed, then added, "settin' on a nail keg."

The sheriff considered the consequences that could likely follow this unexpected outcome of the gunfight. He feared Ned Stark's reaction was going to be violent. Stark had already reneged on his agreement to control his men's behavior in town with the shooting of Tom Parker. After that, it was bad enough for Stark to personally invade the hotel dining room. But then to permit Curly to come into town to kill Perley Gates, Mason was afraid he was going to have to stand up to Stark. He was not sure that he could and damn sure he didn't want to. His thoughts were distracted then when the town people felt it safe to investigate the shots heard.

The first to arrive on the scene was Horace Brooks. Seeing the sheriff standing motionless, Horace asked, "What happened, Sheriff?" He looked near the forge then, relieved to see Perley standing beside his horse. "He got him, didn't he?" Horace asked before Mason had time to answer his first question. "Perley got him! I saw that sidewinder when he rode by the stable. I knew then he'd come to town lookin' for Perley. I was hopin' he wouldn't look for him at the blacksmith. Now, I'm tickled that he did." He walked back to the forge. "Perley, you all right?"

Aware that he should be investigating the shooting, Mason came to join them. "I'm glad to see you're all right. John Payne told me his version of the shooting, although some of what he said didn't make sense. Why don't you give me your version of what happened?"

"Not much to tell," Perley said. "He came in here and said he was here to settle with me for shootin' Quirt Taylor. I told him Quirt didn't give me any choice, but I was willin' to give him a choice. He didn't want anything short of a duel, so we shot it out, and he lost. That about sums it up."

Out of curiosity, Mason had to ask, "What was Payne talkin' about with the nail kegs?"

Perley shrugged and replied, "I don't know. I was sittin' on that nail keg there when Curly came back here. I reckon that's what he meant."

Hearing Perley's answer to the question, Payne insisted, "He was still settin' on that nail keg when Curly drew his gun and he beat Curly to the draw. Put two shots in him before he knew what happened."

"Still settin' on the nail keg?" Mason repeated, doubting Payne knew what he had actually seen.

"I don't know," Payne said. "He was on it, then he

was off of it. It don't make any difference, Curly drew first and Perley cut him down. Dead is dead."

Horace spoke up then. "Seems to me, there ain't much doubt that Perley did what he had to, to keep from gettin' killed. Right, Sheriff?"

"I reckon so," Mason decided, his mind already occupied with what Ned Stark's reaction was going to be when he found out about it. With no way of knowing about Stark's proposition to his men, the sheriff was worried about what was going to happen if any of the other members of his gang came into town today. He feared that he could definitely see the writing on the wall. His guarantee from Stark that there would be no killings in his town was definitely null and void. After this incident this morning, he was sure there would be a meeting with the mayor. For the present, there was nothing to do but assume the posture of a sheriff, so he said, "Payne, I'll tell Floyd to pick up the body. Horace, take his horse down to the stable with you and we'll see if somebody comes to claim it." He looked around him as if checking to see if there was anything else that required his attention. Then he relieved Curly of his gun belt, returned the pistol to the holster, and drew his rifle from his saddle. "Let's see what he's got in his pockets." He went through Curly's pockets until he found a small roll of bills. "Looks like he's got enough to pay Floyd's bill. The rest will go in the city fund. Reckon that about wraps it up."

"Reckon you can finish up with Buck now?" Perley asked John Payne.

* * *

Like the sheriff, Perley had a valid interest in the reaction of the Ned Stark gang to the latest reduction in their number. He accepted the fact that he was the cause of the flare-up in the Ned Stark problem in Bison Gap. But he knew that Bison Gap had the problem before he got there. Trouble was going to happen sooner or later, or as his brothers would call it, Bison Gap was a cow pie waiting to be stepped in. He and Possum had ridden down there to help. He was sorry that he seemed to have made matters worse. The only thing he could do now was to stick around and see if there was anything helpful he could do. With that in mind, he decided to stay in town to be handy if any more of Stark's men showed up. So, he led Buck back to the stable and threw his saddle on him. Buck hadn't had much exercise in the last couple of days, so he would take a little ride, staying close to town and see how comfortable Buck was in his new shoes. Then he would go to the hotel dining room for the noontime meal.

The morning went rapidly, and as far as he could tell, the town was as peaceful as he remembered it when he and Possum left to return to the Triple-G. *Would that it could remain that way,* he thought as he walked Buck back up the street to the hotel, aware of the stares he was attracting from some of the people outside the stores. There was no doubt that the word had spread about the early morning shooting at the blacksmith. Consequently, he was not surprised by the guarded reception he received in the dining room, with the exception of his welcome by Rachael's daughters. They ran to greet him when he came in the outside door. "Perley," Alice announced, "Bess made apple pie!"

"She did?" Perley responded, pretending to be excited. "I reckon we have to eat our dinner before we get any." He let them lead him to the table, aware of the serious concern on the faces of their mother, Bess, and Kitty as they all watched him closely. "I reckon everybody heard," he said, breaking the ice.

"Are you all right?" Bess asked. "You ain't shot or nothin', are you?"

"Nope," he answered and held his arms straight out and turned a complete circle before sitting down at the table.

"Thank goodness for that," Rachael said. "And thanks, Perley, I'm glad that damn snake is dead."

"Mama!" Alice scolded. "You're not supposed to use those cusswords."

"You're not supposed to listen so hard when grown-ups are talking," her mother responded. "Now, eat your dinner and let Perley eat his." Back to Perley then, she asked, "Do you think Ned Stark will send somebody looking for you?"

"Can't say," Perley replied, but he was wondering if it would be better for him to move out of the hotel to keep any trouble away from there. He decided then. "If they start showin' up, I'll move outta here and get the word around town that I ain't here anymore. Then maybe they won't be botherin' you folks."

"That might be a good idea," Emma said, just entering the room from the door to the hotel. "I heard what happened and I'm glad you're all right. I just got back from a meeting with the mayor and the sheriff." She looked directly at him and said, "Perley, the sheriff and the mayor both agreed that it would be best if you left town. Sheriff Mason is convinced that there will be gunmen coming to look for you. And he and Ralph Wheeler are afraid for the safety of the people when the shooting starts.

"What do you think, Emma?" Perley asked.

She didn't hesitate to answer. "I'm sorry, but I'm afraid I have to agree with Ralph and the sheriff. I can't afford to have this hotel turned into the scene of a battle. I've worked too hard to get it to this point."

Both Rachael and Bess appeared to be truly shocked by Emma's statement and turned to Perley at once. "I respect that decision," Perley said. "I'll get my things out of the room right away." He paused, then asked, "Is it all right if I go ahead and finish eatin'? Things are pretty quiet in town right now."

Emma nodded. "I think that would be all right. Perley, I truly am sorry."

"I am, too," Rachael said, "after all you've done for us. We wouldn't be here if it wasn't for you."

"Damn right," Bess exclaimed. "Sorry, Alice." She apologized for her language. "I'm worse than your mama." Back to Perley then, she said, "Yes, sir, you finish your dinner. And then eat a big piece of that apple pie I baked. I reckon it ain't for me to say, but it don't make sense to me. We're talkin' about maybe a bunch of gunslingin' outlaws coming to town and so we send the only man who stands a chance to protect us outta town. 'Scuse me if I think that's the definition of crazy."

"It won't take me long to finish up," Perley said to Bess. "I understand why Emma has to feel that way. She's got everything she has invested in this hotel. And I understand the mayor and the sheriff's thinkin', too. They figure, if they can convince Stark's men that I left town, then maybe they won't waste their time searchin' for me and causing a lot of damage."

Emma returned to the hotel while Rachael and Bess sat at the table to keep him company while he ate. Kitty kept his coffee cup filled and Bess cut a huge slice of pie for him. "It's gonna be hard to camp somewhere after this," he said.

"You oughta hear John Payne tellin' about that shootin'." Bess couldn't help bringing it up. "He said it was so fast, you couldn't see your hand movin'."

"Don't pay any attention to that," Perley said, not wanting to build a reputation. "I don't know what Payne thinks he saw. The truth of the matter is, Curly was just slow, and he let his temper get in the way. That'll slow you down."

"If you say so," Bess responded, tongue in cheek.

When he finished the last bite of apple pie and the last gulp of coffee, he said his good-byes and left to get his things out of the hotel, feeling like he would never have to eat again. There were things he would have to buy, since he was going to have to make a camp out of town somewhere. His first thought after getting kicked out of the hotel was to move in with Rooster. But now he was wondering if he should stay away from there for the same reason he was getting out of town. The picture in his mind of Rooster's little cabin surrounded by a gang of angry gunmen was not one he would care to cause.

When he left the hotel, his first stop was the stable to get some things out of his packs. He was going to need his camping gear. Then he would go to Wheeler's store. He and Possum had used up most of the supplies on their trip from the Triple-G. His plan was to find a spot to set up a camp and after he got everything he needed from his packs, he'd leave the packhorse at the stable, so he wouldn't have the worry of it. He told Horace Brooks of his situation and his intentions, and Horace offered to let him stay in the stable. "Then you'd be right here in town, so you'd know what was goin' on," Horace said.

"I 'preciate the offer, Horace, but I wouldn't want to put you in the same fix the hotel would have been in. I'll tell you what, maybe if they come and search your stable and barn, then I might wanna take you up on that offer. I've got me a spot picked out that ain't too far from town and that'll do me for a while." The spot he had in mind was halfway to Rooster's cabin where a healthy stream emptied into Oak Creek.

His final stop before leaving town was at Wheeler's for some bacon, coffee, and hardtack. He figured, with the supplies he still had, he could make it a few days on that. "Did Emma talk to you?" Ralph asked.

"She did," Perley answered. "I've already moved out of the hotel."

Wheeler shook his head. "That was bad business, that gunslinger coming after you this morning. I talked to Sheriff Mason, and he told me what happened. Nobody here in town blames you for killing that man."

"They just want me to leave town, right?" Perley couldn't resist remarking.

"I don't blame you for getting a little sore about it when none of this is your fault. You just happened to be standing where the lightning struck. But I'm sure you can understand you're now a lightning rod for the town." He watched Perley's face for his reaction. "I hope you know there are no hard feelings on my part or the town's part."

"Nope," Perley said. "No hard feelin's. I understand the problem you're facin', Mayor."

# CHAPTER 7

"Hellfire!" Eli Priest exclaimed. "Where the hell is he? He oughta been back by now." He walked out the front door and stood on the little square porch, peering at the trail leading up to the house. After a few minutes, he came back inside. "That little town ain't big enough for that jasper to hide in."

"Maybe ol' Curly shot him and that sheriff threw him in jail," Carl Leach suggested.

"Hah," Ned Stark grunted. "I got my doubts about that." The only reason he could consider after this length of time was that Perley got Curly, instead of the other way around. Unless Perley Gates had left town, Curly should have found him, shot him, and been back here by now. He expressed as much to his gang. They had been sitting around this small ranch house for too long now. Every one of them was developing rough edges, and nobody had any money left from the last cattle sale to blow off some steam in town. "I reckon we'd best hit that herd down in Blanco County," he said. "They oughta be just about ready. Soon as we finish this business in Bison Gap, we'll get ridin' again."

"I thought we were gonna wait till your cousin got here before we were goin' after those cattle," Jim Duncan said. "Ain'tcha gonna wait for him?"

"I figured I would," Stark replied, "but I thought he'd be here by now." His cousin was supposed to be on his way to join them. He had been released from prison two weeks ago, and Stark figured he'd be there in a week. He wasn't really surprised that he was late. He no doubt had a few things to take care of, like a horse and a weapon and anything else he needed. Stark almost chuckled when he thought of his cousin's way of acquiring the things he needed.

"I want that money you promised for Perley Gates," Slim Garrett said, breaking into Stark's thoughts. "I think that lowlife nailed Curly, and that's the reason he ain't back here yet."

"How 'bout it, Ned?" Frank Deal spoke up. "One of us can go into town and find out what happened to him. Whoever goes in won't get the hundred bucks if he sees Gates and shoots him. That's fair, ain't it? Then it'll be open season on Gates tomorrow and everybody'll have a chance to collect that money."

"That's better'n settin' around here waitin' for Curly to come back," Eli said.

"All right," Stark said. "Maybe that ain't a bad idea. Slim, you ride on into that town and find Curly. Tell him, if he don't find Perley Gates by tonight, he's just gonna have to take his chances with the rest of you to-morrow."

"Hell," Eli protested, "why Slim?"

"'Cause he ain't raised no hell in town for a while," Ned answered. "And you broke out the front window of the saloon last time you went into town."

"How 'bout loanin' me enough to buy a drink while

I'm in there?" Slim asked Stark. "I swear, I'm flat broke."

"Then don't go in the saloon," Eli cracked. "We ain't sendin' you in there to get drunk."

"But if Curly's waitin' around for that jasper, he'll most likely be in the saloon," Slim insisted.

"Well, maybe Curly will buy you a drink," Junior Humphrey cracked, drawing a laugh from the others.

"All right, here's two bits," Stark said. "Now get goin'."

"What about my supper?" Slim asked then. "I'll miss my supper, and you hogs won't save me any."

"I'll send somebody else," Stark said, knowing full well if he gave Slim money to buy supper, he'd spend it on whiskey.

"Never mind," Slim bellowed, "I'm goin', I'm goin'." And he hurried out the door.


"Where's Perley?" Possum asked when he walked into the dining room for supper. He was alone, since Rooster had decided it best if he stayed home, instead of sleeping and eating at the hotel. He figured he was losing too much time for his chores.

"He ain't here," Rachael answered him. "Emma said he had to get out."

"Get out? What are you talkin' about?" Possum asked. "The hotel, the dinin' room, what?"

"There's a lot happened here while you were at Rooster's, so sit down and I'll tell you." She then told him everything that had taken place that day, starting with Curly Williams coming into town, looking for Perley, the shoot-out at the blacksmith shop, and Perley's departure.

"Damn," Possum dragged out. "He shot Curly. . . I'll be . . ." he started, then asked, "Where did he go?"

"I don't know," Rachael said, already feeling sorry that she had not thought to ask. "I don't think he knew where he was goin'. Emma's eviction notice hit all of us kinda sudden-like."

Possum was beside himself. "I've gotta find him!" He looked frantically from Rachael to Bess, and back to Rachael again. "We're partners. We came down here to try to help you folks. I've gotta find him!" No one had any idea where Perley had gone. Finally, Possum got up from the table and started for the door.

"Where you goin'?" Rachael called after him. "Ain't you gonna eat your supper?"

"I ain't hungry right now," he yelled over his shoulder and went out the door. With no place else to look, he decided he would see if Perley was somewhere in town. Since he had already left his horse at the stable, he started walking down the street. He went in every door that was still open, asking if they had seen Perley. The answer was the same everywhere: no one had seen him. Possum went to the sheriff's office on the chance Mason had locked him up. He hadn't. He stopped dead still, startled when he got to Floyd Jenkins's barbershop. There by the front door, stood an open casket. It contained the body of Curly Williams, a neat bullet hole in his forehead, another in the center of his chest. Possum was shocked to find it on display. Surely the sheriff and the mayor didn't know it was there. Floyd must have been out of his mind to display the body. If that didn't rile Ned Stark's gang, nothing would. He hurried along to the blacksmith shop.

Still a little shaken, he checked with John Payne and got a full retelling of the shooting, but like everyone else, Payne had no idea where Perley had gone. He didn't even know he had left.

The only two places left to check were the Buffalo Hump and the stable. The saloon was the closest, so he went in there first. He walked in to find a rather slow evening, even for this early hour. Jimmy McGee greeted him when he walked up to the bar. "Evenin' Possum, what's your pleasure?"

"Nothin' right now, Jimmy. I'm lookin' for Perley. Has he been in here this evenin'?"

"No, not so far," Jimmy answered, "but it's early yet." He flashed a wide grin. "He sure took care of ol' Curly Williams, didn't he? I'da sure loved to have seen that, if it happened like John Payne says it did."

"None of the rest of that sorry crew been in tonight?" Possum asked.

"Nope, nary a one, this afternoon or tonight. It sure has made things a lot more peaceful." He paused, looking at the door, then said, "Until right now, here comes one of 'em in the door right after I said they hadn't."

Possum turned to look. "You know him?"

"He ain't been in lately, but I think he's the one called Slim." Jimmy and Possum watched him as he stopped and looked all around the room before coming over to the bar. "What can I do for ya?" Jimmy asked.

Slim threw his money on the bar. "Gimme a shot of corn likker," he said. He tossed it back as soon as Jimmy poured it before saying, "I'm lookin' for Curly Williams. Has he been in here today?"

Jimmy gave Possum a wink and said, "He was in

here first thing this mornin', sat down right over there at that table to eat breakfast, but he got up and left before he finished it." He didn't tell him that Curly left because the sheriff came in and told him Perley was at the blacksmith shop. "And he ain't been back," Jimmy went on. "Did you look up by the barbershop? Somebody said they thought they saw him there."

"The barbershop?" Slim asked, wondering what Curly would be doing there. "The barbershop ain't open this late, is it?"

"Not usually," Jimmy said and let it go at that when it suddenly struck him that, no matter how harmless the skinny little man looked, he rode with a mean bunch. And their idea of amusement would be the gutting of a smart-ass bartender.

Possum decided to end the mystery for him. "Curly Williams is dead, Mister. If you need proof, his body's in front of the barbershop. He came into town with the idea he was gonna kill somebody. And you and your friends need to know that's what's gonna happen to any other outlaws that come in this town lookin' to kill somebody."

Slim's eyes opened wide in shock, and he backed away from the bar. Possum was afraid for a moment that he was going to draw his weapon, but he suddenly spun around and made for the door. When he had gone, Jimmy gasped, "Are you crazy? I hope to hell none of his friends are outside waiting for him. After what you just told him, there ain't no tellin' what Ned Stark will do."

"Lost my temper there for a minute, I reckon. It don't make no difference, though, does it?" Possum answered him. "Whether they find out tonight or in the mornin'. There's gonna be hell to pay, no matter when they find out." He left the saloon then and walked across the bridge, heading toward the stable.

"I'll be right there," Horace Brooks yelled back when he heard someone calling his name. He put his pitchfork aside and walked to the front of the stable. "Howdy, Possum, forget somethin'?" he asked, when he saw who it was, back after having just left his horse a short while before. The look of concern on Possum's face prompted him to ask. "You lookin' for Perley? 'Cause, if you are, he ain't here."

"Do you know where he is?" Possum asked.

"For a fact, I don't," Horace replied. "He was here, but that was a couple hours ago, maybe more. He said Emma kicked him outta the hotel, so he picked up some stuff from his packs and left. I asked him where he was goin', but he said he wasn't sure." He paused then to watch Possum's obviously worried reaction. "I offered to let him stay here in the stable with his horse, and he said he might take me up on that after he gives Ned Stark's boys time to search the place. Like I said, though, he took some supplies, so I reckon he's fixin' to take to the woods."

*Or Rooster's place,* Possum thought. *Hell, I just came from there. I woulda passed him on the way.* He shook his head, amazed that Horace hadn't told him all that when he was just there. *He must have thought I knew.* He knew he was going to have to go back to make sure, so he told Horace he was going to have to saddle his horse again and go back to Rooster's.

"Are you gonna be back tonight?" Horace asked, thinking he would be locked up by the time Possum rode to Rooster's and back.

"No," Possum answered. "I'll just stay with Rooster

tonight." He walked back to pick up his saddle while Horace fetched his horse.


"That's far enough!" Rooster warned the rider approaching his cabin. "You'd best state your business here."

Possum pulled his horse up short. "Rooster, it's me, Possum! Where the hell are you?" He peered at the little porch, but in the darkness, he could not see him.

"Over here by the fence," Rooster answered as he walked out of the small corn patch near the side of the cabin. "I was fixin' to blow your head off, if you hadn't said who you was," he said, holding an ear of corn in each hand, pointed at Possum like a pair of pistols. "Whadda you doin' back here? You get to missin' me, already? Or did Emma throw you outta the hotel?"

"No, but she threw Perley outta the hotel," Possum answered, "and I ain't been able to find him nowhere. I was hopin' I'd find him out here."

Serious at once, Rooster responded. "What are you talkin' about, Emma threw him out? For what?" Possum got down from the saddle and brought Rooster up to date on everything that had happened since they left the hotel that morning. "I swear," Rooster declared. "And you ain't got no idea where he is?"

"No idea," Possum confirmed. "But Horace Brooks said Perley came to the stable to get some things out of his packs, so he mighta just made him a camp somewhere on this creek."

"Wonder why he didn't come here?" Rooster asked.

"If I know Perley, I'd say it was for the same reason he left the hotel," Possum speculated. "He knows that it's him Ned Stark is lookin' for, and he's tryin' to keep the rest of us out of it. He's most likely thinkin', if Stark's men come lookin' for him here, and he ain't here, then maybe they won't bother you no more."

"Hell, we coulda been ready for 'em, if they came in here raisin' hell," Rooster said. "We'd give 'em more'n they bargained for."

"Perley's thinkin' the same thing I'm thinkin' right now," Possum said. "I don't know exactly how many men Ned Stark's got holed up with him on that ranch of his. But I guarantee you he's got at least enough to surround this little cabin and shoot it to pieces, if we decided to stand him off here. That, or he'd burn the cabin down with us still in it."

"Damn, you might be right, at that," Rooster reconsidered when he thought about it some more. "What the hell are we gonna do? Where you reckon he is? And why don't he come tell us?" They both paused to think about that, then all of a sudden, Rooster's eyes lit up. "I bet I know where he's set up a camp." He laughed when Possum asked where. "You remember when you was down here last year? You remember that day when the horses got out and your'n and mine run off down the creek?"

"Yeah, and Perley's didn't run off with 'em because that fool horse won't go nowhere without Perley," Possum interrupted to comment.

"Right," Rooster continued. "I don't know if you remember, but we found 'em about three-quarters of a mile from here where the creek takes a double bend and a nice stream empties into it. You remember what Perley said?" Not waiting for Possum to answer, Rooster continued. "He said that it was a good spot for a camp."

"Is that right?" Possum replied. "I don't rightly recollect."

"Well, that's what he said, all right, and I'm bettin' if we found that spot again, we'd find Perley settin' there."

"Well, I've run outta places to look, so let's go see if we can find it," Possum said. "You gonna go get your horse?"

"Nah," Rooster replied. "Like I said, that spot ain't but about three-quarters of a mile from here and makin' my way along that creek bank in the dark, I don't wanna take a chance on my horse breakin' a leg."

"You're right," Possum agreed. "I'll leave my horse here." He led the gray gelding into Rooster's corral, then the two of them set out along the creek bank, making their way carefully through the bushes and brush that lined most of the banks. After about fifty yards, they struck a narrow game trail that followed the creek through a patch of thick oaks, and that made the walking easier. A couple of minutes more found them approaching the first loop of the double bend.

"That spot's just around that next bend in the creek," Rooster whispered.

"I remember this place now," Possum declared. He pointed toward the outer loop of the second bend where the trees were the thickest. "If he was here, you oughta be able to see his campfire, and I don't see one."

"Let's get a little bit closer," Rooster whispered. "I can't see in the dark as good as I used to." They inched their way cautiously along the game trail, making an effort not to make a sound, just in case they might be creeping up on a wild boar or a bear. A dozen yards closer, and Rooster held up his hand to signal Possum to stop. He turned back to him and whispered, "There's somethin' down in that bottom, moving near that stream."

"Whaddaya reckon it is?" Possum whispered back.

"Whatever it is, it's big," Rooster whispered.

"Maybe it's a horse," a third voice suggested, this one not whispered.

"Maybe," Rooster said before he realized it was not Possum who said it. "Oh hell!" he blurted then and jumped sideways, bumping into Possum, who was as startled as he. "Perley!" He protested loudly, knowing who it could only be. "Damn it, Perley, you scared the bejesus outta me!"

"What are you two old codgers doin' stumblin' around in the woods in the middle of the night?" Perley asked, as he stepped from behind a large oak tree.

"Lookin' for you!" Possum declared impatiently. "Nobody knows where the hell you disappeared to."

"Good," Perley said. "The main thing I wanted was for nobody to find me in the hotel, the dinin' room, or your cabin, Rooster. It's me they'll be lookin' for. I'm the one who did the shootin'. I just don't want to take a chance on anybody gettin' hurt, just because they were with me. I'm hopin', if they can't find me in Bison Gap, they'll think I took off for parts unknown."

"Well, what's keepin' you from takin' off for parts unknown?" Possum asked.

"The same thing you're thinkin' right now," Perley answered him. "Whether I'm here or not, things ain't gonna be no different than before I shot Curly and Quirt. Matter of fact, they might get a lot worse, because they'll take it out on the town. We came down here to help Emma and Rachael and Rooster, and doggone if I ain't made matters worse. I don't blame

Emma. It's a wonder she didn't shoot me when I showed up in the dinin' room after that thing with Curly."

He interrupted himself to ask then, "Have any of the rest of that gang showed up in town today?"

"Just one man," Possum said. "Showed up in the Buffalo Hump, lookin' for Curly. There's somethin' else you probably don't know. Floyd Jenkins got the crazy idea to stand Curly up in an open coffin right in front of the barbershop."

"Damn!" Perley swore. "What in the world was he thinkin'? All that's gonna do is make Ned Stark mad enough to make some real trouble for the whole town. I hope Sheriff Mason has enough sense to make him take it away before one of Stark's men sees it."

"One already has," Possum said, "the feller that came in the saloon lookin' for Curly. Jimmy McGee said his name is Slim."

It wasn't the first time a slain outlaw had been displayed on a public street. It had been done in many frontier towns as a warning to outlaws, promising swift retribution for crimes committed in that town. Perley was sure that was the message Floyd decided he would send. But most of those other towns that used that warning had some means to back up their warning, like a strong, fearless sheriff, backed by the town and a strong vigilante posse. Bison Gap had none of those assets. The outlaws held the strong hand in this town. He looked at Possum and said, "It's gonna be the end of Bison Gap if somebody doesn't step up and defend the town."

"How we gonna do that?" Possum wanted to know.

"I'm thinkin' on it," Perley said. "I ain't sure what we can do to help. We need a strong sheriff, and I ain't sure if John Mason can stand up to that job or not. From what little bit I've talked to him, I think he would like to fill the job, but I don't believe he's confident enough to think he can. Maybe, if he thought he had some backup from a town vigilance committee, he might find out he's tougher than he thought." He thought about it for a few more minutes, until Possum became impatient.

"Whaddaya think we oughta do?"

"All right," Perley answered him. "Here's what we need to do right now. Let me get my horse. I'm headin' back to town." He turned and headed toward the hollow where he had left Buck.

"We're headin' back to town," Possum corrected him, and followed him. "What were you doin' out here, anyway?"

"I was plannin' to camp here tonight, so I'd be close to town, then set up someplace in the mornin' where I could watch to see who came into town."

"How come you didn't build no fire?" Rooster had to ask.

"Because I ain't cold," Perley replied. "And I ate in the dinin' room before I left the hotel, so I wasn't gonna cook anything."

"Oh," Rooster said, then after a moment, he added, "If you'da had a fire, I woulda seen it back yonder."

"That's another reason, I reckon," Perley allowed with a grin.

By the time they rode back into town, it was already approaching ten o'clock and the only signs of life came from the Buffalo Hump Saloon, and that was relatively quiet. Perley was gratified to see there were only a couple of horses tied at the rail as the three of them rode slowly past. "There it is," Possum said, and pointed to the coffin standing outside Floyd Jenkins's barbershop. Perley pulled Buck to a stop and looked at the corpse for a few seconds, thinking how fortunate he had been to have gotten the best of that shoot-out. When he didn't dismount, Possum asked, "Ain't we goin' in?"

"Not yet," Perley said, and wheeled Buck away toward the bridge over the creek in front of the saloon. On the other side, instead of going to the saloon, he turned toward the sheriff's office. When he pulled Buck to a stop in front of the office, he stepped down, walked up to the door, and knocked, after trying the knob.

After a long moment he heard the key turn in the lock and the door opened just wide enough to allow the sheriff to peer out to see who was calling. When he recognized his visitor, he asked, "What are you doin' here?"

"Me and my associates," he nodded toward Possum and Rooster, "have come to help you."

"Help me do what?" Mason asked, highly suspicious.

"Help you outta your mess with Ned Stark," Perley answered. "If you'll open the door, it'll be a lot easier to talk."

"What the hell are you talkin' about?" Mason demanded. "I ain't in no mess with Ned Stark."

"No? Well, you're gonna be, come tomorrow mornin' and Ned's boys see that corpse standin' up in front of the barbershop."

Mason opened the door, then. "I saw it and I thought about tellin' him that he oughta take it down, but I don't know of any law that says he can't do that."

"Well, then maybe we'd best make a new law right now, 'cause you need to arrest Floyd Jenkins tonight. We'll help him move that body back inside where it's supposed to be, then you can put him in jail."

"Are you crazy?" Mason blurted. "I might be able to talk him into moving that casket back inside, but I can't put him in jail, especially if he does what I tell him to do with that casket." He gawked at Possum and Rooster, then back at Perley, about to come to the conclusion that they were all drunk. "Why would I put him in jail?"

"To save his life," Perley answered. "One of Stark's men has already been in town today, looking for Curly Williams. He found him in a box in front of the barbershop." He turned briefly to Possum. "Slim?"

"Right," Possum responded, "Slim."

"His name's Slim, and he saw what Floyd did with Curly's body. What do you think Ned Stark's gonna do when Slim tells him Floyd's showin' one of his men off like a Christmas turkey? I'll tell you what I think. I think Ned's gonna send enough of his boys in here to hang Floyd up by the neck to show Bison Gap what happens to people who mess with him. That's what I think." He turned again toward Possum and Rooster. "Is that what you think?" Both men immediately said that's what they thought, too. Turning back to the sheriff, Perley said. "That's the reason we came to help you, Sheriff. We'll go with you to arrest Floyd, and we'll help Floyd carry his coffin back inside his shop. When he realizes what he's done, he'll be mighty grateful to you for thinkin' of lockin' him up, so Stark's gunmen can't get to him. And if we do it tonight, you won't have to worry about Stark seein' Curly on display. Seems to me it's a win for you and a win for Bison Gap. It'll even be a sign to Stark that you keep law and order in your town, even if you have to arrest one of your citizens for disrespecting the dead, be it outlaw, or preacher. So, whaddaya say? Strap on your gun and grab your hat, and we'll go save Floyd Jenkins' life."

Sheriff Mason stood stone-still for a long moment, dazed. He wasn't sure what his reaction should be to the storm that had just blown through his mind. A lot of what this crazy man had said made sense in a way, but he wasn't sure everything would work like Perley predicted. Perley, Possum, and Rooster stood silently watching him, waiting for him to do something, anything. Finally, Perley asked, "What do you wanna do about the door? You wanna lock it or do you leave it open when you go to make an arrest?"

"I usually lock it," Mason answered, still in a daze.

"All right," Perley said, "lock her up and let's get it done. We'll leave our horses here and walk over with you. When that coffin is gone, folks here are gonna know their sheriff is lookin' out for them and what's best for the town."

Sheriff Mason locked his office door and started walking toward the bridge with his three escorts for no other reason than his not being able to think of a reason he shouldn't. Over the bridge, then up the street, the arresting party marched up to the barbershop and the offending corpse beside the door. When they arrived, Perley stepped forward and pounded on the door.

Evidently tucked in for the night, Floyd took a little

while before showing signs of life. Eventually the glow of a lamp was seen through the window as it moved toward the front door. A few seconds later, the door opened a crack and Floyd peeked out. When he saw it was the sheriff, he opened the door, only then seeing the three men standing behind him. "Sheriff Mason, what's the trouble?" Floyd asked.

When Mason hesitated to tell Floyd he had come to arrest him, Perley stepped up beside him. "Evenin', Floyd, excuse the late call. The sheriff brought the three of us in case you need help to put Curly back in your shop. Then he's gonna arrest you for improper display of a deceased person."

"Arrest me?" Floyd exclaimed. "Arrest me for what?"

When Mason began to stumble for an answer, Perley came to his aid again. "For what I just said. At least, that's the official reason, but the real reason is to save your life."

This captured Floyd's interest immediately. "What are you talking about? Save my life?" He turned his attention fully to Perley.

"That's right," Perley replied. "You see, the sheriff's smart enough to know that when you parked this corpse out here for everybody to see, you just signed your own death warrant. Ned Stark already sent a man into town today, and he saw Curly, here, standin' up against the wall. So the safest place for you right now is in the jailhouse. Stark ain't likely gonna send his men into the jailhouse after you."

Floyd remained in a state of shock for a few long moments, still trying to make sense of the intrusion upon his bedtime. When he began to realize the possible results of his whim to display the outlaw's body, he saw the reasoning behind the "arrest." It was really a move to ensure his safety. He turned back to address the sheriff. "I don't know where my brain was when I put that body out there, Sheriff. You're right, it wasn't very smart, and I reckon I owe you my thanks for arresting me."

Seeing the bizarre incident turning in his favor, Sheriff Mason found his tongue. "It's just to make sure you're safe, Floyd. If Stark asks, I'll tell him you're under arrest, if he shows up here tomorrow, and that oughta cool him off. If you'll unlock your back door, we'll carry the coffin back inside your shop while you get your clothes on. I don't reckon you wanna go to jail in your nightshirt."

"All right, Sheriff," Floyd said, eager now to get it done. "I'll meet you at the back door." He closed the door and locked it, then hurried toward the back of his shop.

Feeling in command now, Mason said, "All right, boys, let's see if we can carry this coffin around to the back."

"Yes, sir, Sheriff," Rooster responded, and nudged Possum with his elbow.

When Curly was back inside and Floyd was dressed, the party walked back across the creek to the jailhouse where Floyd was shown to his cell. Mason didn't lock it so Floyd would have the freedom to go in and out to the coffeepot, when there was one on the stove, and even to the outhouse out back when it was dark and nobody could see him. "It's gonna be like stayin' in a hotel," Rooster quipped.

"Better," Perley said. "You've got the sheriff to protect you. And since you are officially a prisoner, the town will have to pay for your breakfast in the mornin', sent over from the hotel dinin' room."

"Is that a fact?" Floyd asked the sheriff.

"That's a fact," Mason answered. "They have to feed my prisoners." He turned to Perley and asked, "Do you think some of Stark's men will show up here in the mornin'?"

"I ain't really got any idea what Stark's thinkin'," Perley replied. "Depends on how mad he is, I reckon. So it's hard to say if he's gonna show up early or not, but he's gonna show up sometime tomorrow. You were smart takin' Floyd in tonight just in case Stark's mad enough to hit town early. I expect you're already thinkin' about talkin' to the businessmen here in Bison Gap about formin' a citizens committee to back you up when you have trouble with outlaws."

"Well, I had been doin' some thinkin' about that," Mason lied, "a vigilance committee or something like that."

"That's a good idea, Sheriff," Perley responded. "I can think of a couple of good men right off—Horace Brooks, John Payne, maybe Floyd, here. Rooster, Possum, and I would would be glad to help you out gettin' it set up, if you want us to. I kinda feel like that's the least I can do, since I was responsible for the death of two of Stark's men." He looked toward Possum and Rooster, and they both nodded to show their willingness. "All three of us have reason to help protect the town," Perley continued. "The hotel and the dinin' room are run by friends of ours. We don't wanna see 'em fail because the town couldn't stand up to a gang of lowdown cattle rustlers."

"I reckon nobody wants to see that," Mason replied.

"Bison Gap is mighty lucky to have a sheriff that

thinks like you do. We'll be proud to stand beside you to keep that gang of gunslingers from runnin' over this town." This came from Possum, who figured Perley wasn't the only one who could work on the sheriff's mind. He gave Perley a wink.

# CHAPTER 8

"Late as it is, you might as well come on back to the hotel with me," Possum said to Rooster after they left the sheriff's office. "That cot's still in my room." He paused then and looked toward Perley. "I reckon I've still got a room." He paused again before asking, "What are you gonna do? I expect Horace has locked the stable up."

"Why don't you come on back to the hotel with me and Possum?" Rooster asked. "Emma ain't gonna tell you you can't stay there. She was probably just scared when she told to get out."

"I understand why she did it, Rooster, and I don't want to worry her any more than she's already worried," Perley said. "I picked up some things to get me by for a day or two, so I'll just make me a camp over by the creek somewhere. Might even go back to that spot where you found me tonight."

"Hell," Possum snorted. "Rooster's right, it don't make no sense you sleepin' out in the bushes. Stark and his men ain't gonna show up here tonight. If they were, they'da already been here. You'll likely be gone in the mornin' before anybody shows up lookin' for you."

Perley thought about it for a few seconds before telling them that he had changed his mind about hiding out. The more he thought about it, the more he realized that Stark's men would go through the town like a tornado looking for him, destroying everything and everybody who got in their way. It wouldn't save the town any damage if he wasn't found when they searched. It would minimize the destruction of property if Stark found him. It had occurred to him while trying to build up the sheriff's confidence that the best chance of defeating Ned Stark, and all the other Ned Starks out there, was to build a strong vigilance committee, just like he was preaching to Sheriff Mason. "I ain't thinkin' about hidin' out anymore," he told them. "I'm thinkin' that everything we told Mason is the way this town has to go. So I'm gonna be here when Stark and his men show up. Maybe we'll have some time in the mornin' to get some of the citizens of this town to stand with us."

"Now you're talkin'," Possum said. "I didn't think much of your plan to hide out in the first place."

"You shoulda said so," Perley responded. "Then maybe I'd be sleepin' in the stable tonight."

"You might as well come on to the hotel with me and Rooster. Emma will most likely give you your room back. You can tell her you'll be gone in the mornin', anyway."

"I reckon it's worth a try," Perley said. "She can't do anything but throw me out again."

"Good," Possum declared, "and maybe Bess has got some cold biscuits or somethin' left over. I missed my supper to go out and look for you."

"I haven't had anything since noon, myself," Perley said.

It was settled then, the three friends returned to the hotel. They went by the front desk first to see if Wilbur Ross or Emma might still be there, but the office was closed. "Come on," Possum said, "there'll still be somebody in the dinin' room." So they left their horses in the small hotel stable, built especially for circumstances like theirs, and went to the dining room. Having to enter from the hotel entrance, since the outside entrance doors were locked, they found the lamps all turned down in the dining room, but there was still someone in the kitchen.

"What happened to you?" Rachael exclaimed when she saw Possum come in the kitchen door. She was sitting at the kitchen table, drinking coffee with Bess and Emma. "I see you brought Rooster back with you." She started to welcome Rooster, but stopped short when she saw Perley behind him and looked at once toward Emma.

The smile Emma had flashed for Possum faded immediately, replaced by a look of concern. "Perley," she announced calmly. All conversation ceased immediately.

Judging by the expression he saw on her face, Perley decided his decision to come with Possum and Rooster was not a good one. "I beg your pardon, ma'am. I was just ridin' up this way with Rooster and Possum. I'll be on my way now." He turned at once to leave.

"Perley," she called out, "wait." She got up from the table to stop him. "Don't go. I'm so sorry I acted the way I did before. After all you've done for me and my sister, I'm so ashamed I told you to leave. I want you to stay.

I hoped you'd come back. You'll see, I even left your room key in the door, so you'd see it. I don't know what I was thinking. We're likely to suffer the same damage from Ned Stark's men whether they find you here or not. And who knows? Maybe we can find someplace in the hotel to hide you."

"Well, after I thought about it, I decided the same thing you just said," Perley said. "But I fully understood what you were afraid of and I didn't want you worryin'. And you don't have to hide me. My mind's changed on that one, too. I won't be hidin' anywhere. First thing in the mornin', Possum, Rooster, and I are gonna see if we can round up a vigilante committee to fight for Bison Gap. I think we might even get the sheriff raring to go."

That was exciting news for all three women, but Bess was quick to remind him that Sheriff Mason might not go along with bucking Ned Stark. "I think just about everybody in town knows that Mason is afraid to stand up against Stark," she insisted. "Look at what happened when Curly Williams shot Tom down in the saloon. Mason knew that Tom didn't try to draw on Curly. The eyewitness he believed was Quirt Taylor, for goodness sakes."

"That's right," Rachael said. "And you might have been hanged, if one of the witnesses that saw you shoot Quirt hadn't been the preacher."

"But he did take John Payne's word for that business between Curly and me," Perley pointed out. "I think Mason would really rather be on our side, but he's got to work up the courage to do it. I'm hopin' that he'll get enough support from some of the men here in town to give him the confidence to fight for what's right."

The women didn't look convinced. The evil Ned Stark was capable of had been built up to legendary proportions in the short period since he had suddenly showed up in the county. "Well, I hope you're right," Bess interrupted, then asked Possum, "Did you get any supper?"

"No, I didn't," Possum replied at once. "Don't reckon there's anything left from supper that ain't already been throwed out, is there?"

"There's some ham and beans left that ain't gone stone cold yet and some biscuits," Bess answered. "The oven's still warm. We can heat it up, and I'll stoke up the fire, so we can make some coffee. Don't reckon anybody else is hungry," she japed to see if she could get a rise out of Perley and Rooster. "All right," she said, chuckling, "we'll get it started."

Emma asked where they were before coming here so late, and Rooster promptly answered her question. "We was arrestin' Floyd Jenkins for stickin' Curly Williams's corpse up in front of his shop." That called for an explanation that took up most of the remaining evening.


Some miles away, another group was gathered around a table, discussing a similar topic. "Did you see Curly's body?" Ned Stark asked Slim Garrett for the second time since he had gotten back from Bison Gap.

"I told you, Ned, I didn't take no time to go see him. That one feller in the saloon said he was dead and they stood him up in a casket so everybody could gape at him. He told me that it was a sign for all outlaws to look at, and that's what was gonna happen to anybody comin' to Bison Gap and killin' somebody."

"Damn." Ned scowled. "Who shot him?"

"They didn't say who done it." He threw his hands up in the air, helplessly when he thought Stark was eyeing him in scorn. "I swear, Ned, I was in town all by myself. I couldn't nose around too much."

"Where'd they have the casket set up? Near the jail?"

"Feller told me it was at the barbershop," Slim said.

"At the barbershop? What the hell would it be at the barbershop for? They was japin' you. I shoulda sent somebody else in there," Stark complained. "They mighta throwed Curly in jail. He might not be dead a-tall." He jerked his head back to stare at Slim again. "Did you go by the jail to see if Curly was in there?" Before Slim could answer, Stark went on. "I swear, if that damn yellow belly sheriff has arrested Curly, I'm ready to put him in a box."

"What about the open season tomorrow, Ned?" Eli Priest asked. "It's wide open now, ain't it? Curly ain't come back—dead or in jail or at the barbershop—so he didn't get Perley Gates." His remark brought a few chuckles for the barbershop crack.

"I'm puttin' that off for another day," Stark said, not amused. "I'm gonna take a little ride into town tomorrow and see what's goin' on. I wanna see if that Perley Gates feller is still in town, and I need to talk to that sheriff—make sure he ain't started goin' to that new church they've got. I'm gonna take a couple of you with me, just in case they might be thinkin' about gettin' religion. Jack, Eli, and Junior, we'll ride into town tomorrow. The rest of you get your gear ready for that roundup down in Blanco County." He picked only three, because he didn't want to create the appearance of a cavalry troop invading the town. He was very much aware of the bad relations he had with the people of Bison Gap because of the rough nature of his men. But he needed to keep some appearance of control, because the town was the closest source for his supplies. His cousin came to mind, and he wished he would hurry up and get there. He could make use of his not being known by anyone in the town when it came to buying supplies. So he came with only three, but in his mind, the three he picked were the equivalent of a cavalry patrol.

It was midmorning when the four riders slow-walked their horses down the middle of the main street. Just to satisfy his curiosity, Stark pulled his horse to a halt in front of the building with a barber pole in front. He dismounted, while the others remained in the saddle, and walked up to the door, which he found to be locked. Seeing a young boy coming from the post office, he called to him. "Hey, kid, come here."

Richard Hoover, the postmaster's son, just one month past his fourteenth birthday, did as he was told. "Yes, sir?"

"What time does this barber open up? It's the middle of the mornin'."

"He usually opens earlier than this," Richard answered politely, while glancing cautiously at the three men on horseback staring at him.

"Today ain't Sunday, is it?" Stark asked.

"No, sir, today's Saturday," Richard said. "Maybe Mr. Jenkins is doin' one of his other jobs this mornin'."

"What jobs is that?" Stark asked.

"We ain't got a doctor in Bison Gap," Richard informed him. "But Mr. Jenkins does some doctorin' when folks need it."

"Doctorin', huh?" He started to step up into the saddle. "Maybe he's doin' some doctorin'," he joked to his men. Then another thought occurred to him, and he looked back at the boy, still staring wide-eyed at them. "Mr. Jenkins, does he ever do any buryin'?"

"Yes, sir, he's the undertaker, too."

"Did he have a dead man in a casket in front of this shop?"

"Yes, sir," Richard said, "but my dad said the sheriff made him take it away."

"Damn," Junior Humphrey blurted. "They did kill Curly."

One name sprang to the minds of all four men, Perley Gates. Stark automatically thought Curly died by the hand of Perley, the innocent-looking jasper he had seen in the hotel dining room. A more unlikely looking gunslinger he had never encountered before, but Perley Gates had evidently been contracted by someone in the town to systematically trim his gang down to size. Stark had never heard of a gunslinger named Perley Gates, but now, he suspected it was not the man's real name. More likely, it was an alias, chosen to imply the assassin sent his targets to enter the Pearly Gates. He wondered who in town could have contracted the professional killer. His first thought would have been the mayor. He found it hard to suspect Ralph Wheeler, however, because of the volume of business he did with his store. Who, then? Possibly the two women running the hotel, he speculated. They had the money to build the hotel and dining room. *No matter,* he told himself, *we stop the gunman and the problem's solved.* Shaking his mind free of the puzzle of Perley Gates, he stepped up into the saddle and wheeled his horse away from the barbershop. He led his three men over the bridge and turned toward the sheriff's office.

Not fully recovered from his arrest of Floyd Jenkins the night just passed, Sheriff Mason was not prepared to deal with an early visit from Ned Stark. He almost dropped his coffee cup when he glanced out the window and saw the four outlaws pull up in front of his office. "Quick!" He exclaimed to Floyd. "Get back in the cell! Now, damn it!" He commanded when Floyd didn't respond at once and gave him a shove that caused Floyd to spill half of his coffee as he went through the door to the cell room. Mason quickly closed the cell door barely seconds before he heard the front door of his office open. He hurriedly closed the door to the cell room as Stark walked in.

"'Mornin', Sheriff," Stark said, his greeting somewhat cynical, as was the smile on his face. Led by a sneering Eli Priest, the other three men filed in behind Stark and immediately began nosing around the sheriff's office, like a pack of hungry wolves looking for food. Stark might have told them to wait outside, but their intimidating presence appeared to be working on the startled sheriff.

"'Mornin'," Mason managed to return. "What can I do for you, Stark?"

"I'm hopin' you can solve a little mystery for me," Stark replied. "One of my cowhands came into town yesterday mornin'. I was expectin' him back at the ranch by noon, but he didn't come back a-tall. Curly Williams is his name. I thought maybe Curly mighta got drunk and caused some trouble, and maybe you've got him locked up back there." He pointed to the cell room door. "If you do, I thought I'd take him off your hands. I'm fixin' to drive a sizable herd of cattle to market and I need all my men." When the sheriff hesitated to answer, Stark went on. "You know, I'd expect to pay his fine, or any damages he mighta caused."

"No," Mason replied. "Curly ain't locked up. Curly's dead. He called another man out for a showdown and the other man was faster than he was."

"Was that other man's name Perley Gates?" Stark asked calmly.

"That don't really matter, does it?" Mason answered, hoping to prevent another shooting. "The man didn't do nothin' to rile Curly. Curly came lookin' for him and didn't give him any choice. The man had to defend himself."

"But that innocent man's name is Perley Gates, I'm thinkin'," Stark insisted. "And maybe you've got him locked up back there. Is that about right?"

"No," the sheriff maintained. "Perley Gates ain't locked up. I told you, he didn't go after Curly. Curly started the whole thing. There was a witness who saw it."

"If you say so, then I believe you. Who have you got locked up back there?" Not waiting for the sheriff to answer, Stark said, "Junior, take a look and see who's locked up." When Mason started toward the door, Stark said, "Don't bother, Sheriff, Junior'll do it. You just set yourself down at your desk."

Junior, a simple giant of a man, grinned at the

sheriff and stepped in front of him until he sat down. Then he opened the cell room door. He stepped inside the cell room to gape at Floyd, who had backed up against the far wall of his cell. "I don't know who it is, Ned," Junior called back. "I ain't never seen Perley Gates."

Stark held the sheriff captive with his eyes focused on Mason's eyes while he called back to Junior. "Ask him if his name is Floyd Jenkins."

"Call your ape back," Mason finally found the courage to say, not at all sure how far Stark intended to go. It was clear to him now that Perley had been right about putting Floyd in jail for his protection. The question now was whether or not he could provide that protection. He had no choice. He had to stand firm. "That's Floyd Jenkins, you've got no interest in him."

"Well, now, the hell I don't," Stark responded at once. "That rat stuck Curly Williams's body out on the street for everybody to gawk at. And I don't want my men treated like that, so what's gonna be Jenkins' punishment?"

"That'll be up to the city council to decide by jury," Mason answered, thinking as fast as he could. "But don't worry, there'll be a sentence passed."

"I think he needs to be strung up out on the street, like he did with Curly," Stark said. "I'd like to hear what he thinks you oughta do to him," he suddenly proposed and went into the cell room. Mason jumped up out of his chair, but Eli Priest caught him by the arm to stop him from following Stark.

Standing in front of the cell door, Stark stood glaring at the petrified Floyd Jenkins pressed against the back wall, his eyes jumping back and forth from Stark to the still grinning Junior Humphrey. "What do you think oughta happen to you for what you did to Curly?" Stark asked.

After hearing the conversation in the outer office between Stark and the sheriff, Floyd feared he was to be shot right then and there. He had been trying frantically to think of some explanation for what he did, other than the real one. "It was just a mistake I made," he stumbled, trying desperately to think of some believable excuse. "It wasn't for what it looked like at all." Then a thought popped into his head and he went with it. "It was supposed to be an advertising display. I'm an undertaker, not just a barber, and I wanted folks to see how good my coffins were, so they'd want me to take care of their friends and loved ones." Stark hesitated, scarcely able to believe what he was hearing. Floyd, even more frantic, tried to fill that space with more explanation. "Curly looked so good and peaceful in that coffin, and I wanted folks to see how well cared for he was. That's the only reason I put him outside for a little while. I didn't know it would make anybody mad till the sheriff came and told me."

Stark just continued to stare at the desperate man, deciding whether or not to shoot him down. But Junior was touched. "Dang," the big child uttered. "I wish we coulda seen him." Stark drew his .44, cocked it and aimed it at Floyd, who sank to the floor. Stark held his gun on the cowering victim for a long moment while he decided what the risks might be if he executed a man in the jail. Reluctantly, he released the hammer and holstered the weapon, deciding that action would open an all-out war with the town and cost him a place to buy supplies.

Stark turned around and went back in the sheriff's

office, where he found Eli and Jack on either side of the sheriff. "He ain't worth a bullet," he said, referring to Floyd, who was still huddled against the back wall, weeping tears of relief. "Hey, boys," Stark said then. "Give the sheriff a little breathin' room. Go on outside and wait for me. You go, too," he told Junior, and when they had gone, he turned his attention to Mason again. "Are you all right, Sheriff? My boys can be a little rough sometimes. But I thought you and I had an arrangement about handlin' my men, and all of a sudden, I've got two less men than I had before. And I need all my men to work the cattle, so I can pass along a little money your way."

"Damn it, Stark," Mason complained, speaking softly so as not to be overheard by Floyd through the open door to the cell room. "Those two killings were the fault of your men. How the hell could I do anything to keep them from gettin' killed when they pick a fight with a man who's better at it than they are? The problem is you've got too many men who like to shoot people."

"The problem we've got here right now is this damn gunslinger that came to town. What the hell is he doin' here in Bison Gap?"

"I told you, Stark, Perley Gates was the sheriff here for a little while till they hired me. He's got friends here."

"Maybe so," Stark said, "but somebody called him to come back again, and it wasn't till we took that ranch near here to operate out of. So who was it? 'Cause that's the real problem." He paused when it occurred to him. "Unless, he came back on his own because he wants his old job as sheriff back."

"I don't think so," Mason said. "Ralph Wheeler told

me he tried to get Perley to take the job before he found me. But Perley wouldn't take it. Ralph says him and his brothers own a big cattle ranch up in northeast Texas."

"He don't look like a big cattle rancher to me," Stark grunted.

"He don't look like a big gunslinger, either," Mason couldn't resist saying.

"Somebody here in town sent for him," Stark maintained. "I guarantee it, so who are his friends here?"

Emma Slocum and Rachael Parker naturally came to mind at once, but Mason was reluctant to name them. He had no desire to cause them the kind of trouble Ned Stark was likely to bring them. "Nobody in particular I can think of who knows him any better than anyone else in town."

"You ain't holdin' out on me, are you, Mason?"

"No," Mason protested at once. "I ain't holdin' out on you. It's just that Perley wasn't here but a short time, so nobody got a chance to know him all that well."

"All right," Stark decided. "I reckon it's just a matter of takin' care of Mr. Perley Gates. Then maybe things will get back to the way they were." He walked out to join his men.

When he was sure they were gone, Mason went in the cell room to unlock Floyd's cell, only to find that he had not locked it before. Floyd was still squatting on the floor against the wall. "He's gone now," the sheriff informed him. "Are you okay?"

"I guess I am now," Floyd answered. "But there was a moment there when I pictured myself in one of my coffins. He was fixin' to shoot me. I don't know why he didn't. I reckon he knew you'd arrest him if he did."

"Yeah, I suppose that's so," Mason said. "He knew I wouldn't let him get away with that." Saying it made him feel sick inside. At that moment, he wished with all his heart that he had never allowed himself to become involved with Ned Stark. "You want me to let you outta that cell?"

"No," Floyd said. "If it's all right with you, I'll stay here another night."

"It's all right with me," Mason said, "but ain't you got a body that's gettin' a little ripe about now?"

# CHAPTER 9

Unaware that Ned Stark and three of his gunmen were making a visit to the jailhouse, Perley and Possum were talking to Ralph Wheeler about the possibility of forming a citizens' protective committee. "Vigilantes are what you're referring to, isn't it?" Wheeler responded.

Perley shrugged. "Call it what you will. We're talkin' about a group of men who will protect their town from predators like Ned Stark. 'Cause when a gang of outlaws as big as the one Stark has lands on your doorstep, one sheriff can't handle it without help."

"I don't know, Perley, it's been a long time since I've fired a gun, and I expect it's the same with most of the merchants in town. We're getting too old to think about gunfights."

"There's still a few men around that are young enough to take up arms when the cause is to protect your homes and your families," Possum insisted. "What we're talkin' about for you is to help organize the ones who will fight, if it's necessary. You're the mayor, so most everybody is already used to listenin' to you, and you could head up the committee."

"It looks like we're gonna have to do something," Wheeler said. "I have to agree with you there. It seems like it happened to us all of a sudden—shootings, fights, and destroying property. Tell you the truth, I'm beginning to think I used poor judgment in the hiring of John Mason."

"I wouldn't give up on Sheriff Mason too soon," Perley said. "I think he has to know he has the backing of the whole town behind him. Right now, he thinks he's alone in his fight against people like Stark. Make sure you invite him to come to the council meetings, let him know what's goin' on, and find out how to help him. I think he just needs to know he's got backing, so he knows which side he's on."

"Maybe," Wheeler allowed. "We never have asked him to come to any meetings we've had. I reckon it had to come to this problem with Stark's gang for us to realize we're gonna have to take a stand." He paused, nodded a couple of times, and said, "I'll contact the council for a meeting and see what we come up with. You're invited." Perley and Possum started to leave, but Wheeler stopped them. "Perley, how long are you gonna be here?"

"Well, I think some of the folks here think that I'm the problem because of the two gunfights I was in. But I plan to stay here till Bison Gap's outlaw problem is settled, or till I'm told to leave—whichever one comes first."

"I'll let you know when the meeting's set up," Wheeler said and walked them to the door. Outside, Possum suggested they should talk to John Payne and Horace Brooks to get an idea if they were willing to back the sheriff. Before they stepped off the board-walk in front of Wheeler's, they felt the zip of a bullet pass between them and smash Wheeler's window. Both men dived for cover at the same time they heard the report of the pistol.

"Yonder!" Possum shouted, "Between the jail and the saloon! Four of 'em!" Perley looked where he pointed and saw four men on horseback. Both he and Possum drew their handguns and fired at the riders, already galloping away along the creek bank, and already out of range for their pistols. When they had disappeared from view, Possum got up from beside the boardwalk and brushed the dirt off his trousers. When Perley got up, Possum said, "Danged if it ain't got downright dangerous walkin' around with you."

"That shot passed right between us," Perley replied. "How do you know they weren't shootin' at you?"

"I got a pretty good idea," Possum said.

Thinking it safe to come out now, Wheeler came out complaining. "He shot out my window! Did you see who he was?"

"It weren't a he," Possum answered. "It were a them. There was four of 'em."

"We'd best get down to the jail to see if they're all right," Perley said. "Those four mighta done for Floyd." He started running toward the jail, and Possum followed. They heard Wheeler yelling behind them that he was going to call the meeting for that night.


"What the hell is wrong with you?" Ned Stark demanded after they had galloped their horses far enough to get out of sight and reined them back to a walk.

"Hell, open season," Eli crowed. "You said it would be open season on that feller today. And you said that was him, coming out of the store. For a hundred bucks, it was worth a shot at him."

"You damn fool," Stark cursed him, barely able to control his rage. "We were way too far for an accurate shot with a handgun, and on a horse to boot. You ain't got the brains of a stump. What you just did was cost us the chance to ride on into town where somebody could get a good shot at him. Now, thanks to you, we have to hightail it and try again some other day."

Eli shrugged and said again, "It was worth a shot."

"Who said you had the right to take that shot?" Jack Sledge asked.

"Hell, there weren't nobody stoppin' you from takin' it, was there?" Eli responded.

"The rest of us had better sense than to throw a pistol shot at him from that distance. Like Ned just said, you're dumb as a stump. Now that jasper is gonna be watchin' for us every time he goes outside."

"You know, Sledge, I ain't sure I like your attitude when you're mouthin' off at me," Eli informed him.

"Not likin' it and doin' somethin' about it is two different things," Sledge replied.

Tired of the bickering between the two, Stark finally barked, "You two wanna stop right here and see if you can kill each other? 'Cause I'm tired of hearin' all that jawin'. Eli, you messed things up for all of us with that crazy shot. Now he knows who we are. He'll be extra careful every time he steps out the door."

"We was so far away, he couldn'ta got a good look at any of us," Eli insisted.

"We just came from the sheriff's office, you damn fool," Stark had to point out. "Mason could tell him it was one of us—so could Floyd Jenkins. We're all gonna have to be a lot more careful now to try to get a clean shot at him. You might have to ride into town and call him out in the street to see if you're a better man than Curly or Quirt." His comments gave all three of them something to think about, since all three knew how fast Curly and Quirt had been before they called Perley Gates out. Their best bet was an ambush or sniper shot.

Stark let them think about that as they rode back to the ranch. His mind was still working on who in town was the person, or persons, who called in this gunslinger. There was also Possum Smith to worry about. Mason said he came to town with Perley Gates. He might look harmless—old-looking, with his white beard and long hair in a braid, hanging between his shoulder blades. It was hard to tell how dangerous he was, however. The two of them were in pretty thick with the runty little blowhard, Rooster Crabb. Maybe Rooster was the one who sent for Perley Gates. To be safe, Stark decided it best to eliminate all three of them to get the town back the way it was.

While Stark was simmering over his aborted mission into town, Perley and Possum hurried across the creek to the jail, anxious about the prisoner's condition. Sheriff Mason met them at the door. "I ran outside as soon as I heard the shot," he said, "but they were already gone. So I don't know who fired it. Did anybody get hit?"

"No, they missed," Perley said as he walked on past him to go inside. "What about Floyd, is he all right?"

"Yeah, he's all right," Mason answered. "I wouldn't let anythin' happen to one of my prisoners."

Perley wanted to see for himself, so he went into the cell room where he found Floyd alive but still shaken. "Are you all right?" Perley asked.

"Yeah, I reckon so," Floyd replied, "if I count gettin' scared out of my mind. That maniac drew his pistol, cocked it, and held it on me for what seemed like an hour, tryin' to decide whether to shoot me or just scare me to death."

"Sheriff Mason make him put it away?" Perley asked.

"Hell, no," Floyd responded. "He wasn't even in the room. He stayed out in the office. The only ones in here were Stark and one of his men, that big one that looks like he oughta be swinging in a tree in a jungle somewhere."

That was disappointing news to Perley, causing him to think that maybe he had been holding on to too much hope for the sheriff's turnaround. If he wasn't strong enough to protect his own jail, how could he ever become strong enough to protect the whole town? "Did the sheriff say you had to stay in jail?"

"No," Floyd answered. "He said I could go now, if I wanted to, but I didn't want to, not with those killers in town. Now, I ain't sure what's best. I thought I was safe in jail, till I sat here lookin' at that pistol stickin' through the bars, pointed straight at me."

Floyd's accounting of the visit by Ned Stark and his three men caused great concern for Perley. He thought that jail cell was the safest place Floyd could be, and he knew he was responsible for making Floyd feel safe there as well. Now, it appeared he was wrong, dead wrong, had Stark pulled the trigger. It was doubly troubling because he thought the sheriff had the potential to stand up to his job. Part of his ploy to get the sheriff to arrest Floyd, and put him in jail, was to try to push Mason in the right direction. *Well, my plan ain't working,* he thought, *looks like it's going to be up to the town council to save their town.* Back to Floyd then, he asked, "What do you wanna do now? If you wanna go back to your place, I could stay with you tonight, if you want me to, or you could bunk in at the hotel, like Rooster does."

"I do need to get my shop open again," Floyd replied. "Today's Saturday, and that's usually a busy day in the barbershop." He paused to insert, "And tomorrow's Sunday, and I'm goin' to church for damn sure. If you wouldn't mind, maybe you could sleep in my place tonight. I'd surely appreciate it."

"All right," Perley said. "I'll stay at your place tonight. I'll bring my bedroll. I'll go tell the sheriff to let you out."

"You don't have to do that," Floyd said, "it ain't locked." He opened the door and came out of the cell. "I just thank the Good Lord Stark didn't try to open it."

"I'll be leavin' now, Sheriff, if there really ain't no charges for what I did. I 'preciate your offer to let me stay again tonight, but Perley said he'd stay at my place tonight. That's just in case Stark's men come back again."

Both Possum and the sheriff looked surprised when they heard that. "Wouldn't it be better if you was to come to the hotel and stay with us?" Possum asked.

"Perley offered that, but like I told him, today's Saturday, my busiest day, and I'm already late opening the barbershop. I expect I'll be workin' late tonight, so I'd rather stay at my place. Besides, they might charge me to stay at the hotel."

"What about Stark and the other three?" Possum asked the sheriff. "Ain't you goin' after 'em? They took a shot at us. If you need a posse, I know me and Perley will ride with you, maybe get some other volunteers."

Mason hesitated before answering. "If they were still in town, I'd most likely arrest 'em. But even if I did, we don't know which one of 'em fired the shot. They could even swear that the gun went off by accident, so I figure there ain't much sense in goin' after them, since nobody got hurt." Perley looked at Possum and shook his head. The sheriff's answer was disappointing to hear.

As they walked out the door of the sheriff's office, they were met by Richard Hoover, the postmaster's son, on his way to the jail. Seeing them on the steps, the boy called out, "Mr. Wheeler sent me to tell everybody there's a council meetin' tonight after supper, seven o'clock, at the hotel dinin' room. He said to be sure and tell you, Sheriff."

"The dinin' room?" Possum questioned. "I thought they used to hold those meetings in the Buffalo Hump."

"I expect they shifted this one to the dinin' room so Emma could attend," Perley suggested.

"Hell, Emma's got a lot more bark on her than that," Possum remarked.

As everyone should have expected, including Emma Slocum, there were some who wanted the council meeting held in the saloon as in previous meetings. Foremost among the protesters was Henry Lawrence, quite naturally, since he was the owner of the Buffalo Hump. He maintained that nothing of any substance had ever been decided over a cup of coffee, and several of the others voiced their opinion that Henry was right. When it appeared attendance of this very important meeting might be seriously lacking, Ralph Wheeler found himself with the task of reporting the problem to Emma. She was surprised that afternoon when the desk clerk, Wilbur Ross, stuck his head in her office door to tell her that Wheeler was there to see her. She got up from her desk to receive him. "Afternoon, Ralph, what can I do for you?"

"Howdy, Emma," he responded. "It's about the special meeting of the council tonight." She smiled and gave him her full attention. "There are going to be some hard choices we'll be asking the members to make."

"I understand that to be the case," Emma said. "Possum told me about some of the problems that will be discussed. Is there something pertaining to the Bison House Hotel that you're concerned about? Because I assure you that Possum and I as owners of the hotel are in full accord with what is best for Bison Gap."

"Good, good," Wheeler responded, "I knew we could count on your support."

His voice trailed off and he appeared puzzled. "Ralph, is there something else?" she asked.

"Might as well, just spit it out," he declared. "In a meeting like this, we've always needed a little bit of something stronger to drink than coffee. Strong drinks help make strong decisions." He hesitated, trying to decide how to tell her the majority of the members didn't want to meet in the dining room.

"That's easy enough to fix," she said. "Why don't we have the meeting in the Buffalo Hump?"

Her suggestion caught him completely by surprise. "What? Why, with you being a lady and all, I was afraid you'd be offended and refuse to attend."

She laughed. "I hope you'll find that I'm just as much a lady in a saloon as I am anywhere else. There's more room in the saloon, anyway, and Rachael will be delighted to hear you've decided to change the meeting site."

"That's mighty gracious of you to understand," he said. "You'll attend then?"

"Yes, indeed, I'll be there, me and my partner, Mr. Possum Smith. We're not gonna miss this meeting."


After making sure Floyd Jenkins didn't have any of Ned Stark's men posing as barbershop customers waiting for him to open his door, Perley and Possum stopped by the hotel briefly before riding down to Rooster's cabin to tell him about the meeting. He had left after breakfast that morning to return to his cabin to care for his stock. They knew he would be fighting mad if the town council held a meeting and he wasn't there. In spite of the fact he was not an official member of the council, he made sure his complaints and suggestions were always heard. They found the little man slopping his hogs when they rode down the path from the creek-side trail.

"Hope we ain't intrudin' on a family reunion," Possum called out to him.

Without missing a beat, Rooster answered right back. "Not at all. Relatives are always welcome. Just find you a place at the trough."

Continuing the banter the two always seemed to enjoy, Possum said, "Me and Perley rode out here to tell you there's a council meetin' called for seven o'clock tonight at the Buffalo Hump. The members of the council, of which I am one, wanted me to tell you it's for members only, so you ain't invited."

"Like hell, I ain't!" Rooster erupted to Possum's satisfaction. "I'll have my say about it." He hesitated, then asked, "What's the meetin' about?"

Perley answered him, "They're finally gonna sit down and do some serious talk about settin' up a vigilance committee to protect the town."

"Well, it's about time," Rooster said. "I've been tellin' Ralph Wheeler that for I don't know how long. They already know I'll ride with the vigilantes."

After they talked about what might come as a result of this meeting, they told him about Ned Stark's visit to town that morning and the fact that either him, or one of his men, had taken a shot at them when they were coming out of Wheeler's Store. "Well, if that ain't a sign we need that meetin', I don't know what is," Rooster commented. They stayed with him, helping with some of his chores until it was getting around suppertime and he decided to go in with them to eat at the hotel.

"I've gotta go check on Floyd," Perley said, "make sure he's all right. He was a little shaky after his visit from Ned Stark this mornin'." That led to a discussion about Stark's visit to the jail and Perley promising to spend the night with Floyd.

"Whaddaya have to spend the night with him for?" Rooster asked.

"Stark came after him for proppin' Curly's body up outside his shop," Perley said. "And Floyd said Stark came close to shootin' him in his jail cell. So he's scared Stark might still be plannin' on comin' after him, but I doubt he will now."

Rooster saddled up his horse and the three friends rode into town. When they got there, Perley stopped at the barbershop to see how Floyd was getting along. He appeared to be fully recovered from his morning fright. Still working, he told Perley he'd fix himself something to eat and see him later at the meeting. So Perley went from there to the stable to put Buck away for the night, then he went to the hotel for supper. When he got there, Possum and Rooster were already eating, so he sat down at the table with them.

Seeing him come in, Rachael picked up the coffeepot and a cup, and brought it over. "Thank you, ma'am," he said, politely. "Reckon you're disappointed to hear you ain't gonna host the big council meeting tonight," he japed.

"I wasn't too tickled to hear Ralph Wheeler wanted to have it here in the first place," Rachael claimed. "Just extra mess to clean up." When Possum asked her if she was going to the meeting with Emma, she answered no. "Emma and you are the owners of this business, and I'm not likely to volunteer to ride with the vigilantes, so I reckon I'll just be happy with whatever you and the others decide. Likely, nothing much will come of it, except Henry Lawrence will sell a lot of whiskey."

"Ain't nothin' wrong with that," Rooster remarked with a chuckle.

The discussion focused upon the possibility of the members finally deciding to take up arms and lasted long after supper was finished. When it was approaching seven o'clock, they left the dining room and walked down to the saloon. Ralph Wheeler was already sitting at the head of a long table that Henry Lawrence had arranged out of several small saloon tables pushed together. In deference to Emma Slocum, Ralph had pulled a chair up beside his to set her a little apart from the men. When Emma arrived a few minutes before seven, she went to the other end of the table to sit beside Possum, wishing to be treated as a partner and not a woman. Perley had to smile when Rooster went up to the head of the table and sat down in the chair set aside for Emma.

The meeting started on time, and right from the beginning, it was obvious that the topic to be discussed was of concern to everyone there. Henry Lawrence had taken the liberty of writing an oath of allegiance to the town of Bison Gap and a promise to defend it. After a brief paragraph stating that, he left spaces for everyone to sign the sheet, which he described as a contract to defend the town. It served its purpose, for the signing of the sheet turned into a solemn commitment to the future of Bison Gap. This, of course, came after a heated discussion of the recent course the town had taken toward a wide-open retreat for the lawless. Halfway through this discussion, a late arrival entered the meeting that caused a general pause in the call to arms. Starting near the front door, the noisy pockets of debate subsided like the ebbing of a wave as he moved toward the council table in the back of the room. "I'm sorry I'm late. I hope I'm not interrupting the meeting," he said.

"Why, no, sir, Reverend Poole," Ralph Wheeler responded, obviously flustered to see the Baptist minister appearing in the saloon, especially when practically all the men in town were there to pledge their intent to start a war. "We were just meeting to discuss some of the problems that needed to be fixed." His initial thought was that the preacher couldn't have come at a worse time. And his message of brotherly love and love thy neighbor had a time and place, and the place was in the church, not the saloon.

"I heard what the meeting was about," Reverend Poole said. "And I came to join the vigilance committee. I own a rifle, and I know how to use it."

There followed a moment of shocked silence, broken by a sudden burst from Rooster Crabb. "Hallelujah, Preacher! Have a drink of likker."

"Maybe just one," Poole said and sat down in a chair John Payne pulled out for him.

With the meeting taking on the new feeling of a righteous crusade, the sheet of signatures was soon filled with the names of volunteers. Many of the names were in spirit only due to age and physical capability, but there was a core of a dozen men who seemed capable of forming a home guard, ready to respond in force when trouble threatened. Future "training" meetings were scheduled to follow to organize an effective response. As interested as anyone there, Sheriff John Mason could not help but be amazed by the response of those in attendance and didn't hesitate to volunteer when asked if he would help with the training meetings. It gave him a lot to think about, especially in regard to Ned Stark. He was startled momentarily when Perley leaned over his shoulder and spoke quietly, "Looks like you ain't alone anymore."

# CHAPTER 10

The meeting broke up then, but the drinking continued for a good portion of those who came to observe, much to Henry Lawrence's satisfaction. The Reverend Harvey Poole made one last announcement before he left. "Tomorrow is Sunday, and I'd like to remind you there's another battle that needs to be fought, this one against the devil. You're all welcome to worship with us." Walking out the door, Poole saw Perley outside, talking to Rooster, so he stopped to talk to them.

"Howdy, Parson," Rooster greeted the preacher. "After hearin' you're a fightin' preacher, maybe I'd better come to one of your services."

"You know you'd certainly be welcome," Poole replied. "I couldn't help but notice that you've got some strong convictions about doing what's right." He looked at Perley then. "My wife and I haven't been in Bison Gap long enough to know very many of the people. We just finished building the church a couple of months ago. But I've already heard more than a few people talking about you. And you might guess, I have a strong curiosity about a man with a name like yours.

Is it your real name, or just one that you go by? You have to admit it's an odd name for someone in your business, Perley Gates, unless it's supposed to have a double meaning."

"What kinda business do you think I'm in?" Perley asked.

"Judging by what I heard at this meeting tonight, I mean with the killings of the two outlaws—Curly somebody and I don't remember the other one's name—I assumed that to be your business."

"Hell, no, Parson!" Rooster exclaimed. "Perley ain't no gunslinger. He's just got the gawl-dangedest reflexes the Good Lord ever saw fit to put in a man. And he goes a long way outta his way to try to keep from usin' 'em."

"To answer your question, Reverend," Perley started the explanation he had repeated so many times in his young life. "Perley's my real name, named for my grandpa, but it ain't spelled like the Pearly Gates up in Heaven. It's spelled P-e-r-l-e-y, and the business I'm in is raisin' cattle up in northeast Texas."

"Well, please accept my apology, Perley," Poole said. "I always get in trouble when I assume something before takin' the time to get the facts. No offense."

"None taken," Perley said.

"It's a pleasure to meet you," Poole said and offered his hand. When Perley accepted it, the preacher said, "I'd like to see you in church tomorrow."

"'Preciate it," Perley responded. When Poole turned and walked out of earshot, Perley said, "I'll stop by and pick Rooster up on the way."

"Hah," Rooster snorted. "I don't know how good the preacher built that church of his. It might not be stout enough to keep from cavin' in if I was to walk in it."

Floyd Jenkins walked up to join them then. He had waited until Reverend Poole left. "Looks like we're gonna have us a vigilance committee, don't it?"

"Looks that way," Perley answered. "Once some of these saddle tramps and outlaws find out about it, it oughta make Bison Gap a much better place to live."

"They ain't had time to find out about it yet," Floyd said, "so you're still gonna stay over at my place tonight, ain'tcha?"

"Sure, Floyd. I said I would, if you still think you want me to." After Floyd's apparent change of attitude earlier in the day, Perley had hoped he had changed his mind about that night as well. "I dropped my bedroll off when I was there earlier. I'm just gonna go down to the stable and tuck Buck in for the night. Then I'll see you back at the barbershop." Turning to face Rooster then, he said, "I reckon I'll see you at breakfast." Another glance back at the door of the saloon told him that Possum was still engaged in a discussion with Emma and Dick Hoover. "Possum looks like he's fittin' right in with the other members of the council," Perley said to Rooster. "If he stays here much longer, he's liable to run for mayor." He turned back toward Floyd, who was waiting to walk with him.

After spending a little time with Buck, as well as having some more conversation with Horace Brooks about the way the meeting went, Perley walked back up the street to the barbershop. With his saddlebags on his shoulder and his rifle in hand, he went around to the back door of the shop as Floyd had suggested.

He told him the front door would be locked and he would be in the back where his living quarters were. Perley found the door, located between the barbershop and a modest addition, complete with kitchen, bedroom, and a small parlor. Still farther back, and attached to the house, was what looked like a small barn. This was where Floyd practiced his mortician sideline. Perley knocked on the door between the shop and the house. In a minute, he got a glimpse of Floyd at the window looking to make sure it was him at the door.

"Come on in, Perley." Floyd welcomed him into his kitchen. "I don't know about you, but I needed a little coffee after the whiskey I drank. How 'bout you?"

"I reckon I could handle a cup of coffee," Perley said

They had a cup of coffee, then Floyd wanted to show Perley around the place. "You've seen the barbershop, I reckon, so I'll show you the rest." He led him from the kitchen through a door that opened to a larger room, divided by a curtain to separate it into two areas—a bedroom on one side, and a small parlor on the other. "I put your bedroll on the sofa under the window there," Floyd said and pointed. "I put a chamber pot by the sofa, so you won't have to go outside to the outhouse." Then, pointing to a door in the back wall between the bedroom and parlor, he said, "That goes to my back shop where I build my caskets." He led the way.

Admitting to himself that he wasn't totally disinterested, Perley followed him into the large workroom, filled with stacks of boards Floyd used in his business. Over against the back wall he saw a casket on a table. "That's one of the caskets you build?" Perley asked and started walking over to examine it, purely because he thought it was polite to show an interest.

"Yep," Floyd replied.

He had no sooner said it when Perley stopped in his tracks and took a step back. "Dang! What is that smell?"

"That's Curly Williams," Floyd said.

"You ain't buried him yet?" Perley exclaimed, the odor backing him up some more.

"I ain't had time," Floyd explained.

"I believe I'd take time before I lived with that smell," Perley said, backing all the way to the door.

"I'll put him in the ground tomorrow. I've got two fellows that'll dig a grave and drop him in it for just enough money to buy a few drinks at the saloon.

"They musta drank enough whiskey to kill their sense of smell," Perley commented. "I don't believe I could handle that job." He turned around and went back in the door to the living quarters.

"You go in and tell him," Slim Garrett replied when Eli Priest told him to approach Ned Stark about the whiskey. Stark had been sulking in the little room that served as his private bedroom ever since they came back from town that morning. He never slept out in the front room where the rest of his gang slept on straw pallets like a bunkhouse. But he usually sat out in the room with them until he turned in for the night. This was not a typical night, however, and he was still burning with anger after having to make the hasty retreat from Bison Gap.

"You know I can't go in there and talk to him," Eli

complained. "I thought he was gonna put a bullet in me for takin' that shot this mornin'."

Listening to their discussion, Jack Sledge grunted in amusement. "Yeah, Slim, you go on in there and tell him you've got a complaint. Tell him Eli ain't happy 'cause we've run outta likker. 'Course, he might remind you, Eli, that he was plannin' to go in the saloon and buy some likker before you had to leave town all of a sudden."

"I'm gettin' tired of listenin' to all your bellyachin'," Carl Leach announced. "Mopin' around like a bunch of little babies. "I'm goin' into town and get me a drink of whiskey."

"Yeah, sure you are," Eli said.

"I'm tired of settin' around this damn house," Leach said. "We've been suckin' our thumbs around here for days." He strapped on his gun belt and plopped his hat on his head. "Hell, I wasn't in town this mornin'. Can't nobody point their finger at me."

Realizing then that Leach was serious, Eli said, "Hell, it's too late to go to town now. They'll probably be closin' up by the time you saddle up and ride in there."

"Then, by God, I'll open 'em up again," Leach declared.

"You'd best tell Ned what you're aimin' to do," Frank Deal cautioned, "especially when he's in one of his black moods, like he is tonight."

"I'll tell you what," Leach said, "you tell him when he comes out of that damn room."

"What about that Perley Gates feller?" Junior Humphrey asked.

"What about him?" Leach barked at the simple giant.

"I hope to hell I run into him. I'll buy him a drink, then shoot his ass and claim that hundred dollars."

"Eli missed when he took a shot at Perley Gates," Junior said. "But that other feller is what's got Ned so mad." When Leach asked what other fellow, Junior answered, "That feller that stuck Curly in a box, that barber. I was in the cell room with Ned. He wanted to shoot that feller and almost did. He had his .44 aimed at him and almost pulled the trigger. That's why he's so mad. He's mad at hisself for not shootin' when he had the chance."

"You ain't got no sense, Junior," Eli snorted. "He didn't shoot 'cause he was in the damn jailhouse, and he didn't want anybody in town to hear the shot. Same reason he got mad at me. The only difference is when I took a shot at Perley Gates, it was a gamble worth takin' 'cause, if I'd hit him, that woulda got rid of all our trouble in that town. That undertaker feller ain't no danger to anybody."

"Well, you fellers talk it over all you want," Leach announced. "You're wastin' my time. I'm goin' to get me a drink of whiskey. I'll see you boys later." He walked out the door, leaving them to speculate on what was going to happen when Ned found out. Some of them thought he was bluffing, until they heard his horse loping out of the yard.

"That crazy peckerwood," Eli remarked when it was plain that Leach meant what he said. "If he makes it back here without gettin' shot in town, Ned'll shoot him."

The town had quieted down for the night when Leach walked his horse across the narrow bridge that led to the Buffalo Hump Saloon. He looked around him, right and left, to make sure no one was paying any attention to him. *Saturday night,* he told himself, *and the town's dead.* It didn't seem natural. He almost felt like he was riding into a trap, but he was certain no one saw him ride into town. He considered wheeling his horse around and riding hell-bent for leather out of there, but he thought of the cocky boasting he had done back at the ranch. *Hell,* he told himself, *I ain't been in this town enough times for anybody to be sure they've seen me before.* He rode on up to the rail and stepped down.

He stood just inside the doors of the saloon for a moment before going on in. It was quiet, only a few customers sitting at the tables. In the back of the saloon, there were some tables pushed together to make one big one. Like a meeting, he thought, or a trial. Telling himself he could carry out his bluff, he walked up to the bar and said, "Howdy," when Jimmy McGee turned to see him.

"Howdy," Jimmy automatically returned, trying to remember if he had seen the man before. "What's your pleasure?"

"I think I might drop dead if I don't get a drink of whiskey," Leach answered with a smile. "I've been in the saddle all day and I'm needin' a drink of corn, if you've got any."

"I sure do, mister," Jimmy responded cordially. He reached behind him and pulled a bottle from the shelf. "First time in Bison Gap? You look familiar, but I ain't sure you've been in before."

"I've got one of them faces, I reckon," Leach said, "but you're right, first time in Bison Gap—didn't even know it was here till I rode in on that trail by the creek." He downed his whiskey and tapped the glass on the bar for a second one. While Jimmy was pouring, Leach nodded toward the tables in the back. "Looks like you had a meetin' or a trial tonight."

"Council meetin'," Jimmy told him. "Town's been havin' trouble with a gang of outlaws, and there was a meetin' here to decide what to do about it."

"That bad, huh?"

"I'll say so," Jimmy answered. "We've already had two shootin's in the last couple of days. And one of our citizens, the barber, the sheriff had to lock him in jail to keep him from gettin' killed."

"Well, I'll swear, that is a passel of bad luck," Leach marveled. "Have to keep the barber in jail, huh?"

"Well, he's out now," Jimmy said, "but he stayed there overnight. You'da seen what I mean, if you'd got here before the meetin' broke up. That's the reason it's so dead in here right now. Everybody's drank all they can hold and gone home."

"I'm sorry you folks are havin' outlaw problems. I guess I'd best take care where I make camp tonight, and I reckon I'd best be gettin' along, too. I'll take a bottle of that corn whiskey with me and wish you a good evenin'." He paid Jimmy, picked up his bottle of whiskey, and walked out the door, looking forward to seeing the faces of the rest of the gang when he tells them about his bluff. "With a bottle of corn whiskey to prove I ain't lyin'," he said with a grin.

It was getting close to midnight when he rode back into the yard and went directly to the barn to take care of his horse. Eli was the first to react when Leach walked in the door of the house. "I reckon you rode into town and had yourself a drink of likker," he said, his tone thick with sarcasm.

"I said I was, didn't I?" Leach answered, standing in the doorway, holding his bottle of whiskey behind him.

"Where have you really been?" Stark asked.

"Well, evenin', Boss," Leach crowed. "I'm glad to see you decided to come out and wait for me. Like I was tellin' these jaspers, I decided to ride into town for a little drink of corn whiskey."

"And you just walked right in the Buffalo Hump with no trouble a-tall?" Stark asked. Like the other men, he was convinced Leach was bluffing, just to get their goats.

"Walked right in and ordered a drink, had a couple of drinks as a matter fact, and talked to the bartender for a while," Leach answered, enjoying the skepticism of his partners.

"What are you gonna do to prove you ain't lyin'?" Eli scoffed.

"I reckon you could smell my breath to see if I've had a drink or not," Leach answered him. "Or I could let you have a drink, too." He pulled the bottle from behind him, walked up to the table, and plunked it down in the middle of it. His action was rewarded by a spontaneous cheer from his partners. Even Stark smiled. The cork was out of the bottle immediately and the contents went down fast.

"Damn," Eli swore after the bottle passed by him. "You shoulda bought two bottles."

"You're lucky to get that drink," Leach replied. "I didn't have enough money to buy another bottle. I thought about holdin' up the saloon, but there were too many jaspers in there for me to cover." He caught Stark's eye then. "I brought back some information that I didn't have to pay nothin' for." He went on to tell them about the meeting the town people held earlier in the evening—and the purpose of the meeting. "They've decided to form a vigilante gang to go after outlaws they have trouble with, and the sheriff's supposed to be in it with 'em."

That brought an immediate reaction from Ned Stark. "That stinker," he growled. "We'll see about that." He was still chafed to find Jenkins in jail and brooding over his failure to shoot him when he had the chance. The next statement from Leach lit the fuse on a second explosion of anger in Stark's brain. "Jenkins ain't in the jailhouse no more," Leach said. "He's gone back to his place."

Stark didn't say anything, but the fury in his face was response enough for the men gathered at the table to know what he was thinking. It was Eli who expressed it. "Hell, we could go get him right now," he blurted.

"It's already midnight," Frank Deal said.

"Couldn't be no better time than in the middle of the night," Eli insisted, "catch him while he's asleep." He looked at Stark for his agreement. "Hang him up on his barber pole, so everybody can see him, like he did with Curly."

"He's right," Stark said, "while he's sleepin'. Drag him out and hang him, that'll send a message to the good citizens of Bison Gap—let 'em know what happens to people when they threaten us."

"I'll go!" Eli immediately volunteered. He had been in a killing mood ever since Stark first offered a reward for Perley Gates. "Who wants to go with me?"

"I'll go with you," Leach replied. Having just seen how sleepy the town was, he didn't see much chance they would encounter any resistance from anyone. In fact, he thought it would be a pretty good response to the council's big meeting about protecting the town.

"Hell, why don't we all go?" Frank Deal asked.

"No," Stark said at once. "We all go ridin' in there, we'll wake up the whole town, and I don't want those people to know anything about this till they get up in the mornin' and see him hangin' on that barber pole with his throat cut."

"You're right, Ned," Jim Duncan spoke up then. He didn't want to go, anyway. "How many do you think oughta go?"

"Eli and Leach can probably take care of that cowardly little snake," Stark said at first, while still considering. "Maybe three just to be safe."

"Let me go," Slim said. "I'm broke as the Ten Commandments, and he's surely got some money around that barbershop somewhere."

"That all right with you two?" Stark asked, looking at Eli and Leach.

Eli shrugged indifferently, figuring he could do the job by himself. Leach said it was all right with him. "But we'd better get goin, if we don't wanna end up snatchin' the weasel in the daylight."

The three assassins strapped on their gun belts and started toward the corral to get their horses. Stark walked out with them and talked to them while they saddled up. "Make sure you hang him where everybody will see him," he emphasized. "Slim's right, you oughta be able to find a cashbox or somethin' around there somewhere. I figure any money you find, the three of you can split it, for doin' the job."

"That suits me fine," Leach said. "I just wish I hadn't unsaddled my horse when I rode in."

# CHAPTER 11

The three assassins found the town as sleepy as Leach had described after his visit earlier that night, maybe more so in his opinion. For now, even the saloon was silent. Although feeling as if there would be no risk of being seen if they walked their horses up the middle of the street, they decided to play it safe and ride behind the buildings. When they came to the barbershop, they dismounted and tied their horses at a short length of fence behind what appeared to be a small barn. "You sure this is the barbershop?" Eli asked Slim, since he had only seen the shop from the street in front.

"Yeah, I'm sure," Slim replied. "I think that's where he does his undertaker work. The barbershop is up front."

They moved up beside a barn door, which was padlocked, and stopped to take a better look at the buildings. From there, they could see the shop and another section behind it that had to be Floyd's domicile. "Damn," Leach suddenly complained. "Is that you?"

"Hell, no," Slim answered. "I thought it was you."

"It's comin' outta this barn door," Eli said. "He's

got somethin' in there that's turned. Let's move up a little farther." They moved up past the door to the corner of the barn. "You can see better here, anyway," he said, speaking in a whisper now. "There's a window on this side, I'm gonna sneak up and see if I can see anything." Not waiting for them to caution him, he ran up to the side of the house and squatted under the window. Then he rose up slowly until he could peek inside. After a few moments, he carefully tried the window and found he was able to move it up slightly. Afraid to test it further, he backed away to report his findings to Leach and Slim.

"That window ain't got no locks on it," he told them when he got back to the corner of the barn. "I think we can get in that way. I looked in the window. It's pretty dark in there, but I could see it looked like a parlor or somethin' with chairs and stuff in there. There's a wall or a curtain on the other side of that room. We need to go around and look at the other side. I bet that's where his bedroom is, and there's most likely another window on that side." That sounded like a good idea, so they hustled around the back of the barn to the other side to find that Eli had guessed right. "Wait here," he said and took off running, not waiting for any comments from them. As they watched, he repeated the same move he had made at the window on the other side. He stayed a little longer at that window, and when he came back to them, he explained. "That's his bedroom, all right. I could see a bed up against the wall and it looked like somebody was in it. The only trouble is he's got some pegs holdin' that window shut."

"We need to decide how we're gonna do this," Leach said. "The easiest way is to stand at that window on this side and break the glass, then shoot him when he jumps outta bed. The only trouble with that is we'll wake up the whole town. We've got to get in there without makin' any noise and wakin' him up. As scared as he was before, he's probably sleepin' with a shotgun in bed with him. And if he hears us comin', a blast from a coward's shotgun makes as big a hole as any of 'em."

"The way to do it is for one of us to slip in that window on the other side, meanin' me," Eli suggested. "You and Slim wait by the window in the bedroom. Then, if I can't slip up on him and cut his throat, you can catch him if he tries to jump out the window."

"If that's the way you wanna try it, it's all right with me," Leach said. He looked at Slim and he shrugged indifferently.

"All right," Eli said. "You stay here and watch that window. I'm goin' around to the other side. If I get in there real quiet, I'll take care of Mr. Undertaker. Then I'll tap on the window to let you know you can come on back around to the other side and I'll unlock the door for you." He gave them a confirming nod of his head and hurried back around the house.

"We might as well move on up to that window," Leach said. "We can stand on each side of it and grab him if he tries to come out that way."

It had taken a while before Perley was able to get in his bedroll on the sofa. Floyd was still keyed up from the council meeting and wanted to discuss the possibility of success with a vigilance committee long after Perley would normally have been asleep. He was convinced that the pot of coffee Floyd had made was the only thing that enabled him to keep from passing out. Unfortunately, that quantity of coffee was evidently causing the interruption of his sleep now, as he woke up to a call from Mother Nature. His first thought was to go outside to answer the call, but he considered the possibility that Floyd might hear him going out the kitchen door. The last thing he wanted was to wake him up again. He then thought of the brass chamber pot Floyd had provided for his private use and considered the possibility of his success standing over the squat vessel in the darkness of the room. He was not confident that he could be accurate enough to prevent some loss on the floor. He shook his head in frustration, knowing he was not likely to go back to sleep unless he answered the call. He decided he had a better chance of success if he decreased the distance between him and the vessel. So he slid off the sofa and remained on his knees, then he pulled the chamber pot before him. Now that the target was much closer, he felt much more confident, so he initiated the release of the excess coffee. It was then that he heard the first faint noises around the window, like those a small animal, like a squirrel, might make. He thought to get up to take a look, but he was now fully invested in his acquaintance with the chamber pot and could not find a stopping place. *Maybe it'll go away,* he thought, *whatever it is.* But it continued until, suddenly to his surprise, the window began to inch up, and he realized what was happening. In spite of the pressing need to react to a break-in, his insides seemed committed to finish the job already underway. He tried to reach for his six-gun, but it was hanging on the other end of the sofa out of his reach. Now, the window was up halfway and a head protruded through the opening, followed by a pair of shoulders. It was enough to effectively stop the flow of coffee, but he could not get up to reach his pistol without giving himself away. Down on the floor in front of the sofa, the intruder could not see him. As he saw it, he had only one option. While the intruder struggled to get his shoulders through, Perley grabbed the brass chamber pot by the rims and came up from the floor with it. Eli, startled, tried frantically to reverse himself, but not in time to avoid the heavy brass vessel that came down on his head, knocking him unconscious.

Worried about Floyd now, Perley grabbed his gun belt and strapped it on. One quick look at Eli told him he was not moving. So he slammed the window down to make sure he didn't fall out of the window. Then he pulled the curtain aside that separated the rooms and ran to the window, taking a quick look at Floyd as he did. Seeing no one at the window, he tapped on the locking pegs to make sure they were in firmly. When he did, he saw two men, who had evidently been hiding on either side of the window, bolt toward the back of the barn. "What is it?" Floyd sat up and blurted when Perley ran back to the other side to make sure his prisoner was still hanging in the window.

"Somebody breakin' in!" Perley exclaimed. "Get your gun and follow me!" He paused only a second when he saw Floyd throw his blanket aside to expose a double-barrel shotgun and clamor out of the bed to follow him. "Keep your shotgun on him," Perley said, pointing to Eli, still hanging limp in the window, while he unlocked the door.

Leach and Slim, thinking the tapping on the window

pegs was Eli's signal that he had taken care of Floyd, hustled around the building to arrive at the corner of the barn in time to see Perley removing Eli's handgun from his holster. It was easy to assume Eli was dead, his body hanging lifelessly from the windowsill. Both men automatically assumed they were next and reached for their guns. Left with no choice, Perley stopped Leach with one round in his chest, but held back when Slim dropped his gun and put his hands up, having seen how fast Perley had dispatched Leach, and was waiting for him to make a move.

Perley walked over and picked up both guns, then noticing the three horses tied at the fence, he called for Floyd, who was still inside with his shotgun pointed at the still motionless body of Eli Priest. When Floyd answered his call, Perley told him to come outside and guard Slim. "What about this one?" Floyd called back.

"He'll be all right for a minute," Perley said. "You can watch him just as well outside. I want you to keep this fellow company for a couple of minutes." He waited until Floyd came outside, then said, "Keep your eye on this one."

"Where you goin'?" Floyd asked at once, afraid he was going to be left alone with them.

"To those horses right there," Perley answered. "I ain't even gonna be outta sight." He went to fetch the horses then, led them to the back, and tied them to the back steps. He took a coil of rope off one of them. "Get on your knees," he said to Slim, and when Slim did as he said, Perley grabbed his wrists and tied them behind his back. He drew his skinning knife from his gun belt and cut the excess rope. Next, he went over to the sagging body hanging in the window, who was just beginning to show signs of movement. Perley tied his hands behind his back, lifted the window, and Eli dropped to the ground. He turned to Slim then and said, "Sorry about your friend, but he didn't give me any choice."

"You're Perley Gates, ain't you?" Slim asked, his voice low and his tone tired, as if he knew he was destined to end up this way.

"That's right," Perley answered. "What's yours?"

"Slim Garrett," he answered.

"Well, Slim, I reckon we'll take you and your friend to the jailhouse. Don't look like any of us are gonna get anymore sleep tonight. Might as well wake the sheriff up, too." He looked over at Floyd, who was still holding his shotgun on Eli, since he was showing signs of being alive. "At least we don't have to send anybody after the undertaker," Perley said, nodding toward the body lying near the barn door.


"Who the hell's bangin' on my door?" Sheriff Mason yelled through the closed door.

"Open up," Perley yelled back. "We'd like to make a deposit."

"This ain't no bank!" Mason yelled again. The sound of a key turning angrily in the lock, followed by the door opening a crack, was then followed by Mason's voice again. "Who the hell is it?" Then he saw Perley and mumbled, "I shoulda known when I heard the shot."

"Mornin', Sheriff," Perley said. "I hate to bother you at this early hour, but Floyd and I have got a couple of prisoners for your jail. They broke into his place with the intent to do him harm, I suspect."

Mason opened the door wide, so he could get a better look at the two men, one sitting in the saddle, the other lying across the saddle.

"One of 'em looks more dead than alive," Mason commented. "I notice you've got another horse with an empty saddle. What about that?"

"He is dead," Perley answered. "We left him at the undertaker." He nodded toward Eli. "He ain't dead. He just hit his head on a thunder mug. I expect he'll be all right when his head stops ringin'."

"All right," the sheriff said with a weary sigh, knowing they were Ned Stark's men. "Bring 'em on in here. Who's the one you shot?"

Perley was about to say he had no idea, but Slim answered the sheriff. "Carl Leach," he said.

Perley helped Slim off his horse, then he and Floyd slid Eli off to stand on his feet. After a few wobbly steps, Eli managed to walk under his own power as long as Perley held onto his arm. He even spoke as they walked into the cell room and waited for Sheriff Mason to open the cell. "What the hell did you hit me with? I feel like I got kicked by a horse."

"The first thing I could get my hands on," Perley answered. "You'll be all right in a little while."

"What's this wet stuff on my shirt?" Eli asked then. "Smells like piss."

"There, see, you're gettin' your senses back already," Perley said and gave him a little push through the door. When Mason locked the cell, Perley said, "Back up to the bars and I'll untie your hands."

Eli, his senses rapidly returning now, had something to say to Mason when he walked out behind Perley. "Ned Stark ain't gonna like this," he said.

"Ned ain't gonna like a whole lotta things from

now on, I reckon," Mason responded and closed the cell room door behind him. He felt like a man standing on the edge of a cliff, trying to decide whether to jump or not. When he walked back into his office, Perley was standing by his desk, waiting for him.

"Here are the weapons I took off of the three of them," Perley said. "I figure that's what I'm supposed to do. I'm gonna take their horses to the stable."

"Right," was all Mason said.

"Sorry to ruin your mornin', Sheriff. Let me tell you, mine and Floyd's wasn't much better. When I go to breakfast, I'll tell Rachael you've got two prisoners to feed."

"Much obliged," Mason said.

Outside Floyd was waiting for him. Perley took the reins of the three horses from him and they walked back toward the bridge. When they crossed over to the street, Perley said he was going to take the horses to the stable, then he'd drop back by the barbershop to get his bedroll. "I believe you can pretty much figure you won't be gettin' any more visits from Stark," he told Floyd. "But you might wanna put some pegs in the window in the parlor, too. And you know, Floyd, I ain't sure it's a good idea to sleep with that double-barrel shotgun in the bed with you. Maybe it'd be better under the bed." He left him then to lead the horses down to the stable.

It was still too early for Horace to be open, so Perley put the three horses in Horace's empty corral and pulled the saddles off them. He turned and looked toward the east. There was not a trace of light in the eastern sky. It would be at least an hour before Bess cranked up the first pot of coffee. *Might as well go on back to Floyd's and catch an hour's worth of shut-eye,* he thought. When he got back to the barbershop, he found Floyd struggling to move Carl Leach's body inside his barn. "Here, I'll give you a hand," he said to Floyd as he walked up. "Are you gonna start workin' on him right away?"

"No, I'm just gonna get him outta the yard," Floyd said. "I've got a pot of coffee on the stove. Thought you might want a cup."

"I could sure use a cup," Perley said, "and that's a fact." He took his bandanna out of his pocket and tied it over his nose. "Let's get Mr. Leach inside before he catches a cold layin' out here on the ground."


He left Floyd to fix his own breakfast, as was Floyd's custom, and went to the dining room after he stopped by the washroom to splash some water over his head and upper body. As he expected, he was the first customer to show up. Actually, it was a little before the usual opening time, but he was welcomed cheerfully by Bess and Kitty. He was finishing up his first cup of coffee when Rachael came in, after having squared the girls away for the day, a day she told Perley was going to include church. "I plumb forgot. That's right, today is Sunday," he said.

"You look tired," she said. "Are you getting enough sleep?"

"I reckon it's just because I had to sleep in the barbershop last night." He looked at his coffee cup and was reminded. "I reckon I drank a little too much coffee last night after that meetin'. Floyd made a pot of coffee and we drank the whole thing. That man's a talker. It's a wonder I got any sleep at all."

"Well, I see you made it back from Floyd's, after

your early-morning visit from Ned Stark's boys," Possum sang out as he walked in the door.

"Oh, you know about that?" Perley responded. "How'd you find out this early?"

"Sheriff Mason," Possum replied. "I saw him just now outside the hotel. Said he might have breakfast here this mornin'. He also said you were gonna tell Rachael, here, that he had two prisoners to feed."

"I was just fixin' to," Perley said, having forgotten to do so. Then he turned to her and said, "Sheriff Mason's got two new prisoners in jail, and he'll be wantin' breakfast for 'em." He could see by the look on her face that she was more interested in Possum's statement about the visit from Stark's men. So, he related the events of the night that occurred well past the end of the meeting in the saloon. This he told without a great deal of detail, especially the part about Eli Priest's capture, then changed the subject completely. "I reckon you're goin' to church this mornin' with Rachael and the girls," he said to Possum.

Possum laughed, well aware he was being japed. "Well, I was considerin' it, but I got to thinkin' about what Rooster said and I ain't sure the church roof is strong enough to stand up if a sinner like me walks in. After the preacher showed up at the meetin' last night, ready to ride with the vigilantes, I wouldn't be surprised if some new faces don't show up this mornin' to hear him preach, though."

A little over three miles from Bison Gap, another breakfast-time discussion was taking place at approximately the same time Perley was talking to Possum and Rachael. The atmosphere was drastically different at this one. It was the second time in recent days that someone from Ned Stark's gang had gone into town on a special mission and failed. The first was a simple mission by Slim Garrett to find out what happened to Curly Williams. But this second mission was a special one to seek revenge for the display of Curly's body. "There's only one reason they ain't come back by now." Frank Deal said what everyone else was thinking. "There musta been some kinda ambush set up for 'em." He looked around at the four other men sitting at the table. "All that crap Leach was talkin' last night about how peaceful the town was had to be a trick to make him think that."

"That part about the vigilante meetin' musta been true," Jack Sledge said, "'cause it would take a bunch of 'em to take down all three of those boys."

Stark remained silent, still seething inside with an ever-growing anger, fueled by a sense of betrayal by the hand of John Mason. Mason was on his payroll and lately he had not done the job he was paid to do. "I need to know what happened in that town last night," he suddenly stated as if just then realizing he had been cut down to only four men. He had his eye on a large herd of cattle in Blanco County, and he needed more than these four men sitting at the table with him now. He could only hope his three missing men were in jail and he would go in and tell the sheriff to release them. When he shared those thoughts with his men, there were some who thought that might be a mistake.

"You think they might be holdin' Eli and them just to get you to come in after 'em? Then they'd throw you in jail." Sledge was the first to voice it. "Might be better if one of us went in to see what's what—get an idea if they're tryin' to get up some vigilantes."

"John Mason would play hell tryin' to hold me," Stark replied.

"They ain't likely to arrest one of us if we ain't causin' no trouble," Jim Duncan said. "If he was just goin' to the store and didn't even go to the saloon. They didn't bother Slim when you sent him in to find out about Curly."

"We need some coffee and some flour to make some pan biscuits," Junior Humphrey blurted.

"You might be right," Stark reconsidered, ignoring Junior's interruption. "It might be better to find out what I might be walkin' into."

"Send Duncan in," Sledge suggested. "He's the most harmless-lookin' one of us left, since Slim ain't here."

"You kiss my ass," Jim Duncan responded. "I'll teach you a lesson about harmless." Sledge laughed in response.

"Sledge is right," Stark said. "But what he really means is that you don't look as much like a saddle tramp as the rest of us. You wanna take the job?"

"Yeah, I'll go in alone. I ain't scared of anything or anybody in that town," Duncan answered.

"And he can get some coffee and some flour," Junior spoke up again.

"Today's Sunday," Sledge said. "Wheeler's store ain't open today, so he'll have to go to the saloon." His remark brought a genuine look of despair to the simple giant's face.

# CHAPTER 12

An hour after the bell in his tall bell tower rang out its clear call to worship, Reverend Harvey Poole was gratified to see the extra bodies in the pews on this warm Sunday morning. He glanced toward the organ to exchange smiles with his wife, Nancy, on his way to the pulpit. "I want to welcome you all to worship with us here on this fine morning," he began as he looked over the new faces. Seeing Rachael, he paused for a moment to give her and her two daughters a warm smile. She marveled at the difference between this warm and friendly man and the fierce messenger of the Lord who had appeared at the council meeting the night before. It was a good feeling and one that gave her hope for the town of Bison Gap.

Back in the town, Slim Garrett stood up on his bunk against the side wall of the cell, so he could look out the small window near the ceiling. "Town sure is dead on a Sunday mornin'," he informed his cell-mate. A few minutes later, he caught sight of a solitary rider slowly walking his horse up the street. He thought the rider looked familiar, but he wasn't sure, since the jail was across the creek from the business street. A few moments more, when the rider turned his horse toward the bridge, he recognized him. "That's Jim Duncan!" He turned toward the man on the other bunk. "Hey, Eli, that's Jim Duncan ridin' into town."

"Is he by himself?" Eli asked at once, hoping it meant the gang had come to break them out of jail. Still nursing a headache from his encounter with a brass chamber pot, he stepped up on the bunk beside Slim, so he could look out, too. "He's by himself," he declared. "Hell, he's goin' to the saloon. Where's the rest of the boys?" He pushed Slim aside in an effort to try to see more of the street. "What's he doin' here by himself?" He frowned at Slim as if he expected him to know the answer.

"Reckon he's wantin' a drink of likker," Slim answered Eli's question. It seemed obvious to him. "How come I'm the only one broke and everybody else has got the price of a drink?"

"He'd better watch hisself," Eli said, "or he's liable to be in here with us." He continued to strain his eyes in an effort to see the rest of the gang coming behind Duncan, but there was no one. "What's Ned gonna do, just leave us in this damn jail?"

"He might not know we're in jail yet. But, if he does, he's most likely got a plan to get us outta here," Slim said, believing he was right. "He said he owns the sheriff."

"I ain't so sure about that," Eli pondered, thinking back to Mason's response when they were locked up and he told him that Ned wasn't gonna like it. "The sheriff mighta hitched his horse up to another wagon."

"One thing about it," Slim commented, "we had

us the best breakfast we've had in a long time." His comment was met with a look of disbelief.

At the Buffalo Hump, Jimmy McGee glanced toward the door when he heard Jim Duncan come in. Ordinarily, he wouldn't have noticed, but on this Sunday morning there were very few souls gathered at the saloon. Dixie Bell was standing at the bar talking to him while she finished her first cup of coffee. Usually one or two cups of coffee was all she had for breakfast. She said food early in the day always gave her belly cramps. Glancing at the door at the same time Jimmy did, she commented. "That's one I've seen before. He's one of that Stark gang. I don't know his name, but he's awful shy about goin' upstairs with me." She laughed then and added, "He always wants to go, though."

"Mornin'," Duncan said when he walked up to the bar, then looked at Dixie, nodded and said, "ma'am."

"Good mornin', darlin'," Dixie returned. "You lookin' for a drink of whiskey, or did you come to see me?"

"I'm afraid my wages have been a little short this month," Duncan replied, "and it's still a little early for a drink. What I'd really love to buy is a cup of that coffee you're drinkin'. We've run outta coffee beans out at the ranch and I ain't had no coffee in two days."

"Well, I reckon we can fix you up with some coffee," Jimmy said and went to the kitchen to get him a cup. When he returned to the bar with it, he said, "You're one of Ned Stark's boys, ain't you?"

"That's a fact," Duncan answered, a little cautiously. "I work cattle for Stark."

"I thought you might be in town to find out what

happened to three of your friends last night," Jimmy couldn't resist saying.

"Oh?" Duncan responded, making an attempt to remain casual. "Was some of the boys in town last night? I was ridin' night herd."

"Sure were," Jimmy went on. "They took a notion to break in the barbershop. Two of 'em's in the jail. The other one's in the undertaker's barn."

"Well, if that ain't somethin'," Duncan reacted. "They musta been drunk—robbed the barbershop," he marveled. "What happened to the one you said was at the undertaker?"

"He got shot," Jimmy answered. "Ran into Perley Gates."

Duncan didn't comment for a long few seconds. There was that name again. He just slowly sipped his coffee, not sure if he should ask any more questions. He had no fear of Jimmy but he couldn't help a feeling that there was someone watching from inside the kitchen door, waiting for him to make a move. He wanted to find out which one of the gang was killed, but he was hesitant to ask any more questions. Whoever it was must have been killed in ambush and now he might be set up for one as well. He decided he'd ask one more question. "I swear that's sorry news about one of Stark's men gettin' killed. Do you know who it was?"

"Yep," Jimmy replied. "Sheriff said his name was Carl Leach. I don't remember the names of the two that got locked up. You want some more coffee?"

"No, no thanks. One cup's enough. How'd the sheriff know to have some fellers waitin' in the barbershop?"

"It wasn't nobody but Perley Gates and Floyd Jenkins that done for 'em. The sheriff just locked 'em up."

"Well, that's somethin', all right. I expect I'll get along now." He placed a nickel on the bar and backed away a few steps before turning abruptly and heading for the door.

Jimmy grinned at Dixie and declared, "He seemed kinda nervous when I told him about his friends, didn't he? He didn't waste any time headin' for the door. Said he was ridin' night herd. Kinda odd, ain't it? Ridin' night herd last night and comin' into town for a cup of coffee this mornin'? Seems to me he woulda just gone on back to the bunkhouse."

"He said they was outta coffee," Dixie reminded him.

Jimmy glanced over at the kitchen door then and said, "What you standin' behind the kitchen door for, Ida?"

"I was just waitin' to see if he was gonna want somethin' to eat," the cook said.

Duncan did not spare his horse on his way back to the ranch, and when he pulled up in front of the house, he found Stark sitting on the porch with Sledge and Junior, waiting for him. "They got 'em!" he announced, excitedly as he slid off his horse and came up the steps. "Leach is dead and Eli and Slim are in the jailhouse."

"What the hell happened?" Stark demanded. "Who got 'em?"

"Same one that's gettin' everybody," Duncan answered, "Perley Gates."

"How can that be?" Stark demanded. "Three men who handle guns for a livin' get done in by one man? He had to have some help. I don't care what they told you."

"He said the only one in the shop with him was the barber-undertaker jasper and that's all," Duncan maintained.

"Yeah, and he mighta been japin' you, just for the hell of it," Stark asserted, unwilling to believe this one man was able to cause him so much trouble. In the span of a few days, his gang of nine men had been reduced to four—and by the actions of one man. "I need those two men in that jail, and we're goin' into town and break 'em outta there."

"When you figurin' on doin' it, Boss?" Sledge asked.

"I think Sunday is a good day for a jailbreak," Stark replied, suddenly feeling his old invincibility again. "Get your weapons ready, we're goin' to Bison Gap as soon as we get saddled up." He went inside then to tell Frank Deal to prepare for a raid. In short order, they were all five mounted and armed and ready to ride. Before making the ride into town, he gave them their orders once again. "That town council wants to get up an army to protect themselves—well, I've got my army ready, and we'll strike first. We'll ride straight to the jail first and get our men outta there. I'll give John Mason the chance to get his head straight and start takin' orders from me again. If he doesn't, I'll shoot him. Then we're gonna go through that town like a tornado. I wanna be sure they know we were there today. Anybody not sure what we're gonna do today?" Nobody admitted it. "All right," he shouted, "let's ride!"

Unaware of the attacking force gearing up to descend upon the peaceful town, the congregation emptied out of the First Baptist Church to hurry home for Sunday dinner. In Rachael Parker's case, it was to be the usual roast beef dinner Bess always prepared in the hotel dining room. Alice and Melva always helped serve the Sunday dinner, so Kitty could have a day with her husband. The dinner at the hotel had been so popular that it was becoming a tradition with many of the families of Bison Gap.

Neither Rooster nor Possum made it to church, but they were both early to arrive at the dining room to make sure they were seated at one of the tables. Rachael and Bess, with the assistance of Alice and Melva, hurriedly began to serve the guests already seated. In the midst of their activity Rachael suddenly grabbed Perley by the arm. "Perley," she said, "I forgot about the sheriff and his two prisoners. Sheriff Mason always comes for our Sunday dinner, but he didn't come today."

"I forgot about that, too," Perley admitted. He didn't explain that he had been quite busy all through the night and hadn't gotten much sleep. "The sheriff has got two prisoners that he doesn't want to leave alone to cause mischief. I'll tell you what, fix up a plate for him and I'll take it down there to him. Fix a couple plates for the prisoners, too. I'll take 'em all."

"You're an angel," she said and hurried to the kitchen to prepare the food. When it was ready, she stacked them one on top of the other but thought, "You can't carry a coffeepot, too."

"Never mind," he said. "Mason's got a coffeepot down at the jail. We'll make 'em a fresh pot. They'll think it's Thanksgivin'." He took the plates and headed out the door.

"Open up, Sheriff," Perley called out when he arrived at the sheriff's office. "It's me, Perley. I've got your grub." In a few seconds, he heard the bolt slide, and the door opened. Sheriff Mason took a cautious look out the door before opening it wide. "Here's some dinner for you and your guests. I couldn't carry a coffeepot, too, so you'll have to furnish that yourself."

"I swear, that looks like Thanksgivin'," Mason said when he saw the food piled up on the plates, causing Perley to chuckle at the remark. Perley put the plates on Mason's desk, while the sheriff immediately locked the door again. "I ain't takin' no chances with this pair in the cell room," he explained his caution to Perley. "I'm thinkin' there's a good chance I might get a visit from Ned Stark, tryin' to get these boys outta here. And he ain't gonna be too happy when I tell him I can't let 'em out."

The sheriff's remarks were enough to give Perley some encouragement. If Mason meant what he said, then it would mean that the sheriff had finally made his decision to back the people who paid his salary. He decided to hang around long enough to help Mason while he fed his prisoners, thinking it a good idea to have someone watching them when he passed their plates into them. The next thing was to get a pot of coffee working, which Mason started right away. With Eli and Slim eating their dinner, and the coffeepot bubbling away, Perley was ready to go back to the hotel to get his dinner. "I'm startin' to smell that coffee," he said. "I'd best get myself up to the dinin' room before all the food's gone."

He started to unlock the door, but a glimpse of something through the window caused him to hesitate. He took another look through the window to be sure. "Uh-oh," he announced, "I think you've got company."

His statement captured the sheriff's attention right away. "Stark?" He asked automatically.

"Yup," Perley answered, "Stark and four men with him."

Mason hurried over to the window to see Stark walking his horse toward the jail with four men riding abreast, two on each side of him. Catching a glimpse of the sheriff at the side of the window, Stark called out, "Sheriff, I've come to take my two men off your hands. Open up."

Perley decided it best to stay out of sight to see how this turned out and was disappointed to see Mason go to the door and unlock it. It appeared that the sheriff was still under Ned Stark's yoke. He was surprised, however, when he heard Mason's response to Stark's request. "I'm afraid I can't do that, Ned," the sheriff said. "These two men are under arrest for breakin' in Floyd Jenkins's place of business and attempted murder."

"What attempted murder?" Stark wanted to know. "They was just some fellows that had a little too much to drink and wanted to get in the barbershop to look for more."

"Carl Leach drew on Perley Gates with intent to kill him," Mason said.

"And Leach is dead," Stark replied. "What's that got to do with Eli and Slim? Let 'em outta there."

"Can't do it, Ned. They were in on it with Leach, so they're gonna have to stand trial for their part in the crime. Best just leave this up to the judge and jury and go on about your business."

His temper heating up now, Stark stepped down off his horse and walked toward the door. "Damned if you ain't forgot who's been butterin' your bread for the last year or so," he sought to remind him.

Mason hurriedly closed the door and bolted it, hoping Perley had not heard Stark's comment about buttering his bread. "Any arrangement between you and me is over and done with," he said through the door. "You'd best get along now, before I have to arrest you for disturbin' the peace."

Still standing back out of sight of the window, Perley grimaced as he thought, *Maybe you shouldn't have threatened him with that,* even though he was impressed that Mason was intent upon standing up to Stark. In the cell room, Eli and Slim were standing up at the bars, straining to hear everything said between the sheriff and Stark.

Stark responded to Mason's threat just like Perley feared he would. "Arrest me!" Stark exploded. "You think I'm disturbin' the peace? I'll damn-sure show you some disturbin' the peace, if you don't open that door and let my men outta there right now!"

In the cell room, Eli grinned at Slim and said, "Hot damn! I knew we weren't gonna be in here long." He yelled out at the top of his voice then. "Get us outta here, Ned!"

"Open that damn door!" Stark ordered. "I'll shoot it down, if you don't!"

*Shoot,* Perley thought, *I didn't get my dinner.* After hearing Stark's threat, he went to the gun rack on the wall behind Mason's desk and took a Henry rifle and a box of cartridges. He ducked down behind the desk when Stark suddenly cut loose with his six-gun, firing all six shots into the door. But none of the shots penetrated the heavy, double-oak door. Luckily, the sheriff's office and jail was a solidly built structure. The only vulnerable places were the two windows, one in front and one in back of the office section, so these were the places to defend. "I'll take this one," Perley said, since he was already near the back window. Mason understood and positioned himself by the front window, which was shattered moments later by a blast of gunfire from the five outlaws. Stark quickly sent two of his men around to the back of the office to fire through that window.

While the windows were the only vulnerable spots, they were also the only spots for defensive fire. This proved to be unfortunate for the defenders of the jailhouse, for in order to fire at their attackers, it was necessary to expose their rifle barrels as well as a portion of their bodies. Consequently, it became a dangerous game of trying to pop up, take a quick shot, and duck down before catching return fire. This while their attackers watched for them to try to take the shot. It soon became sport for the outlaws, who were blasting away at the slightest movement at either window. "We got him jumpin' back and forth like a jackrabbit," Junior said. Like his partners, he assumed Mason was alone in the office.

This went on until Perley got a glimpse of one of the outlaws when he looked toward the front of the office to see if Mason was all right. He realized that he had a better line of sight on the shooters through the front window than he did from the window he was guarding. And to find a target, he could move from side to side in the back of the room to get the angle he needed to take the shot. So he told Mason what he was going to do. "Stay back from the window." Then, using the sheriff's desk for cover, he laid the Henry on top of the desk and waited for a shot.

Frank Deal was the unfortunate target when he moved up to get a better angle at the sheriff when he popped up to take another shot. Perley saw him moving closer to the front door. He shifted over a couple of feet until he could see more of him and squeezed the trigger. The bullet went through the front window and caught Deal in the right shoulder, spinning him around to drop to the ground. "I'm shot!" He cried out, then began to crawl back toward his horse. In response, Stark and Junior flattened themselves against the wall of the office.

Inside, when Mason saw what Perley had done, he turned to see if he had a shot through the back window. Perley ducked out of the way while Mason waited for one of the men in back of the office to give him an angle of fire. Not as patient as Perley, he fired as soon as he got a glimpse of Jim Duncan, resulting in a slug swiping a shallow trench along Duncan's side. "Damn, I shoulda waited," Mason swore, but the results of the two shots caused the outlaws to seek cover while they tried to come up with a better plan.

Determined to get his two men out of the jail, Stark sent Junior around the cell room section of the building to see if there was a window in the cells. When he got around to the side, he looked up to see the one small window. Junior was a tall man, as well as big, so he jumped up and caught the window ledge with his fingertips. Pulling as hard as he could, he almost managed to get his head up to the barred window. Then, in a loud whisper, he called, "Eli, Slim, you in there?"

"Yeah, yeah," he was answered at once. "We're in here. Get us out."

"All right," Junior called back and dropped to the ground again. "I'm gonna go tell Ned."

"Can we get a rope on the bars?" Stark asked when Junior reported that there was a window in the cell that Eli and Slim were locked in. "All right," Stark said, "let's go see." They ran around to the back again and Junior pointed to the small window high up on the wall, obviously a window meant only for light and ventilation. "Eli!" Stark whispered loudly, "Can you hear me?"

"Yeah, I can hear you," Eli answered, his voice louder than a whisper, since there had been so much gunfire it seemed unnecessary to whisper.

"If we yank them bars outta that window, can you get through it?" Stark asked. Eli said he sure as hell could, so Stark said, "We'll get the horses and some rope. When we throw the rope up, can you catch it?" Again, it was a yes from Eli, so Stark and Junior ran back to the front to get their horses. "We'll tie two ropes around the bars and use both horses to yank that window out," he told Junior.

Inside the cell, Eli and Slim pulled Slim's bunk out of the way and moved a four-foot bench that served as their dinner table under the window, which was near the ceiling of the cell. By standing on it, Eli could reach the window. Leaving Duncan and Sledge to keep firing through the windows to keep the sheriff occupied, Stark and Junior took their horses around to the back. With Junior in the saddle, he easily handed two ropes to Eli, who quickly tied them to the window bars, then stepped down to watch the show. "I don't know," Slim said. "That window looks awful small. You think you can get through that?"

"Hell, yes," Eli responded. "You can, too."

Outside, Stark and Junior pulled the ropes taut with their horses, then kicked them hard. The ropes stretched and strained, threatening to break until the window, frame and all, suddenly snapped out of the wall. There was no hesitation on Eli's part. He jumped on the bench again, grabbed the bottom of the opening, and pulled himself up. But he couldn't get his shoulders through. The window was too small. Not to be stopped by a minor handicap, he said to Slim, "Let me get on your shoulders, so I can stick my arms through first, then I can pull myself through from the outside. Then I'll pull you through."

Having heard a noise from the cell room, Perley thought he'd better check on the prisoners. He started to go but paused when his eye caught sight of a couple of pairs of handcuffs on Mason's desk. *Might be a good idea to handcuff them to the bars to keep them from doing anything to cause trouble,* he thought, so he picked them up. "Be right back," he told Mason and went into the cell room just in time to see Slim push Eli up to his hips through the tiny window. He drew his .44 and held it on Slim. "Back away," he ordered. Slim backed away, leaving Eli hanging on his stomach, halfway in and halfway out of the window. Perley took the cell key from a peg on the wall and opened the cell next to the one they were in. Then he unlocked the cell they were in and motioned Slim out. With Perley's gun on him, Slim offered no resistance and went dutifully into the other cell. Perley locked him in, then holstered his pistol.

While Slim was being transferred to the other cell, Eli took advantage of what time he had and struggled and strained to pull himself to freedom, successful finally in pulling his stomach through. But that was as far as he could manage, even though he had the use of both his hands on the outside wall. His hips were wider than he had thought. In spite of that, his determination was so strong that he was sure he could still make it, if he twisted and turned enough. "Gimme a hand!" He cried out to his two dumbfounded partners outside, standing fascinated while watching his efforts.

Inside, equally fascinated by Eli's struggles, Perley took a look at the two sets of cuffs he had taken from Mason's desk, then went inside the cell. He closed one end of each cuff around each of Eli's ankles even with Eli kicking to avoid it. Then he picked up one end of the four-foot bench and clamped the open end of one handcuff around one leg of the bench. Satisfied that it would not slip or slide, he repeated the procedure on the other end of the bench. "I declare, Eli," he had to say, "you just don't get along with windows, do you?" He stepped back to take another look at the hapless outlaw wedged in the window with a four-foot bench clamped to his ankles and dangling above the floor. "I'd best see how the sheriff is doin'," he said aloud.

He was turning the key in the cell door where the half-man was hanging when he heard a scream of pain from outside the wall. "No, no! Don't pull no more. You'll pull me in two."

Perley paused in front of the cell Slim was now occupying to say, "You shoulda gone first. I believe you'da made it."

"What was all the noise?" Sheriff Mason asked when Perley came back.

"They were tryin' to escape. Stark musta hitched a horse up to the window 'cause he managed to pull the whole thing out." Mason was at once concerned, but Perley told him his prisoners were still secure. "If Stark pulls Eli out, he's gonna take half the wall with him."

That was enough to cause Mason to have to see for

himself, so he got up from his kneeling position by the door. "Watch yourself, Perley. Whoever that is in the back keeps tryin' to sneak up to the window so he can see the whole room inside." He got up in a crouch and went into the cell room. When he came back, he said, "I ain't even gonna ask how he got himself in that fix. I think that's a good place to leave him." He looked at Perley, who had taken his original position beside the back window. "What I wanna know is, after all that big talk last night about the vigilance committee, where the hell are they? With all the shootin' goin' on, why don't somebody come to help?"

"Sheriff, that's a mighty good question, and I ain't got any answer for it." As soon as he said it, they heard shots coming from the street, just across the creek.

Mason looked at Perley. "You reckon?"

"I reckon," Perley answered and shrugged.

The shooting through the windows stopped and brief seconds later, they heard the sound of horses galloping away. "They're gone!" Mason blurted and ran to unlock the door. He stepped out on the porch in time to see the five horses start across the bridge to Main Street but stop and turn up the bank of the creek instead. Mason put his rifle against his shoulder and fired at the fleeing outlaws. Jim Duncan fell forward on the neck of his galloping horse.

Perley looked toward the small posse of vigilantes, the cause of the outlaws suddenly changing their route of escape. In the lead, he saw Rooster and Possum, charging like wild Indians. The posse was on foot, so they broke off their pursuit when they reached the bridge, then, out of breath, they walked over to the jail.

"Took you a little while," Perley said to Possum when he and Rooster walked up to him.

"Well," Possum replied. "Me and Rooster had to do some talkin' before we could get enough men to go save the jail." He shrugged. "And it bein' Sunday, you know, everything kinda runs slow on Sundays." He paused then to look at the bullet-riddled sheriff's office. "Boy, they were tryin' to chop this place up, weren't they?"

"Shot to hell," Rooster crowed as he walked up to join them. "You know you got a prisoner tryin' to escape out the back?"

"That's Eli," Perley said. "I guess we'll have to pull him outta the window. Don't you reckon, Sheriff? You could leave him there, but you can't get any air in with him pluggin' the window."

"We're glad to see you and Perley made it through that jailbreak, Sheriff," John Payne said as he walked up to join the conversation. "Sorry we didn't get down here sooner. We'll get a little better at it when we get organized. I don't think we were all expectin' to answer the call this soon."

"I think me and Perley are glad to have your support, even if it was after I got all my windows shot out," Sheriff Mason said and managed a little laugh. A couple you fellows wanta help me pull my prisoner back in jail?" They all volunteered, so they went inside.

"What the hell?" Horace Brooks exclaimed when he saw Eli Priest's lower body, from his behind on down, with a heavy four-foot bench hanging from his feet.

Mason chuckled. "That's Perley's method for makin' sure a prisoner don't get sucked out the window if a tornado hits town." They all chuckled with him, including Slim in the next cell, but excluding Eli, who was enduring another defeat at the hands of a window.

It struck Perley that he might be witnessing the evolution of a qualified sheriff. Watching Mason now, talking with the few members of the council who had responded to his call for help, he saw a different man. Decidedly different from the cautious, somber man who was reluctant to challenge Ned Stark. He even had a sense of humor, with that crack about Eli getting sucked out the window. The sheriff had undoubtedly made a commitment to the town when he decided to deny Ned Stark, so Perley hoped the town would back him up.

# CHAPTER 13

"That was one of the liveliest Sunday mornings we've ever had around here," Ralph Wheeler declared when he returned to the hotel dining room where his wife waited for him. He was one of the five men who responded to Possum's call for volunteers to rush to the relief of the two under siege in the jailhouse. It was obvious to those still in the dining room that the mayor was feeling his manhood after his part in the rout of the five outlaws. "I reckon I won't have any more use for this right now," he said to Emma as he returned her shotgun. "I thank you for the use of your weapon." He had borrowed it when Possum and Rooster were asking for help. He and Cora had just come from church to eat dinner in the hotel, and he wasn't wearing a weapon. "I never fired it, didn't have to," he said. He was distracted momentarily when Perley walked in the dining room. "Perley," he called out. "Everything all right down at the jail?"

"Yep, everything's all right," Perley answered, thinking it an odd question, since Wheeler just came from the jail a few minutes before him. He soon realized that the mayor was still on a high after the newly

conceived vigilance committee had responded to save
the jail. He wanted to warn him that a man like Ned
Stark was not easily defeated and might be determined to seek his own vengeance after today. But he
decided to wait and let him enjoy his victory for a little
while. His thoughts were immediately steered to another subject by a question from Rachael Parker.

"You never got to eat your dinner, did you?"

"No, ma'am, I didn't," he answered. "And I reckon
I'm too late to get it now."

"Maybe not," she said. "Bess put a plate in the oven
to save for you, while the oven was cooling. You can
thank Alice for that. It was her idea. I hope it hasn't
dried out by now."

"Doesn't matter if it has," Perley assured her. "I
surely appreciate it, and I'll thank her for thinkin' of
me. Nothin' cranks up your appetite like sittin' in a
little room while a gang of maniacs try to shoot it to
pieces. If you don't mind, I'll just go in the kitchen to
eat it." The dining room was beginning to become
crowded with folks anxious over the first response by
the vigilantes. He was happy to join Bess, who was sitting at the kitchen table, having a cup of coffee after
cleaning up the dinner dishes.

At the hideout that Stark called his ranch, there
was a definitely different aftermath of the failed jailbreak attempt. Junior Humphrey and Jack Sledge
were trying to ease the discomfort of their two
wounded partners while Stark fumed over the disas-
trous raid. Duncan was losing a lot of blood as the
unlucky recipient of Sheriff Mason's lucky shot when
they were riding away. The shot had caught him in the

back, a little right of center, and he had already been bleeding from the graze in his side. "I reckon you were lucky we were that far away when he hit you," Sledge said as he looked at Duncan's back. "It's bleedin' a lot, but I don't think the bullet is real deep in your back."

"Can you get it outta there?" Duncan asked.

"Not without cuttin' a piece of your back out," Sledge told him. "It ain't that deep. You oughta just leave it in there. You can still move your arm, can't you?"

"Yeah, a little bit," Duncan said, "but it hurts like hell."

"There's a lotta men walkin' around with a piece of lead in 'em," Sledge said. "If we get somewhere where there's a doctor, get him to take it out, if you want to. Can you reach over your shoulder with your other hand and hold this rag over it? When the bleedin' stops, I'll try to tie a bandage on you." He went then to help Frank Deal stop the wound in his shoulder from bleeding. Junior was supposed to help him, but he seemed to be unable to do anything but stare at the hole just below Deal's collarbone.

"That sure as hell didn't go the way we wanted it to, did it?" Deal asked Sledge when he moved Junior aside and took a look at the wound.

"Reckon not," Sledge replied. "They were ready for us, all right. Looks like the town was givin' us notice that we ain't welcome there no more."

Overhearing his comment, Stark broke from the angry trance that had taken over his mind. "We'll decide who's welcome in that town and who ain't," he grumbled.

Sledge and Deal exchanged doubtful glances. "You thinkin' about going back any time soon, Boss?" Sledge asked. "We got our asses whipped pretty good today. Looks like they really have organized a vigilance committee."

Stark turned to stare straight into Sledge's eyes. "Maybe they have," he responded, glowering out from under a heavy frown. "But it's a committee made up of the same store owners and shopkeepers with no backbone that have always been there. Them vigilantes didn't do a damn thing but run down the street makin' noise and shootin' in the air. When a couple of 'em gets shot, that'll be the end of the vigilantes. We were just unlucky today. We ran into an ambush and got stopped by two men, that damn Judas sheriff and another man. If Mason hadn't had that extra man, he'da never been able to cover both windows in that office."

"Perley Gates," Sledge pronounced.

"Maybe," Stark responded sharply, reluctant to give Perley any more credit for the destruction of his once formidable gang of outlaws. The man had become a definite thorn in his side ever since he showed up in Bison Gap. "It coulda been anybody in the jail with him."

"I'll bet it was Perley Gates that shot me," Deal said. "I got hit by a shot from the other side of the room—shot me through the window."

"Anybody coulda made that shot," Stark insisted. "He was just lucky."

"I don't know, Ned," Sledge responded doubtfully.

"What the hell's the matter with you two?" Stark demanded then. "You're talkin' like whipped dogs, wantin' to run off and hide in the bushes. They've got two of our men locked up in that jail and I, by God, don't intend to leave 'em there! What if it was you locked up in that jail, waitin' for those mealymouthed shopkeepers to hang you? I reckon you'd want the rest of us to get you outta there." Although his argument was slanted toward his sense of responsibility for the men who rode with him, his real concern was not so noble. He had planned to rustle a sizable herd of cattle down in Blanco County. He needed the money the sale of those cattle would provide. With the four men he had now, it would be hard to herd that many cattle, even if they were all fit. With two of them wounded, it was impossible. If he had Eli and Slim back, it would still be difficult, but it would be possible.

"I ain't sayin' we shouldn'ta gone to get Slim and Eli outta there," Sledge insisted. "I'm just sayin' we ain't in no shape to go after 'em again right now."

"I swear," Stark scoffed, "I never expected to hear that kinda yellow talk outta you—Slim, maybe, but not you." He looked at Junior. "What about you, Junior? You scared to go back after Eli and Slim?"

"Hell, no, Ned," Junior replied at once. "I ain't scared of nothin'. You're the boss. If you say go in there and get 'em, I'm ready to ride."

The simple giant answered exactly as Stark knew he would and that was the reason Stark had asked him. Back to Sledge then, Stark said, "Junior knows, just like I know, that we need to get those boys outta there before they decide to hang 'em."

"Damn it, Ned," Sledge charged, "you know I ain't ever backed away from any job we've tried. I'm just talkin' about the shape we're in right now. Frank ain't in no shape to help, neither is Duncan, so it'll just be the three of us against the whole damn town."

"And we're outta coffee and flour," Junior thought it necessary to remind them again.

Ignoring the childlike man's remark, Duncan said, "I wanna get Eli and Slim outta that jail, but what Sledge says is true. We ain't in no shape to go ridin' back in there for another go-round with Perley Gates and the sheriff. It sure looks like Mason has made a deal with that gunslinger to take over the town. If Slim and Eli hadn't got theirselves locked up, the smartest thing we coulda done is to move on and find a better place to do our business." He paused to see if the scowling boss of the gang was going to interrupt. When Stark didn't, Duncan continued. "You know, we might want to start havin' a lookout at night. After that little party this mornin', they might start thinkin' about payin' us a visit."

"I hope to hell they do," Stark said. "It'd be a whole lot different when they ain't holed up in that jail. It'd be a good chance to thin that crowd out."

"That's another thing," Sledge reminded him. "That jailhouse was built like a dang fort. How are we gonna break 'em outta there? The only way I can think of to open that thing up is to dynamite it, and we ain't got no dynamite."

Back in Bison Gap, the talk about the successful defense of the town jail continued past dinnertime, and most of the folks went across the creek to look at the bullet-riddled structure. Of special interest was the gaping hole in the cell room wall where a window used to be. One of the spectators discussing the damage to the sheriff's office suddenly stopped in mid-sentence when he was interrupted by the sound of a train whistle. "Oh, my goodness!" Gomer Sikes exclaimed and pulled out his pocket watch. "I've let

the time slip up on me. That's the afternoon train."
He hurried toward the bridge over the creek as fast
as a man of his considerable bulk could manage. As
stationmaster, Sikes was usually on hand to receive
the mailbags, as well as any important passengers.
And since the railroad tracks ran behind the stores
on Main Street, he had a good little run to reach the
station.

Sikes made it to the platform mere seconds before
the train ground to a stop at the station. Henry Pea-
cock walked back to the mail car to swap mailbags
with the mail clerk while another employee set up the
ramp for the lone arriving passenger to lead a solid
white horse out of the stock car. Gomer Sikes took
special notice of the man leading the horse. Tall and
slender, he looked around him as if deciding whether
or not the little town was worth his appearance. With
thick black hair and a neatly trimmed mustache, he
looked the part of a professional gambler. But the
fancy black engraved gun belt suggested he might be
proficient in something other than a game of cards.
Seeing Sikes standing on the platform, the stranger
led his horse up even with him and stopped. "Afternoon," he said.

"Afternoon," Sikes returned. "Welcome to Bison
Gap. You looking for the Buffalo Hump Saloon?"

The stranger looked up at him with an easy smile.
"Now, what makes you think that?"

Sikes stumbled over his words, realizing that he
might have offended him. "Oh, uh, I just thought you
might be looking for some refreshment, since you've
been riding in the cattle car on such a warm day."

"This is my first time in Bison Gap," the stranger
said, "and I was going to ask you how to find the hotel.

I assume there's a town over that way somewhere." He nodded toward the train blocking his view of the town.

"Oh, yes, sir," Sikes replied. "Bison House Hotel is right over there." He pointed. "You'll see it as soon as the train pulls out of the way. Fine establishment, just built this year. It's operated by two women, the hotel and the dining room. I'm Gomer Sikes, the station-master."

"Thank you, Gomer," the stranger said but didn't offer his name. He stepped up into the saddle and said, "A drink before supper might be good, at that." He turned the white gelding and crossed over the tracks behind the train.

Jimmy McGee stopped in mid-sentence when he was talking to Ida Wicks about the raid on the jailhouse earlier that day. He was distracted by the appearance of the stranger in the door of the saloon. The man paused there for a few moments while he looked over the busy room. A tight-lipped little smile on his face, he seemed to give the impression that he was amused by what he was looking at. "Howdy, stranger," Jimmy greeted him. "What's your pleasure?"

The smile widened slightly and he replied, "Good lookin' young women and rye whiskey."

"Pour him a whiskey, Jimmy," Ida said. "I ain't young no more, and I never was good lookin', so I can't do anything for him." She turned and walked away. "I'll be cookin' something for supper." The stranger threw his head back and laughed.

Jimmy poured him a shot of rye whiskey. The stranger picked it up, tossed it back, and ordered another. "Here's to older women," he said and downed the second shot. "They're more comfortable."

"What brings you to Bison Gap?" Jimmy asked.

"The train and a snow-white horse," the stranger said, "and I'm gonna need to put the horse in a stable for the night. The train can take care of itself."

Jimmy was not impressed by the glib tongue of the stranger and was inclined to be suspicious of his carefree attitude. "Well, sir," he said, "the stable's at the other end of the street. Are you wantin' to sleep with the horse?"

"Hell, no," the stranger exclaimed. "I wanna sleep in the hotel. Fellow over at the train station—Sikes, I think his name was—said there was a good one here."

"He wasn't lyin'," Jimmy replied. "Bison House, back across the creek, on the north end of town. One of the owners manages it, Emma Slocum. She'll fix you up with a nice room. If you're lookin' for supper, Ida's throwin' something together now." He glanced toward the kitchen, then lowered his voice. "But if you want a little fancier supper, the hotel dinin' room is where you wanna go."

The stranger chuckled in appreciation of Jimmy's careful measures to keep from being heard in the kitchen. "I appreciate it, bartender. My name's Drew Dawson. What's yours?"

Surprised, because he had gotten the impression the stranger was guarding against giving his name, Jimmy answered, "Jimmy McGee."

"Nice to meetcha, Jimmy. Pour me another shot of that rye, then I'm gonna go take care of my horse." He paid Jimmy for the whiskey, started to leave, but paused to ask a question. "When I rode over here, from the main street, there were a lot of people standing around that other building on this side of the creek. What goes on there?"

"That's the jail," Jimmy said. "There's a couple of prisoners in there, and earlier today, some of their friends tried to break 'em out."

"Well, I'll swear," Drew declared. "Did they break 'em out?"

"No, but they shot the jail near-'bout to pieces and pulled a hole in the back where a window used to be."

"I'll bet that woke the town up on a Sunday," Drew said. "Well, I'd best go take care of my horse." He lowered his voice to a whisper and winked at Jimmy. "Then I'll go to the hotel for something to eat."

"You have a good evenin', sport," Jimmy called after him. *Nice fellow*, he thought. *I had him figured out wrong when he first came in.*

"That's a fine-lookin' horse," Horace Brooks was inspired to comment when Drew Dawson rode up to the stable. "What's his name?"

"Thank you, sir," Drew responded. "I'm glad to see you have an appreciation for fine horses. This one will outlast any horse I've ever owned, and I've owned some good ones. His name's Snowball and he's never failed me, so take good care of him for me."

"You can count on that," Horace said. "How long you gonna be with us, Mr. . . . . ?"

"Dawson," he said, "Drew Dawson. I'll just be here overnight."

"All right, Mr. Dawson, I'll take care of Snowball for you. I expect you want me to feed him some oats."

"Unless you don't have any other grain," Drew answered. "Oats make him a little bit windy. But if that's all you've got, give him oats."

Drew pulled his saddlebags off the horse, then let

Horace take Snowball's reins. "I'll put your saddle in the tack room. You want your rifle?"

"Do I need my rifle in this town on a Sunday night?" Dawson asked.

"No, sir, not usually," Horace answered. "I just asked because a lotta customers take their rifle with 'em. But it'll be safe here."

Horace led the white gelding into a stall and pulled his saddle and blanket off. He pulled the horse's bridle off and left it on a peg inside the stall. The saddle and blanket he carried into the tack room and set it on the rail he had made for that purpose. He stopped to admire the obviously expensive saddle. As he set it back squarely on the rail, he felt the workmanship of the leather and when he lifted the skirt, he saw the initials *TC*. He had to pause then, thinking they would have been *DD*. *Must have bought it from the original owner,* he thought.

Drew Dawson's next stop was the hotel where Wilbur Ross put him in one of his finest rooms on the second floor, front, where he would have a view of the street. Drew asked where the washroom was, since he desired to clean up after riding in a stock car with his horse for a good bit of the day. And there was plenty of time before the dining room would be open for supper.

When he went into the dining room, he was greeted by Rachael Parker. He removed his gun belt and holster before she requested it, seeing the sign on the table by the door. She had already been advised by Wilbur that an apparently well-heeled gentleman had checked into the hotel and would be eating in the dining room. "Welcome," Rachael said. "I'm Rachael Parker, and it's my job to see that you enjoy your supper. Sunday dinner is always a busy day for us, but Sunday supper is usually slow, so we just fix more of what we had for dinner. Today it was roast beef. Will that suit you? Because if it doesn't, I'll have Bess fix you some ham or bacon."

"The roast beef will be fine," Drew assured her. "I'll have coffee with that." Alice, who was standing near the kitchen door, heard him and ran immediately for the coffeepot. She was helping her mother in the dining room, since Kitty had the day off. In a minute, she came to the table carrying the big coffeepot. Since the pot was full, Rachael deemed it a little too heavy for her six-year-old to handle the pouring and took it from her to fill his cup. Noticing the look of pride on Rachael's face, Drew asked, "Is this your daughter?"

"Yes, it is," Rachael replied. "This is Alice."

"Well, how do you do, Alice?" he said. "My name is Drew. I'm pleased to meet you." Alice performed a little curtsy her mother had taught her, then returned the big coffeepot to the stove. "Fine-lookin' young lady," Drew said to Rachael. "You must be proud of her."

"Indeed, I am," Rachael responded with pride. "Thank you for your compliments. I hope you still feel like complimenting us when you've finished your supper."

As they expected, the dining room was not busy at all on that Sunday evening. Emma came into the dining room while Drew was still eating, and she stopped to say hello. "Good evening, Mr. Dawson. Is my sister treating you all right?" He replied that she certainly was. "We hope that your visit to Bison House is pleasant enough to make you want to come to see

us again when you're back this way." Having checked
the registration, she knew that he was checking out in
the morning.

Emma stayed for a while to have coffee with Rachael
and Bess in the kitchen, and in a little while, Perley
and Possum came in to eat supper. They seated themselves at a table close to the kitchen. And when
Rachael brought their coffee, Possum asked, "Who's
the slick-lookin' jasper settin' over there?"

"That's Mr. Drew Dawson," Rachael answered.
"And he's not slick-looking just because he's neat.
He's staying in the hotel overnight. I wish we'd get
more customers like him, instead of so many that
would look more natural at a trough."

"She's talkin' 'bout you, Possum," Perley said and
received a snort from Possum in return. "I couldn't
help noticin' the fine-lookin' gun and holster Mr.
Dawson left on your weapons table by the door,"
Perley said to Rachael.

"I saw that, myself," Possum said.

Emma came out of the kitchen and sat down at the
table with Perley and Possum. They naturally talked
again about the unusual Sunday just winding down.
Their conversation was interrupted when Drew got
up from his table to pay Rachael for his supper. He
complimented her on the food, then walked over to
their table to compliment Emma as well. "Well, I'm
pleased to hear we're treating you right," she said.
"This is Possum Smith," she said then. "He's my business partner in the hotel."

Drew reached across the table to shake Possum's
hand. "Drew Dawson," he said. "I'm pleased to make
your acquaintance. Like I've been tellin' Miss Slocum,
I think you have a first-class hotel here."

"'Preciate it," Possum responded with nothing more.

Realizing she was ignoring Perley, she said, "And this is Perley Gates. He's a friend of ours."

"Perley Gates," Drew repeated, like most everyone else when hearing Perley's name. "That's a very unusual name. Is it your given name, or a nickname?"

"Given," Perley replied. "Sounds like the Bible name, but it's spelled different. It was my grandpa's name."

"What's your line of work, Perley?"

"Cattle," Perley answered. "I work on a cattle ranch in Lamar County."

"Lamar County, that's a long way from here. What brings you this far away from home?"

"Just visitin' some friends," Perley answered. I spent some time here about eight months ago, so I thought I'd come back to see how everybody's doin'."

"Perley Gates, that's a good name," Drew declared, "a name that's easy to remember, just like mine."

"Drew Dawson?" Perley repeated.

"There," Drew replied, "see, you already remembered." He took a step back. "It's been good to meet you," he said and took his leave.

"Kind of an unusual feller, ain't he?" Possum asked as they watched Drew stop at the weapons table to strap his gun belt on.

"He's got his own way about him," Perley agreed.

# CHAPTER 14

There was no way the outlaws could know if there might be a posse on its way to their ranch or not. They didn't know if the so-called vigilance committee had been organized to the point where they were ready to ride as a posse. Consequently, Stark thought it was necessary to keep watch, in case they were. He believed that, if they were coming after them, they would have come yesterday, but they didn't. Still, he thought there was no sense in taking a chance on being surprised, so he set up a schedule to watch for two hours at a time. No one was exempt, not even the wounded men. Stark said all they had to do was sit in a chair on the porch and watch the trail that led down to the house. It would not likely do their wounds any harm.

Junior saw fit to remind them that they were out of coffee and flour. Tired of hearing about the need for coffee and flour, Stark told him to kill one of their cows and get some fresh meat cooking while he took the first watch. "Bring me a slab of that meat when you get it done," he told Junior and went out to the porch and sat down. He had not been there long when he suddenly sat up straight in the chair, his gaze caught by a flash of white through the bushes that lined the trail into the yard. He hurriedly grabbed the rifle lying on the porch floor beside him, his eyes focused on the first stretch of the path that was in the open. He raised his rifle and sighted on the spot. In a few seconds, a rider appeared. He was alone and riding a white horse. Stark waited to see if anyone followed, but there was no one else as the rider continued following the path straight toward the front porch. A few yards closer and Stark murmured softly, "Drew." Then he blurted it out. "Drew!" His cousin had finally arrived.

"That you, Ned?" Drew called back and nudged his horse into a lope the rest of the way to the porch. He pulled up in front of the steps and dismounted to exchange handshakes and back slaps.

"Damned if you ain't a sight for sore eyes," Stark said, then yelled back toward the house, "Drew's here!" Back to Drew then, he asked, "Where in the hell have you been? You was supposed to get outta prison two weeks ago."

"I couldn't come straight here," Drew explained. "I had some things to tend to before I could—had to have some money and things. They don't give you much when they let you out of prison." He paused to greet the rest of the gang when they filed out to see him.

After more handshaking and slaps on the back, Sledge asked, "Where'd you get that white horse?"

"Ain't he somethin'?" Drew replied. "He ain't got a handful of black hairs on him. Fellow this side of Fort Worth gave me this horse, right after he died. How you like that saddle? That saddle musta cost two hundred dollars, maybe more." He chuckled then. "I ain't ever priced 'em in that range, so I'm just guessin'. Fellow left me enough spendin' money to get me an outfit, too. I spent a lot of it on this Colt and the fancy holster. I figure that's my business, so I wasn't gonna skimp."

Junior, fascinated with the stark white horse, asked, "What's his name?"

"The fellow or the horse?" Drew japed. "I don't know if he's got a name or not. I didn't think to ask that fellow before he expired. Fellow at the stable in town yesterday asked me the same thing. I told him the horse's name was Snowball. It was the first thing I could think of." He paused to chuckle again, then looked at Deal and Duncan. "You boys look like you've had a little bad luck. Where are the rest of the boys?"

"There ain't no rest of us," Stark answered. "You're lookin' at the whole gang, except for Slim Garrett and Eli Priest, and they're in the jailhouse in Bison Gap."

"That was you they were talkin' about," Drew exclaimed, recalling his conversation with Jimmy McGee in the Buffalo Hump Saloon, "and the jailhouse shot to hell." He shook his head slowly. "Well, I'll be . . . What happened?"

"We ran into an ambush and a double cross is what happened," Stark answered. "The sheriff I had in my pocket double-crossed me. Him and that mayor brought in a gunslinger. I know it had to be the mayor, 'cause the sheriff ain't got any money to hire a gunman. And the sheriff and the gunslinger was settin' there waitin' for us when we tried to break Slim and Eli outta that jail."

"What happened to the rest of the gang?" Drew wondered aloud. "Curly Williams, Quirt Taylor, Carl Leach, they were all good men. Did they cut out on you?"

"No," Sledge answered him. "They were all cut down by that gunslinger I was just tellin' you about."

"How the hell did that happen?" Drew asked, knowing those three men as well as he did. "Who is this gunslinger? Has he got a name?"

"Says his name is Perley Gates," Stark said, "nobody I ever heard of."

Totally surprised, Drew didn't respond at once, having to stop and consider what he had just heard. "Perley Gates," he said the name. "Are you sure about that?"

"Yeah, I'm sure about it. Why? Have you heard of him?"

Drew smiled. "I had supper with him last night," he said. "Well, I oughta say I talked to him in the dinin' room of the hotel. I didn't set down at the table with him." He looked sharply at Ned Stark again. "Are you sure?" He asked again, "Because the Perley Gates I talked to in the dinin' room last night didn't look like a gunslinger to me, and I don't reckon there's two fellows runnin' around here with that name. He said he worked on a cattle ranch." When no one answered, he asked, "How'd he kill 'em? Pick 'em off with a rifle? Shoot 'em in the back? He didn't call 'em out to face him, right?"

"No," Jim Duncan answered, "they called him out."

"Is that a fact?" Drew considered the possibility, bringing the picture of the pleasant-looking young man back in focus in his mind and trying to see him in that role. Curly and Quirt were both fast, not as fast as he, but they were fast. He had to ask Stark a question then. "Is he faster than I am?"

"I don't know," Stark answered. "I've seen you work, and I ain't ever seen anybody as fast as you. But I didn't see any of the draws this fellow had with Curly and the others, so I don't know."

There was a void in the conversation for a couple of minutes when no one spoke. Everyone knew what Drew was working over in his mind. They could not realize the fascination he now had for this unlikely-looking fast gun and the rapidly building desire to prove himself faster. After he thought about it a minute or two longer, he decided he was faster. He could tell by just looking at Perley. He would prove it before he was done with this town. With that settled in his mind, he asked, "What are we all standin' around on the porch for? I need somethin' to eat, and I need to take care of ol' Snowball, here."

"We ain't got no coffee or flour," Junior piped up.

"You ain't?" Drew responded. "Well, why not? Who's supposed to go get supplies?"

"With that business yesterday at the jailhouse, they've got the whole town stirred up, and we're liable to be shot on sight if we go into town. There'll be a gun stickin' outta every window and door," Stark answered him. "But we've got plenty of beef to eat, if you're hungry."

"I swear, cousin," Drew said, "this is a bad situation. You ain't got anybody who can ride into town and go to the store?" Stark simply answered with an apologetic shrug. "Beef's good," Drew continued, "but I need some coffee to go with it."

"And flour," Junior said.

Drew turned to look at him. "Right, and flour, too."

Turning back toward Stark, he asked again, "Are you tellin' me that there's not one of you who can go into town without gettin' shot at or arrested?"

"That's what I'm tellin' you," Stark said. "Problem is, there ain't another store or tradin' post within fifty miles of here."

"That ain't no problem," Drew insisted. "There's a store just three miles from here in Bison Gap, and nobody knows me in that town. So I reckon I'm gonna be the one to go to the store before we all starve to death. I reckon you're all broke, too, but thanks to good ol' T.C., I'll pay for it." His announcement brought a small measure of cheerfulness to the gang of outlaws.

"Who's T.C.?" Deal asked.

"Those are the initials on the side skirt of my new saddle," Drew said. "Our business transaction happened so fast we didn't really have the time to exchange names. I'll buy us some supplies, if somebody will fetch me a couple of packhorses." He was interrupted right away when Junior volunteered. "Good, Junior," Drew went on. "If we're thinkin' about movin' anybody's cows to market, we need supplies, so bring me two packhorses." Junior ran straight to the corral. Drew talked to Stark then. "Whaddaya plannin' to do, cousin? In your letter, you said you were fixin' to start a big drive as soon as I got here. You wanna go ahead and go after those cattle, or you wanna get your men outta jail first?"

"We could sure use the two extra hands," Stark said. "Jim and Frank ain't in too gooda shape to do the job."

"If I see that fellow, Perley Gates in town today, I'll ask him if he wants to help us steal some cattle," Drew japed. "He said he was a cattleman." Joking aside then, he said, "You know, we can't stay here if we ain't got anybody who can go into town anytime we need something. I'll do it now, but we're gonna have to pick up some new faces somewhere. Right now, we can't even go into the saloon to get a drink of whiskey. I can, but none of the rest of you can. How did all this start, anyway?"

"Well, the boys got to raisin' hell a little too much, but it wasn't any worse than Dodge or Wichita. What really started things boilin' over, was when Curly Williams gunned a fellow named Tom Parker down in the saloon. Did you see that woman who runs the dinin' room at the hotel?" Drew said he did, so Stark went on. "Well that Parker fellow was her husband, and he never went for his gun. I owned the sheriff at that time, so he took Quirt's word that he did." Stark went on to bring Drew up to date on everything that happened up to the present.

Drew listened to Stark's account of the situation they were now sitting in, and it seemed ridiculous to him that they could have gotten so bad that their men were banned from coming to town, even in the daytime to visit the stores or shops. "I think there's only one problem and that's the gunslinger, Perley Gates," Drew said. "We get him, and in a week, the town will go back like it was before he showed up."

"Don't think I ain't tried that," Stark was quick to protest. "Quirt called him out and Perley Gates cut him down. Curly went after him and got the same thing. I even offered a reward for anybody that killed him. And he's still there."

"He's gotta be cut down the right way," Drew maintained. "Out on the street, where the people can see it's all fair and square, then it'll be business as usual. We'll buy supplies at the general store and stop in the saloon for a drink. As long as the boys don't get too rowdy, everybody will be happy. Let me go into town now and get to know some of these citizens and we'll see how best to work 'em, Hell, at the hotel and the stable, they already think I'm rich. I'll play 'em like a piano."

"Well, howdy, Mr. Dawson," Horace Brooks called out when he saw Drew ride past the stable, leading two pack horses. "I didn't know you were comin' right back to town."

Drew pulled up and waited to speak to him, seeing that Horace was walking out to meet him. "I didn't know, myself," Drew said, rapidly making up a story to explain his reappearance. "I just had a change of mind, always one of my bad habits, I suppose."

"Where'd you get the packhorses?" Horace asked.

"I ran into a group of hunters headin' north after havin' no luck at all tryin' to hunt buffalo down this way," Drew answered, being unable to think of a reasonable explanation.

"Buffalo?" Horace responded. "There ain't no buffalo down this way no more."

"That's what they said," Drew declared. "They asked me if I wanted to buy a couple of packhorses. The price was right, so I decided, why not? I'll just use them to carry all the supplies I'll need while I'm exploring the country around here. And it helped the hunters, too, since they were down on their luck." He left Horace scratching his head and thinking what a strange man he was.

Having used up most of the morning out at the
ranch, Drew decided he would spend some of his
money on a good dinner at the hotel. While he rode up
the street on his white horse, leading the packhorses,
he was well aware of the attention he was attracting.
He always enjoyed seeing people stop on the street to
stare at him, and he made it a point never to show that
he noticed. As he neared the hotel, his reunion with
the gang came to mind. As strong as Ned was, he had
certain weaknesses when it came to controlling the
men. Being ruthless, himself, Ned inspired that in
the men as well. And Drew decided that was the
reason men like Curly and Quirt provoked unlikely
gunfights just for the satisfaction they enjoyed from
killing. The results of that lack of control would always
be the same. What he and Ned had planned was to
establish the appearance of legitimate ranchers instead of what the town now saw as a gang of outlaw
cattle rustlers. *Don't know if I can turn this around or not,*
he thought. He wasn't inclined to chastise Ned in
front of the men, and maybe not in private either.
Ned was his cousin. Otherwise, he would just shoot
him in the head and tell the men things were going to
change. He would just have to see what he could do.
This setup with a small town in the middle of miles of
prairie was ideal for what he wanted. He didn't want
to give up on it and move on just because his men
caused too much trouble in town. *Too bad I got caught
with that bank money bag on my horse,* he thought. Then
he grinned when he thought, *If I hadn't persuaded that
deputy marshal that the bag fell off one of the bank robbers'
horses when he was making his getaway, I would have been
in prison a lot longer than the two years they gave me.*

"Mr. Drew Dawson," Rachael Parker greeted him

warmly when he walked in the dining room and paused to rid himself of his gun belt. "I thought you had left our little town this morning."

"I had left your little town," Drew replied. "But I found myself thinkin' more and more about the cookin' here in this dinin' room and decided I had to sample some more of it."

Rachael smiled, delighted by the compliment. "Well, I'll certainly tell Bess that you enjoyed her cooking. "Kitty will be serving you today." She signaled her young waitress. "Kitty," she said. "This is Mr. Dawson. Take good care of him, we wanna keep him as a customer."

"Yes, ma'am," Kitty replied. "Pleased to meet you, Mr. Dawson."

"Do I look that old?" Drew responded with a grin. "Pretty young ladies like you can call me Drew." He cocked a roguish eye at Rachael. "And that applies to you as well." He was satisfied to see the slight blush in Rachael's face as she smiled back at him. He figured that it had been a while since she had been thrown a compliment of that nature.

"Are you back in the hotel with us for a while?" Rachael asked.

"No, ma'am, but I'll be poppin' in on you from time to time." When she looked puzzled, he explained, creating it as he talked. "I maybe didn't mention it when I was in last night. The reason I'm here is to buy some land not far from Bison Gap to start up a little cattle ranch."

"Good," Rachael said and stepped aside to let Kitty set a cup of coffee down for him. "Will you be bringing a family with you?"

"No, no family," Drew answered, "but I never give up hope that a family might be in my future one day."

"Well, I wish you luck, Mr. Dawson," she said and turned to greet a man and his wife at the door.

"Drew," he reminded her, "and thank you."

"Drew," she responded with a cheerful laugh. "Enjoy your dinner."

*That I will*, he thought, turning his mind back onto his reason for coming to town. He had made a big score when he opened the safe in T.C.'s office. Evidently, the man had that much cash in the safe for purchasing cattle. It was considerably easier to make money by stealing it than it was to have to rustle a herd and drive them to market for men like T.C. to buy them. But he couldn't always find safes to rob, and unless he got the gang back into the rustling business again, his money would soon run out.

While Drew Dawson was dining at the hotel, John Payne was busy repairing the damaged wall in the jail cell room and replacing the window. Interested spectators, Eli Priest and Slim Garrett, watched from the cell next to the one under repair while finishing up the dinner plates sent down from the hotel dining room. "If you ain't gonna eat that biscuit, I'll take it," Slim said.

"Go ahead and eat it," Eli said, rubbing his stomach and grimacing. "I swear, my belly still hurts from hangin' in that window. Junior damn-near pulled me in two. There's red marks all around my middle."

"You was bigger than that window," Slim said.

"You think?" Eli asked sarcastically.

"I knowed you were too big to fit through that

window," Slim insisted. "Perley Gates told me, while you was still hangin' in it, that I shoulda gone first. He said I woulda made it."

"Is that so? I reckon you're bellyachin' because you didn't get away. But I can't help it if you didn't step up and try it first."

"I'm just sayin' you shoulda told me to go first, so at least one of us woulda got out," Slim said.

"It wouldn'ta been right for just one of us to get out, if the other'n couldn't," Eli declared. "If you had any decency about you, you'd know that. Gimme back my biscuit."

He reached for the half-eaten biscuit, but Slim stuffed all of it in his mouth. When he was able to talk again, he said, "I'll give it back to ya in the mornin'."

"You two sound like a couple of little young'uns fightin' in here," Sheriff Mason said when he walked into the cell room. "Gimme your plates. I'll take 'em back to the dinin' room." He had been waiting for them to finish, so he could take all three plates back. They handed the plates through the bars and he walked over to the other cell and called to John Payne, who was outside. "Hey, John, you need to get in here for anything? I'm goin' across the creek for about half an hour." Payne yelled back that he wouldn't need to get inside for a while yet, so Mason said, "I'm gonna lock it up, then."

"You can leave the key with us, Sheriff, in case he has to get in before you get back," Eli remarked.

"What do you need a key for, Eli?" Mason replied. "I thought windows was your specialty."

"You go to hell," Eli spat.

"You'd best watch what you say," Mason responded.

"You're talkin' like a man that don't want supper." As a precaution, he took the key to the cells with him, then closed the cell room door and locked the office when he went out. Outside, he checked with Payne to tell him he would take a little look around town after returning the dishes to the dining room before he came back.

As a manner of habit, Sheriff Mason glanced at the weapons table as he walked into the dining room. The fancy gun belt with a Colt revolver in the holster caught his attention enough so that he paused to look around the room looking for a fit. The only likely candidate was a lone diner seated at a side table, who was attired in an outfit that seemed to go with the gun belt.

"Sheriff Mason," he heard Rachael call his name. "You didn't have to bring those back. I would have sent for them."

"No trouble," Mason replied and walked into the kitchen with her. "It was mighty good, just like always," he said to Bess, who took the dishes from him. "I even caught my prisoners fightin' over a biscuit," he joked. Rachael and Bess both laughed. It was another sign, as far as Rachael was concerned. She and Bess had discussed the topic of Sheriff John Mason and concluded that there was a definite difference in his demeanor since Perley had come back to Bison Gap. "Who's the slick-lookin' jasper sittin' over at the side table?"

The two women looked at each other and shook their heads. It was the same description Possum had used the night before. "That neatly dressed gentleman is Mr. Drew Dawson," Rachael informed him.

"Is he stayin' in the hotel?"

"He did last night, but not tonight," Rachael said. "He just likes to come in to get Bess' fine cooking."

"He wears a slick-lookin' gun belt, too," Mason said and smiled. "Think I'll go over and welcome him to Bison Gap. He walked across the room to Drew's table. "Afternoon," he said. "The ladies treatin' you all right?"

Wary when the sheriff walked in and paused by his gun belt, Drew had no option other than to remain in character. "Good afternoon, Sheriff," he replied. "Yes, sir, they're treatin' me like a king. Have a seat and join me."

"Thanks just the same," Mason said, "but I've already had mine."

"Well, sit down and have a cup of coffee," Drew invited. "It's mighty good coffee."

"Maybe just a cup," Mason said, and Drew signaled for Kitty as the sheriff drew a chair back. Watching from the kitchen door, Bess and Rachael exchanged wide-eyed glances. They had never witnessed that by Mason before. They were further amazed when they heard him say, "I'm Sheriff John Mason."

"Drew Dawson," he returned. "It's a pleasure."

"Those your horses out front?" Mason asked, and when Drew said that indeed they were, Mason commented on the white horse. "That's an outstandin' gelding, don't believe I've ever seen one whiter than that one. Before I took this job, I was a ranch foreman for a cattle ranch south of here, so I've seen a lot of horses."

"I get a lot of comments on that horse," Drew said, "the saddle, too. That horse cost a lot of money. So did the saddle, but I thought at the time I had to buy a saddle that looked just as rich as the horse." He chuckled and said, "Wish I had that money back, I'd put it on some of this land I'm lookin' at now."

"You lookin' to find some land close to town?"

"Absolutely," Drew said. "I like the look of this town and as soon as I finish eating, I'm going to go to that store down the street and load those packhorses with enough supplies to last me till I'm done lookin'."

Mason took another couple of gulps of coffee and got up. "Well, I won't hold you up. Thanks for the coffee, and I hope you find the land you're lookin' for."

"It was my pleasure, Sheriff," Drew replied, as Mason headed for the door. *Like a piano*, he said to himself, pleased with his introduction to the sheriff of the town. It was not a hopeless case, he decided, in spite of Ned's bungling of it. For now, and maybe for some time to come, he could not let anyone know there was a connection between him and Ned Stark.

Finished with his meal, he left the money for it on the table and sauntered over to the weapons table to retrieve his gun belt. Rachael came out of the kitchen then. Seeing him about to leave, she came over to thank him. "I left the money on the table, if that's what you're after," he joked. "I knew better than to try to get outta here without payin'."

Rachael laughed. "We weren't worried. One of us would have tackled you before you got out the door. Was everything satisfactory?"

"I'll remember that about the tacklin'," he joked. "Maybe I'll try it next time. And the meal, I wouldn't say it was satisfactory." He waited for her to raise her eyebrows in surprise, then said, "I would say it was excellent."

"Thank you, sir," she said with a sweet smile. "Don't be a stranger."

"I can promise you that," he said and took his leave.

"What was all that?" Bess asked Rachael when she returned to the kitchen door.

"What was all what?" Rachael replied.

"All that little chitty-chat at the gun table," Bess said. "I declare, I thought I saw you make a little curtsy there. You ain't gettin' no ideas about that slick talker, are you? And you with two young daughters."

"Bess Curry! Bite your tongue! I just think it's a nice change to see pleasant, polite customers come into the dining room." She pretended to be offended. "Chitty-chat, I don't even know what that means."

Outside, Drew Dawson climbed aboard the big white horse and led his packhorses a short distance down the street to Wheeler's General Merchandise, curious to see the mayor of Bison Gap in his natural habitat, behind the counter of a general store. Ralph was in the store and so was his wife, Cora, so Drew cranked up his charm once again. By the time he was finished, he felt he had impressed them both to his satisfaction. As he started down the street toward the creek, he found himself thinking how disappointed he was to find that Ned had not controlled his men to maintain better relations with the town. Drew believed one could milk a town while still on friendly terms. Near the middle of town, he admired the new bank building. *First Bank of Texas*, he read to himself as he slow-walked his horses by. "That's where they keep the goin'-away present, Snowball," he murmured

to the gelding. "If we ever find we need to leave
Bison Gap in a hurry, we can always stop there for a
little spendin' money." *Yep*, he thought, *this town has
a lot to offer. I only wish I had gotten here sooner, before
Ned established himself with the sheriff. It could have been
handled much better.* There was still time to salvage
most of it, he decided. But for the time being, he reminded himself that he was the only member of the
gang who could go back and forth to town.

# CHAPTER 15

"Here comes Drew," Junior announced, "and he's got them packhorses loaded down." That was enough to cause some measure of excitement among the still-defeated band of cattle rustlers. Everyone went outside to help unload the supplies, even those who could use only one arm. "I sure hope you got some coffee and flour," Junior said to him when he pulled his horse up before the porch.

"There you go, boys, everything you've been missin'. I even went in the saloon and bought a couple of bottles of rye whiskey. Maybe that'll help lift your spirits a little. Ain't that right, cousin?" He grinned at Stark. "I got a good picture of your little town today, even had the opportunity to have a cup of coffee with your sheriff. You know, the one you used to own. Right friendly fellow he was, too. He looked like he owns that town now. Came in the hotel dinin' room and chatted up the ladies, and they were all sweet and friendly to him. Something musta happened to that man, 'cause he ain't the coward you told me about."

"That faker," was Stark's only comment.

"I'll tell you somethin' else I found out when I went to the Buffalo Hump to get the whiskey. Jimmy told me they're fixin' to have another one of their town council meetin's tonight after supper, right there in the saloon. He said just about all the men in town would be there, includin' the sheriff. Jimmy thought that was newsworthy, the sheriff comin' to the meetin'. He said before Perley Gates came to town—back when you were payin' him off—the sheriff never attended a single meetin'. Now, he's invited to every one of 'em." He looked around at the five faces and was aware that he had everyone's attention. Talking to all five of them then, he asked, "You know why that's kinda interestin'?" He waited for someone to say the obvious answer. When no one did, he shook his head, surprised. "That's interestin' because it means nobody will be watchin' the jail."

"What about Perley Gates?" Jack Sledge asked. "Most likely he'll be guardin' the jail."

"You know, Sledge," Drew answered. "I asked the same thing. I thought the sheriff would surely not leave his prisoners unguarded. But Jimmy said Perley has been comin' to the meetin's right regular since they started havin' 'em. And Jimmy ain't never lied to me," he joked.

"You're thinkin' we oughta take another shot at breakin' Eli and Slim outta there tonight?" Stark asked.

"They're havin' that meetin' in the Buffalo Hump," Stark said. "That ain't but about thirty-five or forty yards from the jail. If we go in there and try to hit that jail again, they're bound to hear the racket we'd make. And there'll be every one of the vigilance committee right there, plus Perley Gates." His remarks brought grunts and words of agreement from the other four men, none of them anxious to try the same thing that crippled them the first time.

"That's probably true," Drew said. "But if you wanna try to maybe slip 'em a gun, or two while you're at it, you won't get a much better chance than tonight. Then maybe Eli and Slim can get themselves out of jail." He saw Stark's eyes light up at that.

"That might be the best chance we've got to get them outta that jail," Stark declared. "One man oughta be able to slip up behind that jail without nobody seein' him. Some of the rest of us could hang back on that creek bank just in case somebody sees him."

"I'll do it, Ned," Junior volunteered.

Stark smiled at Drew and nodded his head. "That just might work, cousin," he said.

"Let's cook us up a big supper tonight," Drew said. "Maybe Junior can make some pan biscuits with some of that flour I brought back from town."

"Did you get the jail fixed up all right?" Ralph Wheeler asked Sheriff Mason when he walked into the Buffalo Hump after supper. The mayor had requested a meeting of the council that night to decide what direction the town should take with the Ned Stark gang.

"Yep," Mason answered. "John Payne got the bars back in the window, so I moved Eli back in that cell. Looks stronger than it did before. Hope we don't get it tested again."

"Maybe you oughta just keep Eli Priest in the jail, so he can plug it up again, if somebody else tries to pull it out," Rooster remarked, bringing a few chuckles from the few who were there already.

"Maybe so," Mason allowed. "The only thing that's gonna take a while is fixin' the windows in my office. Almost all the glass was shot out of the front and back windows, and we're gonna have to wait for some glass. John Payne had to board 'em up till we get some."

"That's one of the first things we need to talk about when enough of the members get here," Wheeler said. "What are we gonna do about Priest and Garrett? Give 'em a trial of some sort and hang 'em? Do they deserve hanging? We've never had to deal with this issue before."

Reverend Poole walked in at that point, in time to hear the questions. "I don't know what their intent was when they broke into Floyd Jenkins's place. Maybe they were just going to give him a whipping or something, or maybe they were breaking in to rob him. And if that was the case, they shouldn't deserve hanging. Maybe they should just be turned over to the state for imprisonment."

"Ah, come on, Parson," Rooster replied. "You know those three were goin' after Floyd to kill him for stickin' Curly Williams out there for folks to gawk at."

"That right there tells me we oughta hold some kinda trial for Eli and Slim," Dick Hoover said. "Some of us think one way and some of us the other."

"I thought this was supposed to be a quick meeting," Horace Brooks said to Henry Lawrence. "Looks like I was wrong about that."

"That ain't all bad," Henry replied, laughing, since he owned the saloon. "We ain't even started talkin' about the rest of that pack of coyotes yet." He nudged Horace when he saw Perley and Possum walk in the door. "I wonder how much longer he's gonna hang around?"

"From now on, I wish," Horace said. "I like havin' a fast gun around who's on our side."

"Maybe so," Henry allowed, "but if word gets spread around about how fast that man is with a gun, in no time at all there's gonna be one gunslinger after another showin' up in Bison Gap to try him out."

"I don't think you have to worry about that," Horace said. "Hearing him talk about it, I know he's anxious to get back home to Lamar County, and that's a helluva long way from Bison Gap."

The blacksmith was the last member to show up, saying he had a few things to touch up on the outside of the window. "Don't worry, Sheriff," John Payne japed, "they were still in there when I left." Mayor Wheeler called the meeting to order then, and they started out right away on the question of what to do with the prisoners.

While one member, then another, had their say about the issue, Sheriff Mason came over and sat down at the table beside Perley. "I ain't all that easy about sittin' in here listenin' to this discussion when there ain't anybody watchin' the jail," he said to Perley. "I don't have a vote on what they decide, anyway."

"You might not have a vote," Perley told him, talking in a whisper to keep from distracting those giving their opinions. "But you do have an opinion, and I think they'll wanna hear it. Besides, the jail ain't but about thirty-five yards from here. We'll most likely hear anybody tryin' to break in the jail."

Mason shrugged. "I reckon you're right, but I can't help worryin' about it. Just because we held 'em off once before, don't guarantee they ain't gonna try it again."

"Now you've got me thinkin' about it," Perley whispered. "How 'bout if I go watch the jail for ya? I ain't got a vote, either, and I doubt they wanna hear my opinion. Possum will tell me what you folks decide to do, and I'll go watch your office for you."

"Boy, that would sure make me feel a lot more comfortable," Mason said and offered Perley his keys, but Perley said he wasn't going to go inside.

"Where you goin', Perley?" Possum asked as soon as Perley got up and headed for the door.

"Just outside," Perley whispered, "gonna keep an eye on the jail." He slipped quickly out the door then before Possum jumped up to go with him, which he was likely to do. He thought it was a good idea if Possum participated in the meeting, since he was a bona fide member of the council. As for himself, Possum could tell him what course of action the town decided to pursue, and he wouldn't have to sit in a smoky barroom when it was such a nice evening outside. With those thoughts in mind, he started out toward the jail but paused to take in a deep breath of the fresh night air. He could have taken the keys Mason offered him, but knew he didn't want to sit in the sheriff's office any more than he wanted to sit in the saloon. Thinking of the nice summer nights when he would sometimes sit out on the porch at the Triple-G to watch the moon come up, he decided he could watch the jail from the outside. So he took the liberty of picking up one of the small, straight-back chairs on the saloon porch and carried it out to the lone tree between the saloon and the jail. Anchoring the chair on its two back legs, he tilted it back against the tree trunk. Settled in comfortably, he thought, *now if that gang makes another raid, I can see them before they even get to the jail.* He sat there for about half an hour before the first signs of a full moon began to appear through the trees along the east side of the creek. It was the last thing he remembered before he drifted off to sleep.

Riding a sorrel, since his white horse was too easily seen in the dark, Drew Dawson led the party of four riders up out of the creek and stopped while they drew up beside him. From that point, they could see the jail sitting in solemn darkness, in contrast to the lights and noise coming from the saloon close by. There were two extra horses with them for the two prisoners. Unaware of the sleeping man under the solitary oak tree, Drew said, "Looks just like we expected."

Stark spoke then, after he took a look, "All right, Junior, you know what you're gonna do. Ride up to that new window they just put in and drop the pistol through the bars. You remember what you're gonna tell 'em?" Junior said he did. "Best go do it before that moon gets up outta the trees. Make sure the gun don't hang up on the windowsill or nothin'. We'll wait right here for you, and if you run into any trouble, we'll come a-runnin'."

Junior nodded and rode out of the trees, headed for the back of the jailhouse. As they expected, no one took notice of the lone rider loping across the dark expanse between the creek and the jail. Pulling his horse up by the repaired window, conveniently absent of a screen, he whispered, "Eli, you in there?"

An answer came back right away. "Hell, yes, we're in here. Who's that?"

"It's me," Junior answered.

"Me, who?" Eli answered, impatiently, even though he could pretty well guess. "Junior, is that you?"

"Yeah, it's me," he answered. "I brought you a gun. I'm gonna drop it in the window. Can you catch it?" Eli said he could. "You're gonna have to break out yourself. We ain't in no shape to try to bust you out again. Ned said to tell you we left two horses tied down by the creek. All right, here comes the pistol. You ready?" He dropped the gun and when Eli said he had it, Junior said, "I'll see you when you get out." He wheeled his horse away from the back of the jail and raced back to the safety of the creek.

When he pulled up before them, Stark asked, "Did you remember everything?"

"Yep, I told him everythin' you said, and he got the gun," Junior reported.

"That's all we can do for 'em," Drew said to Stark. "We can just go on back to the ranch and wait to see if they show up."

Hearing his comment, Junior asked, "Go back to the ranch? Ain't we gonna wait to see if they get out?"

Stark held up for a moment. "Was there anybody else in there, besides Eli and Slim?" Junior said there was no one else. "Well, you big dummy, they can't do nothin' with a gun unless there's somebody there to point it at. There's no tellin' when the sheriff's gonna check on them tonight. It might not be till mornin' and they'll have a pretty good chance of gettin' away, if all they've gotta do is run back to the creek for the horses."

"I've got a better idea," Junior said. "Why don't we

wait for the sheriff to come back from that meetin' and grab him when he opens the door? Then we'll let Eli and Slim out and shoot the sheriff."

His suggestion caused them to hesitate, strictly because it came from Junior. "Damn, Junior," Stark replied in surprise. "That's not a bad idea, dependin' on if Mason comes back to the jail by himself." The big simpleton beamed in response to Stark's praise.

"It is a good idea," Drew agreed. "Should have thought of that first, but I don't think we need all of us to take one man. And I'm not ready to take a chance on them findin' out I'm one of this gang."

Pumped up now, since his idea was recognized as a good one, Junior volunteered again. "Shoot, I can jump that sheriff by myself."

"I wouldn't doubt it," Drew said, "but it might be a lot easier if there were two of you, in case he turns out to be more trouble than you expect. And you need to do it without firin' a shot and havin' the vigilantes on your neck. That might be too much for one man, even one as big as you."

"Hell, I'll go with you," Sledge volunteered. "I wouldn't mind gettin' my hands around his gullet."

"Good luck, boys," Drew said. "No use in Ned and me waitin' around here for Mason to show up. We'll see you back at the house."

"We'll get 'em," Junior boasted. After they left, however, he turned to Sledge, who already had his eyes glued to the saloon. "What if Mason ain't alone? What if that Perley Gates feller is with him? You reckon we oughta jump both of 'em?"

Sledge didn't have to give that much thought. "You might wanna jump both of 'em but damned if I do—

not as fast as that man must be. So I say, if Mason ain't by hisself, let's just let Eli use that gun you took him and get out like we first planned."

As it turned out, there was no need to worry about it. In less than an hour, the council meeting broke up, and as luck would have it, Sheriff Mason came out of the saloon, still talking with a couple of the members. After a few minutes of conversation, the sheriff said good night and started walking back to the jail alone. "Here he comes!" Junior suddenly blurted when he saw Mason striding across the empty space between the saloon and the jail.

"Let's go!" Sledge responded, and the two of them galloped out of the trees, each man leading a spare horse, intent upon getting to the sheriff before he reached the door of his office.

Sound asleep, until suddenly awakened by the sound of thundering hooves around him, Perley jumped up out of his chair in time to see the two riders as they passed on both sides of the oak tree. With no time to think, he ran after them, only then seeing their target, as Mason turned to see who was charging toward him. The sheriff drew his weapon when he realized their intent, but he was too late. Junior came off his horse like a great cannonball, knocking Mason to the ground, his six-gun flying out of his hand. Sledge dismounted to join his partner, who was now sitting on Mason's chest, grinning at the sheriff. "Howdy, Sheriff Mason," Sledge gloated, his .44 aimed at Mason's face. "Didn't expect to see us again, did ya?"

"I expect you'd better drop that pistol." The warning came from behind them, startling both outlaws, causing both of them to freeze. Junior just sat there on Mason's chest, not sure what to do. Sledge, after a moment more, slowly turned his head. "Best not think about it," Perley warned. Seeing Perley standing behind him, his weapon in hand, Sledge panicked, suddenly whipping his .44 around to fire. Perley's bullet struck him in the chest, and he dropped to the ground, never pulling the trigger. "Get off him," Perley ordered Junior, but the confused man-child continued to sit there until Perley, confronted with a task that looked too big to take on, put a shot through the toe of his boot. With a howl of pain, Junior rolled off Mason, who promptly rolled in the opposite direction and came up on all fours. In another few seconds, the sheriff was on his feet and had his pistol covering the moaning giant, who was rocking back and forth holding his injured foot. Perley quickly reached down and pulled Junior's gun from the holster. He then checked to be sure Sledge offered no further threats. "He didn't give me no choice," he said in apology.

"That big hog liked to crushed the life outta me," Mason complained. He shook his head as he stared down at Sledge. "Man, I sure am glad to see you," he said to Perley.

"I shoulda got here a little bit sooner," Perley said. He had no intention of confessing that he had been sound asleep while he was supposed to be on guard. They were joined then by half a dozen men, led by Possum and Rooster, responding to the sound of the shots.

"What happened?" Possum exclaimed.

"Perley just saved my bacon," Mason answered. "These two jumped me. It was another attempted jailbreak, I reckon, since they brought a couple extra horses with 'em."

"That one's name is Junior," Rooster announced, pointing to the big man sitting on the ground holding his foot. "The dead one's Jack Sledge." He took another look at Junior and said, "Looks like you might need Floyd to take a look at his foot, but you might need the blacksmith to get his boot off. I reckon you're gonna need two or three of us to help you get him in a cell."

"You got any more orders for us?" Possum japed.

"Matter of fact," Rooster answered and nodded toward Horace Brooks. "Horace, here, might need some help roundin' up these horses. I reckon that's what you wanna do with 'em, Sheriff, put 'em in the stable?"

Mason looked at Possum and grinned. "That's right, Rooster, that's what I want, but I'd like to get this critter in a cell first of all." So several of them got Junior on his feet and he hobbled into the sheriff's office, where Mason relieved him of his gun belt before taking him into the cell room. "I'm gonna need to put these two in one cell and put Junior, here, in one by himself, since he's gonna need some doctorin'."

The profound look of disappointment was painted on both the faces of Eli and Slim when the cell room door swung open and Junior was helped into the room. "Hello, fellers," Junior managed sheepishly. "We was tryin' to get you outta here."

"Who's with you?" Eli asked.

"Sledge," Junior answered. "They shot him dead. He was hidin' out, waitin' for us."

"You fellers are runnin' outta men, ain'tcha?" Rooster crowed. "How many more you gonna have to lose before you figure out Bison Gap ain't a good place for your health?"

Once Junior was in a cell by himself and Eli and Slim were in the other one, the men who had come to help thinned out to return to the Buffalo Hump for another round of drinks before calling it a night. Perley, Possum, and Rooster were the only ones to remain, and Rooster was in between on his decision to go home, or to room with Possum that night. Perley volunteered to go get Floyd Jenkins. Rooster reminded him to tell Floyd to bring his handcart to take Sledge back with him.

While Mason watched, his revolver out and ready, Possum and Rooster struggled to get Junior's boot off. Eli and Slim were huddled together in the farthest corner of the other cell. "Whaddaya reckon we oughta do?" Slim whispered, referring to the pistol hidden under Eli's bunk.

"We can't do nothin' right now," Eli answered, "with all them in here and all of 'em with guns. We'll have to wait till there ain't nobody here but the sheriff."

"Maybe we oughta wait till Junior gets his foot doctored," Slim said, "so he can go with us."

"I don't know about that. We get outta here, we're gonna have to run for it. We ain't got no horses, so we gotta run. I don't see him doin' much runnin'. We'll just wait till we see our chance, then we'll bust outta here."

"I reckon you're right," Slim said. "I'm gonna miss the meals, though. I wish we could get outta here before Perley Gates gets back. Junior shoulda brought guns for both of us." He would have continued rattling on with every thought he had, but Eli told him to be quiet.

When Perley returned with Floyd, he helped Floyd

carry in a large pan that he used to heat water. That was filled and put on the stove in the office. Then he opened his medical bag of medicines and various tools, some of which he would use on Sledge's body later on. He removed Junior's bloody sock and took a look at the wound just below the arch in his foot. "That ain't so bad," Floyd said. "There's an entrance wound and an exit wound. The bullet went all the way through. Did you look in his boot? There oughta be a slug in there somewhere."

As soon as he said it, Rooster picked up the boot to see. "Sure is," he said, feeling around in the boot. "There it is, halfway through the sole." He worked at it a while with his fingers until he pried it loose and held it up for them to see. Then he tossed it to Junior. "There's you a good-luck charm. It'll come in handy when you're in prison."

Junior caught it and examined it closely. "They wouldn't throw me in prison for just tryin' to get somebody outta jail, would they, Sheriff?"

The sheriff didn't answer, but Eli did. "You ain't got to worry about prison, Junior. 'Cause they're gonna hang you right alongside of me and Slim. Ain't that right, Sheriff?" Mason didn't bother to answer Eli, either.

When the water was hot, Floyd washed Junior's foot with some lye soap, which he said would keep it from getting infected, if he changed the bandage once in a while. Before wrapping a bandage around it, he sprinkled a white powder on both wounds. Watching the treatment, Perley was struck with the thought that it was the same powder he had seen in Floyd's barbershop. *Must be good for everything*, he thought.

With his new prisoner bandaged up, Sheriff Mason

locked Junior's cell and told his three guests they might as well settle down for the night and he'd see that they got breakfast in the morning. Then he went into the office to talk to Perley, Possum, and Rooster. Perley left to help Floyd push Jack Sledge's body back across the creek. Possum and Rooster stayed a little while longer before deciding to go to the hotel and go to bed, Rooster having decided he'd just go back home in the morning after breakfast.

The three prisoners in the cell room were talking very little because they were straining to hear any conversation beyond the closed door of the cell room. After a while, when they could hear no one in the office, Junior asked, "Have you got that gun I brung you?"

"Sssh, Junior," Eli scolded. "You wanna tell everybody in the whole damn town? Keep your voice down. 'Course, I've got it."

"I know you're thinkin' I can't walk," Junior said, this time in a whisper. "But you're wrong. I can walk good. It just hurts, that's all."

"When we gonna call him in here?" Slim asked.

"We'll wait a little while," Eli said. "I wanna make sure he's settled down for the night and thinkin' 'bout goin' to bed." So they waited, listening to every creak of a board in the building when the wind blew, wondering if it was Mason moving around, maybe someone else with Mason, or just the wind.

It didn't take Perley long to help Floyd push Jack Sledge's body into his barn, and he didn't linger once they had the corpse inside. He wasn't sure if it was actual or not, but he believed he could still smell the eye-watering stench of Curly Williams in that barn.

So he left to go to the hotel but stopped when only halfway before he started to wonder if Mason might be worried about another visit from Stark that night. *I doubt it,* he thought, then remembered falling asleep while he was supposed to be watching the jail. That turned out all right, but he felt guilty as hell about it. Mason could have been killed. He knew it was going to bother him now unless he checked with the sheriff before he left him for the night. *After all,* he thought, *that was the reason for the signal.* When he had left to go with Floyd, he told Mason, if he was locked up and he came back later, he would tap four times on the back window, which was boarded up, awaiting glass. He would do that instead of knocking on the front door, so Mason would know it was him.

When he got back to the jail, it appeared that Possum and Rooster had left, so he walked around to the back window and tapped four times on the boarded-up window. Inside the cell room, Slim whispered, "Did you hear that?"

"Hear what?" Eli asked. "I didn't hear nothin'."

"I thought it sounded like he was walkin' around in there," Slim said. "Maybe he's gettin' ready to go to bed."

Out in the office, Mason went to the front door and asked softly, "Is that you, Perley?" When he heard an affirmative from Perley, he opened the door. He was about to say come on in, but he heard a call from the cell room.

"Sheriff," Slim called out. "Sheriff!"

"Come on in, Perley. Let me see what he's cryin' about."

Perley came inside and bolted the door behind him while Mason opened the cell room door, stuck his head in, and asked, "What is it, Slim? What are you yellin' about?"

"It's Junior," Slim said. "There's somethin' wrong with him. He's actin' like he's got the fever or somethin'." On cue, Junior moaned painfully.

"He's all right," Mason responded. "That's just a minor wound in his foot. He's just actin' like a baby about it."

"I don't know," Eli said. "He's been doin' a lotta moanin' and groanin' ever since you brought him in. He mighta got it infected. It's in his foot, and you know it's likely he ain't washed it in six months."

"All right," Mason conceded, "I'll take a look at him, but there ain't much I can do for him, if Floyd didn't find nothin' else wrong with him." He stepped inside the cell room and walked over to the bars of Junior's cell. "Why'd he move that bunk over here?" Mason asked when he saw that Junior's bunk had been pulled over close to the bars between the two cells.

"Just so we could talk to each other without havin' to yell, I reckon," Eli answered, as he moved up to the bars facing him. "Who knows why Junior does anything?" Thinking Eli too close, Mason started to step back. "Just hold it right there, Sheriff, less'en you want a bullet in your gut." Mason looked down to see a .44 revolver aimed at his stomach. His natural reaction was to reach for his pistol, but Eli warned him before he could move. "You do and I'll shoot you down."

"You're makin' a big mistake, Priest," Mason warned. "I ain't the only one here."

"Right," Eli scoffed, sure he was bluffing. "If you don't wanna die right where you're standin', you'd best step back up to these bars."

"What if I don't?" Mason replied.

"I just told you, you damn fool. I'll cut you down right there."

"If you do that, how are you gonna get outta that cell?" Mason asked, thinking to stall for time and hoping Perley would realize something was wrong in the cell room.

"I reckon I'll still be in this cell, all right," Eli said, "but I won't be dead like you. So quit wastin' my time and step up here if you wanna live." Mason hesitated, but there was no sign of Perley. He had no doubt that Eli would shoot him and no certainty that he wouldn't kill him after he did what Eli demanded. When Eli cocked the hammer back, Mason had no choice but to do as he said, so he stepped back up to the bars. "Put your hands on them bars," Eli ordered, and when he did, Eli said, "Grab his gun, Slim." Slim reached through the bars and snatched Mason's pistol out of his holster. "Now, Sheriff," Eli continued, "The thing that's gonna save your life is if you walk over by that door and get the key to these cells offa that peg. If you try to walk out that door, you'll go through it with two bullets in your back. You understand?"

Mason nodded and answered, "I understand, but you're makin' a mistake. You ain't gonna get away with this."

"Move!" Eli commanded, tired of Mason's stalling.

With no options left, the sheriff moved slowly back toward the office door and the cell key on the wooden peg. *Perley, wake up!* His mind pleaded silently, as he reached the door. "Whatcha doin' in here so long, Sheriff?" Perley said as he came through the door, causing a chain-lightning reaction. Startled, Slim was the first to fire. He had moved away from the cell wall then and fired at Perley, but his bullet ricocheted off one of the bars and buried itself in the wall. Without consciously thinking what he had to do, Perley re-acted, putting one shot, dead center between the bars, to drop Slim on the cell floor. A second shot nailed Eli before he could fire his pistol, already cocked. Shot in the chest, Eli sagged to the floor, his body hanging by his one arm thrust through the bars.

"Damn!" was the only word that dropped from the mouth of Junior Humphrey as he tried to believe what he had just witnessed.

Every bit as shaken as Junior, but thankful to be alive, John Mason put his hand on the wall for sup-port when he felt a reluctance in his knees. Recover-ing rapidly, however, he walked back to the cell wall and took the cocked pistol out of Eli's hand. When he thought he could talk, he said, "I didn't think you were ever gonna understand what was goin' on in here, but I'm mighty damn happy you finally did."

"Sorry I took so long," Perley replied. "I wasn't payin' much attention to what you were talkin' to them about. But then I heard one of 'em say, 'Move', kinda loud and I thought I'd best see if everything was all right."

Still struck by what he had just seen, Mason tried to seek answers. "I can understand how you got Slim. He fired a shot that ricocheted off one of the bars, or you mighta been hit. But how you beat Eli I'll never un-derstand. His pistol was already cocked. I saw him cock it." Mason had heard how fast Perley was, but this was the first time he had actually seen the mild-mannered young man in action.

"I don't know," Perley honestly tried to explain. What had happened during those critical few seconds was actually a blur to him now that it was over. "He had his arm stuck through the bars, pointin' at you, I reckon. Maybe that hampered him."

"But he had the gun cocked," Mason insisted. "Why didn't he shoot?"

"I wondered about that myself," Perley said. "I don't know what he was waitin' on." Uncomfortable with the subject, he turned to Junior then. "How did he get that gun?"

"I dropped it through the window," Junior answered, without thinking whether he should say so or not.

"I reckon you need to get John Payne to put some screen-wire over that window," Perley said.

"I reckon I'd better," Mason agreed.

# CHAPTER 16

With the reports of gunshots coming from the jail, Possum and Rooster were soon running down the street to find the cause. They, like most of the members of the vigilance committee, had not expected anything more from Ned Stark's gang on this night, especially since it had cost them the loss of two more of their number. They were encouraged to see some of the vigilantes running from the Buffalo Hump to investigate the gunshots, an occurrence that was new to Bison Gap. Before the town decided they could pull together to protect themselves against the Ned Starks of the territory, gunshots usually caused citizens to run the other way.

"What's goin' on?" John Payne called out when he saw Possum and Rooster heading for the jailhouse. Horace Brooks and Ralph Wheeler were running behind him.

"That's what we're gonna find out," Rooster answered him. There were no horses outside the sheriff's office, so he could only guess. He and Possum had some concern, since Perley had not shown up at the hotel yet. Rooster ran up the steps and banged on the office door.

"Everything's under control," the sheriff assured them when he opened the door. He stood aside to let them come in. Possum and Rooster were relieved to see Perley standing inside as well. "We lost a couple of prisoners," Mason told them.

"They escaped?" Wheeler asked, at once concerned.

"No," Mason answered him. "I mean they're dead because they tried to escape." He nodded toward the cell room door. "They're in there." They went immediately to see for themselves. Walking in behind them, Mason told them about the attempt to escape, and the gun that was secreted in to them.

"I was the one that slipped the gun in for 'em," Junior interrupted. The simpleminded giant seemed to take pride in his part of the failed escape attempt. "I dropped it in the window yonder."

"Like he said," Mason went on. "He dropped a gun in the window sometime this evenin'. When they thought everybody was gone but me, they called me in here and pulled the gun on me."

Staring at the two bodies lying on the floor of the cell, Wheeler asked, "What happened?"

"Perley," Mason answered. There was a pause while everyone waited for the story, but that was all the sheriff offered. He could tell them what happened, but he wasn't certain how it could have happened. "Well, they surprised me with that weapon Junior brought 'em and Slim, there, got my gun and Perley walked in and shot both of 'em."

"They didn't give me any chance to just wound 'em." Perley felt the need to explain that he had to shoot too quickly to pick his spots. "I know you were probably wantin' to put 'em on trial."

When they decided they weren't going to get any more details on the actual shooting, they started to file out of the cell room. "How 'bout a couple of you fellows give me a hand with these bodies?" Mason said. "I just wanna get 'em off the floor and lay 'em on the bunks and leave 'em there till mornin'. It's a little too late to call Floyd over here again tonight." Half joking, he said, "That won't bother you, will it, Junior?"

"Nope," Junior replied. "I 'preciate a little company." They laughed at his comment, not realizing the simpleminded outlaw was serious. He felt the need to make one more comment before they left. "That feller," he said, nodding toward Perley, "is faster'n greased lightnin'. I ain't ever seen nobody that fast but one other feller. And he might be faster, I don't know, but he's just as fast." He was thinking of Drew Dawson.

"Is that so?" Possum asked, "What's his name?"

"I can't tell you that," Junior answered. He knew that Drew didn't want any of the gang to let on that they knew him, and he was good at keeping a secret.

"Why can'tcha?" Possum pressed.

"Because it's a secret, and I'm good at keepin' secrets," Junior insisted. "So you're wastin' your time askin' me."

Not at all comfortable with the topic of discussion, Perley said, "Leave it be, Possum. There's lots of men faster'n me. That ain't nothin' to be proud of, anyway." Already he had been forced to outshoot four men before this latest confrontation tonight, and the last thing he wanted was to be saddled with a reputation as a fast gun. He just wished that every time he tried to help a friend, or someone else, he wouldn't end up finding himself forced to act.

"Pass that bottle over here, Jim," Stark said. "I'm partial to corn whiskey, myself, but I'll drink rye, if that's all there is."

"Ah, cousin," Drew Dawson chuckled. "It's a good thing I finally got out of prison, so I can teach you to appreciate the finer things the world has to offer. The problem is you couldn't get anything but corn whiskey back on the farm when you were old enough to steal it out of Uncle Buck's feed bin. As a matter of fact, that's one of the main reasons I came back to ride with you boys again, to inspire all of you to improve your social senses."

"You mean it wasn't because your career in the bank-robbin' business was cut short when that gang you was ridin' with got rounded up and sent to prison?" Stark asked.

"No, indeed," Drew answered, as he poured himself another drink and held it up as if to toast them. "It was really because I missed you boys." His toast was met with hoots and sarcastic remarks. "Which reminds me," he said. "I wonder what's keeping Junior and Sledge. The meeting in the saloon must have been long."

"They might still be waitin' for the sheriff to come back to the jail," Frank Deal suggested.

"If we had known there was not going to be anybody at the jail for that long, we mighta been able to break in and get our men out," Drew commented.

"That jail ain't that easy to break into," Stark said.

"We found that out the hard way, didn't we, boys?" Both Deal and Jim Duncan grunted in agreement.

"Damn place is built like a fort," Duncan said.

"You don't reckon they ran into a trap, do ya?" Deal asked.

"Ain't likely," Stark answered. "We was settin' right there on that creek bank watching the place. And we watched Junior ride right up to the back of the jail and drop that pistol in the window. If there had been anybody watchin' the place, they woulda got Junior."

"Ned's right," Drew said. "They're just havin' to wait for the meetin' to end."

"Maybe somebody came back to the jail with Mason," Duncan suggested, "and Sledge and Junior couldn't jump 'em."

"They'd had to be more than a few to keep Junior and Sledge from jumpin' 'em," Deal declared.

"I guess we'll just have to wait to find out," Drew said. "I just hope we find out before this second bottle of whiskey runs out."

As the hours passed with still no sign of Junior and Sledge with Eli and Slim, Stark became more and more concerned. Well past midnight, he found himself the only one awake and he looked at his cousin, still sitting at the table, his chin resting on his chest, fast asleep. Frank and Jim had long since deserted the table to sit on the floor so they could lean up against the wall, also asleep, both with their shoulders bandaged. What if something did go wrong in town, and Junior and Sledge were captured, or killed? Then this pitiful collection of the four of them was all that was left of his once powerful gang. And if this was what it had come to be, then the reason for it was one man— one innocent-looking saddle tramp—Perley Gates.

He ruled Bison Gap before the arrival of Perley Gates. The hatred he felt for this one man ran through his veins like hot lava, causing every fiber in his being to tense until the glass he held in his hand suddenly shattered, spilling whiskey on his hand. He didn't even let out a yelp when the alcohol began to sting the cuts from the broken glass.

Morning came as a surprise. Stark did not realize he had fallen asleep until Drew woke him. "Ned, what the hell happened to your hand?"

Stark, still groggy from the short sleep just ended, looked at his hand, a patchwork pattern of dried blood covering most of it. He continued to stare at it, trying to remember. When it came back to him, he ignored Drew's question and asked one instead. "They back yet?"

"No, they're not," Drew answered.

"What time is it?"

"Six o'clock," Drew said. "They're not comin' back. Something went wrong last night and I'm gonna have to ride into town to find out what happened. The three of you best be keeping your eyes sharp in case that damn town vigilante gang decides to come out here and finish us off. I'll go in there and hope to hell none of them have told the council who I really am. Maybe we can convince them that we've high-tailed it outta here. I don't know. I'll just have to find out what happened." He looked again at Stark's hand. "Three of you wounded now," he muttered in disgust. "Are you gonna be all right? You look like you got run over by a herd of cattle."

"Don't worry about me," Stark answered. "The only

problem I've got is a head about to blow up from too much whiskey and not enough sleep. If you're ridin' into town, you'd better be ready for trouble. If they took Junior alive, there's no tellin' what that big idiot has told them. He mighta told 'em you're one of us." Stark considered trying to persuade his cousin that it could be too risky for him to ride into Bison Gap, but he desperately wanted to know what had happened after he and Drew left Junior and Sledge on the creek bank.

"Just in case," Drew advised, "the three of you best saddle your horses and keep an eye on that trail leadin' to the front porch, if you're figurin' on stayin' here. 'Cause, you might have to run for it, if there's too many of 'em."

"Well, good morning, Sunshine," Rachael greeted Perley when he came into the hotel dining room. "The two other early birds just beat you by a few minutes," she joked. She enjoyed japing all three of them for their late arrival because, ordinarily, they were banging on the dining room door before she opened for breakfast.

Perley gave her a smile for her efforts to shame him and said, "Good mornin' to you, too. I hope you've got plenty of coffee, 'cause I'm gonna need a lot of it. We didn't get to bed very early last night."

"I heard about the little party you had at the jailhouse last night after the meeting," she said. "Go set yourself down and I'll get you started on some coffee."

"Much obliged," he said and walked back to the table where Possum and Rooster were seated. "Mornin'," he said as he pulled a chair out and sat down. Neither of them said anything in response to his greeting until he looked at them and asked, "What?"

"We was just wonderin' if you was gonna stay in that bed all day," Possum japed and winked at Rooster. "Me and Rooster have been waitin' for you to show up for 'bout an hour. Ain't that right, Rooster?" Rooster grinned and nodded.

"Is that so?" Perley responded in kind. "Well, now you know how I feel every other mornin' of the year, don'tcha? Besides, Rachael just told me you two just barely beat me to the door." While his two friends chuckled, he paused to say good morning to six-year-old Alice when she brought him his coffee. "Why, thank you, darlin'," he greeted her. "My coffee always tastes better when you bring it to me." She smiled sweetly and returned to the kitchen.

"How come that young'un don't ever bring me and Possum any coffee?" Rooster complained.

Overhearing his question, as she brought two plates of food to the table, Kitty Lowery laughed. "You don't like the coffee I bring you?" she asked.

"That was him that said that," Possum quickly replied, pointing to Rooster.

"Next time, I'll let him get his own," Kitty said. She smiled at Perley then and said, "Your breakfast is coming, soon as Bess gets it on a plate."

"Much obliged," Perley said, then turned his attention back to the table. He couldn't help noticing that everyone seemed to be in a downright playful mood this morning, so he commented on it.

"I don't know," Rooster answered his comment. "I reckon after that little shindig at the jailhouse last

night, Ned Stark's gang of outlaws has been whittled
down to nothin'. Me and Possum was talkin' about it,
and as near as we can figure, there must not be anybody
left with Stark but those two fellers that got wounded
when they tried to shoot the jail to pieces that first
time. And that's somethin' to get happy about. There
ain't no tellin' if he's got more men we don't know
about, but I think we're at the place where we oughta
ride out to that ranch and find out."

"I think Rooster's right," Possum said. "And I think
the town is ready to tell Stark it's time for him and his
kind to move along and find some other part of the
state to pester."

"I know we're ready," Rooster declared. "Last night,
when we heard them shots from the jailhouse, did you
see them fellers pourin' outta the saloon to see what
was the matter? And runnin' right with 'em, Mayor
Ralph Wheeler. Ain't nobody ever seen that before."
He had no sooner said it when Possum nudged him
and motioned toward the door as the mayor walked in.

Seeing the three of them, Wheeler walked back
and seated himself at the table next to theirs. "Good
morning, men," he greeted them cheerfully. "I'll sit
over here so I don't crowd you."

"That's a good idea, Mayor," Possum said. "With all
these elbows flyin' at this table, somebody could get
hurt." His comment earned a hearty chuckle from the
mayor. Perley was reminded again of the seemingly
cheerful mood this morning.

As Perley expected, Wheeler was eager to talk
about the night just passed and the course of action
the town council should take to finish the job. "We
was just talkin' about that," Rooster said. "We was

thinkin' it's the right time to ride out to Stark's place to see who he's got left—maybe tell him it's time for him to move on. And if he don't want to leave, hell, arrest him 'cause he's the one responsible for everything his men have been up to."

"You may be right," Wheeler responded. "I was already thinking about a little meeting with the sheriff and a few of the members to decide about that. I imagine you men would want to be in on it." He glanced at Perley. "Especially since you have been involved in damn-near every incident of this war with the outlaws."

The talk was interrupted then when another diner entered the dining room, and spotting them, walked back to greet them. "Good mornin' gentlemen. This looks like an important meeting goin' on. I won't interrupt."

"No," Wheeler responded, "no meeting. Mr. Dawson, right?"

"That's right," he answered. "Drew Dawson." He glanced around the table, smiling at each of them. Perley thought he detected a look of caution behind the smile, but decided it might just be that he was afraid he was interrupting something important. He relaxed completely when Wheeler invited him to sit down at his table and have breakfast with them.

"Why, that would be my pleasure," Drew said, "if you're sure I wouldn't be interfering with any important discussion."

"Better take another look at this table," Possum said. "Does it look like we could be talkin' about anything important?"

Drew laughed and replied, "Looks like you were planning the future of the whole damn town." His glance at Perley went unnoticed. After he and the mayor told Kitty what they wanted for breakfast, he turned back to Wheeler. "As I was passin' the entrance to the hotel, I heard a fellow say you had some excitement in town last night."

"Well, yes we did at that," Wheeler answered him quickly before Rooster could. His impression of Drew Dawson was one of a man who appeared to have a little money, and he seemed interested in the future of Bison Gap. He suspected him of hiding his real interest in the town, thinking he might be considering building a business here, but he was guarding against possible pressure by the mayor's office. For those reasons, Wheeler preferred to downplay any problems the town had with outlaws. "There was a little trouble at the jail after a council meeting last night," he continued. "A couple of outlaws made an attempt to free two prisoners from the jail, but the attempt was prevented by the sheriff with some assistance from the vigilance committee."

"Oh, so now the sheriff has all of them in jail," Drew assumed.

"He ain't got but one of 'em in jail," Rooster informed him. "The rest of 'em are dead."

Dawson had to use all the control he could muster, but he managed to maintain a blank expression on his face. The news was as bad as he had feared, and he pictured Ned's face when he took the news back to him. He couldn't resist probing for more details. "Sounds like you must have been one of those who gave the sheriff assistance," he said to Rooster.

"We all were," Rooster declared, "but we weren't

there in time to make any difference, except Perley.
He's the one that stopped the whole thing."

*I knew it!* Drew thought, but maintained his compo-
sure. "Perley Gates," he pronounced the name grandly.
"Nobody told me you were so handy with a gun."

Perley shrugged, not wanting any of it. "As handy
as the next fellow, I reckon, like everybody born on a
cattle ranch. You learn to shoot snakes and coyotes."

*What if the coyote has a gun and is faster than you, I
wonder?* Drew thought as he smiled at Perley. *I'd like to
call you out in the street right now to see if you really are fast,
or just lucky.* He had to remind himself that this was
not the time to call Perley's hand, but he was determined that the time would come after he and Ned
decided what they were going to do. And he was afraid
his concern was showing in his face. He was saved
when Rachael and Kitty came to the table with their
meals. "I see you've come back to see us, Mr. Dawson,"
she said. "I hope your breakfast is satisfactory."

"Ah, Miss Parker, indeed it is but you knew I would
have to come back here to get such excellent cooking,
served by such charming ladies."

"Mr. Dawson . . ."

"Drew," he corrected.

"Drew, then," she said, blushing. "You do go on. I'll
let you eat your breakfast before it gets cold." She
retreated to the kitchen. Possum gave Perley a sideways glance and shook his head. Perley grinned in
response. He couldn't recall having seen Rachael
blush before.

"Forgive me, gentlemen," Drew said. "I'm afraid
pretty ladies are one of my weaknesses. I'm sure

Miss Parker, or should I say Mrs. Parker, knows I mean no harm and certainly no disrespect."

"I hadn't thought about it one way or another," Rooster said. "Rachael Parker can take care of herself. Ain't that right, Possum?"

"That's a fact," Possum confirmed.

Devouring his breakfast in record time, Drew announced. "I've got some places to go, so I'll say good mornin' and be on my way. Once again, it was a pleasure." He placed some money on the table and got up to leave, waving to Kitty on his way out. There was really only one other place he planned to visit, and that was the Buffalo Hump, for two reasons. He knew he would get more details about the previous night's activities from the bartender, and he needed to replace the whiskey he and the others had consumed.

"Howdy, Drew," Jimmy McGee greeted him when he came in. "I was wonderin' if you'd be back this way any time soon. Shot of rye?"

"Don't mind if I do, Jimmy," Drew answered. "Even if it is a little early." He watched Jimmy pour his drink, then said, "I had breakfast with the mayor a little while ago. He was tellin' me you had a little excitement over at the jail last night."

"I reckon you could say that, all right," Jimmy said. As Drew expected, Jimmy went on to tell him about the attempt by Junior and Sledge to free Eli and Slim that was followed by the shoot-out between Perley Gates and Slim and Eli, resulting in Junior as the sole survivor of the men Stark sent to get his men out of jail. He got every detail from Jimmy, who never left the saloon. But Drew had every detail he needed to paint the picture for Stark. There was every indication that the people were now fully prepared to fight any outlaw intrusion upon their town. Drew could only grimace when he thought about Stark and his two wounded men waiting back at the ranch, compared to the hard-riding gang he was reported to have the day he left prison. He said so long to Jimmy and rode back to the ranch. The only good news he could give Ned was that he was pretty sure there would be no posse coming his way today. The town had to have a meeting before they could do anything.

# CHAPTER 17

Drew was not surprised when his cousin went into a rage upon finding out that Jack Sledge and Junior Humphrey were not going to return alive from Bison Gap and that Slim and Eli were already dead. At this point, Stark had been beaten in every confrontation with the gunman the town hired. And in spite of what Drew told him he had learned, Ned could not be convinced that Perley Gates was not a hired gun. "Why, then, wasn't one of my men killed by someone else, someone besides Perley Gates?" Stark demanded. "I'll tell you why, because that damn mayor, Wheeler, sent for that gunslinger when the sheriff couldn't do what Wheeler wanted." He banged his fist down on the table in a fit of anger, causing his cut hand to bleed again. He stared at the injured hand as if just discovering the bandage wrapped around it.

"Well, what are you gonna do?" Drew asked, when Stark seemed to have calmed down a little. "We're finished in Bison Gap, that's for sure. I've still got some of that money left that I got from T.C. We could head for Arizona or Colorado, maybe get back into the cattle business there."

"We need men to drive cattle," Stark said, "and we ain't got men." He hung his head and sulked for a few minutes more. "I don't know where we're goin', but I know one thing. I've got some debts to pay off before I go anywhere. Ralph Wheeler, John Mason, and Perley Gates, I will see them dead. Then I'll leave this damn town."

"You sure you want to go after those three?" Drew asked him. "They'll be hard to get to without somebody seein' you comin'. And I expect they're ready to shoot on sight, if you go ridin' into town."

"I ain't dumb enough to commit suicide, if that's what you're thinkin'," Stark answered him. "What I need to do is figure a way to draw Perley Gates out somewhere by himself and wait for him in ambush. I need to get him out of the way first, then I could ride right into town and get the other two. If it wasn't so hard to set up with my rifle close enough, I'd just shoot him in town."

Drew listened to Stark trying to come up with a workable plan to eliminate the three men he had come to hate so violently, and he realized his cousin had no idea what to do. "You're right," he told him. "The first thing to do is get rid of Perley Gates. Then we can handle the other two without any trouble at all. Since we can't go in town to get him, we're gonna have to make him come to us."

"How are we gonna do that?" Stark asked, at once interested if Drew had a plan.

"By havin' something he wants," Drew answered, thinking of what Stark had said about the time he surprised the reunion in the hotel dining room when he confronted Rachael Parker. "You remember what you said about Perley Gates then? If you don't, I'll remind you. Jack Sledge told me you said Perley Gates just sat there playin' pattycakes with Rachael Parker's two little girls."

"That's right, that's what I said 'cause that's all he did," Stark said. "Didn't open his mouth the whole time I was there. So what?"

"We get our hands on one of those little girls, we'd have something he wants, and I'll bet something he'd want bad enough to come after it," Drew declared with a confident smile.

"Yeah," Stark responded enthusiastically, "that would sure as hell do it. I remember I told that woman that waited on me that he looked like he'd like to be their daddy. Played with 'em like he weren't no older'n they were," Stark remembered.

"So, what we've gotta figure out is how to snatch one of those little girls and lead him back here after her. It's my guess he ain't ever been out here before, so we'd have to leave him a trail that's not too hard to follow. Since I'm the only one of us who can go to town, I reckon it's up to me to find a way to get to those girls when there ain't nobody to see us. I reckon I'm gonna be spendin' more time in town."

By the following morning, Ralph Wheeler and the members of the town council were beginning to enjoy a feeling of victory over the outlaws who had cast an evil shadow over Bison Gap. It was the common belief of the vigilance committee that Ned Stark's ruthless gang of outlaws had been effectively reduced to one angry man and two wounded followers. And as such, they were no longer a threat to the town. There had been a meeting of the council primarily to discuss

whether or not a posse should be formed to ride out
to Stark's ranch with the purpose of arresting the
three survivors of his gang. Even though morale was
now high in the hearts of the vigilantes, there was a
general belief that Stark was whipped, and he and his
two wounded men would leave the area and look for
greener pastures. One who was opposed to this apparent truce with a man who had brought a lot of trouble
to Bison Gap was the ever-vocal Rooster Crabb.

"We're makin' a big mistake if we don't finish this
thing off proper and put Ned Stark outta business for
good—keep him from takin' his kind of evil to some
other poor unsuspectin' folks. 'Cause that's exactly
what he'll do. It's in the breed for a coyote like him.
He's just as responsible for Tom Parker's death as that
lowdown snake, Curly Williams. It don't matter if it
was Curly that pulled the trigger—it was Stark who
told him he could. So what we need to do is get up a
posse to go after that snake in the grass and hang him
for murder."

There were some members of the council who
agreed with Rooster; Possum Smith, John Payne,
Horace Brooks, and of course, Emma Slocum. However, the majority, led by Reverend Harvey Poole,
voted to leave Ned Stark to fade away from their town's
memory. So the council turned instead to the matter
of the one remaining prisoner in Sheriff John Mason's
jail, Junior Humphrey. They were all in favor of having
a trial for Junior to discuss just how serious his crimes
were, whether or not they justified a sentence of
hanging. So, once again a trial was scheduled for the
prisoner, to be held in the Buffalo Hump on Friday,
two days hence. This was in order to give the prosecu-
tors and the defense time to prepare their cases. As

expected, Ralph Wheeler would take the role as judge, Dick Hoover as prosecutor, and Harvey Poole would speak for the defendant.

An interested spectator at the meetings of the members of the council, always held in the saloon, was the now-familiar stranger, Drew Dawson, who seemed to be spending more and more time in town. When he wasn't having a drink in the Buffalo Hump, it seemed you could find him in the hotel dining room, where he was becoming quite friendly with Rachael and the other women. Good natured and always in a pleasant mood, he enjoyed a joke, even one on himself. After a while, folks stopped wondering why he was still hanging around town, when originally, he was just passing through. His big white horse became a familiar sight on the main street of Bison Gap. The only one who seemed curious enough to ask him where he had set up camp, since he wasn't staying in town, was Rooster Crabb. He told Rooster he had made a camp east of town, a couple miles away.

Two residents of the hotel who became fast friends with the charming stranger were Alice and Melva Parker, especially when he would sometimes stop by Wheeler's store and pick up a couple of peppermint sticks, which he would stick in his vest pocket, half exposed. Then he would pretend not to know they were there and the game would be on. The girls would delight in his games and looked forward to his visits. Rachael was delighted as well that he entertained her daughters every time he came in, thinking it would take a special kind of man to take so much of his time to entertain someone else's children. In a very short time, Drew knew every detail of the two girls' daily routine, including when and where they usually played outside the hotel, if ever.

"Just hold your horses, cousin," Drew said. "I know you're wantin' to do this thing right now, but if you'll wait till Monday, that'll give us a chance to snatch up one of those little girls while the whole damn town is at the trial. We don't have to worry about a posse comin' out here lookin' for us, because in that meetin' they decided you were gonna run. They're ready to just be done with you." Stark considered what he said and agreed that it would be best, even though he still didn't want to wait. "I'll go into town every day, so I'll know if anything changes," Drew assured him.

They went into the kitchen then where Jim and Frank were sitting at the table, a bottle in front of them. "How 'bout it, boys?" Drew asked. "Those wounds startin' to heal?"

"Not so's you notice," Frank Deal answered him. "It ain't hurtin' like it was, but I can't use that arm a-tall."

"Well, you've got a couple of days for it to get better, we might need to put you to work on a little kidnappin' job."

"Kidnappin'?" Frank responded. "Who we gonna kidnap? I don't know if I can do much kidnappin' with one arm in a sling."

Stark interrupted then. "You'd best get that arm outta that sling in two days and go to work, if you still wanna lay around here and eat my grub and drink my whiskey."

Drew waited for Stark to finish his warning, then answered Frank's question. "A little girl, that's all you gotta grab. You oughta be able to do it one-handed—

two little girls, one of 'em's six and the other'n's four. You ain't gotta snatch but one of 'em, and it don't matter which one—just whichever one is handiest."

"Damn, I don't know, Drew," Duncan said. "I ain't ever thought about kidnappin' no kids."

"Then there's no point in thinkin' about it now," Drew responded. "Just go pick up one of these little girls when we tell you to. Nothin' to worry about, we ain't gonna hurt 'em. We're just gonna kill the fellow that comes lookin' for 'em."

There were no more questions from either of the two wounded outlaws on the kidnapping of one of Rachael Parker's daughters. But it was obvious by the expressions the prospect of it left on their faces that they were not comfortable with it. Satisfied they would do what they were told when the time came, Drew considered the matter closed. "Now, as much as I enjoy havin' supper with you fine gentlemen, I'm afraid I've got to ride back to town to keep an ear out for any change of plans by the gallant men of the Bison Gap vigilance committee."

Ralph Wheeler looked up when Perley walked into his store and went at once to meet him. "Horace Brooks said you wanted to see me," Perley said.

"Yes, Perley, thanks for coming by. I wanted to ask a favor of you, if you wouldn't mind."

"Sure, Mayor. What can I do for you?" He hoped it wasn't something that was going to take much time. He was hungry, and he had planned to go to the dining room right after he left his horse with Horace Brooks.

"Well, maybe you'll think I'm a little crazy to ask you, but I thought it was worth a try. To tell you the truth, you're so full of surprises that I thought this might be something else you're good at." The mayor hesitated.

His hesitation made Perley nervous now. "What is it you want me to do?"

"You know we've scheduled a trial for Junior Humphrey, right?" Perley nodded and Wheeler continued. "Well, since we voted not to send a posse after Ned Stark, some of my fellow members and I got to wondering, what if Stark is building up his gang again? That's something we need to know. Sheriff Mason has repeatedly questioned Junior Humphrey about it, but Junior won't tell him. He just keeps sayin' he knows how to keep a secret. So I was wondering if you were any good at getting somebody like Junior to talk."

His question clearly puzzled Perley. "Why would you think that?"

"I don't know," Wheeler said, thinking now that it was a bad idea and he should have known better than to listen to Rooster. But he pressed on. "It's just that you're different in a lot of things. I don't mean different, strange, mind you. I mean it in a good way."

A silent witness to the fumbling of words by her husband, Cora Wheeler could hold her tongue no longer. "Oh, for goodness sakes, Ralph." She turned to Perley and said. "Rooster Crabb thinks you have a special way of figuring things out that most people don't. What my husband wants to know is, can you get the information out of Junior so we're sure there's nobody but that monster, Ned Stark, and two wounded men left outta that bunch he had."

"Rooster said that, huh?" Perley asked, hardly believing they would put stock in any of Rooster's wild claims. "To answer your question, I ain't got any special talents in anything that's worthwhile to anybody." He looked at them and smiled. "But I'll go ask him if there's anybody else at that ranch, if that's all you're tryin' to find out."

"I'd appreciate it, Perley," Ralph said.

"Glad to help," Perley replied, "but I wouldn't count on any success."

He left the store in a hurry, still thinking about supper, also thinking, if the council was worried about additional outlaws at the ranch, they should have sent a posse out there to find out. He found the sheriff in his office and the door unlocked for the first time since the trouble with Stark had started. He knocked a couple of times and pushed the door open far enough to peek in.

"Come on in, Perley," Sheriff Mason called out when he saw who it was.

"Howdy, Sheriff, I just talked to Ralph Wheeler and he's worried that Stark is already buildin' up a new gang."

"I know it," Mason replied. "I've tried and tried to get Junior to tell me how many's out at that ranch of Stark's. And the sniveling sack of slop won't tell me. He just keeps sayin' over and over that he can keep a secret, and he ain't gonna tell me nothin' about Stark."

"You mind if I talk to him a minute?" Perley asked.

"Hell, no, talk to him all you want, but I hope you're not hopin' for intelligent conversation."

"Thanks, Sheriff." Perley went into the cell room.

When Junior saw him, he got up from his bunk and picked up his empty supper tray. "Perley Gates," he exclaimed as if glad to see him. "They send you down here to pick up my supper tray?"

"Yep," Perley answered. "Just slide it right through." When Junior slid the tray under the bars, Perley asked, "How you doin' in here all by yourself?"

"I'm all right." He held his foot up. "My foot's kinda swole up where you shot me."

"Yeah, I'm sorry I had to do that, but you were about to crush the sheriff," Perley said. "You know, you're a pretty big boy." The big grin on Junior's face was evidence that his remark had pleased him. "At least you're better off than ol' Ned Stark."

"Ned's doin' fine," Junior immediately insisted. "Can't nobody beat Ned."

"Nah," Perley said, shaking his head sadly. "Poor ol' Ned, he's sittin' out there at that ranch all alone. He ain't got nobody to talk to, nobody at all."

"He's got Jim and Frank left," Junior blurted. "He ain't by hisself."

"I reckon you're right, Junior. You take it easy. I've gotta take this tray back." When he came back through the office, he saw that Mason's empty tray was sitting on his desk. So he picked it up. "I'll take the trays back to the dinin' room. I'm headed that way now."

"Thanks," Mason said. "Get what you need from Junior?"

"Yeah, there ain't nobody left at that ranch but Stark and the two wounded men."

He hurried back across the creek to the main street and when he got to Wheeler's store, he stuck his head in just long enough to repeat the message he just left with Mason. "Thanks, Perley!" Wheeler yelled after him. He turned to look at his wife then. "I told you he's got special talents."

* * *

"I brought your trays back from the jail," he said to Rachael when he walked into the dining room. "Junior said the food was all right, but not as good as what he'd had at the Buffalo Hump."

"You'd better wash your mouth out after telling lies like that," Rachael fired back at him. "And you haven't even got your supper yet. Maybe Ida Wicks hasn't thrown out the slop yet at the saloon." She pointed at a table in the back with the two trays he handed her. "They weren't waiting for you, so you'll have to catch up." He walked back to join Possum and Rooster who were busy polishing off some pork chops and fried potatoes.

"Where you been?" Possum asked when Perley sat down at the table.

"I was just out ridin' around town," Perley answered, "doin' nothing in particular. Mostly I just wanted to work Buck out a little bit. He's been standin' around in Horace's corral too long."

"You can take him out to my place and hitch him up to a plow," Rooster japed. "That'ud give him some exercise, and I've got a field that needs plowin'."

"Then whaddaya sittin' around here for?" Perley cracked. "Besides, Buck and I are on pretty good terms right now. He'd never forgive me if I hitched him to a plow." He went on to tell them what he had been doing just before coming to supper.

"I noticed you was carryin' a couple of trays when you walked in," Rooster commented. "I figured you musta been down at the jail."

"You can't slip nothin' by ol' Rooster," Possum couldn't resist saying. The carefree banter continued through supper, a reflection of the mood of optimism felt by many people in town and most of the business owners. It was like a great burden had been lifted from the town with the seeming defeat of Ned Stark.

Before the three friends were ready to leave the dining room, Drew Dawson walked in. Seeing them, at the back table, he came back to join them. "Evenin', boys," he greeted them in his usual cheerful manner, a manner everyone in Bison Gap had become accustomed to. "Looks like you're still eatin'. Mind if I join you?"

"Have a seat," Possum responded, "if you can stand the company." He pushed the one empty chair back with his foot.

"I'll just sit at this table next to yours," Drew said. "You boys need the room, and I don't wanna get hit by a flyin' elbow." While his remark caused a chuckle from the three friends, Drew pulled a chair out from the table next to theirs, one that allowed him to sit down facing Perley, although at an angle. He could not ignore his fascination for Perley, nor did he want to. In his mind, Perley was his competition. He wanted to study him, everything about him, his moves, his alertness, even the way he handled his knife and fork. It didn't matter to him that Ned desired to kill Perley Gates by his own hand. Drew knew that Perley was his destiny to determine. That thought was interrupted momentarily when Kitty came to make sure he planned to have supper. "Yes, indeed, fair lady," he responded poetically. "And it looks like I've got a lot of catchin' up to do in this competition."

"I declare, that's good eatin'," Rooster announced. "I've a good mind to start over again, just to keep you company."

"That would be very considerate of you, Rooster," Drew remarked, "but Perley looks like he's got a little way to go yet. I'll try to catch up to him." Perley looked up from his plate when he said it, and Drew smiled at him. "Perley doesn't say much," Drew observed, wondering to himself how a stick of dynamite could look so bland and harmless. It was a mystery he felt he was destined to solve.

"With friends like these two," Perley replied, "you don't have to. They don't leave much to be said."

"I've heard it said that people who don't talk much are listeners, or they have secrets to keep," Drew said. "Which one applies to you?"

Perley shrugged, wondering where Drew could possibly be going with this conversation. "I heard there's a third option," he said. "There's people who ain't very bright, so they keep their mouths shut, so nobody finds out. I reckon that more likely applies to me. Which one are you?"

Drew threw his head back and laughed. "I'd really be surprised if you haven't already figured that out by now." Without pausing, he turned his head and said, "Yes, darlin'," when Kitty held the coffeepot up. Back to them, he said, "But I've been ramblin' on. It's a habit of mine, so tell me what's goin' on in Bison Gap, now that the vandals have been vanquished?"

"The what have been what?" Rooster asked.

"He means what's goin' on since we kicked Ned Stark and his trash outta here," Possum translated.

"Oh," Rooster responded. "Why didn't he just say that?" He looked at Drew and asked, "You ain't from around here, are you?"

"Where are you from, Drew?" Possum asked. "I ain't never heard you say."

"Here and there," he answered. "Kansas City is where I started out—had a business there."

"Is that a fact?" Possum replied. "What kinda business?"

"Guns," Drew answered. He couldn't resist it. It was not untrue. It was there he first discovered he was faster than the average man when it came to settling a dispute, usually having to do with a card game. "That's why I'm interested in the weapon you carry, Perley, since you seem to have success with it." Perley paused, but Possum hadn't satisfied his curiosity yet.

"Guns?" Possum asked. "Whaddaya mean? Did you sell 'em, or make 'em?"

"I modified 'em," Drew answered, and shifted his gaze back to Perley again. But Possum's curiosity had not been satisfied.

"I thought you told us you were scoutin' out the territory around here to start you up a cattle ranch," Possum said.

"That's right," Drew quickly replied. "And that's exactly what I'm doin'. I've always wanted to see if I could make it in that business." Back to Perley then, he asked, "That's the business you said you were in, wasn't it?"

Perley nodded slowly. It struck him that Drew had suddenly become unusually interested in him. "That's right," he said after a moment. "Possum and I work on a cattle ranch in Lamar County. We're just visitin' here for a little while."

Drew picked up on Perley's sudden caution and was quick to apologize. "Excuse me if I'm a little bit nosy. I guess you saw right away that I'm a tenderfoot when it comes to starting a cattle ranch. My friends back in Kansas City told me I was crazy to try to make a success at something I don't know a thing about. I reckon I should stick to guns, something I know about. That's the reason I was curious about what kind of gun you used. You know, did you have it modified for a special purpose—when you're workin' cattle or something?"

"You don't need any special kind of gun," Perley finally answered. "Most fellows carry a handgun for snakes and other varmints, a rifle for huntin'. I carry a Winchester 73 for huntin' and a Colt Frontier Six-Shooter for varmints. Ain't nothin' special about either one of 'em—buy 'em out of the catalog."

"Four-and-three-quarter-inch barrel?" Drew asked.

"No," Perley answered, "five-and-a-half-inch."

"You talk too much." All four men looked up at that. "Drew, you're letting your food get cold," Kitty scolded. "You fellows let the man eat."

"Right," Perley said. "Let's let Drew eat his supper." He had a funny feeling about the smooth-talking stranger. He figured he was up to something and it didn't have anything to do with raising cattle. He thought he'd better warn Emma and Rachael, and Rooster, too, not to enter any get-rich-quick deals or investments with Drew.

"You fellows gettin' ready for the big trial day after tomorrow?" Drew asked, thinking he'd best get off the subject of guns. All three of them were beginning to give him funny looks.

"There ain't much to get ready for," Rooster answered. "They're gonna try to decide if that big dummy in the jailhouse is a real killer or just one of Ned Stark's hound dogs." That started a discussion that lasted through a slice of pie and another cup of coffee. There was no agreement on whether or not Junior should swing for his part in the attempted jailbreak. Drew stayed behind to visit with Rachael and Bess after Perley, Rooster, and Possum left—Perley to bed—Possum and Rooster to the Buffalo Hump for a drink before turning in for the night.

On his way to the washroom, Perley met Barbara Cooper coming from there with Alice and Melva. When the girls saw Perley, they ran to meet him. "What are you two tadpoles doin' out here in the hall?" Perley said as they each grabbed a leg to hug.

"We're going to bed," Alice informed him. "We just had a bath."

"I bet Barbara had a tough time grindin' all the dirt offa you two tadpoles," he teased. "Maybe she shoulda left both of you to soak in the tub all night."

"Perley . . ." Alice pretended to complain.

"Tell Perley good night," Barbara said. "Your mama will be in pretty soon now and you'd best be in bed and ready to go to sleep." Both girls gave his leg a tight squeeze and said good night. Then they released him and raced up the hallway to their room, leaving Perley and Barbara to shake their heads.

"You spend a lot of time with those girls, don't you?" Perley asked.

"Not a whole lot," she answered. "They hang around the dining room most of the day. My job is to take care of Danny. Emma's with him right now, so I took Alice and Melva for their baths. I'll stay with them till Rachael comes in, and that'll be pretty soon now—when they finish cleaning up the dining room and the kitchen."

"Sounds like you have a full day's job on your hands," Perley said.

"I guess so, but I like to do it. Danny's an angel, and

Alice and Melva are a lot of fun. I'm glad they gave me the job."

"Well, good night then," Perley said, then paused when he thought of something else. "It's already startin' to get pretty dark outside. Do you need somebody to walk you home?"

"No, thanks just the same. I don't have to go that far, just down the street next to the bank. We live behind Daddy's harness shop."

"You sure? 'Cause I don't mind."

She assured him that she didn't need an escort, so he went to his room, feeling like the children were being well cared for.

# CHAPTER 18

"I gotta be honest with you, Jim," Frank Deal spoke quietly to make sure Stark didn't hear him. "I ain't too happy about this business of kidnappin' a little girl. I've been accused of doin' a lot of lowdown things in my life. And I reckon I done most everythin' I was accused of, but I ain't ever snatched a young'un before."

"Damn it, Frank, don't start talkin' like that again. I don't like it, either, just like we said when Ned and Drew first told us what they were gonna do. But I don't reckon we've got much choice with the shape we're in right now. Both of us with one bad arm, not a penny left of that last payday we had, Ned and Drew are the only game in town for us. And they're holdin' plenty of cash while we're broke. Like I said, we ain't got no choice."

"He's liable to get us killed," Frank said. "That's what's liable to happen—Drew in town shinin' up to all them people—and Ned settin' in there at the kitchen table, broodin' like a sick mule. What I wanna know is what's he gonna do with me and you after he kills Perley Gates? Him and Drew will cut outta here. What do they need us for? That's the only thing either one of 'em cares about. I heard 'em talkin' last night about goin' to Arizona or Colorado. Didn't hear a word about me and you."

"Evenin', boys." Both men jumped, startled when Drew rode his horse silently up beside the porch where they were sitting. "Good thing I ain't Perley Gates, ain't it? I slipped right up on you." He pointed his index finger like a gun. "Bang, bang, it'da been easy."

"Ah, hell, Drew, you already told us there weren't nobody from town comin' to look for this place. We weren't tryin' to act like lookouts," Jim Duncan complained.

Drew laughed and asked, "Where's Ned?"

"Where he is every night now," Frank answered, "in the kitchen workin' on that last bottle of likker."

"I'll go cheer him up after I put ol' Snowball away for the night," Drew said and wheeled the white horse away from the porch.

"I thought you were gonna stay in town all night," Stark grumbled when Drew walked into the kitchen. "Did you enjoy yourself? I'm surprised you didn't stay in the hotel."

"You know, I thought about that, since I'm gettin' to be like one of the family. Those two little girls think I'm Uncle Drew, and I'll tell you the truth, I think their mama is beginnin' to discover my charmin' ways." He gave his cousin a great big grin. "But then I got to thinkin' about my cousin settin' out here, anxiously awaiting my return."

Stark scowled out from heavy dark brows. "Drew, you're so full of horse droppin's."

"Horseshit?" Drew howled. "It's been hard work sugarin' up those two little brats. But I know everything those two young'uns do all day long, and I know where they're gonna be day after tomorrow at ten o'clock in the mornin' when that trial starts. And those two jaspers settin' out there on the porch can pick 'em off like berries on a bush." He cast a serious gaze at his cousin. "Just one more day of waitin' around, then we'll see how fast Mr. Perley Gates gets on our trail. You might wanna slack up on that bottle a little bit, so you'll be ready."

"Don't you worry your head about me and this bottle," Stark reacted at once. "I don't need nobody to tell me how much I can drink. I reckon I got along just fine the whole time you was in prison."

"I didn't mean to rile you," Drew quickly tried to apologize. "I know you were runnin' the gang just fine while I was gone." *And look what you've done with it,* he thought, *down to the three of you and scared to go into town.* He had been giving serious thought to the notion that he'd be better off without his cousin. Seeing him in the state he was in now added fuel to that fire. Once the matter of Perley Gates was settled, then he would tackle the matter of Ned Stark. "Well, I'm gonna hit the hay and tomorrow I'll get Frank and Jim ready to do their part on Monday mornin.'" He left his cousin still moping over his whiskey glass.

Monday morning broke clear and dry, another day without rain. It seemed to the small ranchers east of Oak Creek that it must have been a month without significant rainfall. In the town of Bison Gap, many of its residents were planning to attend the trial of Junior Humphrey. Although the actual trial would not begin for hours yet, the stage was being set in the

Buffalo Hump Saloon as Henry Lawrence supervised the arrangement of the tables and chairs to resemble a courtroom. In the jailhouse, the prisoner, Junior Humphrey, was not even aware that this was to be the day of his trial. He had been advised that Monday would be his trial day, but that was two days before this morning and he had forgotten.

At the Bison House Hotel, Bess Curry was reviving the fire in her big iron stove in preparation to fix breakfast. Both co-owners of the hotel planned to attend the trial, as did the manager of the dining room. Rooster rode in for breakfast, since he planned to go to the trial, too. Knowing Perley would be there as soon as the door opened in the dining room, Rooster made it a point to be early.

"Good morning," Rachael said when she unlocked the outside door and found Perley and Rooster waiting there. "What a surprise to see you so early," she said facetiously. "Where's the third member of your gang?"

"I'm sure he'll be here any minute," Perley said, seconds before the knock on the door that led to the hotel. Rachael smiled and walked over to unlock that door.

"Good mornin'," Possum said when he walked in. "Everybody gettin' ready to go to the trial?" Everybody said yes but Perley. "How 'bout you, Perley? Ain't you goin'?"

"Tell you the truth, I hadn't planned on it," Perley answered. Sitting in the saloon, watching a man on trial who was probably not intelligent enough to know what was going on, held no attraction for Perley.

"Well, why not?" Possum asked. "You got somethin' else to do?"

"No, I just thought I'd take Buck for a little ride, maybe, get him out of the stable for a spell. I ain't got much interest in that trial."

"Hell," Possum persisted, "you might as well go with us. You're goin', ain't you, Rooster?" Rooster said he wouldn't miss it. Back to Perley then, Possum said, "Emma and Rachael are goin'. You might as well go with us."

"Maybe I will," Perley relented. "But I think I'll take Buck out this mornin', anyway."

They walked back in the dining room, where Kitty and Bess were setting plates and silverware out. Rachael teased Perley as the men sat down at a table. "You pay so much attention to that horse of yours, when are you gonna pay some attention like that to a girl?"

"Yeah, when, Perley?" Possum joined in, thinking of Becky Morris back at the Paris Diner.

"Well," Perley japed, "I've kinda had my eye on Bess lately."

"Ha!" Bess reacted. "I might wear a young boy like you down to a nub."

Perley shrugged and looked at Rachael. "I reckon I'll just have to wait till Alice is sixteen." Everybody chuckled. It was the general mood in the little town on this morning.

After breakfast, Perley went down to the stable to see how Buck was doing. The big bay gelding was in the corral when Perley got there. "Mornin', Perley," Horace Brooks called out from the barn. "You goin' to the trial?" It was the standard greeting on this morning.

"I reckon," Perley answered as Buck ambled over

to greet him, "since that's where everybody else is gonna be."

"You takin' him out?" Horace asked when the big bay nuzzled Perley's chest.

"I think I will," Perley decided for sure when he got the feeling Buck wanted to get out of the corral for a while. "I'll get his saddle. You go ahead and finish what you were doing."

Far different from the casual morning in Bison Gap, there were also preparations underway at the ranch house a little over three miles from town. Content to let Drew call the shots as long as the intent was to lure Perley Gates out to him, Ned Stark looked surprisingly sober, considering the alcohol in his system. With two hesitant accomplices to rely on, Drew was going over their role in the kidnapping once again to make sure they knew what to do. He had decided on a change in plans, dictated by several factors.

He still sensed Frank's and Jim's reluctance to the snatching of a child, and he had been alert through the night in the event they might decide they couldn't go through with it and slip off. However, they were both still there when the sun came up, so he went over some changes in the operation of the kidnapping. He would go with them to show them exactly where they were to take the child.

Both men had questioned him on his plan, mentioning a possibility that seemed obvious to them. If they snatched the child, how did Stark know Perley Gates would come alone looking for them? More likely, they argued, a posse would arrive at the ranch.

Their logic convinced Stark of that possibility as well. "You're right," Stark agreed. "You can't bring that young'un out here. The four of us will play hell tryin' to fight a whole posse. Damn it! I want Perley Gates by himself!"

"Agreed," Drew conceded. "It ain't smart to risk it. That's why we need to take her somewhere else. So, instead of you settin' here waitin' for him to show up, you could go out to that little line shack you told me about."

"That shack's half a mile," Jim Duncan said. "Ain't nobody used it since we took this place."

"That's right," Drew continued. "And I'd be damned surprised if anybody in town knows about it. So, Ned, you ride on out there and wait for us to bring that young'un there. I'd bet everything I own that Perley Gates won't wait for them to get up a posse. He'll come ahead, and he'll have to track us, so we'll make sure we leave a trail. If they get up a posse, they'll come straight out this way, lookin' for this place."

"What if the posse ain't as dumb as you think, and they show up at the line shack and we're settin' there waitin' for Perley Gates?" Ned asked.

"Then I reckon we'll leave the little girl and run," Drew said. "But it's a better chance to get a shot at Perley Gates."

What Drew did not tell them was his intention to kill Perley himself. He couldn't deny his obsession with the thought of gunning Perley down in a face-off to prove who was faster. His real plan was for Perley to never reach Stark, who just wanted him dead. Drew wanted him more than dead. He wanted him beaten, and he wanted it known who beat him. So, when it was time, Stark got on his horse and headed for the line shack. Drew, with Jim and Frank, headed for town.

So as not to be seen by anyone in town, Drew led his two partners along the creek bank until reaching a point almost exactly where he had gotten off the train when he first arrived. He surprised them then when he told them to stay there out of sight and he would bring the girls to them. More than happy with the change of plan, they sat there on their horses and watched him ride across the railroad tracks to the back of the hotel. From where they waited, they could see a small grassy area behind the hotel with one tree in the middle and a rope swing hanging from a limb. They were there, two little girls, one in the swing, the other swinging her. They stopped when the white horse approached.

"Hey, who's that monkey swingin' in the tree?" Drew called out.

"Drew!" Alice cried out gleefully when she recognized her friend. She ran at once to meet him, leaving Melva to scramble out of the swing and run after her. "Whatcha doin', Drew?" Alice asked.

"Goin' for a ride," Drew answered. He looked quickly at the back door of the hotel to make sure there was no one else outside. "You girls all by yourself out here?"

"This is where we play," four-year-old Melva said.

"I know," Drew said, "you told me that. Nobody watchin' you?"

"Barbara's watchin' us," Alice answered. "She'll be back in a little bit. She's changing Danny's britches."

"Would you like to take a ride on Snowball?" Drew asked.

"I would!" Both girls screamed delightedly at the

same time with hands raised, but Alice was quicker to step up by his stirrup.

"All right," he said, "but I can only take you one at a time 'cause I have to make sure you don't fall off." He reached down and took Alice's outstretched hand. "Put your foot on mine," he said and lifted her up so she could. "All right, swing your leg over behind me." When she was settled, with her arms wrapped tightly around his waist, he looked down at Melva. "You stay right here and I'll come back for you." She dutifully took a step back. "Here we go!" Drew sang out. "Giddy-up, Snowball."

He rode out of the yard, up across the railroad tracks to the two men waiting for him on the creek bank. They stared wide-eyed at him as he approached. Seeing the two men, both with one arm in a sling, Alice became frightened at once. "Drew," she cried, uncertain.

"Don't be afraid," he said. "They're friends of mine." When he rode past, they turned and followed.

"Drew, they're coming after us," she cried.

"I told you not to worry about it." This time, his tone was a little sterner, causing her to become even more fearful. A few minutes later, when approaching a low ridge, he reined the white horse to a stop. Jim and Frank pulled up, one on either side of him, both staring at the young girl as if she was some strange animal. "Take her," he said to Duncan and pulled Alice's hands from his waist. He helped Jim get the girl seated in front of him in the saddle, so he could hold her with one arm. "Head for the shack. I'll be along later." He looked at Alice, who stared back, wide-eyed with fright. "He's takin' you somewhere safe. Ain't no use to be afraid." He watched them ride off until they were out of sight. He had never been to the line shack, so when he finished with the business he had planned for this morning, he was going to have to follow their trail. "So now we just wait," he announced, "and we'll see how fast Mr. Perley Gates really is when he's facing a professional." He found himself a spot on the ridge where he could relax against a tree trunk and watch the trail he had taken from the hotel. If things went as he expected, Barbara Cooper would soon find Alice missing, her little sister would tell her that he took her away on his horse, and Barbara would tell Perley. Then when they found his body, they would know it was Drew Dawson who killed their gunslinger.

Drew was almost exactly on the money with his speculation. Melva Parker stood dutifully where she was told to stand and waited for the white horse to come back for her turn. Although it seemed to be much, much longer to the young child, Drew Dawson and her sister had been gone for a quarter of an hour when Barbara Cooper returned to the yard to find Melva alone. "Where's Alice?" Barbara asked. "Did she go in the hotel and leave you out here by yourself?"

"She went on the white horse, and she's supposed to come back, so I can go," Melva said.

"White horse?" Barbara asked. "What do you mean, Alice went on a horse? Did someone put her on a horse?" She immediately began to panic. "Melva, tell me exactly what happened." Melva told her about Drew coming up on his big white horse and asked them if they wanted to go for a ride. Barbara felt somewhat better when she learned that it was Drew who took Alice for a ride. He was a big playmate of theirs. She would have wished that he had waited until she came back before taking Alice away. After another fifteen minutes and they had not yet returned, however, Barbara became worried again, fearing there had been some kind of mishap. Maybe Alice fell off the horse, the horse bucked them both off, or something frightened the horse. She finally decided they had been gone too long for something not to have happened. She grabbed Melva with one hand and Danny with the other. "Come on!"

With the two children in hand, she hurried them through the back entrance to the hotel, down the hallway to the dining room door. When Bess turned to see who was charging in through the door, she at first grinned to see the two children, but one glance at Barbara's face caused her to blurt, "What's the matter?" Kitty heard and came from the kitchen, and Barbara told them what had happened.

"I've gotta go tell Rachael!" Barbara cried. "Can I leave these two here with you?"

"Leave 'em here," Bess said. "I'll look after 'em. You go find Rachael. Kitty can run out to the back yard in case Drew comes back with Alice."

Barbara ran all the way to the Buffalo Hump. She ran into the saloon when Dick Hoover was laying out the charges against Junior Humphrey. Ignoring the heads turning to see who ran in, she paused only for the time it took to spot Rachael, then she headed straight for her. Immediately alarmed, Rachael called her name, "Barbara! What is it?"

"You gotta come," Barbara blurted, causing Dick Hoover to stop in the middle of his charges to see who had caused the disturbance. "It's Alice! She rode off on a horse with Drew Dawson and she didn't come back!"

Sitting next to Rachael, Emma said, "Go! If she's with Drew, she's probably all right, but you need to go."

Rachael got up to leave, and Perley, sitting behind her, said, "I'll go with you." He got up, and they hurried to the door. He hadn't particularly wanted to go to the trial, anyway, and had left Buck at the hitching rail, thinking he would probably ride out to Rooster's with him after the trial. Outside, he led Buck while they hurried back to the hotel, with Barbara telling them everything that caused her concern.

"You did the right thing, coming after me," Rachael told her. "We're probably worried for no reason. Drew is crazy about my girls. I just hope there hasn't been an accident of some kind."

When they got to the oak tree behind the hotel, they found Kitty still waiting there. She ran to meet them. "They ain't come back," she said.

"I'll go see if I can find 'em," Perley said. "But I need to get Melva down here first." Barbara ran into the hotel at once to get her. As soon as the little girl saw Perley, she ran to him and started telling him about Drew riding his big white horse right up to the tree where she and Alice were playing. "Did you or Alice ask if you could have a ride, or did Drew ask you if you wanted one?" Perley asked.

"He asked us if we wanted to take a ride on his horse," Melva said. "But he couldn't take but one of us at a time."

"Do you remember where you were standin' when Drew and Alice rode away?" Perley asked then. Melva nodded her head and walked over to a spot near the edge of the little yard. When she got there, she stamped each foot down hard, then folded her arms across her breast to show she was sure. "Good," Perley said. "Now, can you point where they rode off to?" She nodded again and pointed toward a little gap in the trees on the other side of the railroad tracks. "That's real good," he told her. "You did a good job." To Rachael then, he said, "I'm gonna go see if can pick up their tracks."

She placed her hand on his forearm and begged him, "Perley, find my daughter." Tears began welling up in her eyes, so that she had to step away. "Please," she pleaded.

"I will," Perley said, and leading Buck, he started out in the direction Melva had pointed, searching the ground for tracks that would tell him the child had remembered correctly. He found that she had, for the tracks were easily seen, and there was one set of tracks, coming and going, so Perley saw that as a good thing. Maybe Drew intended nothing more than giving a child a ride on his horse and had no ill intent. It would have been easier to assume that, if he didn't suspect that Drew Dawson was covering up something. He had gotten that feeling when Drew was so interested in his six-gun. He told himself to put those feelings aside and just concentrate on following Drew's trail.

The tracks led him to the gap Melva had pointed toward, and he entered the creek there. Once across, he found more tracks, left by more than one horse. He decided there were two or more horses, and they had stopped there, never entering the water. The multitude of tracks made it difficult to try to guess an exact number, but from the pattern of the tracks, he had to allow that it could have been only a couple of horses nervously stamping around in that one spot. He mentally painted a picture of two or three riders accompanying Drew and waiting there while he went to pick up the girl. It was not a pleasant image. Since the trail leading away from the creek was so obvious, there was no need for close examination. So he climbed aboard his horse and followed.

There were no longer any thoughts of innocent amusement for a child at this point. Whatever Drew Dawson was up to could be of nothing but evil purpose. Kidnapping came to mind, kidnapping for ransom maybe. He might erroneously think Rachael was wealthy, or if not, that Emma would come to her aid financially for the safe return of her niece. The farther he rode, the madder Perley became, and he cautioned himself to beware of a surprise ambush, for he was obviously outnumbered. He looked out ahead of him and scanned the land before him. Nothing but wide-open prairie with only a tree here and there. He could certainly see if he was catching up with anyone and it didn't appear that he was. The prairie led to a low line of hills not too far ahead. There was nothing to do but to follow the trail, which was blatantly obvious. It almost made him think it was intended to be obvious, but he felt he could not afford to break off to find a safer route, for the simple reason he didn't know where Drew was going.

He was closing in on the ridge ahead when he heard the snap of the bullet as it passed over his head, followed a full second later by the sound of the rifle that fired it. *Ambush!* He thought and immediately looked for cover as a second shot rang out. A dried-up streambed was the only cover anywhere close, so he galloped straight for it as rifle shots kicked up sand behind Buck's hooves. He charged into the dried creek, coming out of the saddle as fast as he could, pulling his rifle in the process. He had cover, but the sandy bank was not adequate cover for Buck, so he tried to shoo the horse away with a swat on his rump. He didn't want the bay to catch a wild shot, but Buck took only a few steps and turned to face him. He was confident that Buck wouldn't be shot on purpose, unless he was dealing with a complete fool on that ridge. And he was sure now the shots were coming from the ridge. So he crawled over and took the horse's reins and led him about ten yards along the dried creek bed, then dropped his reins to the ground. Knowing Buck wouldn't move from there with the reins on the ground, he then scurried back to a place where he could see more of the ridge. The rifle fell silent for a time. Perley figured the shooter was moving to a different position to get a better angle to shoot from. That might explain why he had not been hit by the many shots thrown at him while he was hustling to find cover.

He realized that he was in a very bad position. The words *cow pie* came to mind, and he could picture his brother John saying them. "Well, you're right, brother, I've stepped in another one, and this one looks like I ain't gonna be able to wipe it off my boot." It was then that the voice called out.

"Hey, Perley, you kinda rode yourself into a tight spot, didn't you?" The voice sounded familiar, but he couldn't nail it down. "You know, the way I see it, you ain't got a lot of choices. You can lay down there behind that little sandbank until I start takin' aim, instead of just skippin' bullets in the sand to keep you humpin' to get to cover. But I'm a sportin' man, myself, so I'm willin' to give you a chance to walk away from here alive."

Before he said the next word, Perley knew who it was, and he scolded himself for not paying enough attention to his gut feelings about the man. "Is Alice with you?" Perley called out.

"No," Drew called back. "Alice is on her way to visit some folks. She's all right. Don't worry about Alice. Right now, it's time for you to decide what you're gonna do, and you ain't got but two choices. One, you can set behind that sandy bank while I start pickin' it apart with this rifle. And believe me, Perley, I could have put you down at any point I wanted to while you were hustlin' your ass for cover. But I like you, Perley, so I'm willin' to give you a chance to see how fast you really are with that Colt six-gun you carry. And if you're as fast as everybody's talkin' about, then, hell, you can walk away from here and tell everybody you beat the fastest gun in Texas."

Perley didn't doubt Drew when he claimed he could have shot him at any time. He could imagine he was sitting on that ridge somewhere, watching him as he approached. "That does sound mighty sportin' of you, Drew, but how do you know you're the fastest gun in Texas? Texas is a big place."

"I found out the same way you're gonna find out you *ain't* the fastest," Drew called back. "So what's it gonna be? You gonna face me, man-to-man?"

"What if I don't want to shoot it out man-to-man?"

"Then I'm gonna shoot that bay horse you think so much of, and then really start takin' aim at that bank you're hidin' behind," Drew answered.

*That bushwhacker really will shoot Buck,* Perley thought.

"All right, but how do I know you won't shoot as soon as I get outta this creek?"

"Because I don't have to," Drew answered. "Don't worry, you'll get your chance to win a reputation. Let's get to it."

"All right," Perley said. "One last question. Are you one of the Ned Stark gang?"

"I'm not in anybody's gang. Ned's my cousin."

"I was beginnin' to think you had some connection with him," Perley said. "How 'bout tellin' me where they're holdin' Alice, so I can go get her when this little thing between us is done."

Drew couldn't help chuckling. "I like your spirit, Perley. I'm comin' out now. You do the same, guns holstered."

Perley saw him emerge from a deep gully, halfway up the slope. He made his way down to the bottom of the ridge, his gun in his holster, but his hand was hovering over the handle, leery of a trick. As he agreed, Perley climbed up from the dry creek and walked over to a flat area where Drew waited, smiling, finally getting Perley Gates where he wanted him, facing him with ten yards of Texas between them. "There ain't no use for lyin' now," Drew said. "Tell me the truth, did Curly Williams and Quirt Taylor pull on you first?"

"Yep," Perley answered, "both of 'em." His answer gave Drew pause, and during that pause, Perley whipped his six-gun out and put one round in the middle of Drew's chest. With a startled expression of shocked disbelief, Drew fell to his knees, making no attempt to draw his weapon. Perley watched him closely as he walked up to him.

Still on his knees, although fatally wounded, Drew

stared at Perley as he approached, his six-gun cocked and ready if needed. "I wasn't ready," Drew forced out between clenched teeth.

"I was," Perley replied. "I couldn't take a chance. You mighta been the fastest gun in Texas, for all I know, and Alice needs me." He took a step back then when Drew fell face forward, his last breath exhaling on the way down. *Good,* Perley thought, *I won't have to waste another bullet.* He then relieved him of his fancy gun belt and a sizable roll of money. Before going to get Buck, he took one final look down at the body and thought, *I never could understand why a man would want to stand face-to-face with another man and try to see who could shoot first.* To Perley, it was the definition of stupidity.

# CHAPTER 19

"What you're doing is wrong," Alice said to the coarse-looking man who took her roughly by the arm and led her into a small shed attached to the line shack. "I don't wanna go in there. I wanna go back to my mama. Drew didn't mean to give me to you. Please take me back home."

Clearly uncomfortable with the kidnapping of a six-year-old girl, Jim Duncan was hard pressed to think of what to tell her. Ned was already annoyed to have her there, and Jim was afraid if she caused any fuss at all, Ned would severely punish her. "You'll be all right in here, a whole little room all to yourself. Just be quiet, or you're liable to get Ned riled up, and you don't wanna do that. You be real quiet, and I'll bring you a cup of water and somethin' to eat, all right?"

"I wanna go home," Alice insisted.

"Now, honey, don't make a fuss and you'll be all right." He closed the door. There was no lock for the door, but he closed the hasp and secured it with a twenty-penny nail, especially for that purpose. He left her and returned to the line shack where Stark and Frank Deal were sitting at a crude table, using two upended wooden boxes as chairs.

"Where the hell is Drew?" Stark demanded. "He oughta been here by now."

"They musta been a little bit slow findin' out the little girl is gone," Frank answered.

"If he don't show up pretty quick, I'm gonna go look for him," Stark declared. He had been threatening to do that for about an hour. The plan that Drew had agreed to was for him to pick up the girl, since he was sure she would come with him. Then he and Jim and Frank would leave enough of a trail so anyone could follow it when they brought her out to the shack. When Perley followed them, they would bushwhack him. He had come to hate Perley Gates so passionately that he would know no satisfaction unless he personally put the bullet in him that finished him. And now, he was beginning to realize that Drew had gone back on the plan, just so he could gain a reputation for killing him. He had tried to tell Drew that killing Perley Gates wouldn't gain him a reputation, because he had never heard of him before. Drew had always had a big head about his fast gun. Ned should have suspected he was up to something when he insisted that the other boys should go with him to pick up the Parker brat.

"I told her I'd bring her a cup of water," Jim said. "You reckon we oughta give her somethin' to eat?"

"What the hell for?" Stark responded.

Jim shrugged and said, "I just thought she might be hungry and maybe thirsty—thought it might keep her quiet." When Stark didn't respond, Jim said, "I can give her some water outta my canteen. There ain't enough water in that little stream for the horses to drink."

"Hell, it's your canteen," Stark said. "If you wanna waste it on that young'un, that's up to you."

Sitting huddled up in the tiny shed, Alice could hear the three men talking, but she was not sure why they had taken her. Feeling alone and frightened, she held onto the one thought that sustained her. "Perley will come to get me," she murmured softly to herself. In her heart, she believed this, and it was enough to keep her from crying. She pictured her mother and her sister worrying about her, and it almost made her cry. So she told herself again, "Perley will come to get me."

Even as Alice told herself not to cry because Perley was coming, Perley was urging Buck to maintain a steady lope that was rapidly shortening the distance between them. Leading the big white gelding that Drew had ridden, he followed the trail left for him to see. The trail turned when it came to a trickle of a stream, and he followed it for about a quarter of a mile before he pulled Buck to a stop. He had been riding along the stream bank through a sparse copse of trees. But now there were no trees as the stream wound its way across a grassy plain, and he could see a shack of some sort sitting in another small patch of trees about one hundred yards away, backed up to a low ridge. He studied the shack for a few minutes. There were horses in a small corral beside the shack, which he decided must be an old line shack. Had he ridden out of the trees to follow the trail, he could have been easily seen by anyone in the shack.

There was no reason for anyone to be in a line shack this time of year. Even when in use, there was usually only one man. So he figured this was where Alice had been taken. Evidently Stark was holding the girl here, in the event a posse showed up at his ranch looking for her. He was still puzzled over Stark's interest in the kidnapping. Was he thinking of holding Alice for ransom, as he had considered earlier? Drew Dawson had evidently taken advantage of the kidnapping strictly for the purpose of a showdown with him. No matter what Stark's reason was for holding her, Perley's purpose was to rescue her and see her safely home, so he started thinking about how he was going to do it. While he was sitting there on Buck, he looked back at Drew's horse and an idea struck him.

He slid out of the saddle and grabbed his rope, then he tied Drew's horse's reins to the limb of a tree while he prepared to give him a tail. He pulled Drew's saddlebags off and tied them to one end of the rope. Then he played out about fifteen feet of the rope, cut it off, and tied that end to the saddle horn so that the saddlebags would drag about nine or ten feet behind the horse. He took a look at the saddlebags, picked them up and dropped them a couple of times, and decided they could use a little more weight. He removed the pistol and cartridges from Drew's fancy gun belt and put them in Buck's saddlebags. He put Drew's gun belt around the saddlebags and drew it up tight so it wouldn't fly off. "That's better," he said and prepared to set the white horse off to the races. He picked up the saddlebags and gun belt tail and carried it while he led the horse to the edge of the trees. With the reins wrapped around the saddle horn, he aimed the horse at the shack and gave him a slap on the rump. When the horse jumped, startled, Perley pulled his six-gun and fired three quick shots right behind him. When he ran, Perley threw the saddlebag tail up in the air after the charging horse. When it hit the ground, it bounced up behind the frightened horse, causing it to gallop even harder. Hoping Snowball did his part in his plan, Perley jumped on Buck and raced off in a circling direction to come up on the other side of the ridge behind the shack.

"What the hell!" Stark blurted when he heard the shots fired about a hundred yards from the shack. All three men ran out the door, their guns drawn.

"That's Drew's horse!" Frank exclaimed. They watched, astonished, as the riderless white horse galloped across the grassy prairie in front of the shack. The saddlebag tail bouncing high in the air every time it hit the ground effectively chased the confused horse relentlessly.

"What the hell?" Stark repeated, this time a question. "Where's Drew?"

"That don't look too good," Jim said, then uttered what they all thought, "Perley Gates."

"Maybe," Stark responded, then ordered. "Go after that crazy horse before it breaks a leg." He picked up his rifle while Jim and Frank ran to get their horses and galloped after the panicking horse. Out in front of the shack, he watched the woods from which the horse had come, waiting for whoever was chasing the horse.

Alice held her head up when she thought she heard someone whisper her name from behind the shed. Then she heard it again and turned toward the back of the shed to discover someone there. She could see a body through the wide cracks between the boards but couldn't tell who it was. "It's me, Perley," he whispered. "I'm gonna get you outta there." He grabbed one of the boards and gave it a good yank. The rusty nails offered no resistance, so he pulled the board out of the way and grabbed the next one.

He only had it pulled halfway aside when she whispered, "I can get through," and wedged her little body all the way out. She took hold of his hand then and followed him up the low ridge behind the line shack. He paused only once to take a look behind them to make sure her escape had not been discovered. Ned Stark was still standing out in front of the shack scanning the open expanse, his rifle ready. Then Perley ran up the slope at a trot, so Alice could keep up with him. Over the top, they ran to find Buck waiting at the bottom. Alice had not spoken another word until she was on Buck, behind Perley, with her arms locked tightly around him. "I knew you would come to get me," she said softly.

"You can count on that," he told her as the big bay gelding's hooves pounded the dirt in a steady ground-eating rhythm. "I just wanted to be sure you weren't late for supper." With Alice safely behind him, he was not worried about being chased. The two men he saw ride out after Snowball were of no concern to him. The frantic horse was leading them off in the opposite direction to town, and the last glimpse he got of him, Stark was still standing out in front of the line shack with his rifle ready to fire. Since it was not that long a ride back to town, he eased Buck back to a gentle lope.

When they arrived at the hotel, Perley rode Buck

around to the outside entrance to the dining room. When they went in the door, they were met by four worried women, who squealed joyous cries of relief upon seeing the little girl safely home. Perhaps the calmest female in the room was Alice, who stood by Perley's side until her mother came to her with arms outstretched. "Oh, baby, baby," Rachael repeated over and over. "I was so worried. If anything ever happened to you . . ."

"I wasn't afraid, Mama," Alice said. "I knew Perley would come to get me."

"I knew he would, too, darlin'," Rachael replied. She released Alice long enough to give Perley a big hug. "Thank you, Perley. Thank you for my daughter."

Her obvious sincerity embarrassed him slightly, so he took the opportunity to lighten the mood when he felt Melva leaning up against his leg. He placed a hand firmly on top of her head and said, "I don't know if I'da bothered, if it'da been this little scamp, though." She responded by sticking out her tongue at him. He pretended to try to grab it, which caused her a giggling fit.

The gathering of women around him smiled at Melva's giggling. Rachael, watching the happy reunion, couldn't help thinking what a wonderful father he would be. *If I was a few years younger . . .* she caught herself thinking and immediately shook her head to clear it.

Realizing there was no one in the dining room but the four women around him, when he would have expected Possum and Rooster to be waiting there as well, he asked, "Where's everybody else?"

"They're down at the Buffalo Hump," Bess was the

first to answer. "They're gettin' up a posse to go after Alice."

"We shoulda told you that as soon as you got here," Emma said. "You'd better get down there and let them know Alice is back safely."

"I don't know what they're gonna do about Drew," Kitty wondered. It occurred to the women that they were so happy to see Alice's safe return, but there had been no mention of the man who carried her away. They all looked at Perley then.

"They won't have to do anything about Drew," he said. "I reckon I'd best get down to the saloon to tell 'em about Alice." With that, he turned and went out the door.

When he got to the Buffalo Hump, he found the core of the council, the men who were committed to take action when the town required action, gathered to decide what to do. "Perley!" Rooster bellowed as soon as he saw him enter the room.

"Did you find 'em?" Possum called out.

"Did Drew Dawson come back with you?" Sheriff Mason asked.

"I found 'em," Perley answered. "Alice is all right. She wasn't harmed. Drew ain't comin' back. He's dead." The reaction to his statements was predictable, so he was quickly pressed to explain. He told them of Drew's involvement with Ned Stark in the kidnapping, but he could not explain exactly what their demands were going to be. Ransom possibly, he guessed, since he didn't realize the real purpose was to draw him out to his death. He told them that he had been given no choice other than to kill Drew Dawson. He didn't offer any details of the killing. As far as Ned Stark and the two remaining members of his gang, he said that he had no actual contact with them. He just sneaked in and got Alice out. And the last he saw of Stark he was standing in front of a line shack while he watched his men chasing a runaway horse.

His explanation was adequate for the gathering of men in the saloon with the exception of Possum and Rooster. Possum stepped up close beside him and informed him, "You're gonna have to tell me a helluva lot more about it than that, especially the part about Drew Dawson."

"There ain't much to tell," Perley replied. "I'm wonderin' now what these fellows are thinkin' about doin'." Then it occurred to him. "What about the trial?" He looked around him and realized the saloon was no longer set up like a courtroom. His concern for Alice's safety had driven thoughts of Junior Humphrey out of his mind.

"I reckon you're faster than Drew was, right?" Rooster asked, ignoring his question about the trial.

"I ain't got no idea how fast he was," Perley answered. "It just didn't come to that. I was lucky to get a shot at him when he wasn't expectin' it."

Rooster gazed at him with a skeptical eye and was about to call him on his story when he was interrupted by Ralph Wheeler calling the meeting to order. "There isn't any doubt that we're all mighty relieved to know that Alice Parker is back home safe and sound. It's sorrowful news to hear that Drew Dawson was playing us all for suckers. Nobody ever thought he was in cahoots with Ned Stark. That's what you said, isn't it, Perley?"

"Yes, sir, that's right," Perley answered. "Matter of fact, Ned was Drew's cousin." His reply brought a wave of snorts of disgust for their gullibility.

Wheeler continued. "We need to decide if we should take any action against Ned Stark and his two men now."

Sheriff Mason stood up to respond. "It doesn't make any difference if Alice Parker is home safe. Ned Stark and his men are guilty of kidnappin', and that's a serious crime. As sheriff of Bison Gap, it's my duty to arrest 'em and bring 'em in for trial. I'm gonna need some help with three of 'em to arrest, so I'm askin' for volunteers to ride in a posse, the more, the better." His request was immediately answered by half a dozen hands raised. Mason nodded his appreciation for their support. He looked at Perley and said, "I'd like to have you go with us, Perley."

"I figured you knew I would go with you," Perley responded.

"'Preciate it," Mason said. "I reckon we could get ready to go as soon as everybody gets their horses saddled and their weapons."

That suggestion was met with some reluctance on the part of several of the volunteers. The first to speak was Rex Cooper. "It's gettin' kinda late in the day to start out, ain't it? I don't know how many of us have ever been out to that ranch. I know I ain't ever been there. I ain't sure I could find it, especially in the dark."

His remarks were met with general agreement, and no one admitted that they knew where the ranch house actually was, whether they did or not. It was awfully close to suppertime, and it would be a while before everyone could prepare to ride. "I don't know," Horace Brooks remarked, "but does it make that much difference whether we go out there tonight, or in the mornin'?"

They generally agreed that it didn't make a great deal of difference, figuring that Stark would be holed up at that ranch house. Mason was more in favor of going right away, but he was not going without a posse. So the final decision was to ride first thing in the morning. After that was settled, Perley finally learned the outcome of Junior's trial when Wheeler made a final announcement. "I know we said the hanging was supposed to be tomorrow morning, but because of the posse tomorrow, we'll reschedule it for day after tomorrow." Since it was nearing suppertime, most of the crowd departed, leaving the usual evening crowd to consume Henry Lawrence's whiskey supply and rehash the events of the day, a day that was crowded with them.

Rooster decided to join Perley and Possum for supper in the hotel dining room. So they walked back up the street together, with Possum pumping Perley for more details about Drew Dawson's death every step of the way. Finally, Perley gave up and told them how the confrontation actually played out. "So, this whole kidnapping thing was just so Drew could throw down with you to see who was the fastest gun in Texas?"

"I don't know if it was or not, but he decided to wait for me to follow them when they took Alice. Figured it would be a good opportunity to find out, I reckon. He talked like it was important to him."

"But not to you," Possum said. "So you just went ahead and shot him down before he was ready to draw?"

"Well, hell," Perley answered. "I didn't know if he was the fastest gun in Texas or not."

Possum shook his head slowly while he thought that over. "I swear, Perley, you're smarter than I give you credit for."

"Too bad you couldn't hang onto that white horse ol' Drew rode," Rooster said.

"Like I said," Perley explained, "I needed that horse to help me slip in to get Alice outta that little shed they had her in."

"What about that fancy quick-draw gun belt and six-gun Drew wore?" Possum asked.

"The last time I saw them," Perley said, "they were chasing that big white horse of his across a stretch of open prairie."

When they walked into the dining room, the women were anxious to know about the meeting. When they were told that a posse was set to ride out to Stark's ranch in the morning, the news was welcomed by all. Maybe, they hoped, the long reign of lawlessness might be at an end with the destruction of Ned Stark's gang of hoodlums. "I set the tables up to give us one big one again," Rachael said. "So set yourselves down. Bess has made a sugar cake to celebrate Alice getting home safe. So save a little room for a slice of that after you polish off her Texas stew." As usually happened, Perley sat down with Alice on one side of him and Melva on the other.

# CHAPTER 20

Supper was a considerably less joyous occasion at Ned Stark's ranch. Had it been left up to Stark, there would have been no supper at all. He was too angry and frustrated to eat, and only drank coffee because Jim Duncan made a pot of it to eat with the smoked beef he and Frank ate. "You better eat some of this meat, Ned," Frank said. "Need to keep your strength up." He exchanged glances with Jim. They both were hesitant to say much to Stark when he was in a mood like the one he was gripped with now. They knew he was sulking over the death of Drew Dawson. Even though as late as this morning, they thought Ned was almost at a point where he was sick and tired of Drew's tendency to try to run things his way. But now that Drew had been killed, Ned was back to thinking of the loss of his cousin as if he was someone dear. His death served to increase the heat under an already intense fire in Ned's veins to kill Perley Gates. Perley Gates had effectively destroyed Ned's outlaw empire, and now he was killing his kin.

After they had finally stopped Drew's frantic horse from running itself to death and removed the saddlebags and gun belt, they had little doubt that it was the work of one man. And they saw it as a sign of contempt from Perley Gates. The insult, added to the tail he had attached to the horse, was the rescue of the girl right from under their noses. Neither Jim nor Frank could understand why Perley Gates didn't shoot Stark while he was standing distracted in front of the shack. To Stark it was a message of contempt and meant to tell him that Perley could kill him any time he chose. They had not been eager to do so, but Stark insisted they would go to find Drew's body, in spite of the possibility of an ambush. His two one-armed outlaws were relieved to find Drew lying face down on the ground, a bullet hole dead center in his chest. When they turned him over, the expression of surprise was still frozen on his face. With a great deal of effort, due to the fact that both Frank and Jim were working with the use of only one hand, they managed to bring Drew's body back to the ranch. They carried the body into the house, but there was no suitable place to put it down except the one bed that was in Ned's room. After some deliberation, Ned decided to put Drew on the kitchen table. "That'll get him off the floor," he decided. That was possibly the moment when Frank decided, if he survived to see nightfall, he would leave this cursed land before daybreak. Frank divulged his plans to depart that night to Jim.

"You just gonna ride off without tellin' Ned you're leavin'?" Jim asked.

"I think if I don't, he's liable to try to stop me, and the shape I'm in with this lame arm, I don't feel like puttin' up a fight. You know as well as I do that we're finished here. He's rantin' and ravin' about how he's gonna build the gang back up like it was when we joined up. And damned if I can see how that's gonna happen. Word gets out about everybody but the three of us gettin' gunned down, who do you think is gonna wanna ride for Ned Stark?"

"Maybe you're right," Jim said. "I know we talked about it before, but I never thought we'd quit him. I'll admit, I have thought about it some more."

"I swear, Jim, he's just gonna get us killed before this business with Perley Gates is done with. Did you ever think óne man was gonna gun down Curly Williams and Quirt Taylor and Eli Priest and Jack Sledge, and all the rest of 'em?" He shook his head. "I'm goin'. I ain't waitin' to welcome that posse when they come after us."

Jim Duncan bit his lower lip as he thought about what Frank was proposing. With Frank gone, it would just be him left to take orders from a crazy man. He had ridden with a couple of other gangs before, and he had never quit one without telling the other members. But none of those gang leaders had gone crazy with the hatred of one gunslinger like Ned had. "What the hell? I'm in," he decided. "I'll go with you."

"Good," Frank said. "We'll do better when there's two of us." There was no more talk about it at that time, however, for they heard Ned bellow from the kitchen, calling them. "What is it, Ned?" He called back, then to Jim, he said, "We'd best go see what he wants."

"We need to get Drew in the ground," Stark said when they walked in the kitchen. "We gotta dig him a decent grave."

"That'ud be the proper thing to do, all right, Ned," Jim said. "But that ain't gonna be an easy thing to do right now. With both me and Frank with a crippled arm, I don't see how either one of us can do any good with a shovel. You're the only one with two good hands."

"Maybe the three of us could carry him outside and lay him in a gully or somethin'," Frank suggested, "and try to find some rocks to lay on top of him to keep the critters away from him."

Stark didn't respond at once but continued to look at each one of them in turn as if trying to decide if they were trying to jape him. Finally, he spoke. "No, leave him on the table tonight. We'll decide what to do with him in the mornin'."

"Whatever you say, Ned, you're the boss," Frank said. "We'll leave him right there on the table. It's kinda like when the governor dies and they lay him out on a stand, so everybody can honor him before they put him in the ground."

"Yeah, that's best," Stark said. "You boys go on back on the porch and keep your eyes on that path down to the house. I wanna give anybody comin' in here tonight a real warm welcome."

They did as he said and returned to the porch. "I musta missed it when he said he'd dig the damn grave," Frank japed. "He's got two good arms."

"I druther be out here on the porch than in there with him and his cousin," Jim remarked. "But I think if those folks were gonna get up a posse to come out here tonight, they'da already been here. It ain't that far away. I think they'll damn-sure show up in the mornin', but we won't be here to welcome 'em. I know they're not gonna let us get away with stealin' that little girl."

They waited Ned out until he finally became too sleepy to stay awake and came out to tell them he didn't think a posse would show up that night but to be ready early in the morning. They assured him that they would, so he went into his room and went to bed. It now became a question for the two men as to how long they should wait to go into the main room, pack up their bedrolls, get all their belongings, and slip out to the corral to saddle their horses. They sat and waited and listened. Finally they heard Ned break into a chorus of snoring and knew it was time to pack up. Frank tiptoed up to the bedroom door and listened. When he was sure the noise he heard was steady, sound sleep, he looked back at Jim and nodded.

Fearful of being caught in the act of desertion, they hurried to roll up their spare shirts, socks, and underwear in their bedrolls, and picked up their saddlebags and war bags that held personal items. When they were ready, they went into the kitchen and loaded a sack with smoked beef and coffee, as well as the coffeepot, all the while feeling the gaping mouth and eyes of the late Drew Dawson staring up from the kitchen table.

They moved quietly out the front door and headed for the corral, where they quickly saddled their horses and loaded one of the packhorses with the bags of food and extra ammunition. Ready at last, they climbed on their horses, turned them away from the barn and the corral, and headed up the path leading away from the ranch. Suddenly startled by the report of a rifle shot, Frank looked at Jim beside him as he slumped forward on his horse's neck, shot in the back. In less than a second, Frank felt the impact of the shot that struck him in the back. He heeled his horse for speed, but a second shot closer to the center of his back caused him to jerk straight up in the saddle before sliding sideways off his horse.

Stark walked up to stand over Frank Deal, who was hanging onto life by a thread. He poked him in the side with the muzzle of his rifle. "I won't abide a coward," he said, cranked in a new cartridge, and pulled the trigger. In no hurry, he walked slowly up the path a dozen yards to the horse waiting there. Jim had not fallen off but was lying fatally wounded on the horse's neck. Stark took the horse's bridle in hand and calmed the nervous gelding. Then he pulled Jim's boot out of the stirrup and pushed it up to dump him on the ground.

Still alive but helpless to defend himself, Jim lay there, pretending to be dead and praying Stark would be satisfied that he was done. Stark stood over him for a long time, watching him, knowing he was pretending. After what seemed an eternity to the man dying there, Stark was no longer amused by his victim's helpless effort to live. He put a bullet in his brain.

As agreed, the posse was mounted and gathered in front of the stable shortly after sunup the next morning. Since no one had claimed to know exactly where Ned Stark's ranch house was located, Rooster Crabb volunteered to lead the posse. He had scouted Stark's ranch along Oak Creek once. At the time, he was reluctant to try to find the ranch headquarters, but he remembered a couple of trails that looked as if they could lead to it. Like everyone else in Bison Gap, he hadn't wanted to find the actual hideout, afraid that if he did, he might not live to report it. So he led the posse with the sheriff, Perley, and Possum riding close behind him. They were followed by John Payne, Rex Cooper, and Floyd Jenkins.

As everyone in Bison Gap suspected, the posse found that the ranch headquarters was not hard to find at all. Following the first trail that Rooster suggested, they rode up from the creek on a well-traveled path that bore the hoofprints of horses and cattle. It led to a wider trail that went to a stream, then the trail followed that stream to the path down to the house, barn, and stable. Before riding down that path, Rooster signaled a halt.

"What is it, Rooster?" Sheriff Mason asked as he pulled his horse up even with Rooster's.

"Lookee yonder," Rooster said and pointed toward the ranch house.

"Yeah, I see it," Mason said. "That's gotta be it."

"I ain't talkin' 'bout the blame house," Rooster said and pointed again. "Lookee yonder."

The sheriff saw what he was pointing at then, two bodies, approximately a dozen yards apart, lying beside the path. At once alert then, Mason warned the posse. "Looks like somebody's been shot. Get your weapons ready to use."

"They musta been lyin' there a while," Perley said.

"What makes you say that?" the sheriff asked.

"'Cause we've been ridin' between here and the creek for a pretty good while and we didn't hear any shots," Perley said.

"Right, I didn't think of that," Mason said. "I reckon we can move ahead and see who they are." He moved past Rooster and led the way down the path to the first body. "That's Jim Duncan," he said. Moving on to the second body, he said, "And this here's Frank Deal." He was very familiar with the two men.

"Both of 'em shot in the back," Possum said. "If I was to take a guess, I'd say that these two boys decided to take off and leave ol' Ned alone, but Ned didn't take to the idea." He looked over at Perley and asked, "Whadda you think, partner?"

"It looks that way to me," Perley answered. "So I reckon we got just one man to deal with. Whaddaya wanna do, Sheriff?"

Mason hesitated while he decided what best to do. "We most likely oughta search that barn and the stable to make sure he ain't hidin' in there somewhere," Possum suggested, having ridden in a posse before. "You gonna try to holler him outta the house?"

"Yeah," Mason quickly answered, "that's what I'm gonna do." He gave his orders to his posse then. "Couple of you men stay here with me to watch the house. Possum, you and Perley and Rooster go look through the barn and the stable." Then they all rode down closer to the house and Perley and his two partners broke off to ride to the barn. They had not reached the barn when they heard Sheriff Mason call out. "Ned Stark! Come on outta there with your hands in the air! You're under arrest for kidnappin'!" Remembering the two bodies just found on the path behind him, he added, "And murder!" There was no response to his summons, so he called out again. "Stark, ain't no use to try to hide! Come on outta there!"

While the sheriff was calling in vain for Stark's surrender, the three he sent to the barn and the stable were conducting a cautious search. The two bodies just found were evidence enough of the state of mind the fugitive was in. If that wasn't enough, the two horses, still saddled, found in the stable was confirmation. They were not in a stall, just left to wander in and out as they chose. There were no horses in the corral, and the gate was left open. After a thorough search of the barn with no luck, there were only a couple of places left to look outside the house, an outhouse and a smokehouse. From the appearance of both of these outbuildings, they concluded that they had not been used since the original owners of the property had lived there. To confirm it, Possum walked up to the outhouse, completely surrounded by shoulder-high weeds, placed his boot on the side of it and kicked it over on its other side. They checked the smokehouse, which was sitting with the door open, grown up in weeds as well, to find it a maze of spiderwebs. "If he's here, he's in the house!" Rooster yelled to the sheriff.

Mason called out his summons once more before yelling to Rooster, "We're goin' in. You fellows go in the back. Watch out to make sure we don't shoot each other."

The house was small, in keeping with the size of the original cattle ranch. There were not many places to hide, and much to the relief of Floyd Jenkins, Ned Stark was nowhere to be found. Floyd had volunteered for the posse primarily to prove his courage to the rest of the men. The two search parties converged on the kitchen, where they discovered the body of Drew Dawson lying on the kitchen table, causing Possum to remark dryly. "If that's what's for dinner, I reckon I'll pass."

"Well, he ain't here," Horace Brooks remarked, since no one else had stated the obvious. "Reckon we'd best take those two horses back with us, don'tcha think, Sheriff?"

"Reckon so," the sheriff replied. "Let's look around outside and see if there's any sign he mighta left."

He was just as happy to let Stark be gone from there, hopefully to Colorado or somewhere far from Bison Gap. His past dealings with the vicious outlaw were still a burden upon his conscience and he hoped his disappearance would dim the memory of that time with the town council.

Outside, the posse searched half-heartedly for any place Stark could possibly be hiding, but there was nothing for half a mile in any direction but flat treeless prairie. The only recent trail left by more than one horse pointed toward a low ridge in the distance. And from the direction it led, Perley told them the trail might lead to the line shack where he had found Alice Parker. With little hope of finding anything else, and dinnertime approaching before long, it was decided to follow that trail on the chance Stark might have gone there.

They waited while Horace rigged up a lead rope for the two horses. And while they waited, Mason asked Floyd if he wanted to bury the body on the kitchen table, since he was the undertaker. "Nope," Floyd answered. "I say just leave him where he is."

"Suits me," the sheriff said, so they closed the front and back doors and left Drew Dawson to haunt the house.

When Horace had the two spare horses rigged up, the posse rode off to follow the trail. As Perley had figured, it led to the line shack. After another cautious approach, they found that Stark was not there. They looked the place over, just out of curiosity, and Perley showed them where Alice had been kept. With the last of the posse's enthusiasm drained by then, the party turned toward home, taking the same route Perley had taken when rescuing Alice. If nothing else, the posse had accomplished a general feeling that Stark was gone, and logical thinking told them he would stay gone. And that was progress in the town's hopes to become a major city.

Perley was not surprised that Ned Stark had decided his best option was to run to escape the hangman's noose, although it was disturbing to think he might descend upon another settlement to infect with his lawlessness. His thoughts were now naturally about going home. He and Possum had come to Bison Gap to see if they could be of any help to their friends. He was sorry that it had turned out to be another case where he was forced to use his six-gun. It seemed that it was always his destiny to resort to violence, no matter how he tried to avoid it. There was always a cow pie waiting for him. Maybe he should never leave the Triple-G for any reason, but he knew he could never refuse a request for help. Then he had to tell himself it was worth it when he thought about how things were in Bison Gap now that Stark and his kind were gone. The town had a sheriff who was doing the job he was hired for. He had a willing town council to back him up. Emma and Possum's investment in the hotel was now doing well, and Rachael's dining room was thriving. With Stark and his crew gone, all that would continue to improve. He realized he should be feeling pretty good about the situation. "Hell," he muttered, "I could tell John I stomped that cow pie right in the ground."

"What did you say, Perley?" Possum asked.

"What?" Perley started, just realizing he had said

that last out loud. "I said I hope Bess has still got some of that pie around that we had at dinner."

"Won't be much chance of that," Rooster commented, "fast as that pie was disappearin'."

"You was lookin' there like your mind was a thousand miles away," Possum said. "I thought that one little drink of whiskey was puttin' a buzz on you. Maybe we'd best get on over to the hotel and get some supper. That whiskey hits kinda hard on an empty stomach."

Perley looked up at the clock on the wall behind the bar. "It'll be about fifteen minutes yet before Rachael opens the door. And how often does Ralph Wheeler buy you a drink? We better have one more, or he might think we don't appreciate it." It was a rare occasion when the mayor would spring for a drink all around. But he, like everyone else, was in high spirits since finding out that the Stark ranch house was now occupied by someone not likely to give anybody any trouble. In fact, it was already being referred to by some of the council as the "Dawson Place."

As Perley sat there in the Buffalo Hump, watching Possum and Rooster enjoying the company of the major citizens of Bison Gap, it made him wonder if he might be riding back to the Triple-G by himself. Rooster had been transformed from a quirky character not to be taken seriously into a seasoned veteran whose views reflected common sense. And Possum had established himself as a respected member of the town council, in addition to owning one half of the Bison House Hotel. Perley had to ask himself, *why would Possum want to leave what he has built here in just this short amount of time?* He hoped Possum wouldn't give up his newfound status in this growing community because of some sense of loyalty he felt he owed him. *Maybe I'll hang around a little longer, myself. I haven't been away from the Triple-G that long.*

His musing was distracted then when he saw a stranger walk into the crowded saloon. At least he was a stranger to him because he couldn't recall ever having seen him around town. While he watched out of bored curiosity, the stranger walked up to talk to Horace Brooks. They spoke for only a few moments before Horace looked around the room briefly, then pointed toward him. Perley had no time to wonder who the stranger was because he made his way straight to him. "You Perley Gates?" The stranger asked him abruptly. Perley said that he was. "My name's Spade Ramey. You heard of me?"

"Spade Ramey?" Perley had to think a moment. "Nope, I'm sorry but I don't recall the name. Is there some reason I should?"

The stranger grinned at him as if Perley was putting him on. "Maybe you're as dumb as your name," he said.

Perley suddenly realized the stranger's purpose in seeking him out. "Oh, no, uh-uh," he said at once. "I ain't interested in findin' out how fast you are with that handgun."

Interpreting Perley's response as cowardice, Spade was only encouraged. "I heard you gunned down Curly Williams, and I say that's a damn lie. I don't believe you did. I just think you're tellin' people you did. Ain't that about right?"

"I'll go along with that," Perley answered. "Whatever you believe, that's what I'll believe. All right?"

"You tryin' to smart-mouth me? 'Cause if you are,

I'll put some airholes in your hide right where you set." Spade threatened.

"No, indeed, Spamy," Perley hastened to say. "I just met you, but I can tell you're a reasonable fellow."

"Spamy, huh?' Ramey growled when Perley mispronounced his name. "That's all the slack I'm givin' you, Perley. You asked for it, and now you're gonna get it, you yellow dog."

"Did you have to bring my mother into this?" Perley asked. "You'd really see she's a wonderful woman, if you ever met her. Well, it's been right nice talkin' to you, and I apologize for mispronouncin' your name. I'm afraid it's time for me to go to supper now."

By this time, the men close around the table where Perley sat were aware of a disturbance going on in the middle of the saloon. One of them, Possum Smith, knew what was happening as soon as he turned around and saw the stranger, his gun hung low in his fast-draw holster, leaning menacingly over Perley's table. He pushed his way quickly through the crowd gathering around the table. "Hold on, there, cowboy! Get the hell outta here before you get thrown out!"

Quick as the blink of an eye, Ramey's .44 was out and pointed at Possum's face. "You old fool. Who are you, his daddy? I'll put a hole in that old gray head of your'n."

Perley had no choice at this point. "Back off, Possum, I'm the one he wants. No use in you gettin' in the middle of this." To Spade, he said, "Get that gun outta his face, and I'll give you what you want, but let's take it outside. There's too many people in here. Somebody's liable to get shot. All right? That's what you came in here for, ain't it?"

Spade grinned and holstered his pistol. "All right,

Perley, we'll go outside." He backed away to give Perley room to get up, shoving Possum back in the process. "I'll leave your little boy layin' in the street out front, Daddy. You can tell folks that Spade Ramey gunned him down." He made sure he said it loud enough for everyone gathered there to hear his name. Back to Perley then, he said, "If I have to come back in here after you, I'll shoot you down in the middle of this saloon."

"I'll be right behind you," Perley said and got up from the table. He had seen Spade whip the .44 out when Possum threatened, so he knew the man was quick. Quicker than he was, he wasn't sure. "You know, if you change your mind, that's all right," he felt inclined to say as he followed him through the saloon doors.

"Hah," was the answer he got from Spade.

The crowded saloon emptied, because everyone was anxious to see for themselves what only a handful of folks had seen firsthand. They gathered on the boardwalk in front of the Buffalo Hump jockeying for position so as not to have their view of the duel obstructed. Perley made one last attempt. "I don't wanna kill you, Ramey. I don't even know you. If we don't do this, I'll tell people that you're faster than me. Whaddaya say?"

It only served to encourage Spade. "If you don't face me like a man, I'll shoot you down like I would a suck-egg dog," he warned.

They walked out in the center of the street to face each other, causing unsuspecting people passing in wagons or on horseback to suddenly veer out of the way when they realized what was happening. "All right," Perley said, "this is your call. How do you wanna do it?"

"I'm ready," Spade said, still smiling. "You pull whenever you're ready."

"You sure you don't wanna have somebody count to three or something, so that I don't get the jump on you?" Perley asked.

"I'm sure, Perley," he scoffed. "You pull that six-gun as soon as you get up your nerve."

"Okay," Perley said, "if that's the way you want it." Ramey's knees buckled when he suddenly found himself staring at the business end of Perley's six-gun, cocked and aimed at his chest, his own hand having never reached for his .44. Staring death in the face, Ramey froze, unable to move. "Spade," Perley said calmly, "you need to find another line of work."

Ramey remained frozen, unable to believe what his eyes told him, until Possum took him by the arm. "You'd best count this as your lucky day, son. You get on your horse and go on back home." Completely bewildered, Possum stood there and watched until he disappeared past the end of the street.

"What happened?" Someone on the boardwalk asked. "I don't know, I didn't see it," someone else answered. "There wasn't a shot," another voice said. Pretty soon, there was a great deal of discussion with only one or two people claiming they actually saw Perley draw.

"I saw it," Possum said. He knew to keep his eyes glued on Perley's hand. "The damn fool told Perley to draw first." He pushed through the spectators to get to Perley. "Come on, Perley, let's get away from here. It's time for supper." He knew the turmoil churning in Perley's mind.

# CHAPTER 21

Perley did the best he could to keep up with Alice and Melva's expectations from him at supper that night. They expected a good measure of good-natured teasing from him. It was not so easy on this night after the confrontation with Spade Ramey at the Buffalo Hump. Even though no death had occurred as a result of his confrontation with Spade Ramey, it still troubled him that he often found himself in situations like that one.

The senseless contest that men participated in to see who was quickest with a gun was something he would never understand. That was why he faced a man with a weapon only when he was given no choice. The exception was in a case like the outright shooting of Drew Dawson. If Drew had killed him, he didn't know what would have happened to Alice. So he took Dawson's life without hesitation, but not without regret that he had to be the one to rid the world of Dawson.

Possum guessed what was going on in Perley's mind, so he said, "Why don't you girls let Perley rest for a while? He's had a long day." He met Perley's gaze when he glanced at him. "Sometimes you just do what you gotta do, don't you, partner?"

"I reckon so," Perley answered, realizing then that his moodiness must be apparent. So he resolved to break out of it. "Rooster," he said, "I was thinkin' about ridin' out to your place tomorrow to see if you're keepin' it up like you oughta."

"Did you like that ham you just finished a slab of?" Rooster asked.

"Yep, it was good ham," Perley replied.

"Well, that oughta tell you I'm doin' my part in givin' this dining room somethin' to eat besides beef," Rooster crowed. "You can ask Rachael about that."

Rachael took her cue and remarked. "Yes, indeed, Rooster is doing a dandy job with the pork, and chicken, too."

"You come on out and I'll show you what one man can do, if he knows what he's about," Rooster said.

"I'll do that," Perley replied. "You stayin' here tonight?" Rooster said that he thought he would, so Perley said, "Good, we'll ride out after breakfast. How 'bout you, Possum?"

"Might as well," Possum allowed, "might be entertainin'."

With that decided, they didn't linger around the supper table very long, deciding to retire to the front porch of the hotel to give the rocking chairs a workout. Rooster filled his corncob pipe he said he only smoked on special occasions. "What's the special occasion?" Possum asked.

"Why, hell, the end of the Ned Stark gang in Bison Gap." Rooster answered. "Ain't that special enough for you?"

"That it is," Possum said. "If I had a pipe, I'd smoke to that, too."

Rooster got quiet for a full minute while he lit his pipe, took a few puffs, then tamped the tobacco down again and relit it. Content that it would smoke steady then, he became serious. "I reckon it's about time somebody thanked you two for coming all the way back here to help us here in Bison Gap. This town woulda gone straight to hell, if you hadn't come when I sent you that letter. I was just hopin' when I sent it, but I kinda knew you'd come."

"Why, we appreciate that, Rooster," Possum replied. "But I expect it's Perley that was the key to openin' this lock. I just came with him to get him up in the mornin's."

"I'd have to disagree with that," Perley insisted. "It was Possum that decided to come down here as soon as I got the letter. I just came to get away from the Triple-G for a spell."

They were still trying to outtalk each other on who did the most for Bison Gap when Richard Hoover, the postmaster's son, ran by the hotel. Seeing Possum sitting on the porch, he stopped and came back to tell him that the council was calling a special meeting in the morning at the Buffalo Hump at nine o'clock. "Special meetin', huh?" Possum asked. "Well, I expect you'd best tell Mrs. Slocum about it, too."

"Mr. Wheeler said I didn't have to tell the hotel or the barber," Richard continued. "He said it didn't have nothin' to do with them, so there wasn't any use in botherin' 'em. But I saw you settin' here, and I expect he wants you."

"All right, thank you, son," Possum said. "I'll tell Emma if there's anything that might interest her.

Don't hurt to keep up with what everybody is doin'."
After the boy ran on down the street, Possum said.
"Well, looks like I won't be ridin' out to your place
with you and Perley in the mornin', but I'll ride on
out there after this special meetin' is over."

The talk went on long after Rooster's corncob pipe
had burnt out, and it was Perley who surrendered to
the bed first, but his declaration that he was sleepy was
followed by one from each of his two companions.

After a hearty breakfast of hot cakes, sausage, and
scrambled eggs, Perley and Rooster left to get their
horses from the stable, leaving Possum to soak up
some more of the coffee. As they rode the narrow
path along the creek, Rooster was reminded of the
night when he and Possum went looking for Perley.
When they came to the spot where Perley had surprised them, he pulled up. "If you hadda built a fire
that night we was lookin for you, I woulda seen it
from here. And you wouldn'ta got the jump on me."
Rooster saw fit to remind him.

"Why, I expect that's right," Perley conceded, knowing that it was important to the crusty little man. With
that question satisfied in Rooster's mind, they continued on to his cabin, where they took care of Rooster's
daily chores. In Perley's mind, it was a day he needed.
Peaceful and relaxed, with no decisions to be made
beyond whether to feed the chickens or the hogs first.
A little before noon, they saw Possum coming down
the path from the creek trail.

"Meetin' must not have been very important,"
Rooster greeted him when he rode up to the barn.

"I figured it couldn'ta been 'cause Dick Hoover's boy didn't tell me to be there."

"You're right," Possum said as he stepped down from the gray gelding. "I coulda rode out with you two this mornin'. Wasn't nobody there but Wheeler, Dick Hoover, Henry Lawrence, George Gilbert from the bank, and the preacher. Ralph told me he didn't mean to bother me with it. They was just gonna talk about business loans and such. I don't know why Reverend Poole was there—to keep 'em honest, I reckon," he joked. "Anyway, I figured there wasn't nothin' I could do for 'em, so I came on out here."

"Might be you shoulda stayed at the meetin'," Rooster cracked. "Since they had a representative for the Lord, they mighta needed one from the devil, too."

It was an easy day. Rooster took advantage of the extra help and completed some repairs to the stalls in his little barn and replaced some broken boards on his front porch. The day passed too quickly in Perley's mind, but it served to free his mind to return to its usual carefree state. Before he knew it, it was close to suppertime, so they saddled the horses and rode back into town.

"I figured you three would show up as soon as my beef stew was done," Bess greeted them when they walked into the dining room.

"That's right," Rooster replied. "I could smell those biscuits in the oven way over on the other side of Oak Creek."

Hearing Bess greeting them in the dining room, Rachael came from the kitchen to give Perley a message. "Perley, Ralph Wheeler was looking for you this afternoon. He said there was something he wanted to ask you. I told him you'd probably be back for supper, and I'd give you the message."

"Wants to ask me a question, huh?" Perley responded. "He didn't say about what?"

"Nope," she answered. "I didn't ask him."

*I reckon I can guess,* Perley thought, *the same question he's asked before.* "I reckon I'd best go see what he wants before I sit down to eat—catch him before he leaves the store." He had given in to Wheeler's request before, when he agreed to take the job of sheriff temporarily. But he thought now John Mason had shown he deserved the chance to hold that office. And being a sheriff was just not something Perley wanted to do. "I'll be right back," he told them. "I don't think this'll take long."

He hurried over to Wheeler's General Merchandise and was glad to see that Ralph had not closed for the day. "Rachael said you wanted to talk to me," he said when he walked in.

"Oh, yes, Perley, thanks for coming by," Wheeler said. "I hope I didn't interrupt your supper."

"Not a-tall," Perley responded. "I hadn't got started yet."

Wheeler hesitated for a moment as if trying to decide how to begin. "First off, I'd like to thank you on behalf of all the people of Bison Gap for all you've done to rid us of the curse of Ned Stark. Frankly, it couldn't have been done without you, and there ain't anybody in the whole town that doesn't know that's true."

Perley felt downright embarrassed. He had not expected more than a simple "thanks for the help." His natural modesty made it difficult for him to accept such accolades without an attempt at humility. "That's mighty nice of you to say that, Mr. Mayor, but I wasn't by myself. Possum and Rooster and all of the council were all together in getting rid of Ned Stark. And I have to give your sheriff credit for standin' tall when the time came. Truth is, I've got good friends here, and I wanted to help them if I could."

"I respect that," Wheeler said, "and I figured you'd respond just like you did." He grimaced as if something hurt before continuing. "Secondly," he said, "I had a meeting this morning with some of the council members about a problem we feel we're faced with in the future. It has to do with you, and I'm left with the uncomfortable duty to ask you to leave Bison Gap, for the sake of those friends you mentioned." When Perley made no reply, obviously struck speechless, Wheeler hastened to explain. "That episode yesterday at the Buffalo Hump was an example of what the council thinks we can expect from now on, as long as you're in town. Every gunslinger in Texas will be showing up in Bison Gap just like that one yesterday." Wheeler threw his hands up in frustration. "Ned Stark hadn't been gone a day when that Ramey, or whatever his name was, showed up here looking for the man who shot Curly Williams."

After a long pause while he tried to recover his wits, Perley replied. "I reckon I understand why you feel that way. How soon do you want me outta town?"

"Well, the sooner the better," Wheeler answered. "Damn it, Perley, I know you're not one of those gunslingers, and I feel like an ungrateful lowdown dog to ask you to leave town after what you've done for us. But it's just what we feel is best for the town, and I was the unfortunate one who got the job of telling you."

"All right with you if I don't go till in the mornin'?"

Perley asked. Wheeler nodded at once. "I'll need to load up my packhorse and take care of a couple of other things. I'll be needin' to buy a few things from you in the mornin', too."

"Anytime tomorrow will be fine," Wheeler said.

"'Preciate it," Perley said and turned to leave.

After he went out the door, Cora Wheeler stepped out of the storeroom where she had been listening to Ralph deliver his message. She looked at her husband, who was pressing down on the counter with his fists clenched. "That was one of the saddest things I've ever heard," she stated. "That poor man."

"What was that all about?" Possum asked when Perley walked back into the dining room. Thinking along the same lines as Perley thought before, he asked, "You ain't the new sheriff, are you?"

"Not hardly," Perley replied. "The council's givin' me till tomorrow to get outta town." His statement left everyone at the table shocked speechless, just as it had when he got the news.

Rachael was the first to find her voice. "That dirty so-and-so!"

"Mama!" Alice exclaimed upon hearing her mother's language.

"I'm sorry, baby," Rachael quickly apologized, "but sometimes it's all right for your mother to use that language. This is one of those times."

"Whaddaya mean, the council told you to get outta town?" Possum asked. Perley told them everything the mayor had said about the potential for gunslinger problems, if he remained in town. "How can the council tell you to get out, if the council ain't even voted on it?" Possum demanded. "No wonder he didn't want me and Emma at that little meetin' he had this mornin'."

"You practically saved this town right by yourself," Rachael insisted.

"Maybe that's why they had the preacher at their meetin'," Rooster remarked. "They mighta had to ask him if they should nail you to a cross or somethin'."

"Watch your mouth, Rooster Crabb," Bess scolded. "We don't need a lightning strike on top of it."

Her reprimand struck Perley as funny, then suddenly the whole affair struck him as funny and he said, "It's better than being asked to be sheriff again." He grinned at Bess and asked, "Can I have some of that stew now? The mayor said I've got till anytime I want tomorrow." The discussion of Perley's exile from Bison Gap continued on through supper, but after the initial shock, he was no longer bothered by it. Everyone in his circle of friends had their say about what they considered fine treatment for one who had risked his life for no other reason than to help the town. Emma, who came in late to dinner, threatened to call another meeting of the town council of all the members. Perley told her he'd rather she didn't, because he was ready to go home, anyway.

When Perley, Rooster, and Possum went out on the front porch of the hotel after supper, Perley took that time to have a serious talk with Possum. Possum had rapidly become a prominent fixture in the town, so Perley broached the subject of his role in Bison Gap's future. "I'm been wondering if you want to return with me to the Triple-G." He put it this way, "In Bison Gap, you're half-owner of the hotel and a member of the town council. In Lamar County, you're just a ranch hand on a cattle ranch."

"I reckon that is somethin' to think about," Rooster remarked. There was no doubt in Perley's mind that Rooster would love to have Possum stay.

"Every time we come down here, you try to ride off and leave me," Possum said. "Truth of the matter is, in Bison Gap, I'm just a ranch hand tryin' to act like a council member. Back at the Triple-G, I'm an honest-to-God ranch hand, actin' like a ranch hand."

"Does that mean you're goin' with me?" Perley asked.

"I reckon," Possum answered.

"We'll pack up in the mornin' after breakfast," Perley said, "and ride half a day tomorrow."

"I swear, I hate to see you fellers leavin' town again," Rooster confessed. "If I didn't have my place and my livestock, I'd pack up and go with you."

"It just rests my mind knowin' you're here to take care of Emma and Rachael," Possum told him. "Takes care of a lot of my worryin'."

"Well, there's that, all right," Rooster allowed. "I do keep an eye on 'em."

"And they appreciate it," Perley offered. Then it seemed like a good place to call it a night and look forward to breakfast in the morning.

# CHAPTER 22

Perley and Possum went down to the stable before breakfast the following morning, planning to pick up their packhorse as well as their saddled horses. Horace Brooks met them at the door to the stable. "Mornin', Horace," Perley greeted him. "We'll be checkin' 'em out for good this time. How much do I owe you?"

"Not a dime," Horace answered. "Listen, Perley, I wasn't invited to that meetin' Ralph Wheeler had yesterday. I didn't have no part in this business of askin' you to leave town. I want you to know that."

"We never thought you did, did we, Possum?" Perley assured him. "It doesn't make a lot of difference. Possum and I woulda been leavin' in the next couple of days, anyway. The summer will be over before you know it, and we'll start getting back to work again."

"Well, I wanna personally thank you for what you did for Bison Gap, both of you. It was you that got the rest of us out of our holes and gave us enough gumption to take our town back."

"'Preciate you sayin' that, Horace," Possum said.

"Never can tell, we might be back this way sometime. We wish you folks a whole lotta luck, don't we, Perley?"

"That we do," Perley said. They shook hands and led the horses out of the stable. "Looks like we'll have to wait to go to the store," he said as they rode by Wheeler's. "He ain't open yet. We'll hit him after breakfast."

As expected, breakfast was calmer than usual at the big table Rachael had set up again, so that everyone could eat with Perley and Possum, and everyone was there. Emma made it a point to be there early, and Rooster stayed over the night just past. The conversation was low key with questions about what they expected to be their total days in the saddle before reaching the Triple-G. Even Alice and Melva sensed an underlying feeling of a sad farewell and were well-behaved for a change. Afterward, the good-byes were brief but warm. Emma gave Possum a hug and promised to write him from time to time to let him know how the hotel was doing, still unaware that he couldn't read. Perley got hugs from both girls, and this time Melva told him that she would marry him if Alice changed her mind. "I 'preciate that, honey," he said. "I'm gonna hold you to that promise."

Eager to get going then, they got their belongings out of the hotel rooms and loaded them on the pack-horse, then headed to Wheeler's store to buy supplies needed for the trip home. When they showed up at the door, Ralph opened up for them, still a little wary in case Perley had a change of heart and decided to defy the council's request. "Mornin', Mayor," Perley offered when he walked in. "We've got a few supplies we're gonna need for the trip home."

Wheeler was relieved by his friendly tone, but

surprised when Perley said "we," for he hadn't thought of the possibility that Possum was leaving as well. As much as he hated mentioning the subject again, he felt he should make it clear to Possum. "You know, Possum, you are certainly welcome to stay here in Bison Gap. It's not quite the same as with Perley."

Possum puffed up, and Perley knew he was getting ready to let the mayor know what he could do with his welcome. So he quickly cut him off. "Possum knows that, Mr. Mayor, but he's got responsibilities back home." He then started reading off a list of things they would need for their trip.

When they had finished, Wheeler totaled the bill, and when Perley started to pay, Wheeler said, "I'm takin' two dollars off of that total, and we'll just settle for twelve dollars even."

"I swear, if you ain't all heart," Possum couldn't help commenting.

"'Preciate it, Mayor," Perley said. "Every little bit helps. Let's get this stuff loaded on the packhorse, Possum."

"I'll help," Wheeler volunteered and picked up a sack of flour. Perley and Possum each picked up an armful and followed him out the door.

Perley stepped off the boardwalk right behind Wheeler when the bullet struck the bag of flour Wheeler was carrying. Not waiting to hear the sound of the rifle, Perley dropped his packages and dived into Wheeler's legs, driving him to the ground. No sooner did they land when another shot ripped up a spray of dirt under the packhorse's belly. "Get on the other side of the walk!" Perley yelled. "Crawl!" He urged Wheeler. "Possum! You all right?"

"Get by the corner of the store!" Possum yelled as

another shot zipped by close enough to the packhorse to make the sorrel buck and pull away.

"Where they comin' from?" Perley yelled.

"Yonder way!" Possum answered and pointed to the north, so Perley jumped up and grabbed the reins for Buck and for Possum's gray, then led them around to the side of the store while Possum bellowed at him to get down. The sorrel packhorse naturally followed the other two.

Perley slipped cautiously around to the front of the store where Possum was plastered up against the doorway. "Hug that ground," he said to Wheeler as he went past him. When he got beside Possum, he asked, "You sure those shots came from that direction?" Possum said he was sure because he could see the angle the slugs ripped up the ground. "There ain't nothin' past the store but the church," Perley said.

Thinking again about the angle the shots came from, Possum decided, "Those shots came from the church bell steeple," he said. "And I bet it ain't the preacher."

"Ned Stark," they both said at the same time. People were running from the street now as the shots continued to ring out from the church steeple.

"The rat has gone loco," Possum said, "and I reckon he's tryin' to kill as many people as he can."

"This is the second time him or one of his men has taken a shot at me in front of this store," Perley said as he tried to inch his way up close to the corner of the store, so he might see for sure if Stark was really in the church. He peeked around the corner just in time to see a muzzle flash. "You're right, he's in the steeple where the bell is. What worries me is where are the preacher and his wife? Maybe they're in the house."

He looked back at Wheeler, lying as flat as he could up against the edge of the board walkway. "Mayor," Perley called. "If you roll over a couple of times, you oughta be out of his line of fire. The building will block his line of sight."

"You sure?" Wheeler asked fearfully.

"Yeah, but hurry up, we got to do something about that mad dog before he kills somebody," Perley answered.

"Like what?" Possum said.

"We'll think of something, but first, we need to see if the preacher and his wife are okay." Impatient with the mayor's fearfulness, he blurted, "Come on, Wheeler, roll!" The mayor did, three or four revolutions instead of the couple Perley had suggested. Relieved to still be alive, Wheeler hurried inside the store when Perley pointed toward it and followed him inside.

Seated on the floor behind the counter, Cora Wheeler cried out when they came running in. "Get down, he'll kill you!"

"You've got the right idea," Perley replied. "Stay down and stay away from the windows. We're well within range of that rifle he's using. It's just a miracle he ain't hit nobody yet. There ain't no tellin' what he's got on his mind to do, so keep a sharp eye," he said to Possum.

"Where you goin'?" Possum wanted to know, afraid Perley was going to try something stupid.

"I'm goin' to try something stupid," Perley answered. When Possum started to object, Perley said, "I'm worried about Reverend Poole and his wife. I've gotta see if there's any way I can help 'em."

"I reckon you're right," Possum said. "Damn it, be careful."

"I will," Perley said and ran through the stockroom to the living quarters behind the store, then to the kitchen and the back door. Before going out, he opened the door a crack and peeked out to see what kind of cover he could find. He was in luck, because he couldn't see the little window below the bell that the rifle shots were coming from. That meant the shooter couldn't see the back door of the store, so he ran out the door, out of the back yard and into the trees by the creek before stopping to catch his breath. While he did, he checked to make sure he hadn't lost his six-gun on the way. "Cow pie, cow pie, cow pie," he kept repeating under his breath as he made his way down the creek bank toward the house behind the church. Down by the edge of the creek, he saw a saddled horse wandering loose, a sign that told him Stark had nothing on his mind but killing. The parsonage was nothing more than a small cabin. All the money had been spent on the church building. It seemed adequate for Harvey and Nancy Poole, who had no children, a subject that was discussed among the town folk quite often—and a puzzle that was not on Perley's mind as he trotted up to a back window of the cabin.

Using very little caution, because he knew where Stark was, Perley hurried around the side of the cabin, looking inside each window he came to. By the time he got to the front, he knew the cabin was empty. He turned then to look at the church. They had to be in there. Now it was time for caution, he thought as he went to the back door. The door was ajar, so he pushed it slowly open. He saw what appeared to be two bodies lying on the floor before the first row of pews. *Damn,* he thought and stopped to listen. In a few seconds, he heard the sound of the rifle firing and knew Stark was still in the steeple. So he pushed the door wide and walked as quietly as he could toward the bodies. As he neared them, the woman moved. They were not dead but tied hand and foot and gagged.

He removed the gag from her mouth and whispered. "Mrs. Poole, are you all right?" She nodded, then tried to turn to look at her husband. "Just a minute and I'll get you untied." Perley told her.

"He's in the tower!" She whispered fearfully.

"I know," Perley said. "I wanna get you outta here. How bad is your husband hurt?" He thought maybe Harvey was dead, for he had not moved and he could see blood on the side of his head.

"I don't know," Nancy whispered as he worked to untie the knots. "He hit Harvey in the head with his rifle. Harvey didn't move while that man tied him up."

As soon as she was free, she went to her husband while Perley untied his hands and feet. She bent over him and whispered, "He's alive! I can feel his heart-beat!"

"Good," he whispered. "Can you walk?" She nodded. "All right, let's see if we can get him outta here to your house. Have you got a gun in the house?" She nodded again. "You know how to use it?" Once again, she nodded. "Good, let's get both of you in the house." He stopped to listen then, and when he heard another shot fired, he said, "Let's go while he's still at it."

Between the two of them they managed to half

drag, half walk Harvey, who began mumbling and calling for Nancy as they crossed the yard between the church and the cabin. Perley was afraid Stark was going to hear him, but Stark was busy trying to kill Bison Gap. When they got Harvey inside, they lowered him into a chair and Nancy ran to get her shotgun. "Okay," he told her. "I'm gonna go see if I can pull him outta there. You lock this door and don't open it unless I tell you it's me."

"You be careful," she said. "He's crazy."

Since this was his first time in the church, he wasn't sure what he might run into when he opened the door at the front of the church, beneath the steeple. So, to be cautious, he opened the door very slowly and as quietly as he could. What it revealed was a small closet with a ladder up to the bell. Just as he opened the door, he heard the rifle fire, and an empty shell fell to join about twenty others on the floor of the closet. The bell tower was built to hold the heavy church bell and nothing else, so he figured Stark had to be shooting from an extremely cramped position. Maybe that was why his shooting hadn't been that accurate. Perley hesitated before making a decision on whether or not to stick his head inside the closet to get a look at what the situation actually was. *What the hell . . .* he decided, *he won't likely be looking down,* so, with his six-gun in his hand, he stuck his head in the closet and looked up.

Right away, he could see that cramped didn't begin to describe the confines of the shooting platform Stark had chosen. Evidently desperate to rain some hell down on the settlement of Bison Gap, this unlikely steeple was the only position that afforded him enough elevation to see down the street. With his legs astraddle the "A" stands that supported the heavy bell, and his upper body across a narrow access space, he had to support himself with his elbows on the sill of the tower window. Perley's first inclination was to point his six-gun straight up and fire away, but he was not crazy about the possibility that his shots might ricochet off the bell and come back at him. *Should give him a chance to surrender, anyway,* he thought. But how to get him down outta there? Seeing the rope hanging right in front of him, he decided to give that a try.

He holstered his gun and grabbed the rope with both hands. Then as hard as he could, he set to his task with determination. The sudden unexpected clanging of the heavy bell between his legs startled Stark, causing him to drop his rifle when he grabbed the windowsill to keep from falling. Perley increased his efforts on the rope, ringing the bell as hard as he could. Amid the sound of the ringing, he could hear a string of swearing coming from Stark in the confines of his perch. The crazed outlaw struggled to reposition himself so he could draw the handgun he wore. With the deafening sounds of the bell making him even more crazy, he finally managed to get his .44 out of the holster and promptly emptied it into the closet floor below him. Luckily for Perley, he was standing on the other side of the small closet where the rope hung. In an effort to reload his pistol, Stark tried unsuccessfully to reach his gun belt. Realizing what Stark was trying to do, and that he was helpless at this point, Perley stepped up on the ladder and reached up to grab Stark's one free arm. He yanked on the arm with the same enthusiasm he had used with the bell rope and pulled Stark down the narrow opening to land on the closet floor.

Like a raccoon pulled out of a tree, Stark hit the floor hissing and clawing to get to his feet to attack his assailant. Perley backed away, his six-gun in hand, prepared to stop him. He intended to give him one warning before he put him down for good, but he never got the chance. Even though almost out of his mind, Stark was still sane enough to recognize the man he hated above all others. With his eyes locked on Perley Gates, he lunged, only to be stopped cold by the blow of the rifle butt against the side of his head. Startled, Perley looked at the Reverend Mr. Poole, who had just stepped in front of him. Holding the Henry rifle by the barrel, he looked at Perley and said, "Thou shalt not kill."

"Amen," Perley replied.

"The sheriff can hang the useless varmint," the preacher said and handed Perley the ropes he and his wife had been bound with.

They were joined moments later by a crowd of people from the street. After the shooting had stopped and the church bell continued to ring out, everyone rushed to the call. They came in the church, led by Possum and Sheriff Mason, to find Perley tying Ned Stark's hands behind him. Lying still dazed, Stark had blood on the side of his head in about the same location as did Reverend Poole. Nancy Poole came into the church carrying a basin of water and a towel to tend to her husband, who seemed to have recovered enough to say, "I hope that I see this many of you back here on Sunday."

The sheriff helped Perley get Stark up on his feet, and Mason couldn't resist telling the dazed outlaw,

"Things have kinda changed around here, ain't they, Stark?"

Ralph Wheeler looked around him to see many of the members of the town council, so he looked back at the sheriff. "There's enough of the council here to vote on it, so how many vote for a hanging?" He received a quick reply from all those members present. "There's your verdict, Sheriff. I see no point in delaying the execution of the sentence."

Perley stood back, since there were many willing hands to assist the sheriff with his prisoner. He looked at Possum and said, "I reckon that really is the end of Ned Stark."

"I expect so," Possum agreed.

"You still wanna go back to the Triple-G with me?"

"Yep."

"Well, I expect we'd best get goin'." Perley laughed. "I still gotta get outta town before sundown."

*Keep reading for a special excerpt . . .*

## DEAD TIME
A HANK FALLON WESTERN

### Johnstone Country. Try Not to Get Killed.

*In this explosive Hank Fallon thriller, the justice-seeking ex-con goes undercover and behind bars to expose a plot as big, as bold, and as deadly as the American Civil War . . .*

### GET OUT OF JAIL FREE—OR DIE

Doing time in Texas is no picnic. But getting sent to The Walls in Huntsville is a fate worse than hanging. If the guards don't kill you, the prisoners will. And if it weren't for the fact that the man who framed Hank Fallon and murdered his family could be inside The Walls, Hank would never step one foot in that heinous hell-trap—let alone go undercover as an inmate. But this isn't just another assignment. This is his chance for revenge . . .

Inside The Walls, Hank quickly discovers who's boss—as well as judge, jury, and executioner. The only relief from the gang fights and guard beatings is a prison work program that allows inmates to leave The Walls to work for plantation owner J. J. Justice. Hank figures it can't be any worse than jail. But it is. Seems that Justice is ordering the men to commit robberies and murders. He's stockpiling weapons. Building an army. And planning to restart the Civil War—all in the name of Justice . . .

*Look for* **DEAD TIME,** *wherever books are sold.*

# CHAPTER 1

The lousy coffee he had managed to drink for breakfast started rising from his gut when he stepped out of the prison wagon and saw "The Walls."

Harry Fallon forced the coffee back down. He had seen prisons before—too damned many, thanks to Sean MacGregor, president of the American Detective Agency in Chicago, Illinois—but sight of the Texas State Penitentiary in Huntsville did something to his nerves.

*Buck up,* he told himself. *This is no different than Yuma or Jefferson City. And behind those walls, you're going to find the man or men who sent you to Joliet, that murdered . . .*

Fallon shuddered.

"She sure has a way of doin' that to a feller," the deputy marshal drawled as he stepped up on Fallon's right. "Another feller once tol' me that 'The Walls ain't no place to be.'" The lawman snorted, laughed, and spit chewing tobacco onto the cobblestone path cut into the spring grass and pine needles.

The Walls. One hundred thousand square feet

surrounded by a foreboding wall of red brick, fifteen feet high and three feet thick. And inside . . . hell on earth.

"Ready, Fallon?"

"Alexander," Fallon told the lawman in a tight, hard whisper. "Harry Alexander."

The deputy cursed softly. "Sorry," he whispered. "I knowed that. Just ain't good at this private detective business."

"Just don't slip once we're inside."

"Right."

"Let's go."

The chains hobbling his legs and wrists rattled as Fallon walked to the gate, where beefy guards waited to welcome the latest inmate to The Walls.

Those red bricks, the stories went, got their coloring from the blood of every inmate to be sentenced to the prison since it had first opened in 1848.


"Warden," the deputy said, removing his hat, as he stepped inside the dark office behind Fallon, whose manacles had been removed in the anteroom inside the gate. Another prison official shut the door behind Fallon and the deputy.

"Superintendent," the warden corrected. "According to the *Rules, Regulations and By-laws for the Government and Discipline of the Texas State Penitentiaries, at Huntsville and Rusk, Texas.*" He nodded at a four-shelf bookshelf to his left. One shelf held a Bible. The top shelf held what Fallon figured had to be *Rules, Regulations and By-laws* . . . The rest of the case was empty.

Fallon hoped the prison library had more books.

"Besides, I detest that vulgar word, *warden*. And Warden Walter Wilkinson has far too much alliteration."

The deputy stared in complete confusion. *Alliteration* would not be in his vocabulary, but Fallon considered him to be a good man . . . as long as he didn't forget to use Fallon's alias.

Walter Wilkinson, warden—personally, Fallon never cared much for the word *superintendent*—at the Texas State Pen, looked pretty much like every other warden Harry Fallon had known. Sweaty, pale, beady eyes, balding—in fact, Wilkinson was completely bald— whose handshake would be flabby had he dared lower himself to shake hands with a prisoner. Fallon already had the man pegged. A politician, he went to church to keep up appearances, took part in all the fairs, attended the meeting of men of power once a month, and used the underground tunnel that led from the hall to some classy brothel. He took bribes frequently, but not from prisoners. Prisoners didn't have enough clout or influence, let alone money.

"You've been a naughty, naughty young man." Wilkinson shook his head and muttered, "Tsk-tsk." He did not look up but kept right on reading the file the American Detective Agency and the Texas attorney general had prepared. "A life sentence." Wilkinson tsk-tsked again. "Well, you'll be happy to know that when your life is over, we have a very fine graveyard for you."

He had a nasal voice, a heavy gut from too many mashed potatoes and port beer, and thick, dark, unruly eyebrows that contrasted with a bald head glistening from sweat. "I suppose you're innocent, too."

Fallon said, "Why should I be different than anyone else here?"

The warden looked up. His eyes considered Fallon for a long time before he stepped back toward the window, leaned against the sill, and brought the tips of his fingers together.

"Actually," he said, "we have one prisoner who says he's guilty. You'll meet him eventually . . . if you live that long. The first night usually drives the weak ones to kill themselves. But . . ."

The fingertips parted, and the warden shoved his hands into the deep pockets on his striped woolen trousers. ". . . I don't think you're weak, Harry Alexander." He said the name as though he knew it was an alias, but, in this part of the United States, people were always choosing whatever name they wanted, and that wasn't because they were outlaws or running away from someone, or something. Before he pinned on that badge in Fort Smith, Arkansas, Harry Fallon had cowboyed and hunted buffalo, and he had known cowboys and skinners who changed their names with the seasons, sometimes on a whim or bet. Just to freshen things up.

The warden nodded to the assistant who had been quietly standing near the door and the deputy marshal who had escorted Fallon the one hundred and fifty or sixty miles from Austin to Huntsville. Once the assistant signed a receipt and handed it to the deputy, the lawman looked at Fallon, nodded, thanked the warden, and opened the door. The assistant closed the heavy door behind the departing lawman, and Fallon slowly, discreetly, let out a long breath.

So far, so good.

The man in the dark uniform spoke in a dreary monotone, as though by rote.

Fallon would be issued a uniform, of white and brown stripes. This being summer—it was actually spring, but spring usually seemed like a figment of one's imagination in Texas—Fallon would be given shoes, pants, shirt, and hat. Socks, drawers, and a jacket would be provided in winter.

"If he's still alive," the warden said, sniffed, and searched for a handkerchief in his coat pocket.

"You may keep any drawers, undershirts, socks, or handkerchiefs that you brought," the assistant said, "or may receive any through friends, or purchase them but only after receiving permission from Superintendent Wilkinson, the assistant superintendent, or the sergeant."

Fallon learned about the bedding he would receive, how to handle mess call—once again, no prisoners could speak while eating—bathing (once a week), privileges (like Fallon would ever be granted any of those), visitations, punishments, and work details.

"Start him out tomorrow in the mill," the warden said.

The assistant went on. Fallon had heard it all before. Maybe one time, Fallon thought, he might hear it coming from someone who cared. *Wouldn't that be something!*

"Questions?" the warden asked.

"No, sir," Fallon answered.

"Peter." The warden had found his handkerchief and wiped his nose. Spring, Fallon realized. Hay fever. Fallon grinned. It was good to see a man like Walter Wilkinson suffer. Fallon had never been allergic to anything, though he wished he were allergic to prisons.

"Get him . . ." The warden sneezed. "Outfitted. Show him . . ." Another violent sneeze that almost doubled over the lout. This was only March. Wait till all the cedars started doing their damage, the wild-flowers started blooming, and the winds picked up. "His cell. Then . . ." This time, the sneeze provoked a vile oath from the warden. "Turn him over to Sergeant Drexel."

The assistant chuckled. "Barney loves breaking in the fresh fish."

Every muscle in Fallon's body tightened. He had been inside The Walls for no more than thirty min-utes, and everything—all the planning they had spent—could be jeopardized. Fallon had mentioned the possible risk, but the Texas attorney general and Sean MacGregor had waved off his concerns.

*"What would you say the chances are of you actually run-ning into someone you know in Huntsville?" MacGregor had asked. "As a deputy marshal for Judge Parker in Arkansas and the Indian Nations, the men you sent to prison went to the Detroit House of Corrections."*

*"I ran into them in Joliet," Fallon had reminded the Scot. "And in Yuma. And in Jefferson City."*

*"But Huntsville's Texas," MacGregor had scoffed.*

*"I cowboyed in Texas," Fallon had reminded him. "A lot of men I chased out of the Nations rode south to Texas."*

*The attorney general hadn't bought that argument, either.*

*"The chances are slight," Malcolm Maxwell had said. "And it's a risk you'll have to take."*

*Fallon had corrected him. "You mean it's a risk I'll have to take."*

*"If you want out, Fallon," MacGregor had said, "say the*

word." He had spoken that so smugly, condescendingly, that Fallon had found himself grinding his teeth. "Say it, Fallon. There's always room for you at Joliet. Just remember, this isn't just a chance to bring justice to a madman. To help your country. But more than that, this is your chance, your only chance, to right your name. To avenge the murders of your wife and daughter."

Now, thinking about that meeting, Fallon saw their faces then. His wife, Renee, so young, so beautiful. His daughter, Rachel, a sweetheart of a baby . . . who would be approaching young womanhood had she not . . .

Fallon shuddered.

The warden laughed, and the images before Fallon, those recurring, haunting memories, stopped instantly, bringing Fallon back into the office of the superintendent of The Walls.

"It happens all the time, doesn't it, Steve?"

The assistant chuckled softly.

"The Walls have a way of sending a chill up your spine. Especially when you know that you'll be here for the rest of your scum-sucking, miserable life." The warden sneezed again. "No. No. Not a life. You don't have a life anymore. You have an existence, and maybe that's only a figure of speech. Get him out—" Another violent sneeze rocked the warden, and the assistant, Steve, opened the door and nodded for Fallon to follow.

*Barney Drexel*, Fallon kept thinking as he picked up his clothing, exchanging his denim pants, cotton shirt, and boots for the scratchy, ill-fitting summer uniform of white and brown stripes, rough shoes, and a cap that had to be one size too small. At least he had socks, relatively clean, and summer underpants. Those shoes would cripple a man without socks.

Barney Drexel.

Fallon hadn't thought of him since Judge Parker had fired the lout back in Fort Smith maybe twelve years back. Drexel had pinned on a badge after Parker had just been appointed as the only federal judge serving western Arkansas and the Indian Territory. Drexel had brought in most of the men he went after dead, but Fallon had also killed his share. The rule of outlaws in the Indian Nations was: die game. Certainly, it beat hanging on the scaffolds outside of the old army building that now held the jail and the judge's courtroom. Even if, sometimes, you'd get to hang with your friends. Judge Parker's gallows could hold up to six doomed men at a time.

Drexel should have wound up on those gallows himself. He shot another deputy marshal dead while both were off duty in a saloon on Garrison Avenue. Put four .45 caliber slugs into Deputy Marshal Flint Logan's stomach, and another in the back of Logan's head while he lay in a pool of his own blood on the saloon's sawdust-covered floor. He would have put another bullet in Logan's corpse but the Colt misfired the last chamber.

That shooting had not surprised Fallon. Drexel had always been a brute and a bully, and too often went for his Colt or Winchester. What saved Drexel from the gallows was the fact that Flint Logan's reputation also smelled like a coyote's carcass, and witnesses couldn't, or wouldn't, say that Drexel drew first. The argument seemed to be over a prostitute, but she couldn't be found after the shooting. The U.S. marshal, U.S. attorney, and Judge Parker agreed that they had rid the U.S. Marshals Service of two bad apples. Flint Logan was dead. Barney Drexel was told not to show his face in Arkansas or the Indian Nations again.

So Drexel had wound up as a sergeant of guards in Huntsville.

Such was Harry Fallon's luck.

He made it through the prison doctor's evaluation in rapid time.

"You seem to attract a lot of bullets, sir," the bony, white-haired old-timer said.

"And knives," Fallon told him. "Clubs. Broken bottles. Fists. Hatchets. Fingernails."

"I've performed autopsies on bodies with fewer scars. Take a deep breath. Exhale." The doctor lowered the stethoscope. "You're in remarkable condition for what should be a corpse. Have a peppermint stick, Mr. Alexander. And welcome to The Walls."


Now he had been turned over to a guard, a red-headed man with a thick mustache and blackened teeth. As the guard escorted Fallon across the prison yard toward Sergeant Barney Drexel, Fallon kept thinking that maybe, just maybe, after all these years Drexel wouldn't recognize him. A dozen years had passed, and ten of those years had been hard, brutally hard on Harry Fallon. The Illinois State Prison at Joliet certainly had earned its reputation for aging a man.

"Sergeant Drexel," the black-toothed guard said. "Fresh fish for ya."

Big, ugly, bearded Barney Drexel turned around

and rapped a big stick into the palm of his beefy left hand.

Barney Drexel looked the same.

Fallon muttered a curse under his breath, but he was saved by another savage curse.

His escort stopped, and stepped aside.

Fallon turned toward the curse and saw a man in the uniform of a Huntsville inmate running hard.

"You turncoat yellowbelly," the man said as his lowered shoulder caught Fallon's middle.

# CHAPTER 2

Josh Ryker.

Fallon recognized him just before the wiry onetime cowboy knocked the breath out of him. Landing hard on his back, Fallon managed to bring his knees up, and then he kept rolling, somersaulting, sending Ryker sailing toward Sergeant Barney Drexel and the other guards and inmates gathered around the whipping post.

Josh Ryker. The last person Fallon expected to find in Huntsville. Who else could be here? Not that it mattered. What had Fallon expected the American Detective Agency to do? Go through a list of every inmate housed in the state pen and see if Fallon recognized the names? Hell, half the men Fallon had arrested in the Indian Nations and Arkansas had been using aliases.

Fallon rolled to his side, pushed himself up on elbows and knees, trying to get his lungs to work again. He heard cheers, curses, and shouts coming from inmates who now provided a wide arena for the fight. Maybe some of the guards were cheering, too. Fallon also saw Josh Ryker running toward him.

Fallon let him come. At the last second, he dived to his right, lifted his left leg high, and managed to trip Ryker. The man cursed as he went sailing into a wall of men in brown-and-white or black-and-white uniforms. The prisoners shoved Ryker back into the circle. He fell onto his back, spread-eagled, and slowly came up, shaking the cobwebs out of his head.

By then, Fallon had pushed himself to his feet. He stood waiting.

"Go get him!" an inmate shouted.

"Kill him!"

"Stomp his head into the dirt!"

Fallon shook his own head. He wasn't moving. He was still trying to remember how to breathe.

And the spectators in prison uniforms and guard uniforms weren't all cheering for the fresh fish.

"Ryker, you's a-fightin' like a Baptist deacon's wife!"

"Get off yer ass, ya puny sack of snake turds, an' kill dis new meat!"

Ryker came to his feet, turned, staggered, straightened, and began moving cautiously, ready now. He probably expected Fallon to be the young green pup he had been back during their cowboying days, back when they had first arrived in Fort Smith. Ryker was the older of the two, the one who could outdrink, outfight, and outride anyone he ever met. Fallon had been the tagalong kid still in his teens and wet behind the ears.

Now Ryker knew that fifteen years had hardened his onetime pard.

*He doesn't know the half of it,* Fallon thought as he brought his arms up, fists clenched, and began countering Ryker's feints as he drew closer. *Ten years in Joliet for a crime I didn't commit. The riots. The knifings.*

*The weeks in solitary and the whippings just so the guards could let everyone know who bossed the prison. And then, pardoned by the governor, only to find myself back in prison—this time working for the American Detective Agency. Yeah, that'll harden a man until his skin and fists are like iron, and his soul and heart even harder than that. Yuma in Arizona Territory, known, rightfully so, as The Hellhole. Jefferson City in Missouri, called the "bloodiest forty-seven acres in America." And now inside these god-awful Walls in eastern Texas!*

Yeah, Fallon wasn't that kid Ryker had punched longhorns with in Texas, Indian Territory, and Kansas. Wasn't that puppy dog who had followed Ryker to Fort Smith to gamble.

Ryker swung a right. An easy punch to avoid. Fallon felt it pass over his head, and he came up quickly, bending his head so that the back of his skull caught Ryker's jaw. He heard the crunch of teeth and saw Ryker fall backward. Fallon straightened, shaking off the pain in his head, and raised his right foot. He slammed the ill-fitting shoe down toward Ryker's bleeding face, but Josh Ryker wasn't the same youthful cowboy Fallon had ridden with from Dodge City to Fort Smith all those years ago.

Yes, Ryker had learned a few things, too. He grabbed Fallon's foot, twisted it, and sent Fallon spinning into the ground. Now Fallon rolled into the feet and legs of the prisoners who had formed a circle to watch the brawl. They kicked him, hissed at him, and rolled him back toward Ryker.

Fallon turned and rose off the ground, just in time to feel Ryker's kick that caught him in the left shoulder and drove him into the dust and sand. Fallon brought his legs up again, catching the diving Ryker, and once again sent the cowboy sailing. Again, Fallon rose quickly, rubbing his shoulder, already feeling the beginnings of a big, painful bruise. But his collarbone hadn't been broken.

"Quarter pound of tobbacy says the fresh fish takes that little punk."

"Bet."

"I'll let you see that tintype of that whore I met in San Angelo if Ryker loses this fight."

"I've seen that picture. And never want to see it again. Give me nightmares, it did."

Eighteen months, Fallon remembered. That had been Ryker's sentence. The scenes replayed in Fallon's head.

*They had been drunk, Fallon and Ryker, not an unusual state for those two young fools. Pretty much cleaned out by Fort Smith's gamblers, they had been shooting out the street-lamps the first time, only to be stopped by a man that Fallon guessed to be a preacher. The stranger turned out to be Judge Isaac Parker. Fallon should have learned then that Ryker wasn't the type of saddle pal you wanted to be with. For a moment, Fallon thought Ryker would murder the judge, and maybe he would have had a lawman not come along then. Fifty dollars or fifty days. Ryker had to sell his horse and saddle to get them out of the Fort Smith calaboose, then lost most of what he had left over in a craps game. And decided to steal a saddle on display at a saddle shop.*

*Fallon had tried to stop Ryker. Ryker wasn't one to be stopped. They had fought. Ryker had won. And then another lawman came around, and after an insane and intense few seconds, Fallon had stopped his pard from murdering the lawman in cold blood. The lawman whose life Fallon had saved was a deputy U.S. marshal for Judge Parker's court. When Fallon had been brought to the judge's office, there had been no plea deal, nothing like that. The judge and the U.S. marshal, after hearing how Fallon had saved a deputy's life, offered Fallon a job.*

*"It's not a gift," Judge Parker had warned him.*

*And it most certainly wasn't. Fallon had moved up from driving a prison wagon for deputy marshals to becoming a federal deputy himself, one of the youngest, and best, in Parker's court. Till that all came crumbling down.*

*Josh Ryker had spent eighteen months at the Detroit House of Corrections for assault on a federal lawman. He could've gotten more had the state pressed for charges of breaking and entering, attempted burglary, and unlawful discharge of a firearm.*

Well, Fallon thought as the convicts and guards cursed and cheered, he couldn't really blame Ryker. From the look of the inmate, life had never turned out the way the gambling, foolhardy cowboy had thought it would. Detroit was the first step. Now he was in Huntsville.

*Why don't the guards stop this?*

Fallon threw a punch, ducked another, as the cheers and the curses grew louder. The dust blinded him.

He answered his own question. *They wouldn't have stopped it in Joliet, Yuma, or Jeff City. They wouldn't have stopped it in the dungeon in Fort Smith where men awaited trial. Unless it got out of hand. Huntsville's no different.*

His nose was bleeding. So were his lips. His back hurt and shoulder throbbed. He swung, missed, ducked, swung again, connected, felt a punch that almost took off his right ear, and responded with one that Ryker deflected.

Ryker brought his prison shoes down hard on Fallon's right foot. Fallon wrapped his arm around Ryker's neck and drew it close. He tried to flatten Ryker's nose, but Ryker caught the wrist and held it tight, trying to twist it off. The men grunted, squirmed, attempted to break free, but neither man was willing to give.

"Hell, they ain't doin' nothin' but waltzin'," a Texas accent drawled. Fallon didn't know if that came from a guard or an inmate.

"*No más. No más,*" a Mexican prisoner shouted.

Ryker tried to spit in Fallon's face. His breath stank of bad tobacco and worse coffee. He was missing several teeth. Scars cut through his once-handsome face, but, well, after all those years of hard time, Fallon wasn't going to win any beauty contests himself.

"Been waitin' . . ." Ryker heaved. "A long time . . . for this."

Fallon said nothing. Ryker's grip was so tight on his wrist, he felt his hand growing numb. They weaved this way and that. The shouts and curses sounded all around them, but by now the dust was so thick, the sweat stinging his eyes, Fallon couldn't see much beyond Ryker's bloody, sweaty, grimacing face.

"I read . . . about . . . your . . . kid and wife," Ryker said. His eyes gleamed. He laughed.

Which was all Fallon needed.

*"You're a softhearted kid, Hank,"* a deputy marshal once told him in Fort Smith. *"Too nice for this job, I often think. But when you get riled, it's like I don't even know who you are no more."*

\* \* \*

Josh Ryker now saw what Fallon was like when he was riled.

Fallon's knee came up, caught Ryker hard in the groin. The grip relaxed, and Fallon broke free and slammed his flattened palm against Ryker's throat. The inmate's eyes bulged as he tried to breathe. Had Fallon hit harder, Ryker would be dying, but Fallon had not lost all control. He had just lost his temper.

He slammed a right into Ryker's jaw, buried a left into the man's gut. When Ryker doubled over, Fallon brought up his knee again, catching the man in the mouth, smashing his lips, knocking out two more teeth. Fallon reached with his left, grabbed Ryker's shirt, hoping to pull him up and keep pounding his face until it was nothing but an unrecognizable pulp. But the cotton ripped, and Ryker fell into the dust. He was lying still when Fallon landed on top of him. He swung a left, a right, again, again, and again.

Then he felt the stick of a guard against his skull, and Fallon rolled off the now-unconscious Ryker.

Fallon saw stars first, then dust, and finally a burly, bearded face just above him.